DIE FOR ME

JESPER STEIN

Translated from the Danish by Charlotte Barslund

MIRROR BOOKS

First published by Mirror Books in 2020
This paperback edition published in 2020

Mirror Books is part of Reach plc
10 Lower Thames Street
London EC3R 6EN

www.mirrorbooks.co.uk

ISBN 978-1-912624-19-5

Typeset by Danny Lyle

1 3 5 7 9 10 8 6 4 2

'Who doesn't love a maverick cop with a chaotic personal life?!'

Ian Rankin

sustained tension in Stein's plotting — a gripping combination.'

The *Times* and *Sunday Times* Crime Club

'Utterly mesmerising.'   **Raven Crime Reads**

'If you like your Nordic Noir, urban, fast, gritty and are fond of the police procedural format then this is the book for you.'   **Nordic Noir**

'I enjoyed this and would recommend this especially if you enjoy a maverick detective.'   **A Crime Reader's Blog**

'The plot is as ever is complex, dark and uncompromisingly emotive.'

The Quiet Knitter

'Chilling, engrossing, it kept me on the edge of my seat.'

It's All About The Books

'A a read that will keep you on the edge of your seat. Riveting from the first page to the last.'   **Hooked From Page One**

'Stein has written a psychological thriller with real depth that is a tough uncompromising read.'   **NB Magazine**

'A slow, addictive and compelling burn towards an emotionally resonant resolution.'   **Liz Loves Books**

'A well-rounded novel, that brings you thrills, chills, and most importantly the impact such crimes can have on the victims, and the police officers who investigate them. Such a complex novel this is!'

Keeper of Pages

Reader Reviews

★★★★★ "Dark and gritty"

★★★★★ "The plot is tense and terse, the characters well fleshed-out – a rollercoaster ride of a thriller"

★★★★★ "Axel Steen is a cross between Alex Cross and Martin Riggs"

★★★★★ "Cleverly written, with great dialogue... A real eye-opener"

★★★★★ "Absolutely brilliant"

★★★★★ "A hard-hitting crime story, a fantastic read and a compulsive page-turner"

★★★★★ "A first-rate Scandi thriller"

★★★★ "Full of twists and turns"

★★★★ "A darkly disturbing psychological thriller... I was hooked from beginning to end"

★★★★ "I highly recommend this to everyone"

★★★★ "A gritty, intelligent thriller with interesting characters and false leads"

★★★★ "A great police procedural"

★★★★ "Had me on the edge of my seat"

★★★★ "Dark, gritty and fast-paced"

★★★★ "Outstanding"

★★★★ "Enthralling, dark and atmospheric"

★★★★ "A whirlwind ride from start to finish"

★★★★ "Fantastic. A first rate Scandi thriller"

★★★★ "A hard hitting crime story based around Copenhagen, a fantastic read, a compulsive page turner"

★★★★ "Dark and gritty, had me hooked"

Jesper Stein was born in Aarhus, Denmark. He began his writing career as a crime reporter and made his literary debut in 2012 with the crime novel *Uro* (*Unrest* – July 2018 UK release), the first in the Axel Steen series.

Winner of the Danish Crime Academy's Novel of the Year 2018, he has received massive attention for his sharp eye for detail, rich and innovative plotting and confident prose. Praised by critics as a writer who will keep readers on the edge of their seat, Stein has positioned himself as one of the most talented authors of crime fiction in Scandinavia.

To Finn

NØRREBRO

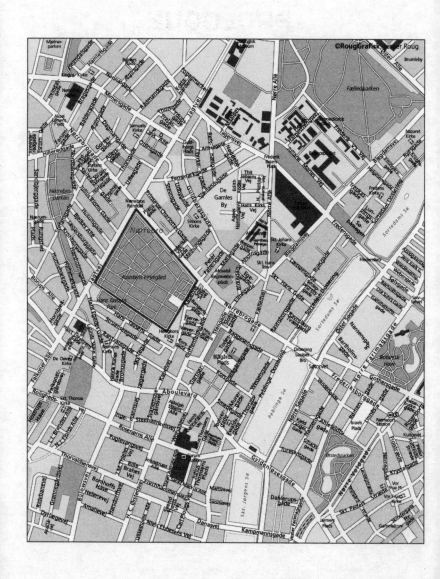

PROLOGUE

Ørsted Park, Copenhagen, June 2004

Swarms of tiny insects buzzed around the motionless air. It was a baking hot Monday morning in the middle of summer.

DCI Axel Steen looked at the line disappearing into the green water. 50 centimetres of visibility at best. The line was attached to an orange buoy bearing the logo of the Frogman Corps, which rested on the surface of the lake a short distance from the jetty.

He scanned the shore. Willow trees sagged under the weight of their green coats; orange, red and yellow flowers surrounded the water, which shimmered in the heat haze.

There was a faint tug on the line and the buoy began to stir in the water.

Axel turned to the frogman, who had just surfaced after 30 minutes of futile searching. He peeled back the rubber hood of his wetsuit and removed his diving mask. The skin on his face was completely white. He shook his head.

A pond skater darted erratically across the glossy surface. Axel watched as tufts of white clouds drifted across the pale blue sky, reflected in the green mirror of the lake. Then another burst of bubbles rose from the deep. They popped enigmatically as they reached the surface.

'…can't be sure that she's down there,' he heard a voice behind him saying.

It was his partner, John Darling, the officer responsible for cordoning off the park. He was the Homicide Division's wonder boy: tall, broad-shouldered and blond, he looked like a menswear model and wore the tightest trousers in the force. He insisted on doing everything by the book, but he wasn't the brightest spark at a crime scene.

Axel rolled his eyes.

Darling turned to the frogman.

'How long will it take you to search the lake?'

'You mean the whole lake?

'You tell me. How long will it take?'

'Searching the whole lake is a big job. It could take us up to 24 hours. It's four metres deep. But if she's down there,' he turned to look at the water in front of them, 'we'll find her. Soon.'

'Could she have been carried away by the current?'

'Bodies don't float around down there. There's hardly any current. The water's stagnant.'

Darling turned to Axel and picked up where he had left off.

'What's your problem? I have a point, don't I? Just because we've found her clothes, doesn't mean she's down there. She could be anywhere. She might not even be dead. She could be in bed with some guy having the time of her life. Maybe they went swimming in the lake, and she forgot her stuff—'

Axel put his hand on his colleague's forearm and squeezed it. Looked him in the eye. The uncertainty was fuelling Darling's fear. And he was trying to suppress it by babbling.

'Why do you think she's in the lake? If she's dead, her body could be anywhere. She could just as easily be—'

'Stop it,' Axel said. He turned to the line again. Bubbles. Otherwise no movement. 'She's down there.' He looked at the candy-striped plastic tape that stretched across the path 50 metres in both directions. There were people everywhere, not just behind the cordons, but also on the grassy slopes opposite. People pointing at them, their movements frozen. A man with a telephoto lens was busy taking pictures.

'Did you bring any blankets?' he asked the frogman.

'No.'

He turned to Darling.

'Get some blankets.'

'Why?'

'Now.' Axel turned to the lake again. 'I want her brought up with dignity.'

His mobile vibrated. It was Cecilie, his wife. He declined the call.

Ørsted Park, of all places. No other green space in Copenhagen saw more action. It was a 24-seven anal paradise for cruising gays and a green sleeping mat for backpackers on a tight budget.

The square park, which dipped down towards the lake from the surrounding streets, had been built in the 1800s on the remains of Copenhagen's fortification ring. The recently renovated lake lay eight metres below street level and was bordered by lawns and fertile slopes; it was a pocket of beauty surrounded by some of the city's busiest traffic arteries.

Three coots and a swan swam majestically towards them. They looked hopefully up at the men on the jetty.

The line twitched. Once. Twice. Three times.

'He's found something,' said the frogman next to him.

Axel's heart contracted. He could hear it beating like an ominous pulse in his ears. He prayed to God that the 'something' wouldn't turn out to be Marie Schmidt. But he knew there was no God. Especially not in Ørsted Park.

Marie Schmidt had been missing for 36 hours. That wasn't unusual for an 18-year-old who had just finished sixth form, but it was unusual for Marie. She had been to a leavers' party at Bellevue beach and had caught the train home to Nørreport around midnight. At 00.23, she had texted her father to let him know what time her train would be getting in. Their flat in Nansensgade was a 10-minute walk from the station. But she never made it home. And her mobile phone had been turned off just one hour later. That was never a good sign. And yet they had treated it as just another missing person case.

At least, they had until four hours ago, when a gardener had found a bag, a traditional red and white school leaver's cap with a black visor, and some clothes in the bushes in Ørsted Park, at the northern end opposite Israels Plads. Axel and John Darling had been the first to arrive at the scene. After a brief talk with the gardener, they had fought their way through the waist-high fern growing between the exit to Israels Plads and the lake. The heat was suffocating and vicious. There was toilet paper scattered around, along with red leaves from last autumn, broken branches and all kinds of rubbish. The smell of soil and excrement. Five metres in they found the cap, a small leather handbag, a jacket, and the item that made Axel straighten up and instruct two uniformed officers, who were waiting on the path, to contact HQ and have the entire area cordoned off: a white, sleeveless dress trimmed along the hem with flounces and lace. It was soiled and had been turned inside out. The gold threads woven into the Indian silk sparkled in the few rays of sunshine that penetrated the foliage. In a bush they found a torn G-string.

The clothes and the bag matched the description of what Marie Schmidt had last been seen wearing. They were scattered across the ground. The earth and the leaves had been disturbed, as though someone had been lying down. Axel had picked up the small handbag. It contained cigarettes, a purse, a lighter, but no mobile. In the purse he found a monthly travel card for the capital's trains and buses, with a photo of a smiling young girl. He felt acid flood his stomach. Not only because the scene suggested the girl had been raped, but because he knew she was dead.

The park had been secured and searched by officers and dogs, but they hadn't found any further traces of Marie. Crime scene technicians had arrived and were busy working in the bushes, but the police photographer, the pathologist and the rest of the Homicide Division regulars were waiting up the street. They had no body. Not yet.

On the path behind him was Sergeant Tine Jensen, the family liaison officer assigned to Marie Schmidt's father. The girl's mother had died from cancer five years ago. Axel had called Tine Jensen the moment he heard they had found the missing girl's clothes and bag, and had asked her to warn the father that the police were searching Ørsted Park and that the media was likely to report on it soon. Tine Jensen had arrived at the park one hour later and taken a look at the clothing. Now she was wandering around the path behind him, waiting and smoking. He called her over.

'They've found something,' Axel said, and she stopped in her tracks. Tine Jensen was in her late twenties, a head shorter than Axel's 1.9 m. She came from darkest Jutland and had very short, blonde hair, blue eyes that sat far apart, a dimple in her chin, a stud in her nose and 10 excess kilos.

The orange buoy twitched and was dragged across the surface.

Axel knew what it meant. It was the diver marking his discovery so he would be able to find it again. They stared into the water and saw a series of oxygen bubbles and a cloud of mud rise towards them, before the head and body of the frogman appeared and broke the surface.

He stayed in the water, removed the mouthpiece to the oxygen tanks and nodded briefly – not as a greeting, but to confirm what they already knew.

'I can't tell if it's her, but it's definitely a woman. She looks young.'

Axel felt the heat wrap itself around him, as if his entire body was being squeezed by a giant hand. He took a deep breath.

'Are you able to bring her up?'

'Yes, sure.'

'Hang on a moment, would you? We need to get the pathologist down here first and I want to screen off the area for privacy.'

He heard John Darling radio for more officers in order to clear this end of the park completely.

Axel was about to ask him to cordon off the whole park when he heard shouting. It was coming from the path 100 metres away, close to a café in the park. He turned and saw a man surrounded by journalists and press photographers rushing towards the cordon.

'Shit, that's her father,' Tine Jensen said.

'What the hell is he doing here? He can't be here when we get her up,' Axel said. Tine Jensen made a beeline for the man, who had reached the cordon and was remonstrating with a uniformed officer holding the candy-striped tape in front of him.

'Let me through. I'm her father.'

He was in his fifties, with curly blond hair that made him look younger than he was. He was dressed in jeans and a blue-and-white-striped Breton T-shirt that looked inappropriately cheerful, given what awaited him.

'What's happening? Have you found her?' he asked them in a loud and anxious voice that was close to breaking.

Tine Jensen told two officers to get rid of the press, placed her hand on the man's shoulder, raised the tape and ushered him towards the curved steps leading up to Israels Plads. She bent towards him and pulled his head close to hers. Axel couldn't hear what she was saying, but the man straightened up and exclaimed:

'It's my daughter down there.'

Then he buckled and slumped to his knees on the path. Axel saw the photographers go into a frenzy.

'Oi, you.' The frogman rapped his knuckles against the wooden jetty. 'How about it? How long am I expected to stay in this soup?'

Axel's shirt was sticking to his body and sweat was pouring down his stomach. He called out to Darling, who was coming towards him with a pile of ambulance sheets.

'We need to clear the area before we get her up. And we need the park searched with a fine-tooth comb. The more spectators we have wandering around, the bigger the chances of them ruining any evidence. I want her brought up now.'

Tine Jensen had handed over the father to two uniformed officers, who ushered him away. She returned to Axel. Behind him Darling was busy issuing instructions to a handful of officers to lock the gates and move the public to the far end of the park, so the police could work undisturbed.

They stepped out onto the jetty, which protruded three metres into the water. Axel signalled to the diver. The frogman's colleague had put on his mask again and was heading back into the water.

'Right, let's get started,' Axel said.

The divers submerged in a cloud of bubbles. Tine Jensen chewed her nails. John Darling was shifting his weight from foot to foot on an unfolded sheet.

'How long before they're back up?'

Axel's mobile vibrated again. Yet another call from Cecilie. And a text message. 'CALL NOW!!' it said. He replied: 'Busy with homicide. Will get back to you.' Then he turned off his mobile.

It was two minutes before the divers resurfaced. Axel could think of nothing but the girl. He reviewed what he knew about the case. Marie Schmidt had been walking home. Drunk, most likely. From Nørreport station. Before ending up here. Where she was raped, judging by the evidence. Then dumped in the lake. 36 hours ago. They had to piece together her movements from Bellevue beach to the park. Had she spoken to anyone? Had anyone seen her? Was she on her own? There had to be witnesses. Ørsted Park was busy at night. They would carry out a detailed search of the whole area tonight and look for anyone who might have seen or heard something.

The line jerked and a series of bubbles rose, along with mud and leaves. The masked heads of the divers were the first to appear, then a blurred white shadow between them that turned into a body – the body of a dead girl, waxy white, the skin on her hands and feet shrivelled. Scratches to her neck. Dark shadows. Strangulation marks? Her blonde hair undulated weightlessly in the water like in a shampoo commercial. Open, watery, green eyes that stared blankly at the sky. She wore a pair of high-heeled white shoes with ankle straps through which her flesh was pressing. Apart from that she was naked. Small breasts, her upper body glistening with water and mud, her shaved sex, legs and arms; her face showed no visible injuries, but on her left ankle there was a tattoo of a blackbird. Marie Schmidt's nickname.

The divers eased a plastic stretcher into the water and draped an ambulance sheet over the body before they lifted it onto the stretcher.

'Oh, shit,' said Darling, who rarely swore.

'Will you inform her father?' Axel asked Tine Jensen.

Heavy footsteps hit the jetty.

'Gentlemen, none of you touch her until I'm done – and take that sheet off her now. If you want to protect the body from nosy bystanders, you'll have to find some other way.'

No one ever disagreed with Denmark's leading forensic pathologist, Lennart Jönsson – better known as the Swede. He was tall, with a potbelly and huge bags under his eyes. He greeted Axel and Darling, nodded to the others, opened his old doctor's bag, and put on his white coverall and surgical mask. He took out a pair of latex gloves, inflated them, slipped them on and squatted down on his haunches next to the stretcher, which was now resting on the steps leading down to the jetty, and began examining the body from head to toe. Everyone looked at him. In silence. He paused at the eyes, produced a pair of tweezers, raised an eyelid, mumbled something, turned her head and looked behind her ears. Axel knew that he was looking for petechial haemorrhaging. The Swede took out a small camera and photographed her face.

'Axel, how long was she in the water?'

'We don't know. We think 36 hours.'

'What do you know about her?'

Axel knew that the Swede was only interested in information that might explain the state of the body.

'Not a lot. Evidence in the bushes that she was raped or the victim of some other kind of sexual assault. She was last seen Saturday night, probably in a state of intoxication on her way back from a leavers' party. Apart from that, nothing.'

'She's a sixth-former?'

'Yes.'

'Fuck. Promise me you'll get the son of a bitch.'

Then he opened the girl's mouth and Axel saw something that looked like washing-up bubbles.

'My initial opinion was strangulation because she has scratches to her neck, bruises, petechial haemorrhaging in her eyes and redness behind her ears, but this is froth. And that means she drowned.'

He examined the rest of the body. Took scrapings from her nails while the police officers watched in silence.

'Will you find anything, given how long she's been in the water?'

'It varies. There might be DNA evidence. Any semen in the anus or vagina will be well preserved. Skin cells under her nails will probably have been washed away,' the Swede said, turning the body onto its side and inserting an electronic thermometer into the girl's rectum. He waited, took it out, and shook his head.

'She got too cold. She's the same temperature as the water. I can't tell you anything about the time of death. What do you know about her sex life? Was she a virgin? Probably not, wouldn't you agree? Given her age. Given the age we live in.'

Darling coughed as if he was about to throw up, and left hastily. The Swede raised his eyebrows.

'Delicate stomach. Right, there's not much I can tell you now, because she's been in the water for so long. I need to get her to the Institute, then I might have something for you, but for the time being it's my opinion that someone tried to strangle her and then threw her in the water. She had probably lost consciousness by then, but she was alive and so she drowned. We'll know for sure once we get a look at her lungs.'

He got up. Removed the surgical mask. Peeled off his gloves and took out a tin of chewing tobacco. Looked up at the treetop above them.

'Japanese pagoda tree,' he stated, and stuffed a wad of chewing tobacco under his lip. 'I'll go write my preliminary autopsy report. I'll be in my car if you want me. She's all yours.'

The police photographer came over. He had been working in the bushes along with the forensic technicians. Axel walked up to Darling, who was on the phone to the head of the Homicide Division. He was ashen.

'We need the whole department working on this. We need officers to talk to the family, map her life, boyfriends, school friends, the beach party at Bellevue, surveillance cameras from Nørreport station. And the park must be checked for any witnesses last night, tonight and onwards. Axel and I will be in charge of the case.'

That meant Darling would do the organising, while Axel would find the killer. It suited him just fine.

'We'll meet at HQ in one hour.'

Darling ended the call.

'You look worried,' he said to Axel as he returned the mobile to his pocket.

Axel was soaked in sweat.

'I have a bad feeling about this.'

'Why?'

'I don't know. Like it's already slipped through our fingers.'

'It's the heat. Or this place. It stinks. Who the hell strangles a sixth-former? It beggars belief. Perhaps you need some time out. I know I do. We'll be working round the clock for the foreseeable,' Darling said.

Axel returned to the jetty and took a last look at the body of the girl, who was being photographed from all angles. She looked horribly exposed, exhibited in her nakedness. The strangulation bruises to her neck were like innocence brutally ripped away from her. He walked up the curved steps and left the park.

He sat down on a stone on Israels Plads. A group of sixth-formers was sitting on some benches not far away. Pissed out of their minds. Cigarettes dangling from the corners of their mouths, bottles clattering, their clothes and smiles far too fresh. They were raucous. Axel made eye contact with a girl, who looked at him with glassy eyes in a drunken stupor.

'Hey, man, give us a smile!'

Axel turned away. Switched on his mobile. He had three text messages from Cecilie. He rang her back without reading them.

'What's wrong?'

'You useless bastard. Why haven't you called me? I'm at the Rigshospitalet. Emma's in intensive care. And it's your fault.'

CHAPTER 1

Thursday, 26 June 2008

Deputy Commissioner Jens Jessen pulled himself up onto the edge of the pool and sat down on the tiles. He was warm. He could feel his pulse falling. Three km of breast stroke and crawl under his belt and the whole swimming pool all to himself. It was 5.30am. A perfect day awaited him. He would be at HQ in an hour. Before anyone else. Timing was everything. But you couldn't time anything unless you were the first person in.

Straight out of PET, the police intelligence service, he hadn't been the popular choice as the new Deputy Commissioner, but he was too high up the ladder and too well-connected for anyone to do anything about it. He was going in to prepare for his meetings with the Police Commissioner, the senior management team and the Police Complaints Authority. The big priorities battle was approaching. It would be bloody. And they would hate him even more than they already did after his first round of efficiency savings.

He took off his goggles and went to shower. He sat down on a wooden bench, feeling the boards under his warm, throbbing muscles. He grabbed the cold steel underneath and squeezed hard. Then he trailed his hands along his legs, down to his feet and up across his hairless body. Time for a shower and a little oil.

Cecilie was turning 37 this Sunday. She was flying home from The Hague with Emma so they could start their summer holiday. Something had to change, that was for sure. He couldn't live with this uncertainty for much longer. They would celebrate her birthday tomorrow at Custom House with Darling and his psychologist wife, who would inevitably drink too much. It was one of those days where nothing could be allowed to go wrong. Cecilie tended to get irritated unless she got her own way. For the most part, he obeyed her. She was simultaneously pure, innocent and steely-eyed – that slight squint and the challenging smile that pinned you down. Oh, how he loved it. And her.

Emma would be staying with her father. That was fine. Children were unpredictable. But he was learning. He had read up on them. He had had no choice. There was nothing from his own childhood he could copy. Cecilie had made it quite clear that setting boundaries and being strict was her job. He was to be an avuncular figure, the nice stepdad who spoke funny through his nose and used strange words.

'I authorise teddy to fetch an ice cream from the freezer.'

Wide eyes, half-open mouth.

'But seeing as teddy can't walk, I'm giving you power of attorney to fetch it on his behalf.'

'Why do you talk funny?' she smiled. 'What do you mean, Jens?'

You couldn't pull the wool over children's eyes.

'I mean that you can have an ice cream.'

She looked at him suspiciously.

'Then why didn't you just say so?'

He had found a middle ground between playing the clown, the rocksteady adult and the attentive stepfather. But it required constant adjustment and fine-tuning. He had to rehearse how he behaved. Had Cecilie seen through his insecurity? She probably had, but if he was lucky it might be one reason why she had fallen for him in the first place – the fact that he didn't know how he was supposed to act. That, for him, each day **was** another big emotional multiple-choice test.

He turned on the scalding-hot water, closed his eyes and let it cascade over his body.

Could he give her what she needed? He thought about yesterday. They had had such a good chat. He was convinced that they had connected, just like the old days when he was away on business and they had Skype sex. For a moment he lost himself in memories. He would watch her lie in front of him on the screen, touching herself. Her perfect form, the curve of her legs, her skin, her sex. He would turn down the volume without her knowing it. But he could see her. She was the less shy of the two of them. She had brought him out of his shell, taught him to let go as he had never done with a woman before.

Yesterday he had felt just as close to her as in the early days of their relationship. His doubts were gone. She had seemed happier than she had done for ages. She had said that she missed him, that she was looking forward to coming home and starting their holiday. But when he had suggested that they took off their clothes and anticipated the pleasure of their reunion in cyberspace, he could read his error in her stiffened body and dull eyes before he even got to the end of his sentence.

He turned off the water and stepped out of the shower. Looked at himself in the mirror. His hair was beginning to curl again. It was definitely time for a trim. He dried himself, combed his hair. A little wax. Unscented deodorant. A fresh pair of underpants. The starched purity of the Hugo Boss shirt, the suit newly dry-cleaned. He looked good. He felt good too.

He had had others.

Dorte from the Foreign Ministry, a lawyer from Greenland with crooked teeth, who liked deep drilling with the lights off. She was great at working a case, but had no idea what made a relationship work.

Mette, an expert in EU law, an elite runner, who used heart rate monitors and stopwatches when she competed with him. She had made it very plain that dating him was just another step of her career plan.

And when he started in PET, there was Lena from the Swedish intelligence service, a myopic human resources psychologist with fat ankles who knew everything about intimacy and was very keen to promote cross-border cooperation – but she was ultimately too Swedish and predictable.

Nice girls, good girls, but all of them lacking what Cecilie had. He had known it from the moment he saw her in the DPP in the summer of 2004. She was a young, ambitious lawyer, kick-starting her career after maternity leave. Yes, she was married, but when he learnt that it wasn't a happy marriage, he was ready. He had carried out a background check on her past. There were no obstacles. Even with Axel Steen on her CV.

CHAPTER 2

Axel Steen sped arrowlike through the night sky. The milky way of Nørrebrogade flashed past in one dazzling second, the Lakes a fading memory bathed in light, Nørreport station a neon glow, Vester Voldgade a burst of brilliance, Rådhuspladsen an explosion of colour, floating weightlessly over the glowing river of traffic on HC Andersens Boulevard. The city was his body, his flesh and blood. He left it behind in a chaos of light and speed.

The feeling of lightness evaporated. His pulse was beating hard, his body full of fluids, nausea and piss. And with his body, his consciousness came crawling back. Slowly, his mind surfaced, like a picture being developed in a sweaty bath of pain and thirst.

His eyes flitted around the room, touching every object they landed on, working out what it was, where he was, until his sticky, panicked gaze came to rest on the Egon Schiele poster above his bed. His mobile was flashing.

There was something he was meant to be doing today, not that he cared. Today. Tomorrow. The day after. None of it mattered. He closed his eyes again. He lay very still, trying to make sense of his life. How far had he got?

He had had five days off in lieu and they had disappeared into nothing. Hash, television, sex with Dorte Neergaard, more sex, more hash, then television, hash and red wine in town, then sex with Dorte

Neergaard yet again. In between, he had messed about with three old murder cases. Spent hours in treacherous fogs of occasional clarity on the sofa with 'Gimme Shelter' playing in his ears, a joint in the ashtray, rereading the files, hoping for sudden revelations to burst through the haze, only for them to vanish as quickly as they had appeared. He couldn't let go of the past, didn't want to let it go. They were cases he was supposed to solve, but they lost their appeal even when he worked his way through the familiar information stone cold sober, finding no way to unlock them. Yesterday he had simply smoked himself high as a kite. Alone.

It was over, his little five-day pocket of freedom, of wallowing in a downward spiral. Now he was going back to work. He tossed the duvet aside and stepped out onto the floor, knocking over the ashtray as he did so.

He smoked every day now. Two or three joints when he wasn't going to work. One every evening. More during the weekend. He didn't feel lethargic, but he knew it was eating him up. And that it would ultimately wreck his career. A stoned police officer. It was a big no-no. The fear of his own death remained, and it rocketed when he woke the following morning. Like now. His heart was in his throat again. His wretched, beating heart.

But there were also days when he didn't smoke, and that proved he wasn't an addict. He would eat healthily, work hard, exercise, but he was unable to sleep – and after one or two weeks he would be so tired that he started smoking hash again. He only did it to help him sleep. And seeing as he wasn't an addict, why not enjoy a joint every now and again? The past year had passed pretty much like this. Up and down. Mostly down. He had promised his ex-wife, Cecilie, that he would stop, but he hadn't. And when she told him she was moving to The Hague for a year and would be taking Emma, he had smoked his pain and rage away.

He had agreed that Emma would live with Cecilie when she walked out on him three and a half years ago for a PET boss; he had put up with the number of contact days getting smaller, and holidays and custody agreements being changed again and again because it suited Cecilie. Then, six months ago, this. He had tried to talk her out of it, but to no avail. She had offered him every third weekend and the holidays. When he had said no, she had threatened him with the family court. And that was the last thing he wanted to put his daughter through. He never wanted to have to explain to Emma that her parents had been so hostile that they had ended up in court – never ever. But after two months he had called the court administration anyway, only to be told that he was too late to file an objection. He told himself it was the final nail in the coffin of their love. But was it? On the one hand, he was reluctant to concede a millimetre after she had taken the most precious person in his life from him. Missing Emma made him hate her. On the other hand, she had moved abroad. Away from Jens Jessen. What did that mean? That she was in the process of leaving him too? That she loved her job more than him? One thing it did mean was that the three of them were no longer living happily ever after in their luxury flat on Islands Brygge. Axel had his doubts. And he hated speculation and uncertainty, looking for signs that she might… might what? No, he would have to be exceptionally naïve to view the move to The Hague as an improvement in her relationship with him – but then again, it didn't improve her relationship with Jens Jessen either, did it? Whenever he starting thinking along those lines, he felt so disgusted with himself that he wanted to throw up. But that was how it was. He missed her. Cecilie.

The flat was hot. He went over to the bay window, pulled the blinds and opened a window. The air outside nearly knocked him over. Dry heat. Saturated with the exhaust fumes of Nørrebrogade, it became almost tangible.

He had to try to make sense of his life. Emma was coming tomorrow evening. And then what? He would have her for two days. And afterwards everything would go back to normal. Grey and pointless. He was fed up with work. John Darling was trying to get him to join a work group looking into investigation efficiency, and Axel had refused. Although Darling was his boss, he was also his former partner, which meant that Axel usually got away with refusal. But Darling had insisted – and they had agreed that Axel would think about it during his time off. Unless he could come up with something better to do, he would have to say yes.

He closed the window and looked down Nørrebrogade. The tarmac shimmered in the heat haze. The morning traffic was at its peak, and the sun glanced off the windscreens of the cars and rolled over glazed roof tiles. Red and blue estate agent signs stuck out from many properties. Now that prices were plummeting, everyone was trying desperately to sell.

He closed the blinds and went to the kitchen. Poured himself a cup of yesterday's cold coffee. Tasted it, threw it in the sink. Then he showered, cleaned his teeth, got dressed. It was a start. He took his wallet from his jacket and walked down the stairwell. Opening the door to the street was like stepping off the plane on a package holiday. The heat enveloped him and he gasped for air.

Down-and-outs and drug addicts were crowding the entrance to the bank. Flabby, chalk-white skin peeked out through ladders in cheap lilac leggings, scabs over bruises and fading tattoos, eyes barely open or fixed on a crack in the tarmac. They were queuing, squabbling over their places; a fat man in a black tracksuit was sitting on his rollator, pushing people away. In front of him was a short and bony woman, tanned like a dry date and just as shiny and wrinkled.

'That's my spot, you arsehole,' she shrieked at the fat man, who grunted menacingly by way of reply.

Axel glanced at the church clock. It was 9.35am. Benefits could be collected in 25 minutes: it was payday for those at the bottom of society.

He crossed the road. The heat wafted across the street, which was bathed in a shiny white light. He opened the door to the bakery, where he ended up behind two customers with all the time in the world to decide their orders. Separately and one item at a time. Coffee. One crusty roll. One cinnamon whirl. They carefully placed their copies of *The Watchtower* on the counter as they unzipped their wallets and counted out the money with servile saviour smiles.

Axel waited. I can't focus anymore, he thought. Every detail is important. So nothing is. Everything matters equally. I have to snap out of this. His eyes caught the tabloid headlines. The biggest story was the one trickling down his upper body. The record hot summer. News recycled from last week.

He ordered black coffee and a crusty roll, asked them to butter it, grabbed a newspaper and took a seat on the sofa at the back of the room. The coffee did him good. His head cleared. He even discovered his appetite, and wolfed down the roll in two mouthfuls as he read the inane article splashed across two pages, accompanied by a massive picture of two topless girls on a beach.

He left the paper and the bakery. In the street, he was shaken out of his reverie by the sound of a gas horn. An army truck full of sixth formers drove past him. It was decorated with balloons and birch twigs. Cheering and singing faces stuck out between the boards on the side of the truck. They had beers and cigarettes in their hands, and relief and hope in their eyes.

The flashback cut straight to his heart. The Blackbird case.

The truck pulled up outside the bank, where the flock of impoverished benefit claimants slipped into a kind of silent paralysis at the sight of the whooping, tipsy young people wearing their white leavers' caps.

On the side of the truck was a banner with the words:

We drink
We party
We moon
We're the Rysensteen Sixth Form

Axel looked at the lost faces on the pavement, some of whom waved happily to the youngsters.

Hopeful futures and failed existences side by side.

He went back to his flat. Pulled up the blinds and opened every window. Took out his mobile. He already knew there would be messages from Cecilie. She always called early in the morning or late at night. To check up on him, he guessed. Tomorrow she'd be flying back to Denmark with Emma. He would ring her then.

Three calls from Darling. One from yesterday and two today. He listened to the voicemail message.

'I need to decide on this working group, Axel. I know you're off work, but please call me when you get this message.' That was yesterday. There were no messages left from the two calls today. Axel had to get himself an investigation quickly or he would be assigned to Darling's group. But it was tricky to invent an investigation, even for the Copenhagen Police Homicide Division's degenerate star investigator. He needed a body.

Axel was feeling far from perky when he reached HQ just under an hour later. The massively off-putting home of the Copenhagen police had been built in the 1920s. It was a four-storey triangular colossus whose nose had been cut off at one corner and replaced with an entrance area, whose only decoration Axel now leaned his bike against: a big iron cage with a gold morning star at the top.

He walked into the perfectly round, neoclassical courtyard, and glanced at the memorial to fallen officers as he always did before crossing the courtyard and walking up to Homicide. Even after 15 years, Axel could still get lost in the unmarked darkness of the stairwells, but he had been in Homicide for almost 10 years now and could walk there in his sleep, which was pretty close to the state he was currently in.

He was soaked in sweat after cycling through the city, and his mood didn't improve when he reached his office and saw there was nothing new waiting for him – except a yellow Post-It note from Darling, asking him to stop by.

He flopped down on his office chair, leaned back so far that it creaked, and asked himself what the hell he was doing here. He looked around the office. All he could feel apart from this sodding heat was apathy and queasiness after yesterday's high. He leaned forward and turned on his computer. Ever since Darling's appointment to management, internal communication had mushroomed. It was the first thing you saw when you logged on – a list of priorities. And then the usual 'Please note' relating to schedules, reports of vehicle usage, forms for registering the use of electronic and technical aids, forms to request examinations of everything.

Fuck, how he hated it. It had Jens His Majesty Jessen written all over it. In recent years the amount of form-filling and measuring had risen – but ever since Jessen's appointment to Deputy Commissioner, they had been bombarded with paperwork and record-keeping. As if there wasn't enough bureaucracy already. Axel had never been very keen on desk work and report-writing, which took up so much of a police officer's time, but he had been able to cope as long as it helped solve the case. It also doubled up as a mental review for him, but this obsession with recording how every single second was spent at work was pointless. The factors that cracked a case had nothing to do with any of this.

He got up, walked through the offices, which were interconnected with internal doors, and greeted the secretary, who told him that Darling was in a meeting on the management corridor. He went back to his desk, turned on his computer and started reading the duty officer's reports from the last five days in the hope of finding something, anything, that could save him from having to join Darling's efficiency review.

CHAPTER 3

Jens Jessen studied the photographs he had received in the internal post. Six grainy pictures of a face he had instantly recognised, handed in at reception in an envelope with his name on it. No sender.

He slid the photographs back in the envelope, put it in a drawer and looked around the office. Apart from the view of the harbour basin, there was little to boast about. The interior didn't reflect the status of the post. But it did say Deputy Commissioner on the door. The cherry-tree furniture and Kvium paintings would just have to wait.

After his years with PET, this was perfect. He regarded this office as a shortcut. First this job. Then a year or two with the DPP or the state prosecutor, so he would be ready when a vacancy came up. National Police Commissioner. Head of PET. The Ministry of Justice. Or this place. He thought of the Police Commissioner's office further down the corridor. The mosaic floor in the front office, the ceiling rising in the shape of an enormous seashell, and behind it the mausoleum of power with its panelled walls of Danish pine, and oil portraits of Copenhagen's former Police Commissioners in every dark, carved square. Cold granite faces that had taken God knows what sins with them to their graves. His portrait would hang there one day.

King of Copenhagen. Nothing was bigger than that.

There was a knock on his door and they entered – police officers who had made it to management the hard way. He would have to watch out for them. And the lawyers who had been in this corridor long enough for them and everybody else to know they would never go any further. He let each of them set out their own little stall. He widened his eyes and sat in his chair like a coiled spring. He would nod and ask sharp questions whenever they lacked clarity.

He told them he was meeting with the Police Complaints Authority, which had alerted him to several complaints. They laughed mechanically with fear in the corners of their eyes, and dismissed it. That wasn't his style. He didn't dismiss anything. He killed it. He loathed stains on the force. There would be nothing for the media. If a fire starts to smoke, it must be put out. There was a reason why he was known for his ability to clear up internal problems without the slightest leak. And to get rid of the useless, the lazy, the low-level offensive, the corrupt, the anabolic-steroid junkies and the drunks.

He looked at the man at the opposite end of the table. Assistant Commissioner Rosenquist. He was known as Comb-over amongst the rank-and-file officers because of the grotesque and impressively thin strand of hair covering his scalp from left to right. He gave a report on the risk of gang warfare and police efforts in Christiania, the controversial community in Copenhagen where drug use and dealing was rife. He was ripe for replacement. Though not if you asked him. Hadn't he turned 62 recently? Next to him was the Homicide Chief, John Darling, the only one here Jens could count on for genuine support. Ambitious and diligent. Unfortunately he was a recent appointment, so it was too soon to line him up for Comb-over's job. But he was an obvious successor. Jens would have to come up with an interim solution and handle Comb-over with kid gloves until then. He had to manage this situation delicately — especially since Comb-over was as retirement-ripe as a rotten apple. People like him were capable of anything. Some plods became quite uncontrollable when they had to cut the cord after 35 years of loyal service.

Then it was his turn. He placed both hands on the file with the latest reports from the finance office. He would bamboozle them with numbers and a couple of new top priorities. Which they definitely wouldn't like. How the hell did you get to be popular? It was life's big question. Well, not compared to the really big question, which he had yet to articulate. He brushed it aside.

'We're 274,567,918 kroner over budget. Distributed equally across the divisions, but with the biggest overspend in violent crime.'

He circulated a piece of paper with a smile. Fortunately, he had already struck a deal with the Police Commissioner.

'We need to fix that. It'll mean officers taking time off in lieu on a major scale. By doing that we can save 100 million kroner this year. I'll move things around to find the rest.'

'What about the Police Federation? Won't they kick off?'

'Of course they will, and I'll deal with them. However, this is the crucial point.' This triggered a small avalanche of tics. 'It's holiday time. Not just because it's hot right now. But for the rest of this year. This applies to all divisions. I know what you're going to say. It'll affect Christiania. And yes, it will – we're closing everything down. We won't have a presence out there for the remainder of 2008. There won't be anyone on Vesterbro, no raiding the hash clubs. A 15 per cent reduction in hours over the next three months. Send everybody off on a nice long summer break. Including those who don't want one.'

They gasped for air like the guppies he used to fish out of the aquarium and study until they got so weak that he tossed them back into the algae soup. Flatfoots with a veneer of politeness over their thuggish behaviour and inflated self-confidence, who crumbled when faced with real power. They would hate him, and he needed to fix that. He hated being hated.

Now for the hard part.

'We've done a little restructuring of areas of responsibility. It's the express wish of the National Police and the Ministry of Justice that we improve the co-ordination of our efforts against terror. As you know, I've previously worked with PET and the Ministry, and I have been asked to make sure that our efforts are optimised. This means that from now on all investigative units will report directly to the Deputy Commissioner – i.e. me.'

Take that, Comb-over. An enemy for life. One of the sycophants leaned forwards with a cough.

'Well, I think that makes a lot of sense.'

Not to Rosenquist it didn't. His face tightened like an old leather sack. He twirled his yellow pencil frantically between his fingers. Up until now he had reported directly to the Police Commissioner, who never interfered in anything, which meant that homicides and terrorism were Comb-over's domain. Up until now. Jens Jessen looked him right in the eye.

'I want you to know that the idea didn't come from me originally, but it has been agreed with the Commissioner and the Ministry, so there's nothing we can do. We'll find a way.'

They believed it. That was the difference between police officers and lawyers. The former took language at face value, the latter knew that words could lie faster than a horse could run, and that it was common for words to mean the exact opposite of what was said.

'That's all. And remember my door is always open if there's anything you want to talk to me about – problems, concerns. That's what I'm here for,' he said, and smiled to Rosenquist, who remained deadpan.

He got up and ushered them out. They left the meeting with their heads bowed. No one said anything. Times were changing. Now we'll have to see how many of you can adapt, he thought. Comb-over lingered behind.

'What's this about? Are you trying to railroad me?'

'No one is trying to railroad you, Rosenquist. This is about terror. Things need to be simpler. Smoother. I have contacts and friends in PET. We can't have any more friction and conflicts when we investigate their cases. The National Police has tasked me to deal with it. Besides, I also have operational experience.'

Was this a step too far?

'Operational experience,' Rosenquist snorted with derision. 'You might have friends in high places, but you have no more operational experience than a rookie from the police academy. And I won't have you poaching on my preserves. Homicide is my department.'

Some linguistic massaging was required.

'You misunderstand me. Homicide is indeed your department and I won't interfere, but I must be kept informed of any major investigations and anything related to terror.' He paused briefly. 'And I've had an idea. I want to do some work experience.' Rosenquist's jaw dropped, then he went crimson. Was he going to turn violent? He had undoubtedly beaten up plenty of suspects in the good old days. 'Yes, work experience. I intend to visit every division and spend several days with our staff to see what they do, get to know them, break down the barriers a little. And don't worry. I promise not to interfere in your work. Unless it becomes necessary.'

Rosenquist looked far from convinced. His cheeky monkey grin had frozen on his face. Jens patted him on the shoulder and sent him back to his own office.

The door slammed behind him. Jens Jessen walked up to the window and looked across the harbour. Three months in the chair. He already had them under his heel, which added four cm to his 1.79 m. They hadn't liked it, but they had swallowed it. Now he would try the carrot, a charm offensive.

His mobile buzzed. A text message from Cecilie.

'Good to talk to you yesterday ☺ Give me time, Jens. Will be arriving tomorrow with Emma. Miss you. Cecilie'

What should he reply? What were you supposed to say? Don't put it off. Do it now. She was impatient. He wrote:

'I love you. We have all the time in the world. Can't wait to see you and Emma. Or is she going straight to Axel? Jens x.'

He put the mobile on his desk, slowly pulled out the drawer, took out the envelope with the photographs and opened it. They showed a man in a hoodie buying hash or harder drugs. Somewhere in Nørrebro, he would guess. On the back of the first picture someone had written the abbreviation DCI – detective chief inspector – and the officer's badge number, and below that the words 'Business or pleasure', followed by a very big question mark. He studied the man's face, his features and scars, the gaze he encountered whenever he looked into his stepdaughter's eyes. Scarface, as he had been nicknamed after a spectacular homicide investigation last year – one he had solved single-handed in a fight with the killer in a burning shipping container. Axel Steen. His girlfriend's ex-husband.

CHAPTER 4

The call Axel had spent four years waiting for came just before noon. He had buried himself in a summary of what sounded like the start of a turf war between Hells Angels and the immigrant gangs in Nørrebro. He had reviewed a number of stabbings and shooting incidents over the last two months that weren't directly related, but suggested a pattern because of the individuals concerned. He had made a table with three rows indicating attacks on biker gangs, immigrant gang members and random people who didn't fit the pattern, but were probably associated with one of the factions in the smouldering conflict.

It looked like a piece of sheet music where the skirmishes danced merrily up and down the lines, replacing one another in a clear structure of payback. The attacks often happened spontaneously and were characterised by excessive force. Guns were rarely used – mostly they involved knives, clubs or other blunt instruments. The groups were as bad as each other when it came to brutality, but there had been five shooting incidents. He had called Brian Boldsen, the king of forensics with whom Axel preferred to work, to get an idea of what sort of guns and ammunition had been used in the shootings. If a turf war was brewing, it was essential to stop it in its tracks, and one way of doing that was to trace the origin of the weapons.

When his phone rang, he presumed it to be BB returning his call.

'Axel Steen.'

'It's Kaspersen from the DNA unit at the Centre for Forensic Services. I've got a note to ring you regarding a case we've got a new match for. A murder. Unsolved.'

Axel stiffened. He had very few unsolvable murders as lead investigator. He could hear his own voice crack when he said:

'Go on?'

'Well, it says here to contact you in case of any developments regarding this investigation. Marie Schmidt. Summer 2004.'

His stomach knotted.

'That's right. What do you have?'

'We have a match to a sexual assault that took place four weeks ago. In the sample section of the DNA register. We don't have a name, but I can tell you that saliva from the rapist matches a mixed profile found in the saliva on Marie Schmidt's leaver's cap.'

'You're saying it's the same perpetrator?'

'What I'm saying is the mouth of the man who raped a woman four weeks ago came into contact with Marie Schmidt's leaver's cap four years ago. What happened to her? Was she raped?'

'We don't know. There was no semen.'

'Do you want me to send you what I've got?'

'Yes. Now, please.'

Axel rang off. He closed the gang war file on the desk in front of him. The desk dated back to well before the Second World War: it was sturdy and made from light-coloured wood, designed by Hans Wegner. Axel had found it in the basement under HQ when he started in Homicide. In order to protect its surface against coffee stains, he had ordered a solid glass sheet measuring two metres by one. Beneath it the faces of three murder victims stared up at him. Mirlinda, Stina and Rajan. Everyone in Copenhagen who could remember 20 years back knew of the two young women and the seven-year-old girl. Killed in the city. Their murders never solved. They were a part of every police officer's, every relatively well-informed resident's knowledge of the sacrifices which life in the city had demanded but never rewarded. And a reminder to Axel of why he was at this desk in this place. Marie Schmidt wasn't among them, but she should have been. He knew that. And he knew that the time had come.

There's no statute of limitation for unsolved murders. The file is never closed and archived in a corner of oblivion in a warehouse: it stays with different investigators in case of any new developments. Axel looked towards the cupboard that contained the case in 15 big ring binders held together with broad elastic bands. Then he cleared his desk completely, got up, opened the cupboard, took out the ring binders one by one, dusted them off and spread them across his desk. 01K1-73111-00003-04. He knew the 16 digits by heart. 01K1 was the code for the Copenhagen police district. 73111 was the code for homicide. 00003 was the serial number and indicated that it was the third murder that year, and 04 was the year itself. Below it, it said: The murder of Marie Schmidt. He sat very still as he felt it wash over him. The case he had never solved. The case he had been unable to set aside. Until the end. When it had cost him Cecilie. And Emma. And which he, for that very reason, had buried deep inside himself and hadn't had the courage to go near for four years. Had the time come? Had he been given a second chance?

CHAPTER 5

When he had recovered from the shock, he opened his emails to read the report from the National Police DNA register. He wanted to see the facts in black and white. As nothing had arrived, he rang Kaspersen.

'How sure are you?' he wanted to know.

'As sure as I can be. I ran it past Forensic Genetics. A million to one. You can't ask for better than that.'

'So you've known about this for several days?'

'Since Monday.'

Axel tried to remember what he had been doing on Monday, but found only a haze of absence.

'Why wasn't I told straightaway?'

'I informed your colleague, who is investigating the sexual assault, and your boss immediately. It wasn't until I wrote my report that I came across the note to contact you. It's not actually my job to do that, but I thought you would like to know. Everyone knows—'

'Everyone knows what?'

'…that you can be very insistent.'

'Would you send me the report now, please?'

'I'll email it to you in five minutes.'

Axel had already started looking for information on the four-week-old sexual assault before he rounded up the conversation.

On the night between Friday and Saturday 31 May, a 23-year-old woman was raped in her flat on Refsnæsgade in Nørrebro. She had walked home from Nørreport station and let herself into her flat. She had left a window open due to the heat, and the attacker had entered her flat via scaffolding put up outside the building, which was due to have its windows replaced. He had threatened her with a knife. Axel skimmed the summary. It was ugly, very ugly. The manner of the rape made his stomach churn. He scrolled down to the name of the investigating officer: Tine Jensen.

What the hell? Tine Jensen had been there from the start four years ago. She had stuck with it long after everyone else had given up, as they hit nothing but dead ends and the investigation had slipped further and further down the list of priorities.

He went out into the corridor, through the rotunda and into the next corridor, which housed Violent and Sexual Crimes. Tine Jensen shared an office with two colleagues, and everyone was at their desks when Axel entered. He could tell from the look in her eyes that she knew why he had come. And he could sense from her two colleagues that they had been expecting him.

'Axel Steen, there you are,' she said.

'Why the hell wasn't I told?'

'Ask Darling, it's not my responsibility. Besides, it's no big deal.'

'What do you mean?'

'It's just one of 26 different DNA traces on that leaver's cap. Mixed profiles galore. It might mean nothing. I heard you were off work, and I was waiting for you to get back so we could discuss it.'

'And that's what we're doing right now. Please explain why you think it doesn't matter?'

'We did the best we could with that sexual assault. But we weren't getting anywhere. And I'm snowed under with other cases. This heat makes people do crazy things.'

'Go on?'

'I've got no leads on the perpetrator. And the DNA match to the Blackbird investigation doesn't help me.'

Axel said nothing, but continued to glower at her as if she hadn't answered his question.

She heaved a sigh and squirmed on her chair, scrabbling around for yet another argument.

'The MOs don't match.'

'Screw that. There was no MO in Blackbird. We had no idea how the assailant operated.'

'Really, I seem to recall you made up quite a few.'

Axel had a flashback and his stomach knotted.

'That was just me speculating. It was better than nothing. The rest of you had given up.'

Was this about the Blackbird investigation? Was that the real reason she didn't want to work with him again? Axel tried to recall how far he had gone. Eventually Tine Jensen had said enough was enough and asked to be taken off the case. Yes, he had gone too far, way too far, but that wasn't important now.

'What's this about?'

'What do you mean?' she said, and Axel could see her vacillating between something she wanted to say and something she was reluctant to say.

'Are you out of your mind? Has everyone gone mad? Is this about priorities? Don't you get it? This is a call from the past. Someone has sent us a message. We might be clutching at straws, but at least we have a straw. Do we just turn a blind eye? Don't we owe it to Marie Schmidt to follow this up? The Blackbird killer might also be a rapist. Shouldn't that be investigated?'

'What do you mean, investigated?'

'Don't we need to look at the cases again? Compare them? Cross-reference them down to the smallest detail?'

'I haven't been told to do that.'

'Is that your way of saying you'll only do it if you're told to?'

She rearranged two files on her desk, making sure that they lay completely straight before fixing her gaze on him.

'I want to catch the bastard just as much as you do, Axel. And if that bastard is the same bastard who raped Jeanette Kvist in Refsnæsgade, then I want to catch him twice as much, but there are many uncertainties. In the rape case too. And you and I have a history that didn't end very well.'

'That attitude will get you far,' Axel said, and walked out.

He returned to his corridor, but rather than go to his office, he carried on straight to Darling, who was sitting in front of his screen entering figures from some Excel printouts on the desk next to the computer.

'Why didn't you tell me?'

Darling straightened up slowly, took off his reading glasses, popped one temple into the corner of his mouth, and leaned back.

'About what?'

'The DNA match between the rape and the Blackbird case.'

'Tine is dealing with it just fine.'

'Fuck you, what's really going on?'

'Hold it right there.'

'You're informed of a DNA match between the Blackbird case and an aggravated sexual assault. And you don't tell me?'

'In my opinion the connection was too weak. Besides, you were having time off.'

'I never take time off from something like that, you know—'

'And you didn't return any of my calls. And besides—'

'Besides what?'

'Well, you know what I mean. The Blackbird investigation. It blew up in your face, you were obsessed with the case and you burned out

25

because of it. And the business with Cecilie. I didn't think you would want to relive it.'

And I don't, Axel thought, but sometimes the call just comes. And you have to show up.

'And I don't want you losing yourself in a tenuous link to an old, unsolved homicide. Now that we're in a period with no urgent investigations, I need you to help me streamline the division and investigations in general. I think you would be good at that.'

What the hell makes you think that? I mean, we have been working together for 10 years, Axel thought. He took a deep breath. It was time to negotiate.

'Please give me some time to check it out. A chance to compare the cases. It would be madness not to explore what we can learn about this man, seeing as he features in two investigations. If it turns out there's nothing, then I'll streamline.'

Darling scratched his chin.

'You have until Monday.'

'That won't work. I have my daughter this weekend.'

'Monday, and you have to work on it alongside your other duties. If I were to say no, you would do it anyway. But please don't go digging up all sorts of things that will cost us an absolute fortune in new tests.'

Axel sat down in front of his screen and looked up the sexual assault. He wondered why he hadn't heard about it. He had been at work four weeks ago, but he had no recollection of it being mentioned at any briefings. Jeanette Kvist was a 23-year-old medical student from Hørning who lived alone in a shared-ownership flat her parents had bought for her. She was a Carrie Bradshaw fan and had been to the preview of *Sex and the City* in CinemaX on Fisketorvet with a female friend on Friday 30 May. Afterwards they had taken the train from Dybbølsbro to Vesterport and gone to Rosie McGee's on

Rådhuspladsen, where they had each had two small draught beers. At 11.12pm Jeanette Kvist had said goodbye to her friend, who had tried to persuade her to stay as they had got talking to some recruits from the police academy, but Jeanette was keen to get home because she was revising the next day. She had taken the train to Nørreport and had been intending to catch the bus back, but changed her mind and decided to walk home in the warm summer night.

Nørreport station. The same station where Marie Schmidt had got off shortly before she was killed. The busiest railway junction in Copenhagen was crammed with CCTV, but there was nothing in the summary to indicate that it had been checked. Axel wrote *compare faces on CCTV cameras from the two cases* at the top of his list.

At 00.09am she had let herself into her stairwell and then into her flat. She had checked her watch. She hadn't noticed anyone following her. She knew that access to the scaffolding was secured, so she had opened both windows due to the heat and hasped them. Then she had undressed down to her underpants and a T-shirt, brushed her hair and her teeth, and was ready to go to bed when she heard a noise. She thought it was a cat that tended to hang around the building, and went to her living room, where she discovered a man standing in the middle of the room in the darkness. She had time to scream before he got to her and pressed a knife against her throat. The first thing she had noticed about him was that he had a nylon stocking over his head.

'Do as I say or I'll cut your throat,' he had said.

Her upstairs neighbour had heard her scream, gone out onto the landing and called out 'Hello? Is everything all right?' Meanwhile she had stood rigid with fear in the living room with the man who had pressed a gloved hand over her mouth and caressed her throat with the blade of the knife. When her neighbour had gone back inside, the man had repeated his threat to kill her. He had led her to the bedroom, where he had tied her hands behind her back with the cord from her dressing gown. He had spent a long time doing it, methodically, bordering on pedantic, and he had made sure that she could not escape. For the next hour and a half he had raped her in her bed and on the floor, anally, vaginally and orally. He had terrorised her and made her choose where she 'wanted it next' – his exact words – and when she refused to choose, he had put both hands around her neck, squeezed tight and forced her. 'The victim believes that he ejaculated in her vagina, but a subsequent examination at the Centre for Victims of Sexual Assault found no traces of semen', the report said.

At 2.15am he had presented her with an evil variation on the rapist's old threat. He had ordered her to state her civil registration number. Her profession. Where she worked. And then he had said, 'I know where you live. I know everything about you. If you tell anyone, I'll kill you.' Then he had gagged her bruised mouth and left.

Jeanette Kvist was described as a strong woman who had been convinced that her attacker would kill her, but she didn't obey his final threat. It had taken her a few minutes to free herself of the restraints that had kept her captive for one and a half hours. Then she put on her dressing gown. Without the cord. And screamed.

'She alleges.'

This particular expression was repeated so often in the summary that Axel began to wonder where the real problem lay and why he hadn't heard about the case until now.

The perpetrator had taken great care not to leave any evidence. Remarkably great care. He wore gloves, he was dressed from head to toe so that the victim at no point was in contact with any skin other than his genitals, and was wearing the nylon stocking to mask him, but also because he was afraid of leaving any hairs behind. He had even ordered Jeanette Kvist to rinse her mouth with cola, which he had found in the fridge, to eradicate all traces of semen.

And yet he had left his genetic fingerprint behind – although he was probably unaware of it. And if it hadn't been for Jeanette Kvist, Axel's colleagues would have missed it. She had contacted the police three days after the rape with additional information, which was the reason Axel was now looking at her case. She knew something about forensic genetics and the examination of rape victims from her medical studies, and she had seen something she couldn't forget. While the man was raping her from behind and bending over her, she had detected a thread of saliva hanging from the nylon stocking by his chin. When he had lowered his head very close to hers and whispered that she was his bitch, the thread was gone, and Jeanette Kvist guessed that it had landed on her bed. Technicians had found the DNA evidence on her bedspread at a subsequent examination.

Axel had noted down 12 points about the perpetrator's MO, which he wanted to look into, but he was far from happy with the level of detail in the description of the sexual assault. There was nothing in this case that he could link directly to the Blackbird case, but that didn't mean there were no similarities. All it meant was that they still had no knowledge of what had happened to Marie Schmidt. But for the first time since he had seen the girl's naked body in Ørsted Park four years ago, there was a chance of finding out.

He picked up his phone. Time to re-engage Tine Jensen. For better or worse.

CHAPTER 6

The description of the attacker from the sexual assault in Refsnæsgade was simultaneously detailed and lacking, but the latter wasn't because of the victim. It was because of the man's precautions.

Jeanette Kvist was 1.78 m tall. The rapist had stood close to her and she thought that his mouth was at her ear level – he was slightly taller than her, so an estimate of 1.82 m to 1.83 m seemed plausible. He was slim. Muscular. Definitely strong. He had been wearing trainers, and forensic technicians had found prints from an Asics GT 2150 trainer on the scaffolding and a shoe print on the living room floor of the same brand in a size 43 – it was one of Denmark's most popular running shoes, but useful nevertheless if it recurred in other cases. Jeans. Black anorak with a hoodie, which was drawn tight around his face to begin with. He had pulled the hood down, but the nylon stocking had rendered pretty much any kind of facial identification impossible. However, Jeanette Kvist could say that he had hair on his head, that his head had an ordinary shape, it wasn't pointed or narrow, his cheekbones perhaps a little broad. His nose small.

Tine Jensen had agreed to re-interview the victim with Axel to try to expand on the information. Axel had had to discuss it with her at length, and had finally managed to convince her that he wasn't rubbishing her efforts so far, but was trying to gather more information about the rapist's MO and behaviour. They would need such details for their search. If the perpetrator in the two cases was identical, Axel knew that he must have a longer track record. There had to be more cases hidden in the system. He hadn't mentioned to Darling that that would be the direction his investigation would then take, and neither did he plan on saying anything else until he had more information, but he had to get Tine Jensen on board first. Axel had already prepared a memo listing 31 points of behaviour, which he would circulate to every police force in Denmark as well as Sweden, Norway and Germany in the hope of a bite.

That was what they were discussing in her car as they drove to Nørrebro. The open windows helped ease the heat that lay like a mirage across the tarmac. Every smell was intensified, and the exhaust fumes were choking on HC Andersens Boulevard.

'You don't do anything by halves, do you? Has Darling approved this?'

'He has given me some time.'

'But has he approved it?'

She got on well with Darling. Would she go running straight to him if he told her the truth? Christ, she was hard work.

'Our focus is the two investigations and the link between them. He has approved that. What's your problem? Aren't you bored with violent assaults? Don't you want to be a homicide investigator? You're never going to get on unless you take the initiative.'

'I've seen what you mean by taking the initiative. I don't want to get reacquainted with that again.'

'Imagine what it could do for your career if we were able to connect several cases.'

'I just want to go through the appropriate channels.'

'If this turns out to be a dead end, you'll soon be rid of me.'

'OK, as long as it doesn't get out of hand.'

Every time they stopped at a junction, the heat in the car intensified. Axel was irritated with her and constantly on the verge of a furious outburst, but his misgivings about her investigation would soon be confirmed or dismissed, and he would have to take it up with her later. He needed her. For now. He had followed Tine Jensen's career since the Blackbird investigation and knew that she had attended several professional development courses and was one of the division's database specialists.

'I need your help.'

'Eh?'

'If this man killed Marie Schmidt and brutally rapes a woman four years later, he must have done it before.'

'Why?'

'Because of how it was planned and how callously it was executed. Because there's a four-year gap. This wasn't an isolated moment of madness. This is a man who gets off on it. And he does it again and again.'

'Yes,' she said. That was all. As if the only thing she cared about was making the case go away.

'So we need to structure the evidence in detail, his MO, any signatures, how he got in and out, what he said and did. Succinct and precise, and then run searches on every accessible database.'

'I understand, but it can take time. More time than you have.'

'It doesn't matter. I'll just have to do it in my own time. What other evidence do you have to move the investigation forward?'

She didn't reply immediately – it was as if she needed a moment to organise her thoughts.

'Nothing. We've spoken to every witness without getting anywhere. All that has happened is that I've been lumbered with you. And six violent assaults from the weekend,' she said ironically.

'If I put together a piece of paper with the details, please would you do the searching?'

She hesitated. Come on, for fuck's sake, a voice was screaming inside him. She nodded.

'Don't get your hopes up.'

Axel had already looked up unsolved stranger rapes from the Copenhagen area. He had found three cases which he would take home and read up on, but he said nothing about that to her.

They drove out of Tagensvej's roaring traffic and turned via Fensmarksgade into the Guldberg quarter – originally a working-class area built in the 1920s in red brick. In contrast with the rest of Nørrebro, there were wide streets with air between the houses, small green front gardens in a few places, and plenty of benches where the neighbourhood's generous assortment of dropouts, fraudsters and junkies could enjoy life in the sun. They were all out today.

As they got out of the car, his mobile vibrated in his pocket. A text message from Cecilie. 'We land tomorrow at 5.40pm. No need for you to pick her up. I can bring her to yours.'

'I'll meet her at the gate,' he texted back.

He was pleased that Emma wouldn't be flying home alone. They had had big discussions during the last six months about whether a six-year-old girl could fly on her own from The Hague to Copenhagen. Cecilie hadn't been worried about it, but Axel had been so strongly opposed to the idea that the first three times when Cecilie wasn't coming back to Denmark and intended to let Emma fly alone, he had flown to The Hague to pick up his daughter. He had struggled to afford it, but had managed to arrange a couple of meetings at Europol HQ in The Hague so he could put it on expenses. It wasn't that Emma was scared of flying. It was Axel who panicked – the mere thought of his daughter being without her mother or father in a plane that might crash was unbearable to him. He had discussed it with the Swede, who had persuaded Axel to let it go. He had been able to do so mentally, but not in his body. Twice since she had flown home to Copenhagen alone, proud and happy, and had met her father in the gate, which he was able to access by flashing his badge. A man of nearly 40 who during the one hour she had been in the air had felt as if he was past 60.

Cecilie offering to drop Emma at Axel's wasn't a sign of rapprochement. It was because she wanted to spend as little time as possible with him. And he wasn't going to the gate to irritate her, but because he missed his daughter so desperately. Or so he had believed when he had sent her his reply – but on top of his longing there was something else. The case he had to solve. His work was his life, and the prospect of a second shot at solving Marie Schmidt's murder was his chance of redemption. This new information propelled him in a direction he knew and loved. He could see the entrance to the tunnel, and knew he had to stay in there until the bastard was caught. Only he couldn't enter it until after his weekend with Emma.

A woman in her thirties, whom Axel thought he recognised, was smoking outside Jeanette Kvist's apartment block. She had chestnut hair cut in a bob and was wearing light-coloured linen trousers and a raw white silk shirt. She had a short summer jacket and a bag over her arm. The moment she spotted their car, she dropped the cigarette on the pavement and squashed it.

'Did you call her?' Axel said.

'Yes, they're entitled to one.'

Ea Holdt was a lawyer who worked at the same firm of solicitors from which Axel's ex-wife was currently on leave. She specialised in personal injury and legal aid cases, and it was a legal requirement that victims of sexual assault should be offered someone like her from their first interview, but in practice many allowed themselves to be talked out of it by police officers, who had a deep rooted antipathy to lawyers, in order to get the interview over and done with.

Ea Holdt offered them a measured smile. She shook hands with Tine Jensen and turned to Axel.

'We've met before. At a works do, I believe. Cecilie Lind is... was my colleague,' she said, shaking hands with Axel firmly and looking him in the eye, completely neutral. 'I gather you need to talk to my client again,' she said without the slightest hint of reproach in her voice.

They entered the stairwell. Axel asked them to stop for a moment.

'Who lives here?' he said, addressing his colleague. 'Have you been through all of them?' According to Tine Jensen, everyone had been interviewed and the mix of residents reflected the neighbourhood, which, like the rest of Nørrebro, had started rising up the social ladder. An old stoner on the ground floor and two old women on the first floor were evidence that the past was still alive, but apart from that the residents in the spacious two and three-bedroom flats were exclusively young people like Jeanette Kvist and a few couples with young children.

'Do you also want to talk to the neighbour who heard Jeanette scream?' Tine Jensen said. To Axel it sounded like a challenge. If he said yes, he would be signalling that he didn't trust her interview of a witness, who had only heard a sound. He declined. It would have to wait, but he was thoroughly fed up with her already. Besides, he was outside his area of expertise. Interviewing a rape victim was enough of a challenge for him. He had investigated many different cases in his 15 years as police officer, but he had never sought out sexual assaults. In fact, he had tried to avoid them, because he was a man and they made him feel guilty. Ea Holdt pretended not to notice the slightly strained atmosphere and merely waited with her hands folded for the two police officers to finish.

Jeanette Kvist opened the door herself. She was tall and blonde, she had blue eyes and was wearing a grey Reebok tracksuit. There was no evidence of the attack on her face except for her eyes, which were dead.

'Hi, Jeanette. We need to talk to you. This is my colleague, Axel Steen.'

She let them into the flat without saying anything. Nor did she speak as they came in. No 'any news?' Or 'have you caught him yet?'

'How are you?' Ea Holdt asked her.

'Managing,' the woman said.

'Please may I have a moment with my client?' the lawyer said, pulling Jeanette Kvist aside, though not so far to prevent Axel hearing their conversation.

'It's completely normal for the police to re-interview you. It means that they're still working on your case. Like I told you the last time, it's very important that you're as precise as possible with the details. Even though it's unpleasant. And hard. So when they ask you, you need to describe the rape with specific words, like we talked about. You should use medical terms, penis, vagina and so on – it's important that you do. For a future trial, so the police can catch the man, and as part of a compensation claim.'

It was miles from what Axel usually heard lawyers say, but then again, he only knew them from interviews where their client was the suspect rather than the victim.

Jeanette Kvist nodded.

'I know,' she said.

Tine Jensen slid her thumbs around her belt, took a deep breath and looked Jeanette Kvist up and down. Axel immediately sensed antipathy from Jeanette Kvist.

'I know it's unpleasant for you to talk about, but—' Tine Jensen said.

'It's all right…' she said, but looked at her lawyer before turning to Axel, who seized the chance to take over.

'We need to go over what he did and said once more. To see if there are similarities to other cases.'

She looked to the side, chewed a nail and withdrew into herself. Axel was convinced that she would shut down completely, but instead she raised her head and looked him right in the eye.

'Funny you should say that. I'm sure there are.'

'What?' Axel said.

'That he has done it before.'

'Why?'

'Because he was so controlling, so vicious. It was like being in some sick American psycho movie. At times I thought I was going to die. At times I thought it was a nightmare, that it would stop… but it didn't.' She began to shake. 'But when he started to… to rape me, I realised that he had done it before.'

'How?'

'Because he… he… was enjoying it… he was in no hurry at all… and at first… when he stood there with the knife to my throat… and we were waiting for my neighbour to go back inside… it wasn't until the light in the stairwell went out… that he pulled me into the bedroom.'

'I want to make sure I've understood you correctly. What exactly did he do from the moment you saw him in the living room?'

'I saw him and I gasped, I think. Then he came up to me. He grabbed my hair. He had a knife. Then he took a hold of me and turned me around. He said: Do as I say or I'll cut your throat.'

'Those were his exact words?'

'Yes. He covered my mouth with his left hand. I could taste the glove. It tasted of leather.'

'When did you scream?'

'He removed his hand and I screamed. I didn't want to, because I was sure he was going to kill me if I did. It felt as if it was what he wanted. It just happened. He put his hand over my mouth again. Very calmly. Then I heard my upstairs neighbour call out 'hello'. He put his head very close to my ear and whispered 'shhh'. And I could feel the blade against my throat. He ran it up and down. As if he was caressing…'

She began to cry. Ea Holdt put her arm around her shoulder. What the victim had just told him deviated in so many ways from what Tine Jensen had written in her report, and Axel felt sick – not at the victim's explanation, but at his colleague's handling of the case.

'I'm OK. We stood there and he just waited. He was patient. And completely cold. As if he was enjoying it. He enjoyed waiting.'

'So he prolonged it? And he let you scream?'

Both women looked at Axel. Why? To make him shut up? Or to ask him if this was really necessary? It was.

'He moved his hand and then I screamed. And we stood there waiting, as if he was in no hurry and wasn't afraid to be caught.'

'Did he say anything?'

'Only that he would kill me… And then shhh.'

'And then when your neighbour went back inside, he led you to the bedroom?'

'No, we stayed where we were. I don't know how long for, but when my neighbour went back inside, he removed his hand from my mouth. And he kept running the blade up and down my throat. It wasn't until I heard the click when the light in the stairwell went out that he put his hand back over my mouth and led me to the bedroom.'

'What did his voice sound like?'

She hesitated.

'Was it angry, calm, snarling, menacing, nasal?'

She fell silent again, and in the stillness Axel could hear the sound of heavy traffic out on Tagensvej.

'It felt as if he was whispering. Whispering into my brain.'

For the next hour she gave a detailed account of the assault, which was ultimately an uninterrupted series of assaults that Axel wished he'd never have had to listen to. And which the woman should never have had to endure. The only word that could describe it was evil.

Several facts emerged that Axel hadn't seen mentioned in the interview reports. For example, the rapist had put music on Jeanette Kvist's sound system and turned up the volume. A detail that could have given forensic officers an opportunity to check the sound system for evidence, had they known about it.

Ea Holdt intervened several times and asked her client open questions, not least when it came to the specific description of which positions Jeanette Kvist and her rapist had been in. He had raped her in the bed and on the bedroom floor. Standing up and lying on top of her. From behind. Except when he had forced himself upon her orally. Then he had said: If you look at me, I'll kill you.'

'I was sure he meant it. I asked him at one point to make sure I wouldn't be able to see him because I was afraid that he might kill me if I could identify him.'

'What else did he say to you?' Ea Holdt said.

'He said that I could choose whether I wanted it "in my mouth, my cunt or up the arse". To start with. When I refused, he grabbed me by the throat and squeezed. Then I said mouth…' She shook her head, she couldn't say it. 'Then it'll be from behind,' he said, and laughed. He pushed me onto the bed, and I thought I was meant to lie down, but he pulled me back so I ended up standing and bent over the bed instead.'

Her account was precise, but she couldn't maintain chronological order, so they asked about specific details and returned to them repeatedly. It was a well-known technique when interviewing witnesses to check that they were telling the truth, but Axel didn't doubt for one second that Jeanette Kvist was.

Tine Jensen asked the fewest questions, but at the end she said:

'You have stated that he ejaculated, but we found no traces of semen on you. How would you explain that?'

Axel was startled at the implied accusation in the question, but feigned indifference. Ea Holdt didn't react either.

'He ejaculated twice. Once in my mouth. Then he told me to drink cola afterwards. To rinse out my mouth. And the second time in my vagina.'

'Did he pull out beforehand?' Ea Holdt said. Axel was about to interrupt her because she was interfering, but she held up a hand to signal for him to hold off.

Jeanette Kvist thought about it.

'Yes, he pulled out at one point and paused.'

'What did he do then?' the lawyer asked.

'I think he unzipped a pocket. It must've been one in his anorak. It sounded as if he was opening a packet. 'Stand very still,' he said, as if he was concentrated on something. I thought he was putting on a condom. Then he resumed. And ejaculated.'

It was a crucial piece of information. Normally rapists were in a hurry, in a great hurry, so the information about the rapist taking his time, so much time that he paused in his abuse of Jeanette Kvist to make sure any DNA was caught by a condom, was important. Axel had never heard of this before. Tine Jensen, however, wasn't following that train of thought.

'How could you know that?' she said instead.

For the first time Jeanette Kvist seemed offended. She glared at Tine Jensen.

'He panted and pulled me close. His thrusting grew faster. Like men do. Before they come. Or perhaps you wouldn't know about that.'

She raised her hands to her face and rubbed it. Then she said in a louder voice:

'I didn't drink anything or clean my teeth afterwards, I know that's important. In case there were traces of his semen in my mouth. But although I said this to the first officers I spoke to, it was three hours before they took me away to be examined. Until then I waited here in one of your white coveralls for two hours. All I did was wait. No one had told me to take extra clothes, so I was driven home in a hospital gown in the morning. After being interviewed for two hours at Bellahøj police station. It wasn't a good experience. I know about rape cases. I've done work experience at the Centre for Victims of Sexual Assaults, where they talked about police work and how victims weren't believed in the bad old days. That we had asked for it. I thought that was all in the past. But it doesn't seem like it.'

'I'm sorry if that was your impression. It's not the case here. We believe you. How sure are you about the condom?' Axel said.

'Quite sure.'

She fell silent, narrowed her eyes slightly, and he could see how agonising it was for her to remember.

'His trousers were down around his ankles. I saw that at one point. And I heard a zip so that must have been in his anorak. I didn't see him put on a condom, but I'm sure that he used both hands for something. It sounded as if he tore something in half. A condom wrapper. What else would he be doing at that point?'

They were done with their questions, but Jeanette Kvist wasn't done with hers.

'Why are you here? Why do I have to go through it all again four weeks later?'

Axel turned to Tine Jensen. Ea Holdt looked at him with a frown. And he realised that neither the lawyer nor Jeanette Kvist had been informed that they had found evidence that linked the rape to an old homicide.

Over to you, Axel thought.

'There has been a new development which I can't tell you about, but we're reviewing your case because there might be a link to another investigation,' Tine Jensen said.

'Your colleague has already said that. What is it?' Jeanette Kvist said.

'Wouldn't it have been better for all parties if my client had been informed of this at the start?' Ea Holdt said.

'Yes,' Axel said. 'Definitely. My colleague and I have misunderstood one another. We apologise. We can actually tell you a little more. We've just got your attacker's DNA. And that's actually thanks to you, your observation of his saliva on the bedspread.'

'I knew it,' Jeanette Kvist said.

Tine Jensen looked utterly hacked off.

'So we have a piece of forensic evidence, but his name isn't in our database. However, something that looks like his DNA profile was found in an unsolved case four years ago. The murder of a young woman.'

He looked Jeanette Kvist right in the eye.

'So you were right. And you did the right thing. You didn't resist. And that was good.'

Or you might be dead now, he thought.

Tine Jensen was fuming once they were out in the stairwell, but Axel stopped her.

'Keep your mouth shut until the lawyer is gone, and then we need to talk.'

They walked down the stairs with Ea Holdt, who asked several questions about the murder case. Axel answered them all, but stressed that although the DNA evidence was a full match, they couldn't conclude that it was the same perpetrator because the DNA in the Marie Schmidt case was saliva found on her leaver's cap, and they had no idea how it had got there. In contrast with the saliva on Jeanette Kvist's bedspread.

Outside in the street the sun beamed down between the buildings. The cobblestones shone like beaten silver. Tine Jensen's mobile rang, and she stepped away from them. Ea Holdt lit a cigarette.

'Thank you for telling my client about the DNA match. I could tell from your face that you understood how important it was. Unlike some people.'

She glanced at Tine Jensen, who had concluded her call and was now getting into the car, slamming the door shut behind her.

'If you remember anything or hear anything from your client, please call me,' Axel said, and said goodbye to Ea Holdt.

He was about to get into the car when he remembered a detail from the interview that had puzzled him.

He went back over to her. She lowered the car window and looked up at him.

'Excuse me...'

'Are you looking for a lift into town?' she said with a smile.

'Eh?'

'You don't seem to be on the same wavelength, you and your colleague. And I have to be honest and say that it was good to see someone finally taking Jeanette seriously.'

'Yes. No, but thanks for offering. We have a lot to talk about, but I'm here because I have a question for you.'

Friendly grey-blue eyes looked calmly into his.

'Yes?'

'How did you know about the condom?'

'It was just a hunch.'

'Why did you ask her about it?'

'What do you mean?'

'It made her uncomfortable. I thought you—'

'...were supposed to protect my client against nasty police officers. Yes, that's a part of my job, but the best thing that can happen for my client is that you catch her attacker. And you'll only do that if you're thorough. Is it a problem that I helped you?'

Axel felt somewhat embarrassed.

'No.'

'All right then. Call me if you need help some other time. Have a good day, Axel Steen,' she said, chucking the cigarette butt into the street and starting the car with a smile playing on her lips.

There had been something else he had wanted to ask her, but now it was gone. Axel returned to the car and a still fuming Tine Jensen.

'Why were you trying to undermine me in front of two people?' she hissed.

'Drop the act,' Axel said. 'I can see right through you. You didn't believe her. You thought she was lying. You thought she made up the rape. That's why you did so little.'

'I've no idea what you're talking about.'

'Oh yes you do. I read your report and it's a disgrace. Your distrust of the victim has screwed up the investigation. Why did no one check CCTV from Nørreport station? Why didn't you check out any convicted rapists or sex offenders living in the area before you got the DNA profile? Why didn't you issue a description to the media? Why didn't you try to track down every man at Rosie McGee's that night?'

She was about to say something, but Axel held up a hand.

'Shut up, I'm not done yet, Tine. Why didn't you even circulate a description of the man to patrol cars? Because you never believed her. She didn't fight back. It says so three times in your report. She can't describe her attacker, she had left the windows open, and is that really a good idea in Nørrebro on a weekend night, you ask her – in the report, for God's sake – and then there's the semen. You thought she was lying about him ejaculating because there was no semen, but you never asked what could have happened. It was something her own lawyer brought to our attention just now, for crying out loud. He put on a rubber in order not to leave any evidence. It's a crucial feature about him. Which you overlooked!'

Tine Jensen protested once more, but Axel didn't let her get a word in.

'Yes, we need to be suspicious, Tine, but this is way, way beyond that. Jeanette Kvist is one of the most credible victims I have ever met, but you didn't believe her, and so you made a total pig's ear of the investigation. You didn't know that he played music or that he pulled her hair or that she didn't scream until after he had grabbed her. You didn't get her to tell you half of what he said. Fuck you!'

There were beads of sweat on her upper lip and red patches on her neck.

'You're wrong.'

'And last, but not least: you hadn't told her that we had a DNA match. You hadn't even told her that we have a DNA profile of her attacker. And now you're pissed off with me for telling her. Fuck you. If it hadn't been for her, we never would have got it. Because you've carried out the patchiest and shoddiest review of a crime scene I've seen for a long time. If this ever comes to trial, then she deserves millions in compensation – and not just from the rapist, but also from us, because you've screwed up big time.'

She said nothing for several moments after he had finished his rant. His rage was all the more intense because he had believed it was his behaviour during the Blackbird case that had alienated her – not that she was scared someone would find out she'd messed up a new investigation. When the DNA result came back, she must have known that it was only a matter of time before he came after her. That explained why she had been so defensive.

But if he had thought their clash during the Blackbird investigation had been forgotten, he could think again.

'And there's the Axel I know. You take out all your frustration with an investigation on your colleagues. You acted out for six months last time until you forced me into a corner, told me I was pathetic, and I walked. I'm not putting up with this. No wonder I had doubts. You're insulting me just as I knew you would. I've dealt with several rape cases over the years, and a false statement isn't unusual.'

Axel was well aware of that, just as he knew that victims putting up physical resistance or crying for help was always a contentious issue. An open window would always make an investigator wonder whether the victim herself hadn't let in her attacker. Police officers were like that, and they probably had to be. The absence of signs of a struggle and information that the attacker had ejaculated – although there were no semen traces – were factors that couldn't just be dismissed, but needed

45

to be eliminated as part of a thorough investigation. But she hadn't done that. And that made him furious.

'And another thing. The DNA test. Why did it take three and a half weeks to get the result? That's outrageous!'

'You're clearly used to working with homicide. Rapes go to the back of the queue. Even a stranger rape like this one.'

Axel was indeed used to getting the results of DNA tests in a matter of days if it was urgent, and he couldn't conceive why something which in his eyes was almost as awful as homicide, had to wait. But they had to move on. They had so much fresh information. Axel wasn't Tine's immediate superior, but he was a DCI, while she was only a sergeant, and he had to put a lid on their disagreement.

'I'm aware that it's only natural to be sceptical when investigating rape. Now let's put our differences aside. Surely you would agree with me that what we've learned – plus what you've discovered – indicates that this attack was extremely brutal and planned?'

'Yes.'

'And that it requires us to devote everything to solving it, and check whether it can be linked to other cases?'

'Yes.'

'Normally a rapist is in a hurry – especially in the case of stranger rapes. Am I right?'

'Often, yes.'

'This guy takes his time. He even enjoys exposing himself to risk by taking his hand away from her mouth so she screams, and afterwards caresses her throat with a knife while he savours her silence as a demonstration of his control.'

'Yes, it's creepy.'

'It's more than that. For me it's a sure sign that he's responsible for several more attacks apart from this one – and the murder.'

'So what do you suggest?'

'We carry on as we've agreed. You search the databases and write up the investigation. I'll see what I can find in the archives and I'll reopen the Blackbird case.'

'You'll be working alone. I'm not interested. In fact, I'm not interested in any of it. We can investigate in parallel, and we can compare, but I want to carry out my own investigation without you there slinging mud at me.'

'I promise to leave you alone as long as you do your bit. If not, then let me know, and I'll do it myself. I intend to start tonight by retracing Marie Schmidt's route on the night she died.'

'What for? Didn't you get enough of it last time?'

'I never get enough of a murder investigation until it's solved. It's a way of bringing it back to life. Tomorrow I hope we'll have a list of cases we can link to this one so we can check if there's any evidence that wasn't DNA tested – old evidence.'

Homicide was Axel's world. And in homicide investigations every resource was deployed from the beginning. Those who worked with violent crimes, which following the police reform was a merger of robbery and homicide and also serious assault, sexual assaults, child sexual abuse, arson and terror, worked cases that were subject to prioritising. And priorities weren't always based on the seriousness of the crime. Rape, for example, was further down the list than biker gangs and other gang cases. The shifting political tides also mattered. But within each category of crime there were also priorities. If they had overwhelming evidence of a rapist, witnesses, a description, surveillance footage, it would shoot to the top of the list, but as a case clogged up and time passed, it moved further down the list. It was what had happened in the case of Jeanette Kvist, but that didn't get Tine Jensen off the hook. She had buried the case herself. And he found it hard to forgive her for that.

They drove to HQ in silence. Nørrebrogade was now a dizzying symphony of pedestrians and cyclists, girls in short dresses or shorts and bikini tops, bare-chested men, groups of young people with sound systems sitting around drinking beer. Camping for the Roskilde Festival would open the day after tomorrow and they were preloading for nine days of partying. He would have the city all to himself. Together with Blackbird's killer.

He thought about Ea Holdt, who exuded a factual coolness that fascinated him. And he wondered that he had lived long enough to see the day when a lawyer would help him with the investigation of a case. He thought of her gaze, which concealed a quizzical and teasing laughter, her warm and appealing eyes. What was it he had wanted to ask her but that her poise had made him forget?

Then he thought about his daughter, whom he would be seeing tomorrow. He had to get as much done as he could before she arrived. He could read up on the case and write reports when she was sleeping, but otherwise he would have to be there for her.

And finally he thought about Jeanette Kvist: strong, shaken, destroyed by a twisted man's desire and sadism. He had met rape victims who never recovered, and no one was ever left unscarred, but Jeanette Kvist might be one of those who coped better than most. What on earth made a man treat a woman like that? He remembered women who had asked him to be rough with them, pull their hair, force their head backwards while he fucked them, put them in handcuffs and smack their buttocks. The sheer number made him feel sick. As did the memory of how much he had enjoyed it.

CHAPTER 7

Lists. Who doesn't love a list? Ever since he was a child, Jens Jessen had organised everything. Lists of playmates – they were short. Lists of outstanding homework – even shorter. Lists of skills he wanted to acquire – they were long. At one point he had started making lists of things he liked. Countries. Spiders. Teachers. Sweets. Symphonies. Girls. Trivial matters, his father had said.

And now this job. Lists of everything. Time usage. Reports. Priorities. There had been no mention of this when he read law. But he loved it. Figures. Columns. Bottom lines. They could moan about burglaries, Nigerian prostitutes in Istedgade or hash clubs. You couldn't argue with numbers.

He was definitely in the top five most hated bosses in the Copenhagen police force due to his efficiency measures, but the National Police and the Ministry had seen the latest reports. He needed nine months and the financial ecosystem would balance once again. He looked at the bare wooden floor. Took three steps across it in his Henri Lloyd shoes. There were no rugs here underneath which anything could be swept. He was putting a stop to that. No more politically horse-traded priorities, no more additional grants to combat trafficking or fight honour-related crime, nothing that would end up being spent on replacing the tyres on patrol cars or paying overtime to workaholic staff. In any other profession, people jumped at the chance to take time off in lieu. Police officers, however, wanted to work themselves to death and be paid extra for it. Work regular, contracted hours. It was the only solution. Apart from redundancies. But that wouldn't go down well with the politicians. 'The police officer and the doctor have replaced God. Sack them and your career is over,' a Social Democratic justice minister had said when Jens, then a young civil servant still wet behind the ears, had served as his secretary in the late 1990s.

He had a goal. He would clear up the mess without blotting the force's copybook. True, they were the guardians of justice, but he must never sow any doubts about their infallibility. Rugs might have their uses, memory lapses might occur, but there was no doubt that the ideal solution was to make difficult cases go away for good.

Justice must be done, of course, but it mustn't cost anything. Because then the system would break down. And that was what most people failed to understand. In particular, the guy inside this envelope.

He was meeting with the head of Human Resources in five minutes. He opened the envelope again and looked at the photographs of Emma's father. The scars after the burns to the left side of his face had bizarrely only served to make him even more, well, what could you say about a man? When you were a man describing another man? Not beautiful, not raw, but authentic and… something else. He had been a big shot since the Youth House murders. While hunting the killer he had ended up having his face and hair burned off. Cecilie had also burned him – or had she got burned by him? There were things he didn't know.

Axel Steen had a better clear-up rate than anybody else. There were rumours of hash abuse. And now this. Axel Steen was a psycho cop, a rogue missile, a damaged man spiralling towards rock bottom. And Jens Jessen didn't mind him ending up there. But then again, he is the father of my stepdaughter, Jens Jessen thought. And this could backfire on people other than those directly involved and end up right at my own front door.

He closed the envelope. The question was the origin of the pictures. The text on the photograph more than hinted that it was internal, since the sender knew Axel Steen's badge number. There were many possibilities. Friends in PET, the Drug Squad, the National Police – yes, it could even have been sent from the outside to someone in house, who had then forwarded it to Jens Jessen. Axel Steen had upset at lot of people. But this was more than someone upset. This was an enemy. Yet another enemy. Apart from himself.

CHAPTER 8

Nørreport station. The gateway to the city centre. Traffic and pedestrian chaos above ground, city sewers with tiled lavatory walls and the smell of piss and diesel fumes below. Everyone was going somewhere, but no one going together. Tine Jensen had dropped him off without asking what he was doing, and he was standing in the middle of the intoxicating bustle on the cobblestones outside the station entrance, surrounded by roaring traffic lanes, pedestrians waiting to cross the road crowding around the lights, their numbers swelling like a doughnut, while a hardy few cheated and dashed across the street to the sound of car horns. Sausage stalls, abandoned bicycles in rusty intercourse with one another, Metro lifts, squashed paper cups from McDonald's, and bottle collectors rummaging around the bins for recyclables. He moved through the Functionalist station, past two kiosks, down to the level with the ticket machines, timetables and photo booths, and knocked on a door. At first the face was quizzical, then the head of security recognised Axel.

'You again,' he sighed.

'Yes.'

'I haven't missed you.'

'I need to see some CCTV footage.'

'Again? Have you fished another body out of Ørsted Park?'

'No.'

'You never caught him, did you?'

'No.'

'All right then. In you come.'

They walked downstairs to a low room with screens on the wall. The man sat down and sucked cola from a paper cup.

'I helped you back then, and you suspected me of having killed the girl.'

'Yes, that's my job. I had to investigate that possibility.'

'Investigate that possibility, yes, I guess you could call it that, though I would call it harassment.'

Axel remembered how he had shaken the man, who couldn't believe Axel was serious when he ordered him to tell him where he had been at the time of the murder. And if anyone could provide him with an alibi. He had laughed nervously. Then he had refused, grown angry, and Axel had grabbed him, shaken him and screamed into his face that if he didn't produce an alibi, he would drag him to HQ and interview him under caution.

'If it helps, I would like to repeat my apology from back then. I crossed the line.'

'You don't say. What do you want now?'

'Friday 30 May. Between 11.00pm and 11.30pm. A young woman gets on a train from Vesterport and gets off here.'

'Are you asking if I have an alibi?'

Axel returned his smile.

'No, but it's a serious incident. Can you also access cameras at Vesterport station?'

'Yes, but it could take a while. Friday 30 May, did you say? It's your lucky day. We only save the stuff for four weeks. It'll be deleted tomorrow. Let me have a look.' He tapped on his keyboard for a while. 'Here we go.'

He pointed to six screens on the wall, and Axel could see the platform from six different camera angles.

'I believe that she left Vesterport between 11.18pm and 11.22pm.'

'OK, we'll look at that afterwards.'

The cameras were positioned in the ceiling and showed the whole two hundred metres of the platform and the track.

At 11.21pm Jeanette Kvist got off the train at Nørreport. She was in view on one camera for three seconds, before she reached the next one, which was mounted at the steps leading up from the platform. Three seconds and then she disappeared out of the picture.

'Can you slow it down for me?'

There were many other passengers in the picture, but Axel could quickly eliminate most of them. He was looking for a man, 1.8 m tall, wearing trainers and jeans. There was only one. And he got off the train two seconds after Jeanette Kvist and went the same way as her.

'Can you take a still of that guy? Play it again. Stop there! Can you find the footage from Vesterport?'

'Yes, it means we're looking for the A line.' He checked the timetable. 'The 11.19pm from Hundige. This will take some time.'

The head of security turned back to his computer screen. Axel looked at the grey tunnels, the platforms and tracks on the screens. Everything was bathed in a crackling grey light. Passengers milled in and out like ants every time a train stopped and the doors slid open. People waited impatiently to board, their frozen faces preoccupied with everyday concerns. Then there was a pause as those waiting for the next train were left behind. They didn't talk to one another. Civil servants in suits, yummy mummies, university lecturers and lawyers travelling home to North Sjælland were standing next to shop girls from Købmagergade, schoolchildren from the city centre, sixth formers, homeless people, junkies, leery drunks, lost tourists, bus drivers, window cleaners, police officers.

A few never boarded any trains, but were sleeping or drinking on the benches, and he was familiar enough with the city to know that the likelihood of them ever reaching a destination of any sort was microscopic.

'Here we are.'

There were four cameras at Vesterport station, which was enveloped in darkest night.

Jeanette Kvist was seen running onto the platform and jumping on board the train.

'Go back a bit.'

Jeanette Kvist rolled backwards and disappeared out of the picture. There was no sign of the man.

'What about the other monitors?' The head of security was silent. He was just as focused as Axel on finding the man. He brought up several screen images. Nor was there anything on the next film. He opened the third camera. Bingo. There he was, appearing at the same end of the platform where Axel could work out that Jeanette Kvist had come running. He was even further away than on the pictures from Nørreport, but he was there.

And he got on the same train.

'I guess you'll want to talk to him. What has he done?'

'You bet I do. And I need those clips. Please would you email them to me?'

'Yes.'

'Today?'

'You'll have them in one hour. I just need to make a copy.'

Back at HQ Axel went to brief Tine Jensen about the man on the platform, but she wasn't in her office.

'She's in the library,' her colleague said. Axel was about to make his way there, but was interrupted by a call from Dorte Neergaard.

'Are you free tonight?'

'No, I have work to do.'

'So you've finally crawled out of the woodwork. What are you doing? Do you have anything for me?'

'No, neither work nor pleasure. My daughter gets in tomorrow.'

'In that case, I'll have to find someone else to play with this weekend. Speak soon.'

She rang off before Axel could say anything. He didn't owe her anything, did he? They had sex and talked shop. She was a reporter on TV2's crime magazine and one of the country's brightest crime reporters, they smoked a joint once or twice a week, depending on how bad things were with him. The worse he was, the more often he would see her. He didn't know what she saw in him and nor did he want to, if it meant more commitment than their current relationship.

His mobile rang again. He was convinced it was her.

'What is it this time?'

'Don't speak to me like that, you Danish bastard,' he heard the Swede's offended voice. 'You never call these days. Have you gone completely to the dogs?'

They saw one another regularly, he was Axel's closest friend, but in recent months their contact had been intermittent, and it wasn't the Swede's fault.

'No, I've just been a bit busy.'

'Nonsense. I stopped by on Tuesday. But you were taking time off.'

'You sound like my stepmother.'

He heard a mixture of coughing and laughter.

'What are you working on?'

'We have evidence that links the Blackbird investigation to an aggravated sexual assault that happened a month ago.'

'And you're investigating that?'

'Yes, it's not an obvious one, but I do have something to go on.'

'Excellent. It'll do you good to clear up that nasty business. I'm coming to Nørrebrogade tomorrow morning. How about breakfast?'

Axel said yes and they ended the call. Then he went down to the basement to find all the archived items from the Blackbird investigation, including the old surveillance videos from Nørreport.

He carried two boxes back to the office. One contained Marie Schmidt's clothing, leaver's cap, handbag – everything wrapped in plastic bags. There had been significant progress in DNA analysis since 2004, so he would send them off for retesting. He opened the second box. It contained her diary and a portable hard disk with a backup of her computer and letters. And six discs with the old recordings from the train, from Nørreport and from Klampenborg station.

He put them into the DVD player and reviewed them one after the other. It took him 30 minutes and brought old memories back to life. Emma at the hospital. He couldn't bear to think of that.

There was no man resembling the one from Nørreport on any of them, but that didn't mean it couldn't be him. He chucked five of the discs back into the box and rewound and watched the recording where Marie Schmidt got off the train at Nørreport station four years ago. She was a tall, slim, almost skinny girl, who wobbled a little on her high heels, swaying her hips while keeping her upper body almost still in something a female investigator had described as a catwalk, her dress was elegant but short. She was a temptation, provocative, even for an 18-year-old girl. She smiled as though she was in a world of her own. He watched it again. And again. Did she know at this point? Was there something in her eyes giving the slightest hint of knowledge about what would happen to her moments later? Axel had asked himself that question a hundred times. There was no answer this time either.

He turned off the DVD player. It was coming up to four o'clock in the afternoon. The head of security at Nørreport station had sent him an email. He opened it, rewatched the man on both clips and made four still photographs, printed them out and took them to radio control. He asked for them to be circulated to all police officers along with information about when and where the man had been seen, adding that the police would like to speak to him in connection with an aggravated sexual assault four weeks ago, and that it was top priority. Axel went back to his office and emailed over an electronic copy.

He looked at the summaries of the three investigations he had printed out earlier that day. He opened them one after the other and made a note of the investigating officer. He recognised all the names, but he had a tolerable relationship with only one of them, and so decided to start with him. He was aware of his own reputation within the force – he was known not only as Scarface, the hero from the Davidi investigation who had had half his face burned off, but also for being difficult, obstinate and confrontational. There were several notes in his personnel file, and not all of them concerned the rough treatment of suspects. Some of his colleagues had also had a taste of his temper. The fact that it hadn't cost him more than it had was down to his clear-up rate. He enjoyed a certain degree of tolerance, but he was well aware that it had its limits.

He called Johnny Schlichtkrull, a sergeant at Bellahøj police station, an experienced investigator who was ten years older than Axel. He had dealt with a rape as far back as 1998 in Brohusgade in Nørrebro. The victim was a 22-year-old woman by the name Anne Marie Zeuthen. Initially there were four similarities that Axel could see. Her attacker had entered through a window via some scaffolding. He had worn gloves. He had threatened her with a knife. The crime scene was Nørrebro, a side street to Åboulevarden. Four similarities, but there could be many other less obvious ones hidden in the report. Aggravated sexual assault was all it said. Johnny had gone home. And he wasn't answering his mobile. Axel left a voicemail and asked him to call.

The other case was 12 years old. The name of the victim was Line Jørgensen and she was only 19 years old. She had been raped in Nørrebro Park, just half a kilometre from Axel's flat. The attacker had been masked and threatened his victim with a knife, but information was sparse and there was nothing else to link it to the Jeanette Kvist investigation. The officer who had dealt with the case had now retired. Axel made a note of his address and phone number. The third case was from an allotment garden association by Borgervænget in Østerbro, close to Nordbanen and Nørreport. Lulu Linette Larsen. Aged 17. Summer 2003. Knife and mask over the face. It didn't say which type. The investigating officer was Sergeant Julie Thomsen, who had since been promoted to chief inspector and was a personal friend of Darling, so he decided to check if those files were in the basement before he contacted her – which would indirectly let his boss know that he was stirring up the swamp of shelved investigations.

He worked for another hour with his MO list from the rape of Jeanette Kvist, before emailing it to other police districts. There were 27 points on it. Five of them were so specific that he asked to be contacted immediately if they had come across any one of them at all. A gloved hand over the mouth, the condom, the stocking, rinsing the mouth, and ordering the victim to choose how she wanted to be raped. The other 22 points were supplementary, and he asked to be contacted should three or more of them occur together.

He went down to the archive in the basement under HQ. A mausoleum of human misery, but also a place that concealed secrets that couldn't bear the light of day. After searching for an hour he found two slim files with the paperwork from the Lulu Linette Larsen case and brought them back to his office, where he added them to the summaries from the other cases to take home. Along with the Blackbird investigation.

He rode past Folkets Park on his way home and bought three grams of hash. Nørrebrogade was filled with cyclists on their way to and from the city, buses and cars close together, and Axel wondered what would happen when the city council closed the street to through traffic after the summer. He stopped to buy a kebab, stood outside while he waited for it and felt the sun on his face. He was on the way, he could feel it, on the way towards something that could drag him out of the mire.

Back in his flat he ate quickly. He had a little time to read up on the cases before he headed out for a night walk that would take him back to the summer of 2004.

CHAPTER 9

Bellevue beach on heat. Posh boys' convertibles roared in competition with modified cars driven by dark-skinned youngsters. The smell of grilled sausages, marinade and disposable barbecues, swallows, bats, whooping teenagers, songs in the crisp night air, a deep blue, transparent darkness. It was still warm. Axel walked quickly and sat down under a tree at the edge of the beach. He could see the profile of the Knud Rasmussen statue further down Strandvejen peering across the Øresund.

Here, under this tree, Marie Schmidt and her classmates had partied after several days of drinking following their exams. They would be riding through the city in a horse-drawn carriage the following day, but Marie never got to do that. That Saturday night there had been hundreds of people on Bellevue beach – school leavers, a couple of football teams, and people who had gone to the beach, got carried away by the summer mood and were now enjoying the afterglow of the sun on the sand or the grass or at one of the many restaurants along the road. Marie Schmidt had been in a group from which police had been able to name 56 people. They were mainly school leavers and students, but also a few from other groups of partygoers. It had been an enormous task to piece together the events of the evening, and Axel had constantly had a feeling that they had missed something. At seven o'clock Marie and her friends had met up on Bellevue beach with beers, cider, spirits and fizzy drinks and had had pizzas delivered. They had brought along a sound system, they had drunk heavily, some had thrown up, there had been the beginnings of a fight with another group of young people, and everything had been merry mayhem.

Marie had kissed a young man from another class, Niels Bak, which had sparked tension because she had previously been seeing another boy from her class, Rasmus Berndt. Both of the young men had been interviewed thoroughly. The unsuccessful rival had left shortly after Marie, and Axel had spent 48 hours with him before they let him go. They had mapped the 18-year-old girl's sexual relationships, which had proved to be extensive. Over six months she had slept with four young men from her year, and they described her as 'wild in bed', 'up for anything', 'horny', 'a bit slutty'. Blow jobs in a park, sex in a classroom and anal sex with one of the young men. An experienced and forward young woman.

They had found DNA from a total of 29 different donors on her clothing, leaver's cap and handbag, and they had managed to trace seven of them: her father, two friends, three boys from her class she had been involved with, and her own; the rest were mixed profile DNA for which no donors could be found. One explanation for that could be that the young people had played a kind of game where they tossed their caps onto different sticks that had been stuck into the ground, and Marie's cap was one of those that had been handled by many people, including some not from her school.

She had gone home around 11.30pm, and had agreed with Niels Bak that she would come to his house about 1am. He had subsequently sent her several text messages when she failed to show. They had also brought him in for lengthy interviews. He didn't leave Bellevue beach until 00.30am, but it was a fact that apart from her text message to her father from the train, they had no evidence of the time of her murder – so the young man could in theory be the killer. His alibi, however, was backed up by his parents. He had come straight home to Frederiksberg and couldn't possibly have had time to attack and murder her in Ørsted Park.

Axel walked up to Klampenborg station exactly as Marie had done four years ago, and as he himself had done many times, far too many times in the subsequent months. They had carried out a standard reconstruction of her movements right after the murder, they had done it again precisely a week later at the same time, but it hadn't been enough for Axel, who every subsequent Saturday evening and night had made his own reconstruction and later had replayed her movements to himself night after night when the case had stalled. He had gone to Bellevue beach, had sat where Marie had sat, walked up to the station, caught the train to Nørreport, walked up along Nørrevold and through the gate to Ørsted Park. Exactly as he was doing now.

First he had followed her movements to the minute, later he had taken time to study each location, sensed the people around him, the air, and all the tiny little signals that might point him in the right direction. He had tried putting himself in her shoes. It lived on like a sick, black deadweight in his memory of a time where everything imploded for him, where he had failed to attain his goal, and in his blind hunt for it had lost sight of everything else, his wife, his daughter, his common sense.

Emma had been two years old. One night Axel had come home to find Cecilie sitting in bed, waiting for him, her hands folded and smiling with joy.

'I think I'm pregnant.'

Axel had stopped mid-movement. In shock.

'What's wrong?'

'I'm… I'm just surprised.'

'Yes, you are, but you're also not happy, I can see that.'

Ever since her birth, Emma had devoured their relationship. Everything that had brought them together had been marginalised, and what remained was breast feeding, nursery, nappy changing, broken nights and endless worries. He had had no idea that having a baby would be like this. That you would get so little back. That the tiny, non-verbal lump of flesh could do nothing but eat, scream, crap or sleep. It got better as she grew older, but Axel and Cecilie's relationship was changed for ever.

The Swede had told him that a man should think very carefully about the consequences of saying no to having another child with a woman who wanted one. Axel had said yes, not to the child, but to Cecilie.

But by then it was too late. His hesitancy had come between them. The following week a doctor's appointment confirmed that it was a false alarm, that there was no child.

'I guess you're relieved,' she had said. She had completely stopped making eye contact with him by then, but now she looked as if she hated him. From then on they slept back to back in bed – when they even slept in the same bedroom. And on the rare occasions they had sex, he felt as if she was tolerating him, as if she just wanted to get it over with.

The C-line train to Køge pulled in. He boarded the second carriage and sat on the very seat Marie Schmidt had sat on four years ago. On the train two young guys from Skovshoved had started to chat her up and tried to invite her out. Unsuccessfully. She seemed to know where she was going, one of them had said. They, too, had been interviewed for hours, but they were one another's alibi and had carried on to Vesterport, where they had been caught on CCTV.

'Do you fancy coming with us to In? Go on, we'll buy you a drink, we're gentlemen,' the two young men had pestered her.

'I'm going home. I'm busy,' she had said. Flirting. According to an old male passenger who had sat diagonally across from Marie Schmidt.

The whole case came alive in his head. He had never in his career re-read reports and interviews so many times, and the case contained more than 1,500. There were few people he hadn't interviewed more than once. This had led to several complaints from witnesses who felt they had been harassed unnecessarily when they had already given their statement to the police. The suburban idyll of Hellerup whizzed past against the backdrop of the blue night sky, framed by trees, roof ridges and solitary chimneys.

They had interviewed Marie's father over and over to find out if he might have killed her. It had been tricky due to his grief, but as it is most often parents who kill their children, Axel had approached the task the only way he knew – by making the man aware of that fact and being straight with him. The job had been assigned to him to begin with, but Tine Jensen and Darling had soon taken over when Axel had crossed the line and caused the father to break down. Their family consisted of just the two of them. The father had been alone with her since she was 13 years old. Her mother's death from cancer had hit Marie hard, and she had fallen behind at school. She had spent a year at a continuation school on Funen. The loss of her mother, who had taught at the Conservatory of Music, had badly affected the girl, who had been a talented singer but started to act up in sixth form. At times it seemed as if she had given up hope of the future that was otherwise mapped out for her, as one of her friends had put it. Her father had been shocked at the number of Marie's boyfriends and the extent of her sex life, and was utterly crushed by grief. He had lost his entire family in five years.

They had done the rounds of her circle of acquaintances and had pointed the spotlight at any potential killers, scrutinising their movements and links to the victim. Especially Rasmus Berndt, who had been in a rough and dominating sexual relationship with Marie. A teacher and two other young men discovered just how far the police would go to eliminate them as suspects. Rumour had it that Marie had been seeing an older man, but they had never managed to identify her secret lover. She kept a diary and there were entries from the last fortnight that they had been unable to decode, including one where she had written: 'Now I've told her. Asked her to help me so it will stop.' None of her friends or those closest to her knew what it meant.

During the early weeks, as they worked their way through every possible motive of every suspect who knew Marie Schmidt, the focus shifted from a killer she knew to an unknown one. It meant that the investigation had to be expanded, the net cast wider, and the mesh grew bigger and bigger. They were convinced that they were dealing with an impulsive rape and murder where there had been no previous contact between the victim and the killer. And that was like searching a haystack in the dark, blindfolded – until someone places the needle in your hand, and that someone might just be Jeanette Kvist.

The train pulled in at Nordhavn station. Behind the window in an apartment he caught a flash of a woman blurred by curtains, a mobile pendant with clowns lit up in a child's bedroom, two young people playing football with a beer can on Nordre Frihavnsgade.

Then Østerport station. The overground train was sucked into the underground section towards Nørreport. Axel followed her route, getting out on the right-hand side, stepping onto the platform to the smell of burned rats, piss and a chaos of drunken teenagers. He wondered who might have been walking behind her.

He walked up the stairs and emerged in the same place he'd been standing earlier today. The cobblestones outside Nørreport station. He looked up at the buildings. It was the most beautiful place in the city, a big-city dream, a stylistic confusion of old and new. NØRREPORT was bent in red neon over the beautiful old Functionalist building. On the side facing the city centre he could see the neon ad for Bikuben Bank, a yellow hive with bees buzzing around it, and on the side facing Nørrebro a tower block loomed on Frederiksborggade, a totem pole in sterile 1950s concrete with a thorny crown of mobile transmitters on the roof. The air was heavy with young people intoxicated by the freedom of the night, fleeting hopes, laughter, bubbling anticipation and desire. Including desires like the one that had killed Marie Schmidt.

A witness had seen the girl move across the right-hand lane of Nørre Voldgade and walk up towards the park, and Axel followed the road – but he was losing heart, because what was the point? He walked to the gate to Ørsted Park and looked down towards the lake and the small jetty from where they had pulled her out of the water. He stopped and listened. He could hear rustling in the bushes not far away.

After the murder they had put up notices asking anyone who was in the park that night to contact them, but it had produced few results. In the weeks that followed they had raided the bushes favoured by the gay community night after night in the hope of finding potential witnesses. They had spoken to 127 men who had been to the park. One thought he might have heard something in the bushes where Marie had most probably been killed, and had been on the verge of going there in the hope of taking part in what he hoped was rough group sex, but had then been approached by another man and had gone off with him. One had seen the girl walk into the park, and a third thought he had seen her emerge on the other side by Farimagsgade, but he had been on all fours in the bushes and was in the process of being 'rogered to high heaven', so he couldn't be sure.

Axel had carried on by himself. Not only in order to find more witnesses, but in the fragile hope that the killer might return to the scene of the crime. He had brought along his torch, but never caught anything other than frightened men busy giving blow jobs or having sex in bushes, up against trees or under the pedestrian bridge across the lake, which was popularly known as the Bridge of Sighs. He had become the terror of the gay community. The crazed detective who chased them around the park at night in search of witnesses, and who would go nuts if they had been there on the night of the murder and not come forward.

His mobile rang.

'Axel.'

'Hi, it's Tine. I've seen your email with the surveillance pictures. It's a good lead.'

'Yes.'

'I've spoken to Darling in connection with that, and he doesn't think that there's enough for us to go public with it.'

'No, there isn't, but there are other options.'

Two young people came riding on a messenger bike down the hill. They were whooping.

'Where are you?'

'Ørsted Park.'

'What are you doing there?'

'Doesn't matter.'

'Have you been retracing Marie Schmidt's footsteps?'

'I'm walking the route she took, yes.'

'Well, I don't want to interfere.'

'Nor should you. What do you want?'

'I've typed up the case and sent it to you. And I've been through the databases.'

'Which ones?'

'We're a bit wary when it comes to registering sensitive personal information, but other countries have extensive registers that list MO and signatures for comparison. Canada, USA, Austria, Switzerland. I've called some contacts I have. I've searched the criminal records register and it has thrown up a lot of cases, but we'll need to open each individually to see if there's anything useful. Then there are the child porn databases, if you think they might be relevant. We have one in Denmark, and there are many more options with Europol and the USA. However, they list information on the victim, not the perpetrator.'

'What would that give us?'

'Nothing, probably, but it can't do any harm. It's not terribly comprehensive. Infomedia came up with six rape cases which I've also emailed to you.'

'Thank you. I'll check them out.'

'And I'll be putting officers in the area around Refsnæsgade from 11.00pm to 2.00am tomorrow morning, then we'll have to see if anyone remembers anything from four weeks ago.'

'Good. I look forward to hearing about it.'

'Yes.'

She ended the call. Axel walked down the path to the lake. He sat down on one of the green benches not far from the jetty where they had fished out Marie Schmidt's body four years ago. She hadn't been strangled. She had drowned. She had been unconscious due to the strangulation when she was thrown into the water; she might have survived, but she had drowned in the green water. He was tired and craved a joint.

The case blurred for him. Why would there be a link between the sexual assault and the Blackbird case? Might the DNA evidence be coincidental? Was Tine right to be sceptical? What if it was just him, who was fixating because he had been brought back to the biggest defeat of his life?

A serial killer? Was that what he was hunting? Denmark didn't have any of those – that was what people had said ever since the phenomenon was scientifically established by the FBI guru Ressler in the USA in the 1970s, and every Danish criminal investigator with sharp elbows and ambitions had attended courses with the FBI in Quantico in Virginia, including Axel. But in contrast with most of the others, he believed that there were one or more serial killers at large in Denmark. There were serial rapists, serial wife beaters, serial paedophiles, serial bastards for every paragraph of the Penal Code, so there had to be a serial killer with the worst of all crimes on his conscience. Only they hadn't caught him yet. He thought about Darling, who had been featured as an expert in TV crime documentaries many times, and every time the conversation turned to serial killers, would invariably dismiss it with the words 'well, of course you should never say never, but I don't think so'. Not in Denmark, this neat and tidy country where every citizen was kept in check, the country of civil registration numbers, a health service and social service that kept people on a leash, not to mention the tax office. Where no one lived off the radar, where women, children and organs weren't trafficked, where there were no drug labs, where you couldn't be anywhere for very long without the state finding out. A saccharine picture postcard with the Little Mermaid in the centre, which had nothing to do with his reality of homicides and rapes, random street shootings, families who moved addresses frequently to avoid detection by social services and treated their children as farm animals and sex slaves, girls who were raped in plain sight in Copenhagen while people watched without lifting a finger. And serial killers. Of course they existed. Of course this one existed. And he must be found.

He took out his iPod, put in his earphones: 'Love Shop'. He looked up at the sky. Took out a joint, lit it and inhaled. He calmed down immediately; he opened his mobile and looked at the picture his daughter had sent him from a beach somewhere in The Netherlands. Her two front teeth still stuck out between her grinning lips, tiny freckles across the fine bridge of her nose and the biggest brown eyes in the world. She sat with Cecilie, who was squinting at the sun, one hand shading her eyes while the other held the camera. He took another drag, inhaling deep into his lungs. Looked at the face of his ex-wife. Closed his eyes and heard Jens Unmack sing about 'the woman, who dragged him down on a bed in a big rush of lies and desire'.

He visualised Cecilie. Her lips, soft and full, the hunger in every part of her body when she reached up to him and opened her mouth so that he could kiss her. Pull her up towards him and feel that he had her.

CHAPTER 9

When she straddled him and rode him, the freckles scattered randomly over her shoulders, collarbone and cleavage where they sat very close together, the flat nipples that now pointed proudly out into the air, the faint smile of pleasure and desire, her dark eyes, the slight squint which made her look crazy, the feeling of her skin against his hands, her breasts that dangled slightly and around which he closed his hands and squeezed, and her putting her hands on top of his and squeezing harder. She would look into his eyes. Look right into him. Moments of happiness that were gone and now only existed in the movie playing on a loop in his head.

He let the music envelop him, he was high enough for that now. Everything would be fine. Even though he had lost everything. And only had Emma. And his job.

He sucked the joint greedily, filling his lungs with the smoke, keeping it in; he lay down on the bench, looked up at the endless sky and then exhaled. He felt good. Then he closed his eyes and disappeared into a pitch-black labyrinth where he chased Blackbird's invisible killer. And caught him.

CHAPTER 10

In his dream he was wet. He was lying under a spring. He opened his eyes and saw three men with scarves pulled up over their noses, standing over the bench. He yanked the earphones out as he tried to understand what was going on. Yes. This was really happening. The middle one of them had unzipped his trousers and was pissing on him. They roared with laughter.

He barely saw the first blow, dazed as he was from sleep and hash. But he knew two things. He was about to get beaten up. And he had to be quick to escape them. Nothing in the world is faster than violence. It's over before you realise what's happening. He had seen it in the eyes of stab victims and people who lay beaten to a pulp on the tarmac. As if they still couldn't grasp what had happened, or were desperately trying to piece movements together and make sense of them, while their life seeped red out of them. Violence wasn't about strength but about speed, and the slowest always lost. And right now he was the slowest.

The blow would have broken his nose if he hadn't jerked his head to the side. He pushed himself down the bench, took yet another punch and rolled off the back, down onto the ground. But they were already on top of him, kicking him, calling him a 'queer' and a 'poof'.

He grabbed the leg of one of them and pulled him down on the ground, broke his nose with his elbow and got onto his feet. The two others froze as the guy who had pissed on him squirmed on the ground, clutching his face.

Three losers, two Arab and one white, out on a gay-bashing. Oh, this was good.

'Are you carrying knives?' Axel asked.

'What?'

'Then get them out, because I'm about to fucking kill you.'

He was back on the path now. In a fighting stance. He squared up to the boy closest to him, who was still trying to work out how a fun bit of gay-bashing had turned into a full-on one-against-three fistfight. Before he had time to decide, Axel sent him reeling with a right hook, grabbed him by the shoulder, kicked his legs away from underneath him and stamped on his left arm which, judging by the look on the guy's face, broke.

'Come on then!' Axel shouted at the third guy. 'Come on then. I thought you wanted to bash some queers? Three against one? That's your idea of a fair fight? What, have you lost your bottle?'

But he couldn't provoke the 60 kilos of terror standing in front of him.

'Relax, man. I just thought you were queer.'

'I am queer,' Axel said with a grin. He lunged and hit him twice in the kidneys, then kneed him in the face as he went down.

Axel yanked him up so their faces were very close together. The boy's nose was crooked. He was sobbing.

'How many times have you done this before?'

'It's the first time, we've never done this before.'

'Fuck you, you piece of shit. If I ever see you again, I'll knock your nose so far into your brain, they'll need tweezers to get it out. Now get the hell out of here!'

He flung him down on the path and watched him stagger to his feet. They half-ran away from him. One of them groaned, clutching his arm.

Axel was wide awake again. The violence had given him a lift. As if he had managed to knock past losses out of his body. He mustn't lose his focus now.

He got up to go home. He felt a little dizzy and touched his face. There was blood near his temple. He walked through the park, to the exit by Teglgårdsstræde and up onto the pavement by Vester Voldgade. It was two o'clock in the morning. He looked down towards the neon advertisements of Nørreport, flickering in front of his eyes. He had to go home and get some sleep. The only people left on the streets were on nights out. And yet. A man was coming towards him, a man Axel thought he recognised.

He came closer. White trainers. Blue-black running clothes. Same face. A face he had first seen on a surveillance camera eight hours ago. And for whom he had issued a wanted notice across all of Sjælland in the hope of catching him. Now. Here. Ten paces away from him.

CHAPTER 11

Jens Jessen was standing on the balcony on the twelfth floor of the Wennberg Silo on Islands Brygge, looking across the harbour basin with a glass of white wine in his hand. He had worked on the budget all night until the early morning hours. The water below him lay like a sheet of slate glistening in the darkness. They had lived here for two years. For most of the last six months he had been on his own. And it had transformed the apartment into a clinical stage set that reminded him of life before Cecilie. Gone was Emma's screaming and her uncontrollable joy and delight, gone was Cecilie's warmth, her presence, which gave him a feeling of homeliness that he had never had before, of not being alone in the world. He was finding her absence unbearable.

Certainty. That was the difference between him and guys like Axel Steen. Jens Jessen wanted certainty before he acted. And so he had called one of his old PET colleagues to ask about the photographs. Kristian Kettler, a working-class bulldog, practically devoid of sympathetic qualities, but highly effective – especially when it came to the dirty work. He knew Axel Steen from the investigation into the dead Albanian, and the two men had been on course for a head-on collision from their very first meeting – they had very nearly come to blows a few times – so he was a good bet.

Did he know anything about photographs of Axel Steen? No, not at all.

'You've never seen them before? Remember, I'll find out...' Jens Jessen had said.

The man had hesitated.

'Is this an official request?'

'Kristian, now is not the time for playing games. If this stems from our surveillance, then I want to know.'

'It might be one of ours, but—'

'You want to get on, don't you?'

'Get on?'

'Kristian, for God's sake. Up the ladder. Bigger salary. Career, am I right?'

'Yes, I guess we all do.'

People who do don't answer so defensively. There was that chip on his shoulder again.

'I can help you and you know it,' Jens said. Though I'm damned if I will. 'But first we need to get a handle on the extent to which we're shitting on our own doorstep. And this is not on. I know you loathe Axel Steen, but I need him. He's off limits. I want all the material you have on him.'

'Why can't we go after him?'

'Because—'

'He's mental, smokes hash, buys it from street dealers. Mixes with all sorts of unsavoury types on Nørrebro.'

'There's a time for everything, Kristian. I'm the one clearing out my backyard, not you, not PET and definitely no one else. In the meantime, I want you to do something for me. I want everything, original files, copies, everything. If you're sloppy, it'll be the worse for you. And afterwards, be patient. There'll be something for you soon.'

'We didn't actually take these pictures. Someone sent them to us.'

'Who?'

'We don't know.'

'Are you telling me the whole truth now?'

'Yes. That's what happened.'

'So you didn't send them to me?'

'No.'

One step forward and two steps back.

'I want all the material anyway. And if you find out who took those pictures, then you call me.'

And now he had reached the real reason for his call.

'There's a small thing you might be able to help me with. Something I want kept ultralow profile. My girlfriend has complained about getting calls from an unknown number which either hangs up when she answers or there's someone on the other end who doesn't say anything. And she's worried – no, that's an overstatement – she's bothered by it. We have an idea of who it might be, and it's something that we can put a stop to ourselves, but you know that guesswork gets you nowhere, so please could you get me a list of every call to and from her mobile over the last 12 months?'

Was he actually snorting? Could he see through the lie? Never mind. He did as he was told.

He washed down the wine and went into the darkness of the apartment. Three hours of sleep before yet another day. But a day with Cecilie.

CHAPTER 12

He had three options: Follow the man and keep him under surveillance. At the risk of losing him. Fling him up against the steel fence and arrest him. Axel had no handcuffs on him, nor had he brought his warrant card. Stop him and speak to him nicely, then bring him into HQ.

He glanced up at the eye of the moon, pale and sickly in the sky over Nørrevold, as he made up his mind.

When they were three metres apart, he stepped into the man's path. He experienced a moment of doubt. Was it really the man from the Nørreport surveillance tapes, or was his mind playing tricks on him? It was only one hour at most since he had got high. His body was heavy and humid from heat and drugs. If this was the rapist, where was his knife? The man wore nothing but running clothes. Axel felt confused, outside himself, as if everything was a slow-motion recording with him as a floating, maniacal extra. He needed to get a grip of himself.

'Excuse me, do you have a light?' he said and stopped in front of the man.

The other man's face was broad, the eyes steel grey, the look in his eyes suspicious and doubtful at once. It wandered around Axel's face, stopping at his cheek. Then he shook his head.

'No, I don't smoke.'

His voice was slightly hoarse, neutral.

He stepped to the side to get past Axel. Evaded his gaze as if he didn't want anything to do with him.

'Could I have a word with you?' Axel said. Axel recognised something in his eyes. As though he had just been caught doing something he shouldn't. Axel raised his right hand, but when he went to place it on the man's shoulder, the man stopped and took a step backwards.

'Leave me alone!' he said in a loud and angry voice.

The man bashed his hand away.

'Hey, I'm a police—'

He got no further. The man spun around and started running back to Nørreport. He was sprinting.

'Stop, you idiot. I'm a police officer.'

Axel chased after him.

The man already had a head start. He turned the corner of the entrance by Ørsted Park, ran along Linnésgade and kept increasing the distance between them. Axel didn't have a snowball's chance in hell of catching up with him if he could keep that speed up.

'Police, stop!' Axel called out as the man turned into Ørsted Park by Israels Plads and disappeared down the curved steps leading towards the point where they had found Marie Schmidt. Not that sodding park again. 'Stop, for fuck's sake, I just want to talk to you,' Axel roared furiously. Why hadn't he just pushed the man up against the fence and called a paddy wagon?

He was too quick. And Axel far too slow. He ran along the lake, but he had already lost sight of him in the dark. He stopped. He thought he could hear the man's footsteps in the gravel further ahead along the lake. He started running again, pushing himself to the limit. He reached the opposite end of the park, tasting blood in his mouth, his muscles refusing to do any more. The man was gone. His heartbeat was in his throat, choking him. His legs wobbled as he stood on the path by the lake in the darkness. He couldn't even hear the other man's footsteps, he was as far ahead as that in what, two minutes? Axel bent forwards, his head hanging limply, gasping for air. The vomit came in spasms from his stomach, the doner kebab from earlier spewing out in acidic bursts, cola and chilli and the overpowering taste of hash. He fell to his knees and puked on the gravel until there was nothing left inside him. He could feel sand and gravel under his palms; he looked at the contents of his stomach close up, saliva and mucus hanging in threads down towards the ground, and another fluid. He was crying.

CHAPTER 13

Friday, 27 June

Someone was knocking. He got out of bed and staggered through the living room to the hall in yesterday's underpants and shirt. He opened the door a crack.

The Swede looked him up and down.

'Having a lie-in, are we?'

His eyes bored into Axel.

'Sweet dreams or a hard night? Are you going to let me stand out here all day?'

'Come in. I just need to get dressed.'

Axel returned to his bedroom.

He heard the Swede groan behind him.

'Christ on a bike.'

He followed him.

'What a dump.'

The Swede's gaze wandered around the floor from one overflowing ashtray to another.

'You look like a bloody junkie.'

He sniffed the air.

'And this place smells as if you are one. What the hell is going on? Who lives in this flat? Where the hell is Axel Steen?' He looked at Axel. Focused on the right side of his face. 'What happened to you?'

Axel wasn't sure whether he was referring to the beating he got yesterday or his burned-out state in general. He held up a hand to the left side of his face and felt swelling and a scab.

'Now you've got scars on both sides of your head. Well done. So tell me what you're up to. I'd been buzzing your intercom for 30 minutes before the bloody postman let me in.'

Axel told him about the rape of Jeanette Kvist, the link to the Blackbird case, his trip from Bellevue beach to Ørsted Park, the attack and his encounter with the suspect from the surveillance footage.

'But you're not sure if it's the same man as on the cameras?'

'No. It was dark. I was tired. But he ran. And he kept running. Even when I told him I was a police officer.'

'Perhaps he was scared.'

'What do you mean?'

'A man reeking of piss with blood all over his face accosts him at 2am saying he wants a word with him? I would have legged it. And I bet you were off your face on that crap your bedroom is full of.'

'I had smoked a single joint, true, but I was fine.'

'Aren't you too old to be running around Ørsted—'

'What the hell do you mean? Too old to follow up a lead in an unsolved murder case?'

'You know what I mean. Too old for this.' He gestured to the floor. Picked up an ashtray, counted the remains of at least seven or eight joints. Held up a lump of resin from the bedside table.

'What's happened to you? Have you thrown in the towel? What about the dead girl? Doesn't she deserve a police officer who's all there? And what about your daughter, for Christ's sake, what about Emma? What are you? A bloody junkie, drowning in self-pity.'

Axel was speechless.

'I'm too old to be wasting time on a loser like you,' the Swede said, turning around and heading for the hall.

'Hey, wait. I can control it. Where are you going? I thought we were going out for breakfast?'

The Swede turned round and gave him a weary look.

'No, we're not. Life is too short for addicts. Call me once you have it under control. Or if you need help with rehab. I mean it, Axel. Until then, goodbye.'

CHAPTER 14

He saw the dark splodge near his eye reflected in the computer screen. He tried to read his emails, but he was rattled. Not by last night's events, but by the Swede's reaction. He was Emma's godfather and had been Axel's best man. They'd known each other since Axel became a detective. It was the closest Axel had ever had to a father-son relationship. And now his friend had dropped him. Or had he? Axel knew he wasn't an addict, but he had to quit cannabis in order to clear his head. He had an investigation to solve. Then he had to mend fences with the Swede afterwards.

For the first time he began to worry about himself. Was the Swede right? He hadn't had many good days recently. In the last year. Emma was coming tonight. And then what? Who was he then? Daddy for three days? Was that all that was left of him? That and his job? If it was, it wasn't enough. All the unanswered questions made him feel sick. He had to get away from his own self-pity. And he knew only one way. The investigation. The Blackbird investigation. And to get there, he had to find the man whose face was now gliding out of the printer, grainy due to magnification, but clear enough to be used for identification. He knew Darling would never give him permission to release the pictures to the media and ask the public for help, as they had nothing else on the man. But there was one possibility. And she lived on Refsnæsgade.

He called ahead and rode there on his bicycle. Friday was tangible. The weekend hung in the air like unbridled laughter. The heatwave had drilled its way deep into the tarmac, which glistened in the sun. He stopped for a red light by Runddelen. A tarmac truck with metal containers stood still as men in fluorescent green work clothes swept the new road surface into place. The smell of oil and tarmac stung his nose as a long-legged woman in sandals and a very short dress crossed in front of him. He stood still and took it all in.

Jeanette Kvist let him into the stairwell the moment he pressed the intercom.

She was wearing the same type of clothes as the last time: a loose fitting tracksuit, slippers, her hair was in a ponytail. She wasn't wearing make-up and looked tired. Subdued.

'Are you going out?'

'Not right now, but I don't want to be in the flat. I don't want to sleep in my bed. I've put it on the market and I'll be moving in with a girlfriend next week.'

Axel wanted to say something, but he didn't know what would help.

'You wanted to show me some pictures?'

'Yes. We're not sure that it's him, but we have some pictures from Nørreport station of a man who caught the same train as you.'

'OK.' She gulped. Placed one hand on her chest.

'I have four pictures of men on the platform. I'm going to show them to you, one after the other. I know you didn't see his face, but you do see something through a stocking. Try to relax. Study them carefully. Take them in.'

She nodded. She gulped again.

Axel placed the file in front of her and turned over the first picture. She looked at it.

'No, that's not him.'

Good.

He put it aside and turned over the next picture. Gave her time to study it.

'No, that's not him either.'

Two clear answers.

Then he turned over the picture of the man at Nørreport station.

She studied it. She took more time than with the two others. Clasped her mouth. Axel felt his stomach somersault.

'It looks like him. The clothes are the same.'

'Are you sure?'

'It could be him. Or… I don't know.'

She looked at Axel, confused.

'Try looking at it again.'

She took plenty of time. Her breathing was sharp and shallow.

'I don't know. It was so dark. They could be his clothes. Perhaps. But I'm not sure about his face. I don't think it's him.'

She looked at Axel again, read the disappointment in his eyes. Then she broke down.

'What do you want me to say? It could have been anyone. I can barely look a man in the eye when I go outside now. He's everywhere.'

Axel got up and sat down next to her. Suddenly he doubted whether this was the right thing to do. He put one arm around her shoulder and held her. Gently.

'It's all right. It's fine. You're doing well. I will catch him. I promise you.'

She dried her eyes and got up. Had he overstepped the mark?

'I'm able to not think about it. And yet it's there. All the time. Like a stomach cramp.'

'He won't come back.'

'Who is he?'

Axel thought she was referring to the man in the picture.

'We only have this one picture. He boarded the same train as you at

86

Vesterport station, got off at Nørreport station and headed for the same exit as you. We know nothing about him.'

'No, I meant what kind of person would do this? Is he even human?' She shook her head and started to cry.

'I don't know.'

'I didn't know it existed. That kind of evil. Of course I've read about it, seen films, but experiencing it is completely different. It's unimaginable that someone can behave like that. As if they're not human at all, but just hard and cold and evil. With no compassion. Consisting of nothing but their own sick needs.'

Her eyes were red and wet. She looked at him as if she was expecting an explanation.

'He will be stopped. I promise you, I will stop him.'

Axel hadn't got what he had come here for, but he left with yet another insight into the corrosive and insidious effect of rape. And with an even stronger desire to catch the bastard who had fucked up Jeanette Kvist's life. And killed Marie Schmidt.

CHAPTER 15

He went to Tine Jensen's office when he returned to HQ and briefed her on his experiences last night – minus the joint, the vomiting and him collapsing on the path. She had kept quiet since their row yesterday, but he sensed she wasn't best pleased that he had visited Jeanette Kvist and tried to get her to identify the man without informing her first. In his own office, his landline phone was flashing with a message. It was Johnny Schlichtkrull returning his call.

He called back. 'Hi, Johnny, it's Axel Steen from Homicide.'

'Axel. How are you? Can you find your own head after the police reform or is it up your arse?'

'Oh, it's business as usual, as far as I am concerned. Still too many chiefs and not enough Indians.'

'What can I do for you?'

'I have a rape and a homicide with certain similarities,' Axel said. 'But no attacker. They're four years apart, and I've been reviewing several cases to see if there might be a link to more. One of them is a case you investigated in 1998, a rape that took place on Brohusgade in Nørrebro, of a 22-year-old woman, Anne Marie Zeuthen. It took place in her flat at night.'

'Yes, I'm not likely to forget that in a hurry. I would have liked to get my hands on the piece of shit who did it. He threatened to kill her, he used a knife and he took his time. But the worst part was—'

'Yes?'

'…that the sick bastard fucked his victim in every orifice and forced her to pick where she wanted it.'

Axel's heart started to pound.

'That sounds familiar. Would you find it for me, please?'

'I can look for it on Monday.'

'I need it now. Tonight at the latest.'

'We're busy with two robberies of Pakistani jewellers in Nørrebrogade and our cells are filled to bursting with a crazy Serbian gang that we need to interview, get before a judge and write reports on. But if it can wait until tonight, I'll try and do it then.'

'I'm not just looking for the files. I want all the evidence from it. Is that at your station?'

'I've no idea where it would be, but I'll find out when I retrieve the file.'

Axel made him promise that he would send him everything as soon as he located the file. DNA registration in Denmark in 1998 was still at an embryonic level. They would not have taken DNA samples in a sexual assault case unless they had an actual suspect with which the samples could be compared. This was his chance. The only factor against him was time. Even in cases of homicide, a DNA test could take up to a week unless it was urgent. However, Axel had a solution to that problem – all it took was a white lie and cashing in an old favour or two.

Then he went to see Darling. He was hoping to convince him to issue a wanted notice to the press for the man from Nørreport station.

'He has a visitor,' his secretary said.

'External?'

'No…' And that was as far as she got before Axel opened the door. It was a tradition that the door of the homicide chief was always open. Axel regretted his decision the moment he saw who the visitor was.

Jens Jessen. Axel had met him many times since he had been appointed Deputy Commissioner three months ago, but he hadn't got used to him. He was at once strong, in total control and ridiculously bizarre. There was no doubt that he was the National Police's or the Ministry's long arm when it came to cuts and efficiencies, and for that reason he ought to have been much more hated than he was. Jens Jessen had joined HQ's squash club, and you bumped into him everywhere, always with a boyish and slightly over friendly greeting. Some referred to him as His Majesty, but even more people just called him JJ. As though he was one of their own. And I'm closer to him than all of you, Axel thought. My daughter spends more time with him than she does with me.

He interrupted them in mid laughter. The two men looked up at him, smiling, and Jessen jumped up from his chair like an uncoiled spring. Pinstripe suit, dark blue shirt. It had to be too warm, but it fitted perfectly.

'Axel, what a surprise.'

His maniacal eyes beneath the helmet of frizzy white hair wandered over Axel's face, fixating first on the side with the scars and then the other with the new injury.

'What happened to you?'

He turned to Darling with raised eyebrows.

'You need to take better care of your men, Darling.'

'Last night in Ørsted Park I bumped into some young immigrants who thought I was gay.'

'It was nothing serious, I hope? I trust you gave as good as you got? Taught them a lesson?'

Jessen looked expectant as he spoke. When Axel didn't respond, he went on:

'We need to root out these hate crimes or we'll have the gay mafia in Parliament up in arms. Or the Jewish community. Or the Equality and Human Rights Commission. Or all three at once, do you follow? This won't do. We must make sure we start some investigations to keep them happy. Could this be one of them?'

'There's no case. And I'm not here to discuss some minor incident in Ørsted Park or a few scratches to my face. I want to talk to Darling about some investigative steps that can't wait.'

Jens Jessen raised his hands, but rather than make his way to the door, he sat down, looked from one to the other and smiled.

'This is precisely what I've been looking for, John,' he said, addressing Axel's boss.

John? Axel, wrong-footed, didn't know what to think.

'This is exactly what we've been talking about. I've just started here and I really need to get a sense of everything we do, so I know what it is I'm upgrading or downgrading, if you know what I mean.'

He winked at Axel.

'So do you mind if I listen in?'

Yes, I bloody well do, you twat. Sod off back to your office on the star corridor, and let the rest of us get on with our job, Axel wanted to scream at his face. But he could tell from Darling's smile that he was on his own.

'Do stay, Jens. After all, you already know one another. Axel is working on an old, unsolved homicide, which turns out to be linked to a recent sexual assault – a faint connection, admittedly. Marie Schmidt, a young woman who was found dead in the lake in Ørsted Park four years ago, if you remember.'

Axel was sure he remembered it. It was the case that had taken over Axel's life, when Jens Jessen struck and stole his wife.

'I've heard of it,' he said with a little smile.

'Go on, Axel. You found something yesterday on surveillance footage from Nørreport station related to the rape investigation?'

91

He had no idea where to begin. Jens Jessen's presence had knocked him off course. He had pretty much made up his mind to tell Darling that Jeanette Kvist believed that the man in the picture was identical with her attacker although it wasn't true, in order to win time and get the wanted notice out so they could bring in the man and DNA test him, but Jens Jessen's presence made him drop the idea.

He told the same story about last night that he had told Tine Jensen. Darling listened to him for a long time with a confident, professional smile that concealed what he thought. Jens Jessen looked mesmerised, as though he was being initiated into a mystery.

'And it's my opinion that we need to issue a wanted notice for him,' Axel concluded.

Jens Jessen looked expectantly at Darling. It was as bad as it could possibly be. If that moron hadn't been here, he might have been able to persuade Darling, but now Darling wanted to show leadership.

'I have a bad feeling about this, Axel. You turn up looking like God knows what. Battered, attacked by some immigrants in a park. And then, quite by accident you bump into this man straight afterwards, and you claim that he ran away from you when you identified yourself as a police officer, and on that basis you want us to start looking for him. We don't issue wanted notices with photographs unless we're almost certain that the people in question are essential to our investigation, and we have nothing on this man. He might not even have seen your victim.'

'He got on the same train as Jeanette Kvist. He got off at the same station. His clothes match the description. He did a runner when I tried to talk to him. And Jeanette Kvist reacted immediately when she saw his picture.'

Jens Jessen interjected.

'Perhaps he was just scared of you? I know I would be if you approached me on a dark street in the middle of the night.'

Axel glared at him icily.

'Has she identified him? Positively?' the Deputy Commissioner demanded to know.

'I don't know what you mean by positively. She hasn't identified him for the perfectly valid reason that he wore a stocking over his head while he raped her, but she says that it could have been him.'

'That's not what I've heard,' Darling said. 'Tine Jensen contacted the victim to try and get her to come in here for a formal identification of the photos, and she told her that she didn't recognise him.'

Axel felt his irritation turned to anger. So Tine had already snitched to Darling.

Jessen got involved.

'Then it's a negative and that's no use. I daren't even think of the consequences if we release a photo to the media of an innocent man wanted in connection with an aggravated sexual assault linked to a murder. The press will join the dots in seconds. What if he has absolutely nothing to do with any of it? Will you pay his compensation out of your overtime? Only joking. But I agree with John, we can't do that.'

I agree with John! Axel wanted to throw up at the double act playing out in front of him. Two alpha males spurring each another on.

'And this gives me an opportunity to emphasise another matter,' Darling began. 'This is a team effort. You must work with Tine Jensen and you will not interview the victim in her investigation without conferring with her first. Even though you're a DCI. You're not her boss. I am, and I must be kept informed.'

If they had to report every tiny investigative step to Darling, they wouldn't have time for anything else. It was outrageous. And Darling knew it. This was purely for the benefit of the Deputy Commissioner. Axel's anger was turning dark red. There was no way he was putting up with this. He thought about the Davidi case, which would never have been solved if he hadn't followed his instincts and hunches rather than listen to two career-climbing morons. Jens Jessen, his staff and their car crash of an undercover operation, and Darling, his partner for years, who throughout the case had had his tongue right up the arse of Jessen and Rosenquist and everyone else in the top salary bracket.

'I'm here to solve murders. And I've been doing that for 10 years. Many of them wouldn't have been solved if we had stuck to the rules. There are times when you have to do something to get a case moving. We're talking murder here, for Christ's sake. It's more important than overtime claims or clear-up rate statistics. And the day it isn't, I quit. There are times when you have to cross the line. If your bosses won't let you, they bloody well have to think of something else instead. But clearly I can't expect any help from you. So if you don't mind, I'll be leaving now, because I need to catch the man who has wrecked the life of a 23-year-old medical student and probably murdered an 18-year-old school leaver.'

He left the office before they had time to say anything. Darling's jaw had dropped, but Jessen looked as if he had enjoyed Axel's closing speech. The door hadn't been shut, and the secretary sat stunned, staring at him. As did the investigators in the adjacent offices as he walked back to his own. He closed the doors to both neighbouring offices. Then he paused for a few seconds before he slammed his clenched fist six times into a bookcase. The wall shook. He flopped down on his office chair, ruffled his hair, opened the drawer and found an old packet of cigarettes. He had quit smoking five years ago, started again last year, then stopped, but given that he smoked two or three joints on some days, it barely mattered. He needed a cigarette right now. He took the packet and his mobile and went down to the colonnade. The latest regulations insisted that smokers leave the premises altogether, but he didn't give a toss about that.

It was 11am, he would be picking up Emma at the airport at 5.40pm, and he had to get home and tidy up first. He couldn't risk going out to work on the case during the weekend. Cecilie would give him hell if she heard that he had brought Emma along on yet another homicide investigation, but he could review cases at home and work on his laptop.

He was quite sure that there would be a fallout after today's encounter with Darling and Jessen. He had to have something ready for Monday that could justify him keeping the investigation, preferably a list of cold cases they should review. And he had to submit a request for a new DNA test today in the case that Schlichtkrull had called him about. He was furious, he was hungry, and he needed a joint.

He had only just lit his cigarette when his mobile rang. Unknown caller.

'Yes?'

'It's Ea Holdt.'

'Yes?'

'Is this a bad time? You sound cross.'

'No.'

'I gather you have met with my client and that you now want to bring her into HQ in yet another attempt to identify a man she can't recognise. We're not going to agree to that. It seems utterly unnecessary to me.'

Axel decided she was angry that he hadn't called her before going to see Jeanette Kvist.

'The first part is my responsibility. I apologise for not letting you know. I've got nothing to do with the second part.'

'I thought it was your case?'

'Yes, but… it's a bit complicated. I'd be happy to explain it to you, but I'm busy right now. Besides, there's something I want to ask you in connection with the interview. Can we meet?'

'Yes. Let me check. I'm due in court at two o'clock. If we meet somewhere near the courthouse around 12.30, then I'll have an hour.'

'Works for me. Do you know a place that isn't a Burger King or a kebab shop?' He presumed that lawyers knew more about good restaurants than police officers.

She laughed.

'Yes. I'll book a table at the House with the Green Tree on Gammeltorv. Danish open sandwiches, if that's OK with you.'

'That's fine.'

'See you there.'

CHAPTER 16

Jens Jessen had spent most of the day visiting the line managers of various divisions to air his idea of shadowing individual officers. Some had looked as if they thought it sounded like the basis for a reality TV programme, others had said it was a good idea, though he wondered whether they had done so purely out of polite deference. Two dinosaurs from the times when coppers wielded truncheons had told him frankly that they thought it was a complete bloody waste of time. Whatever happened to proper policing? He much preferred them. People who wore their hearts on their sleeves.

He had done the same when he worked for PET. Spent time with close personal protection officers and the tactical unit, AKS. The AKS iron men had been the highlight. He had been allowed to train with them, and it had proved to be one of his most fulfilling experiences. He was loath to admit it because he was a lawyer, a boffin, but when they had been marksmen training or practised with replica weapons, he had felt more alive than ever before in his career. While he was shadowing personal protection officers during an exercise, the door had been opened to a world which up until then he had known only on paper in the form of words like schedules and priorities. He had taken part in exercises including night shooting, sweeping vehicles and locations for weapons and explosives, procedures for securing lifts and emergency exits, evacuation scenarios, and a huge party when it was all over. He had loved it, and every now and then he wondered what would have happened if he had chosen that path, become an elite soldier, a close protection officer, a policeman, rather than a senior lawyer with a photographic memory who shaved his legs to reduce water resistance during long-distance swimming competitions.

It was not to be. His father had been a permanent secretary. And his son's career path had been mapped out from the moment he was born.

But at least he had now laid the groundwork for some distraction, and could choose where to go. Not traffic, God no, or fingerprinting or radio control, no, it would be drugs, trafficking, robbery, and then homicide.

He felt tired and irritable after the encounter with Axel Steen in Darling's office. He had so many conflicting feelings towards Axel Steen. He had a no-nonsense quality, none of the beating about the bush that Jens was so used to, and he liked that about him, but Axel was also insufferably single-minded and could see only his own solutions. No corner was so sharp that it couldn't be cut, no rules so rigid that they couldn't be bent. It was part of his appeal, which was simultaneously infuriating and fascinating. He had seemed feral, weary and worn down, the scars and the injuries to his face made him look intimidating, and rage emanated from his blue eyes whenever he was obstructed. He was trying to solve the murder of the girl in Ørsted Park four years ago. Cecilie had mentioned it as a case her then-husband had gone to pieces over. And of course it was commendable that officers took their work seriously, but for heaven's sake! The man's behaviour was shocking. Darling was on the edge too – he could sense it.

And now the drug pictures. He would have to act on them. There was a great deal weighing against Axel.

However, on the other side there was Emma, who loved Axel Steen more than anyone in the whole world. Not that Jens felt any kind of jealousy, because Emma had welcomed him, she was fond of him, or at least he felt she was. But she worshipped her father. God only knew why.

Now that he thought about it, he realised that the roots of his irritation lay elsewhere. Cecilie and Emma were coming home tonight and he had been looking forward to picking them up at the airport, except that wasn't going to happen.

'Axel will be picking us up, he'll be picking Emma up, I mean. I know it's massively irritating, but at least it means I can come straight to yours,' she had said.

Axel is picking us up. Axel, Axel, Axel, what was it about him. Axel? Why was he everywhere? Why couldn't Jens just drive to the airport to pick her up? She was his girlfriend, not Axel's. Axel was nothing but an extra on the cast list of their movie. Or at least he ought to be.

CHAPTER 17

Axel walked down Strøget, central Copenhagen's tourist and enter-tainment trap, also a nightly violence and open-air drinking venue for young people from the poorer suburbs and hormonally challenged immigrant boys. Past his regular kebab shop and down to the cobbled squares of Nytorv and Gammeltorv.

Justice lives on Nytorv, if you believe it is meted out in the court-house, which Axel doubted from experience. The building is about as appealing from the outside as Copenhagen Police HQ and provides a strong contrast with Gammeltorv: a symbol of mercy in the form of the Caritas Fountain, its vast copper basin supporting a pregnant woman with a baby on one arm and her son by her side.

Axel sat down on one of the green benches opposite the fountain. On the Queen's birthday golden apples would leap about in the basin. Axel had twice brought Emma here to watch them dance on the water. His daughter had quickly lost interest in the golden baubles in favour of the spray coming from the boy's willy and the mother's breasts.

'Look, Daddy! He's doing a really big wee!'

He was early, and lit another cigarette as he sat watching the fountain and the three golden, water-spouting dolphins at the woman's feet. The sound of the water and the monotonous murmur of voices and footsteps sent him into a trance. He closed his eyes for a second, turned his face to the sun and felt battered all over, his heart beating restlessly, exhausted and resigned in his chest.

'What happened to you?'

He opened his eyes. Ea Holdt's face moved closer to his cheek. He must have nodded off.

'Are you all right?' she asked, concerned.

'Oh, that? Yes. I was just lost in thought.'

'With your eyes closed? You looked like you were in a coma. What's that on your cheek?'

Axel touched the scar from the burns.

She grinned.

'No, the other one. Though I can see it's difficult when you have so much to choose between.'

'It's nothing. Some kids from Blågårds Plads wanted to discuss whether it's natural for two men to kiss.'

'And is it?'

'Yes, it is.'

'Was it serious?'

'No, we were allowed to finish kissing.'

She looked baffled. Then she laughed.

'OK,' she said, stressing the second syllable.

She turned around and looked across the square, which resembled an overexposed postcard in the bright morning light.

'Lovely here, isn't it?' she said delightedly as she took off her dark blue blazer.

Axel studied her figure. She was wearing matching trousers that tightly fitted her arse, which stuck out under the curve of her back. She was slim, not that tall – she looked fit and attractive. She stood there long enough for him to realise she was expecting him to notice her body. That was OK, but also a somewhat confusing message. He had intended to tell her about Emma and the apples, but suddenly struggled to find the words.

'Yes. I come here a lot. Or I used to. My daughter went to nursery school in Vartov. We would often stop here and look at the fountain on our way home.'

'And now you sit here alone? Do you miss her?'

Axel hesitated. She was getting too close. Too quickly. The conversation had reached the stage that always made him tense because it was about deep feelings, loss, and things that only made sense if you talked about them honestly – but intermingled with a teasing dance around the eternal question of whether they would be naked. Together. One day. He could feel that they both wanted it.

'Yes. Do you have children?'

'I have two boys. Seven and nine.'

She looked at him and gave him a reassuring smile.

'Every other week.'

He squirmed. Had he really looked that disappointed?

'How about we go get something to eat?' he said and stood up.

Linen tablecloths, blue fluted china, dark wooden, waist-high panelling and the rest of the wall covered with old maps and historical pictures of Copenhagen. People were practically sitting on top of one another. The waiter greeted Ea Holdt and showed them to a table for two in the corner. They ordered water and open sandwiches with herring in a curry dressing for them both, then chicken mayonnaise for her and steak tartare on rye bread for him.

'Would you like a schnapps? My treat,' she offered cheerfully.

'No, thank you,' Axel said.

'I can't appear in court after a beer, but a schnapps is OK. And you can't eat herring without a schnapps. I won't have it. Are you sure you don't want one?'

'I'm sure.'

Their drinks arrived.

'Let me just make one thing clear: I don't mind you talking to my client, but I would like to be informed first. I can't promise to be there every time, but I would like to be told.'

'I'll bear that in mind.'

'What's on the pictures you want Jeanette to look at, and why do you want her to look at them for a second time?'

Axel explained what had happened: the pictures from Nørreport station and his encounter with the young men in Ørsted Park last night.

'I want them released to the media so we can identify the man, but my bosses don't agree. My colleague wants to bring Jeanette in to see if she recognises him.'

'Because they don't trust you? Or because you tried to make them believe that she did recognise him?'

Axel was a fan of plain speaking, and he was fast becoming a fan of Ea Holdt.

'Both.'

'Hmm, it's a big step to publish a picture of a man you can't even link to the crime, isn't it?'

'It is. But either it's him or it isn't. Then we can start looking elsewhere.'

Their herring arrived. They ate. He looked at her polished nails, her smooth, slim fingers, the round wrinkles on the joints that stared at him like the eyes of a little old man. Shit, he was still high. She swallowed and looked up at him.

'I appreciate the way you treated Jeanette yesterday.'

'You did?'

'Don't get me wrong. I'm not about to criticise the way the police work, I know you have to treat victims with cynicism, but—'

'There are times when we take it too far, I'm sure.'

Axel had let rip at Tine Jensen, but he wasn't willing to throw her under the bus to Ea Holdt.

'I know you have to ask questions, including unpleasant ones, but there's an automatic distrust of rape victims, which often characterises the whole process from the very first interview all the way to trial. And it's not necessary.'

'We get many false reports.'

'Yes, I'm aware of that and they must be investigated, of course, but they can usually be dismissed quickly. All victims of crimes are entitled to respect, but victims of sexual assaults have particular needs.'

'Why?'

'Because they're alone with their experience. It's very difficult to share. And it doesn't make it any easier to be confronted with a male police officer who – although every piece of evidence supports what you're saying – is fundamentally sceptical. Or a female officer, like your colleague who was prejudiced from the start.'

'No, that's no good.'

'Women are their own worst enemies, as they say. Sadly, that's true in many of these cases. Rape is the only crime I know where the victim becomes the suspect. There's a constant undercurrent of "are you sure you didn't ask for it?" Or "it's a pretty dumb idea to wear a see-through blouse", as a police sergeant once said to a 13-year-old rape victim.'

'I thought that was all in the past.'

'Then I'm going to have to disappoint you. It's not. Female officers are either deeply suspicious or very empathetic. Male ones are different. Either they're very matter of fact and professional – that's actually best. Or they're frightened or uncomfortable.'

'Why?'

'I don't know. I think it's about gender. That men rape. And that they're men. That's why they find it uncomfortable.'

'That's how I feel. I've never wanted to work those cases. I prefer the dead.'

She paused and looked at him quizzically. Then she laughed out loud.

'What is it?'

'You should have seen the look on your face when you said: I prefer dead women.'

'That's not quite what I said.'

'No, but it was what you meant,' she said and laughed out loud again. She knocked back her schnapps in one go. Inhaled sharply. Then she placed a hand on her chest, belched and said, 'oops'.

Their next round of sandwiches arrived. They ate. Looked at one another. Smiled. He could see it in her eyes, her joy. They both knew that there would be more.

Ea Holdt checked her wristwatch.

'I'm due in court in 15 minutes. Did you want to ask me something?'

'Yes. When we visited Jeanette Kvist and you asked her about the condom, I wondered if you had heard of that happening before.'

'Indeed I have. It's pretty standard these days that criminals have seen every episode of CSI and do whatever they can to avoid leaving DNA evidence, isn't it?'

'Yes, but that business with the condom isn't standard. Which case was it?'

'If you can link it to the same rapist, nothing would please me more. A teenage girl was raped on her way home from a party. She was forced into an allotment shed. It happened four years ago, I believe. I think a condom wrapper was found at the scene, but you never caught her attacker. To say the police believed my client would be an exaggeration.'

Axel felt as if he had been given an electric shock.

'Why?'

'She was drunk. Why do you look at me like that?'

'Because it sounds like a case I read up on earlier today. A 17-year-old girl was raped in an allotment garden on Østerbro. Lulu Linette Larsen.'

'Yes, that's her. It's not that easy to forget. The name or the case.'

'How much do you remember?'

'I don't remember the details, but I had the same bad taste in my mouth I also got with your colleague last month when she interviewed Jeanette Kvist for the first time. Lulu Linette Larsen was asked repeatedly whether the rape had really happened the way she said it had, and whether it might not just be sex she had initially consented to and later regretted, and whether the injuries she had sustained might not be as a result of falling off her bicycle. So on and so forth.'

'What do you mean?'

'She had been raped from behind and ordered about inside a shed where her sadistic attacker had also threatened to kill her. I do also have experience of cases that turned out to be false. The girls or women who make them up need help. I can tell the difference. But on that occasion I had no doubts at all.'

CHAPTER 18

When he returned to his office, a cardboard box containing four ring binders and a black bin bag was sitting on his desk. There was a case number on the ring binder below the name Anne Marie Zeuthen. The crime was sexual assault, the year was 1998 and the police district was Copenhagen. It was Schlichtkrull from Bellahøj police station who had been busy.

He opened the bin bag. Small, everyday objects told their own horrifying story: a pair of women's knickers, a T-shirt and a tea towel, all in separate plastic bags. The cord from a dressing down and two belts were in the same bag, as were three water glasses. A bed sheet and a bedspread lay unwrapped at the bottom of the box underneath the other items.

He assumed that everything had been tested for blood type, hair or saliva enzymes, the DNA evidence of its time, and had been kept for any future trial. But the way the items had been stored could only be regarded as evidence contamination of the worst kind. He wouldn't get anything from the unwrapped textiles, which had probably sat in the basement of Bellahøj station for a decade, exposed to light and temperature changes. Besides, there was a very real risk that they had been contaminated by anyone who had handled them. Keeping more than one item in the same bag was also unprofessional, as DNA from different donors could easily transfer. Axel hoped that they had been kept because they contained fingerprints – not that they had anything like that in the Jeanette Kvist or the Blackbird case, but it was another type of evidence that could help them expand their search for the man.

Among the cases he had found the day before, he took out and read the file on the rape of Lulu Linette Larsen in the summer of 2003. She had been knocked off her bicycle and dragged into an allotment garden by Borgervænget that ran parallel to the old railway yard by Svanemøllen Barracks. "The victim was dragged into a shed and threatened with a knife. There she was ordered to kneel while the attacker sexually assaulted her from behind. She alleges that her attacker tried to strangle her, but there were no bruises to her neck or bleeding in her eyes, nor were any traces of semen found during the medical examination. The victim alleges that the attacker interrupted intercourse in order to put on a condom. She has injuries to her hands and a scratch to her left cheek, but these could have been sustained from falling off her bicycle. The victim was intoxicated at the time of the crime. Her blood alcohol level was 1.25. Her clothes had not been damaged. There was no physical sign of rape."

Reading between the lines it was clear that the investigating officer had regarded the report as false, and if Axel had only known about the attack from the police report, he would have reached the same conclusion. But only one hour ago he had heard Ea Holdt talk about it. And she had had no doubts that the girl had been raped.

Forensic technicians had found several finger and hand prints belonging to the victim and the owners of the shed. Otherwise no technical evidence. The girl's clothing, a condom wrapper and a piece of chewing gum were supposedly stored in the basement under HQ, but had never been DNA tested.

Axel went for another trip to the basement. First he found the box containing the file on the sexual assault in Nørrebro Park in 1996 of 19-year-old Line Jørgensen. Three ring binders suggested that the investigation had been thorough. He opened the first and found seven pictures of the woman from her examination at the Rigshospitalet. There were close-ups of different injuries to her body. On one photograph he could see faint red and blue bruises around her neck, but it was the expression in her eye that caught Axel's attention and made his pulse quicken. Fear. Terror. Breakdown.

He had to catch this man.

He returned the photos to the ring binder and started looking for bags or boxes with evidence from the case, and the file on the sexual assault of Lulu Linette Larsen. After searching for half an hour among confiscated slot machines, historical police uniforms, the wheelchair from the Blekingegade gang's robbery in Nørregade, motorbike parts and bizarre regalia from raids on biker gang strongholds, and endless archived cases, cardboard boxes and bin liners, he had to give up. He found the retired inspector who looked after the basement, gave him the case numbers and asked him to try to locate the boxes.

Then he returned to his office. Julie Thomsen, who had been the investigating officer of one of the cases, answered her phone immediately.

'Axel Steen, to what do I owe the honour?'

'I'm looking for the evidence collected in connection with a 2003 rape that you investigated. Lulu Linette Larsen, does that mean anything to you?'

'Possibly, what's this about?'

'It's a routine check in connection with a fresh sexual assault. I haven't been able to find the evidence here at HQ. There are some similarities in the MO and it might be a long shot, but I would like to test the victim's clothing for DNA. After all, they can do a bit more these days than they could five years ago.'

'You can forget about that. That girl was never raped.'

'Are you sure?'

'Why do you want to know?'

'I'm just asking where the evidence is.'

'But why? There's no case.'

'That's not what I've been hearing.'

There was silence on the other end.

'Is it that lawyer? Has she been talking to you? She's unbelievable. She got in our way and put everyone's backs up, let me tell you. Said we didn't do our job properly. Crazy bitch, if you ask me. There was no case, no technical evidence at all, no one heard anything even though there's a residential block right next to the allotment garden. The girl was simply pissed out of her mind and fell off her bike. Yes, anything is possible, but it was very hard to see how she was attacked in any way. And we just weren't getting anywhere with her case.'

Did you even try, Axel was tempted to ask.

'That's OK, I believe you, but do you know where the evidence is?'

'You don't give up easily, do you? You don't believe me. I would have thought you had better things to do than piece together evidence from false rape allegations to find a non-existent rapist.'

'If you know where it is, why don't you just tell me? Or are you too important to give a regular cop a helping hand now that you're management?'

'If it's the only way I can get rid of you, then check the basement of Store Kongensgade police station. Goodbye, Axel Steen.'

Axel quickly put the evidence from the rape of Anne Marie Zeuthen back in the box and placed it next to the box with evidence from the murder of Marie Schmidt.

Five minutes later came the expected footsteps as Darling marched into his office.

'Are you in a better mood now?'

'There's nothing wrong with my mood.'

'What are you up to?'

'What do you mean?'

Darling glanced at the boxes in the corner.

'You can forget about that right now. You won't be sending a billion samples from old rape cases off for DNA analysis without having very good reasons.'

'I haven't sent anything off. Yet. We're working on the Blackbird and Jeanette Kvist investigations. We're trying to find out if in the last 15 years other rapes were carried out in the same area by the same type of attacker, displaying the same type of behaviour.'

Darling listened. He wasn't a complete idiot.

'And there were. Three at least.'

Axel briefly described the cases.

'1996, 1998 and 2003,' Darling repeated. 'All in the Nørrebro area around midnight. The attacker masked his face. Had a knife. Hmm. I mean, there's not an awful lot to go on. Being masked and carrying a knife are fairly common in rape cases.'

'Yes, but the condom isn't. Nor what he says to them. No rapists match the blueprint completely, but there are similarities that link each case to the next. It would be madness not to investigate the connection.'

'Yes, it would, but why the urgency? Those cases are ancient. They're not going anywhere. Why can't you deal with them when you've got nothing else to do?'

'They're connected to a murder, have you forgotten that?'

'No, I haven't forgotten the link to the Blackbird investigation, but it's tenuous. The DNA evidence doesn't automatically link us to the killer.'

'No, but it's the best lead we've ever had in that case.'

'You're busy now, Axel. You're especially busy trying to convince me. On Monday I want a written review which we'll then meet to discuss, to decide whether we'll have the evidence from the historical cases brought in. And if you can't convince us, I need you to work other cases.'

Axel gave in. Mentally he was already on his way to Forensic Services with his bin bags to get BB to start testing the evidence today. But Darling hadn't finished.

'Listen, talking to the new Police Commissioner like that wasn't a smart move.'

'Don't you mean Deputy Police Commissioner?'

'Whatever.'

'Well, it was his idea to tag along with us. And that's how we talk to each other.'

'You're not doing yourself any favours, Axel. And given that he's Cecilie's boyfriend, it's not a wise move either. Are you fighting about Emma?'

'That's none of your bloody business. Or his.'

'No, it isn't. It's just a piece of friendly advice, from one colleague to another. He's actually a nice guy. He's funny and genuine.'

'Do you want a tissue?'

'Why?'

'Before you start weeping in admiration.'

'You're so black and white in your judgement of other people. How about moving on? Yes, your wife left you for him. And, no, it wasn't yesterday. It's been years, Axel. And Jens Jessen isn't here to make your life difficult. He's here because he's a brilliant lawyer, one of the smartest and brightest in Denmark, so perhaps you should take it down a notch. And, in contrast to some of our other bosses, he's not vindictive in the old-fashioned way. In fact, I was struck by how favourably he spoke about you after you stormed out.'

'What did he say?'

'He suggested he shadowed you for a day or two.'

'You have got to be joking.'

'It was just a suggestion. To show a bit of goodwill.'

Axel shook his head.

'Next thing I know I'll be showing school kids around crime scenes. This is a shit show.'

'You've changed your tune. I heard you took your daughter to a post-mortem last year?'

'That was an accident.'

Darling went over to the window. Fiddled with a file.

'The next time we're in a meeting with Jens Jessen or anyone else, I would like you to show a little more respect.'

Respect wasn't Axel's strongest point when it came to senior management in general, but he struggled with Darling in particular because he had been his equal for years. Axel knew Darling too well, knew his weaknesses and shortcomings as an investigator, his complaints about his private life, his semi-alcoholic wife, his pedantic need for order, born out of his fear of losing control. He had been too close to him to be able to bow and scrape to him now.

'I'm your boss, not a colleague you can send out to get lunch. Those days are over. If you can't accept that, you can't work in this division. And that's not a situation I want to see arise.'

There was no hint of threat or reproach in his voice.

'I hear what you're saying.'

Darling smiled contentedly. Fidgeted with some paperclips on Axel's desk. Was there more? Suddenly he looked apologetic.

'We're going out with them tonight, as it happens.'

'We? Them?'

'Cecilie and Jens. My wife and I. We're going to Custom House.'

Axel knew he had to restrain himself, but this was a bridge too far. Darling had been his partner before, during and after the divorce. He knew what it had done to Axel. This was unbelievable. Or was Axel the problem here, because he wanted nothing to do with his ex-wife's new boyfriend, and found it deeply intimidating to imagine Darling talking to his ex-wife and Jens Jessen over dinner?

Would they be discussing him? Agreeing what a moron he was? The thought enraged him.

'Anything else? I'm busy. And I'd rather not be talked about at private get-togethers between you and Cecilie and Jens Jessen.'

'Relax. It would never even cross my mind. If anything I would put in a good word for you.'

'I don't need that.'

'All right. Have a nice weekend.'

Axel was seething. And he felt vulnerable and alone. He had Emma. No one could take her from him. He was scared of dying. Dying beside his daughter while others lived it up at Custom House. He knew that the two weren't connected, but it felt as if they were. He had to invite someone over as he usually did. As security, so there would be someone if he suddenly collapsed. So that Emma wouldn't wake up alone in the apartment with a father she couldn't rouse, a dead father.

BB answered his phone with a grunt. Axel imagined the myopic man hunched over a piece of evidence, completely lost in a world where a scratch, a nose hair or a botanical detail meant the difference between acquittal and sentencing.

'Forensic Services.'

Brian Boldsen was one of Copenhagen's most experienced forensic technicians and a man Axel had worked with for over ten years.

'Don't tell me you have more ballistics for us to test? Or mobile phone records for 35 Hells Angels hangouts and all of the Blågårds Plads gang?'

'No, but it's urgent.'

There was another grunt down the phone.

'Express DNA testing. Two cold cases, evidence from sexual assaults from 1998 and 2003, probably never tested.'

'It'll go to the back of the queue, Axel, you know that. We're drowning in work. This heat is driving us crazy. And it's clearly driving everyone in the streets crazy as well. There should be a ban on committing any crimes when the temperature goes above 25°C.'

'I need them done now, BB, they're connected to a case involving a terror suspect,' he lied, because he knew that invariably ensured top priority.

'In that case, you're in luck. We'll do them as a matter of urgency… You're not having me on, are you?'

'If I were, would you want to know?'

'Stop talking. Are they on their way out here already?'

'I'll have a patrol car bring them in an hour. How quickly can you do it?'

'We'll be sending DNA evidence to Forensic Genetics early tomorrow morning. If you're lucky, we can include yours. But I don't know how quickly they can do it. You'll have to ring Sigurdsson yourself and sweet-talk him. Good luck,' he said with a laugh.

Claus Sigurdsson, the head of Forensic Genetics, was a man Axel had met on several old cases and a few times with the Swede, who was a colleague of his. He was professional to his fingertips and could seldom be manipulated. Axel could hardly expect the Swede to help him after his lecture this morning, but he remembered that Sigurdsson collected rare Scotch whisky and decided to go down that route instead. He had time before going to the airport.

His next move was to call Store Kongensgade police station and speak to the man in charge of archive and evidence storage. He went to the basement and found a box from the rape of Lulu Linette Larsen, while Axel was on the phone to him.

'Have you opened the box?'

'Yes.'

'What's in it?'

'Clothing. It looks like a pair of knickers, trousers and a T-shirt. It smells of moths.'

'Any of it wrapped?'

'No, it's just in the box.'

'Please close it again. Then send a patrol car to Forensic Services with it and tell them not to open it.'

'OK.'

'It's urgent. And tell them to stop by here on their way, would you? I have a box that needs to go with it.'

'Of course. The boys just love acting as cabbies for Homicide. I'll give you a call when they've left.'

CHAPTER 19

The Teilum building lay next to the Rigshospitalet, but while the Swede and his fellow corpse carpenters performed autopsies on the lower floors, the forensic geneticists had an unobstructed view of the Fælled Park football pitches from the fifth floor. Claus Sigurdsson was in his office, which was plastered with framed pictures of him and his colleagues, symposium photographs, posters and diplomas from international conferences. On the windowsill were three purple orchids and an unopened bottle of Glenmorangie, presumably because Sigurdsson regarded it as too common to drink. He was a man in his late fifties with short white hair, a small moustache, a long face and wistful bulldog eyes that gave the impression that nothing could surprise him any more. His voice was better suited to his character, light and scalpel sharp. He was wearing a pale brown corduroy suit that was a little too small for him.

'Axel, what a pleasure, it's been a long time.'

'Yes, it has. It was at the Swede's whisky tasting, I believe?'

'At Professor Jönsson's, that's right. Do sit down. Would you like some coffee?'

'Yes, please.'

Axel took a seat in front of a desk with several framed photographs of Sigurdsson with various colleagues, some posed, others where they were dressed up for festive occasions, such as Christmas parties.

He took one of them and studied five happy people wearing dressing gowns at Helgoland Lido with a background of icy water. Sigurdsson, two of his female colleagues whom Axel had met, and two faces he didn't recognise.

'Winter bathing. God help me. It was a colleague,' he pointed to a woman in the picture, 'who talked us into it some years ago.'

'A cold dip would certainly be welcome in this heat,' Axel said, painfully aware that this kind of small talk, when the truth was he was really here to ask for a favour, wasn't his strong side.

'Absolutely. Copenhagen is unbearable right now. You live in Nørrebro, I believe.'

'Yes, it's a sauna.'

'It must be awful. My daughter lives in Guldbergsgade. We made a big mistake two years ago. We bought her a flat. The bank was only too happy to lend us the money, a good investment, they said. It's already worth less than we paid for it. We thought the market could only ever go up, but seriously, paying 2.5 million kroner for a three-bedroom flat in a side street to Nørrebrogade – we should have known better.'

Axel had kept the flat when Cecilie left and bought her out. He had inherited half a million kroner from his father, but that money was gone now, and he very much doubted that he would be able to sell the flat and pay off the outstanding mortgage today, had he wanted to.

'True, when the banks write to you these days it's a different story.'

'Bastards.'

Axel was taken aback by the strength of Claus Sigurdsson's outburst.

'The bank sent us six bottles of red wine when we signed the papers. Probably to help us swallow their useless advice. They saw us coming, let me tell you.'

'Yes, you should have bought your daughter a flat a few years earlier.'

'I don't need you to tell me that. One of my colleagues bought a place in Nørrebro in 2000.' He pointed to another of the winter bathers. 'Paid one million kroner for a four-bedroom flat. He sold it for three million two years ago. Quit his job and off he went... Do you know what our banking adviser said?'

Apart from his passion for whisky, Axel had inadvertently unleashed Sigurdsson's other passion: his hatreds of the banks – a sentiment he shared with most of the population after the financial crisis. Axel was forced to listen, though the whining sickened him. Bankers might be greedy, but they hadn't put a gun to people's heads and forced them to sign. And greed came in many guises, he thought, as he nodded sympathetically through Sigurdsson's tale of woe.

'Right, that's enough of that. What can I do for you?'

'Do you remember the Blackbird case?'

'Yes, we all do. Any new developments?'

'Yes. We found a DNA match in a rape case.'

'So one of my colleagues told me.'

'And I've looked into other rape cases where either no DNA samples were taken or they were taken only from the victim. I've sent the evidence to Forensic Services for examination.'

'And now you want me to prioritise them?'

'Yes, that's why I'm here. I know it's asking to jump the queue, I know that you're snowed under as it is, but it's a potential breakthrough in one of the worst unsolved homicides in Copenhagen in recent years.'

'Yes, my daughter left school around the same time. That poor father, I feel for him,' Sigurdsson said, though he looked unconvinced.

'And I was thinking that I could bribe you with this so that you have something to wash down the extra work with.'

Axel produced a bottle of 16-year-old Lagavulin from his bag. He saw Sigurdsson's eyes light up, before he checked himself and they fell slumbering back into his deep eye sockets. He leaned back in his chair.

'Ask BB to let me know when the tests are ready. And now get out of my office. I never accept bribes, but on this occasion…'

Axel walked down the corridor a happy man. Finally something had gone right, and now his daughter was waiting.

CHAPTER 20

He showed his warrant card at the staff entrance to the airport. Ea Holdt called him just as he was heading to arrivals.

'I've found the case. Lulu Linette Larsen, 2003. You're welcome to come and take a look at it.'

'When and where?'

'We can go through it together. You can't copy my notes, but I believe I have a different take on the victim's experience from the one you can read in the police report.'

'I'm sure you have. I've seen the report.'

'You work fast.'

'And I've spoken to the investigator.'

'OK, and now you see things differently?'

'No.'

'I could stop by with it during the weekend, if you're free.'

'My daughter is back from The Hague. She'll be with me.'

'Her name is Emma, isn't it?'

'Yes. Perhaps we could meet on Monday?'

They agreed to do that.

He was in the arrivals hall, his loathing of airports growing. There was nowhere else on earth where people were more self-absorbed than in this sterile architect-fantasy of a perfumed hell. The cold clip-clop of soles against the floor, the neutral but masterful smiles of businessmen, the bubbling expectation of children and the mechanical laughter lines of the staff. Most travellers had already arrived mentally at their next destination and it was only a matter of three, five, 12 hours before they were reunited with their body in Rome, Sharm el Sheikh or Vancouver. He found the flight from The Hague on the arrivals board and remembered how his daughter had broken down in tears when he was flying with her back from The Netherlands for the first time, and security staff had confiscated her blunt-ended scissors.

'You can't bring them, Emma.'

'But they're my scissors, Daddy.'

'We're not allowed to take scissors on the plane.'

'Why?'

'They're afraid that you could hurt someone with them.'

'Hurt someone? How?'

'You might stab someone with them.'

'I don't stab people with my scissors. I just use them to cut paper.'

'We have to let them have them, sweetheart. Or we won't be allowed on the plane. I'll buy you some new scissors.'

She had sobbed all the way to the plane. She didn't want a new pair of scissors, of course she didn't. Even if Axel had promised to buy her a hundred pairs, it was no good. The man who had taken her scissors was bad. She wanted to get back what she had lost. He could relate: he was even worse at letting things go than Emma was. A cabin crew member with a teddy bear and a tube of Smarties stopped the tears and they flew home in high spirits. But Emma would regularly bring up the scissors, often just before she fell asleep, and Axel had asked himself over and over what it was really about.

He had put on clean clothes, jeans and a white shirt, and shaved. He saw Cecilie's brown eyes first, a gaze that sought him out with recognition but not much warmth. Then he made eye contact with Emma, who started jumping up and down while she shouted 'Daddy, Daddy, Daddy' and ran, jumped, landed in his arms and nestled her head under his cheek as she always did. His heart defaulted to zero. And filled to bursting.

She withdrew her head from the crook of his neck and looked at him with sparkling, happy brown eyes. Then she opened her mouth wide. Closed it and opened it while the words stumbled out of her mouth.

'Two of my teeth have fallen out, Daddy. Look!'

Cecilie had reached them.

'What happened to you?' she asked.

'I fell. It's OK.'

Wrinkles formed around her eyes, her lips parted slightly. Was she worried about him? Or about leaving her daughter in his care?

They started walking down the pier away from the gate. Axel held Emma's hand. Her trainers squealed against the marble floor. She gave him her teddy and held her mother with her free hand. He tried to catch Cecilie's eye.

'We have a new lead in the Blackbird case.'

She looked as if she had no idea what he was talking about.

'This time I'll get him, Cecilie.'

'Who?'

Emma looked up at them from one to the other.

'Blackbird's killer. He won't get away this time.'

It was then that Axel realised she didn't care.

'You look tired,' she said.

'You're not tired, are you, Daddy?' said Emma, the only one of the three not to realise that tired was another way of saying he looked like shit.

Axel ignored Cecilie. Emma looked up at him, then at her mother again.

'How was the flight?' he asked her.

'It was bumpy. I'm glad you weren't there, Daddy, you wouldn't have liked it,' she laughed.

Cecilie smiled.

'We're here for three weeks. You need to bring her back Monday morning, and then you'll have one week of holiday together later. But I would like to meet with you and talk about various things.'

'Of course.'

'What will you be talking about? Is it about me? I want to come home soon. Please would you tell Daddy that, Mummy?'

'Yes, darling, that's the sort of thing Daddy and I will be talking about.'

Axel offered to carry Cecilie's suitcase, but she said no, so he took Emma by the hand and picked up her teddy and suitcase. The little girl clasped her mother's hand again.

'I'm parked out here,' Axel said.

The heat hanging in the motionless air stuck to his skin immediately. Cecilie peered towards the queue of taxis.

'I'll take a cab, it's fine. I need to go now, Emma, but I'll see you on Monday.'

'Mummy no go.'

'I have to. Have a nice time with Daddy,' she said and rubbed noses with her daughter as she swayed her body slightly from side to side and gave her a hug.

'Mummy no go.'

'Come on, Emma, let go of me now. You're going with Daddy.'

'Mummy no.'

She let go and Cecilie blew her a kiss and headed for the taxis. Axel produced the world's most confident and reassuring smile, as his daughter's loss made him scream inside.

She stood completely still, looking at her mother.

'Teddy,' she then said.

Axel passed it to her.

'Mummy stay. Mummy no go. Mummy stay with Emma. Mummy live with Daddy and Emma.'

CHAPTER 20

Her talking like a two-year-old irritated him.

'Why the baby talk, sweetheart?'

'Mummy no go,' she replied.

CHAPTER 21

'Does Axel Steen have any problems?' Jens Jessen said to Darling. Cecilie had stepped outside the restaurant with Jytte, who was a smoker. 'Could he be mixed up in anything? Any confidentiality concerns? Is he too close to the local criminals in Nørrebro? Any addiction issues?'

The astonishment in Darling's face told its own story.

'I'm purely speculating. I've no interest in hurting him, I acknowledge his talent, but many people would like to see the back of him. And wouldn't mind giving him a helping hand. And if he makes any mistakes, that becomes a real possibility.'

'He's my best investigator. I'll have a word with him.'

'Please don't. I'm just asking you to keep an eye on him.'

At least he had established one thing. Darling knew nothing of the contents of the envelope. That was reassuring, because Darling was so straitlaced that he would have logged it and probably informed the state prosecutor – unless his veneration for Axel Steen prevented him.

He was tempted to ask Darling about Axel and Cecilie's relationship – no, ask was the wrong word, cross-examine him, fling him up against the wall and extract every bit of information from him. Darling wasn't friends with Axel Steen, but he had worked closely with him during the years Axel had been married to Cecilie, and he had hinted that her leaving him had been dramatic. Jens only knew

Cecilie's side of the story, and ultimately that wasn't much. She had told him about their disagreements about Emma, how Axel had been an irresponsible father on many occasions, but would fight tooth and nail to see her as often as possible, how he had pleaded with Cecilie not to be reduced to seeing the child every other weekend. But their past, their marriage, she hadn't brought that up, she was very private. And he didn't know why.

Cecilie entered. Her face was flushed although she hadn't been drinking. The same could not be said for Jytte Darling. She had knocked back the Puligny Montrachet in a manner that annoyed Jens. And carried on with the full fat Napa-cap as though it was squash. At 1,100 kroner a bottle. He loathed drunk women. Especially when they leaned over him with their sugary, metal breath and started calling him 'Jensy-wensy'.

Cecilie looked at him beseechingly.

'Jens, I'm not feeling very well, is it all right if we leave now?'

He nodded. She was unwell. Of course.

So not tonight either.

CHAPTER 22

'I've got a cinema in my head, Daddy.'

'Tell me more, Emma?'

'They sell sausages. And candy floss. It's full of candy floss. And the Tivoli Gardens are in there as well. And Mummy is there. And Jens. Because they're coming to Tivoli with me. And it's the summer holidays there the whole time. And it's in Denmark. Not The Hague.'

She looked up at him, noticed something in his face and said quickly:

'Oh, Daddy, you're there as well, of course you are. Don't be sad. You're always there. Even when you're not.'

He read her a story, they sang a song and while she lay chatting to herself, he went to the living room and sat down in front of his laptop. He hadn't been online since about four o'clock in the afternoon, and he had 16 new emails. 12 of them from colleagues in various police districts who had reacted to his email about the MO in the rape of Jeanette Kvist. He counted as he read through them: three murders, nine rapes and six assaults that he would need to look at. At the top of his list he put the ones which had been carried out in and around Copenhagen. He would forward it to Tine Jensen, and ask her to follow-up.

Then he got to work on the three files. He started with Line Jørgensen from the summer of 1996 in Nørrebro Park because it was the oldest, made a table of the MO and signature, the time, the year, the location, the age and appearance of the victim, access to the victim, and any details that might tell him something about the attacker. There was a list of technical evidence and copies of fingerprints, photographs and various shoe prints. He continued with Anne Marie Zeuthen, who had been raped in 1998. Axel was hoping that the evidence might produce a DNA sample that would match those taken in connection with Jeanette Kvist, and his expectations rose when he saw that shoe prints had also been taken in this case. He put them aside, read through the file and carried on with Lulu Linette Larsen, who was raped in 2003. Shoe prints had been found here as well, and the MO similarities were so obvious that it was an outrage the cases had never been compared before. He decided to make a table of common features, but was overpowered by exhaustion before he got started.

CHAPTER 23

Saturday, 28 June

Islands Brygge Harbour Bath. They had ridden their bikes there. Emma on her new bike, Axel by her side with his hand on the back of her neck when the traffic was at its densest. The plan had been to teach Emma to swim, but after an hour the pool was so full of screaming kids that Axel had started getting claustrophobic. Emma refused to stay in the water on her own, and now they were sitting on their towels reading *The Brothers Lionheart*.

Something had happened to Emma. She wanted him near her all the time. And she spoke baby talk and kept calling him Da-da. He didn't know if he was reading too much into it, but it was as if she had travelled back in time. He thought she was yearning for something in the past, but he couldn't be sure he wasn't projecting his own longing onto her.

They were sitting near a skate park where a group of boys were kicking a ball around. They were about Emma's age and she began to move towards them. Axel was delighted because it was the first time today that she had left his side. He checked on her regularly, while he flicked through a free newspaper he had found on the grass.

She was of slim build, tall for her age and her two front teeth still stuck out. She wore a lime green bikini with white daisies. For a while she ran around with the boys, who played aimlessly. Then she stopped in front of two of them. She hesitated. As if torn between staying and leaving. She said something to them, but her manner was defensive. Her entire body language signalled sadness.

Then she left them and half-ran towards him.

'Daddy, what's a whore?'

Axel got up from the towel and looked towards the boys. Rage surged inside him like a black tower of hatred. The boys looked back at them and began retreating to a large group of men, women and young children sitting by the skate park. They were barbecuing. The women wore headscarves and were fully clothed despite the heat.

'Why do you want to know that?'

'They said I had rabbit teeth. And when I said you shouldn't say nasty things to people, they called me a whore.'

Axel took her hand.

'Come with me,' she said.

She took his hand and followed him. Without much enthusiasm.

'There's nothing to worry about, Emma, but they need to speak properly to you.'

Axel stopped in front of the families. He looked at them. Then he raised his voice:

'One of your boys just called my daughter a whore.'

'It was the one in the blue swimming trunks,' Emma whispered.

Axel looked at the boy. He was standing next to two other boys, glancing nervously at them. Axel took them to be eight or nine.

A man had got up and came over to Axel.

'What's the problem, mate?' he said. Then he noticed the injuries to Axel's face and held up his hands to signal that he wasn't looking for any trouble.

'Is that your son?'

'Yes, mate.'

'I'm not your mate. And you're the one with the problem unless you make him apologise right now. Your son just called my daughter a whore.'

The man glared angrily at his son, who said something in a language Axel guessed must be Turkish or Kurdish. They shouted back and forth. The boys came up to them. One of them spoke up in Danish:

'That's not true. He said bore.'

'Listen, mate, seems like you're the one with the problem.'

Axel was silent. He looked at the boys. Then at the man. He wondered what to do next.

'Don't lie to me. There's no sentence in the Danish language where you could confuse bore and whore.'

'Are you being racist?'

'No. I'm angry. My daughter is six years old, and nobody calls her a whore, understand? Tell him to apologise. Right now.'

'Or what?'

Emma tugged at his hand.

'Daddy, I want to go home, please.'

'I don't want to argue with you, but I'm not leaving until your son has apologised.'

'He has nothing to apologise for.'

'Daddy, please.'

'Do you think I've come here with my daughter on my day off to have an argument with you?'

'Are you accusing my son of lying?'

'Don't you understand what I'm saying?'

'Are you saying I don't understand Danish?'

'Oh, don't play the race card. How would you feel if I called your wife or daughter a whore?'

Some of the other men in the same group were starting to get up.

'Please, Daddy, I want to go home.'

Axel looked at Emma. She looked scared. 10 people had surrounded them now. Adult men and boys.

An old man intervened.

'What's the problem?'

A stream of words, which Axel didn't understand, cascaded over the old man.

'He says that you have insulted him. You called his wife a whore.'

Axel looked the man in the eye.

Emma yanked his arm. 'Daddy, please can we go now?'

'I haven't offended anyone. That boy there called my six-year-old daughter a whore. I want an apology.'

Everyone started talking on top of one another, or so it seemed to Axel, because he didn't understand what they were saying. Emma pulled his arm harder.

The old man threw up his hands apologetically to Axel.

'No one can agree who said what,' he said.

'Shut the fuck up, grandad, and you,' he jabbed his finger into the chest of the first man he had spoken to, 'you get that brat of yours to come over here and apologise to my daughter. Or I'll make him myself.'

'You're threatening my son.'

'No one calls my daughter a whore, understand? He crossed the line. He needs to understand that you just don't do that. Never. And I'm not budging until he apologises.'

'What are you going to do? Hit him? Are you looking for a fight?' the man wanted to know.

Axel exploded.

'Are you fucking deaf? I want an apology. You're his dad? How can you live with yourself knowing that your son runs around calling girls whores? Does he have a sister? What would you do if she came home one day and said that some boy had called her a whore? Would you just throw up your hands and say, well, you'll just have to get used to it, sweetheart?'

Emma was now pulling his arm as hard as she could. 'Stop it, Emma, we need to sort this out first.' She let go of his hand and started to walk away. Axel looked from her to the men and the boys and back again. The group was still talking over one another.

'If my daughter hadn't been here, you wouldn't have got off so easily,' he snarled, turned his back to them and left. He had to clench his fists and tense the muscles in his arms in order not to boil over with rage. He caught up with Emma, who was standing with her back to him. He could see from her shoulders that she was crying.

'I just want to go home, Daddy.'

He put his hands on her shoulders and turned her gently, but firmly. She glanced at the group they had just left, then quickly looked up at Axel's face without looking him straight in the eye.

'There are some things you shouldn't put up with, Emma.'

She shook her head, but he continued to hold her firmly.

'Listen to me. Don't ever let people get away with calling you names. Never.'

Except he just had, hadn't he? His daughter was sobbing. And he carried on. He couldn't let it go.

'Please, I want to go home, Daddy. It doesn't matter what they said, they didn't upset me.'

'Then why are you crying?'

'I don't like you arguing with people. Because of me. Please can we just go home?'

They cycled home to Nørrebro. The mood was glum. Axel was still seething on the inside. He was ashamed to have walked away. He had no doubt that he would have seen the confrontation through to its end, whatever that was, if Emma hadn't been there.

The mood rose a few degrees when Axel suggested they stop off at Isværket, a local ice cream and chocolate bar that also served great coffee, on their way home. The queue in front of the shop stretched out into the street.

Axel's mobile vibrated. It was a message from BB saying he had sent off 38 DNA samples to Forensic Genetics for testing.

'You'll have the answer on Monday', the text concluded.

Axel noticed that he had missed a call. Number withheld. He ignored it.

They shopped for dinner and rented a movie before returning to the flat.

Emma was tired and irritable, and Axel put on the film, a Japanese animation about a girl who got lost in a forgotten city populated by witches. He sat down on the sofa with his arm around her and watched the film until it ended. Every time it got scary, she would press herself against him, and he felt satisfaction at her trust in him. But the feeling of not having stood up for his daughter earlier was eating him up.

Once she was asleep, he returned to the three files. They each contained several prints, not just of fingers, but also of hands. He had started to spread them out on the coffee table when he noticed a message on his mobile. Number withheld once more, but from the message the caller had left, he concluded that it was Kaspersen at the DNA unit. He said he would call back later, that it was important. Perhaps it was about the DNA tests. But how could they have the results so soon? Axel was much too impatient to wait. He called the switchboard and got Kaspersen's mobile number.

'Kaspersen speaking.'

'What's going on? Do you have the results already?'

'No, I'm calling on another matter. I've got a second DNA match for the man whose DNA you found in connection with the murder of Marie Schmidt and the rape of Jeanette Kvist.'

'How?'

'Pure chance. I discovered it yesterday, but I decided not to call you before I had checked it with the Forensic Genetics. And I was right. We have his DNA from an attempted rape.'

'When?'

'June 2004. A 17-year-old girl from Ballerup, Lone Lützhøj. She managed to get away.'

'That's about the same time as the Blackbird case. That's brilliant.'

'Well, I'm not really sure it is.'

'What do you mean? Surely it's boosting our chances of catching him? Is there a description? What do we have on him?'

'The problem is that case was solved.'

'Come again?'

'Yes, the case was solved. The attacker was caught shortly afterwards. He got 18 months.'

'Based on what?'

'Based on DNA evidence, witness testimonies. He left his DNA under her fingernails and her blood was on his clothing. He confessed.'

'But that makes no sense.'

'I'm telling you that we now have DNA from the same donor in three cases: Marie Schmidt, Jeanette Kvist and Lone Lützhøj. One murder, one rape and one attempted rape. But a man has already been convicted of the attempted rape because his DNA was all over the victim. Yet your attacker left something that could be a nose hair on that same victim's clothing.'

'That's insane. What does it mean?'

'That's not my job to find out, and thank God for that.'

'But what the hell—'

'Beats me.'

Axel tried to piece together the information in a way that made sense, but all he could see was darkness and behind it, disaster. He tried to compose himself.

'I need the Lone Lützhøj file. And for the time being you'll keep this to yourself, OK?'

'Yes.'

'What about the guy who was convicted of the attempted rape, how much time did he serve?'

'One year. Good behaviour, but—'

'Where's he now?'

'That's what I was about to tell you. He didn't stay good once he was released. He was subsequently convicted of assaulting a 10-year-old girl and is currently in Herstedvester Prison.'

'And he's been there the whole summer?'

'I don't know about that, but he was sentenced to five years in 2007, so I'm guessing he's not eligible for unaccompanied leave yet.'

'What the hell? Let me just make sure I've got this right. He was convicted of the attempted rape in 2004 based on DNA evidence, but in that same case we also have a hair from the man who murdered Marie Schmidt and raped Jeanette Kvist?'

'Yes.'

'On the victim's clothing?'

'Yes, that's what it says here.'

'But… what the hell is going on?'

'I don't know, but I dread to think what might have happened. And for that reason we've commenced a complete review of the entire register, because there are some profiles in the sample section of the DNA register that don't come up automatically when you search. There would appear to be a problem with the system that we need to solve.'

Axel thanked him and ended the call. *Dread to think what might have happened?* That was an understatement, to put it mildly. If their perpetrator's DNA had ended up in the investigation of a rape he couldn't possibly have committed, then that would destroy the credibility of the whole DNA register. And if evidence from different cases really had been cross-contaminated, the entire system would break down. Though the possibility remained, of course, that their attacker had somehow been involved in the attempted rape of 17-year-old Lone Lützhøj in 2004.

First his daughter had been called a whore. Now the DNA register was in meltdown. He was snatched out of his frustrations by the doorbell. He checked his mobile. No one had called. It was half past midnight.

'It's Dorte,' he heard in the intercom.

He buzzed her in. Opened the door to the stairwell and lingered in the doorway while he waited for her.

'Hi. Are you going to let me in?'

She was happy, but not really present. Intoxicated. Not a lot, but enough for him to tell from her almond-shaped, Asian eyes, which were glassy and stood out under the hidden eyelids even more than usual. Her pupils were tiny.

'You're already here,' he said.

She opened her bag, pulled out a bottle of red wine and waved it.

'Can I come in?'

'Sure, but you'll need to leave soon. Emma is here. And I'm working.'

'I've brought you something else.'

She stuck her hand into her pocket and pulled out a generous lump of hash, three to four grams. Axel had cleared the flat of every trace of the fog of the last few weeks. Not only had he emptied the ashtrays, he had fine-combed the rooms with crime scene diligence yesterday afternoon and gathered up everything – joints, a chillum, small bits of hash resin – and chucked it all out because Emma was coming. He needed to have a clear head now. There would be no smoking. There would be no drinking. There would be no sex with Dorte. He had a horrible feeling that if he let her in, he would end up doing at least one of those three things.

'There's enough here for me to arrest you for supplying,' he said, and she laughed. 'Right, in you come.'

She wore stilettos, but was still a head shorter than him at least. She dumped her bag in the hall. She was dressed in a black skirt, a small silk jacket, a transparent blouse with no bra underneath as far as he could see. She saw his gaze and smiled. Sat down on the sofa.

'What's this?' she asked when she saw the numerous papers and copies of fingerprints spread across the coffee table. 'This isn't one of your old cases. This is new. What are you up to?'

'Come with me,' he said. 'We can't be in here. Come to the kitchen.'

He wanted to get her away from the files. She was an expert at getting him to talk. She mustn't know anything about the Blackbird case. Yet.

'Is it because I'm not allowed to see what you're doing?'

'No, Emma is asleep. She'll wake up if we make too much noise.'

He regretted it the moment he said it. She could take it to mean that he expected them to have sex. And they wouldn't be, he tried telling himself. She stopped behind him in the hallway, kicked off her shoes and dumped her jacket. Came out into the kitchen with the wine bottle in her hand.

'I was deeply hurt yesterday. Because you were too busy to see me.'

'Sometimes you're too busy to see me.'

He opened the bottle of wine.

'That's different.'

'It's not different. I have my daughter. And my job. And the two of them come first. It's the same for you.'

They clinked glasses. She drained practically her entire glass, but shook her head at the same time so a little wine trickled down the corner of her mouth.

'Apart from the fact that I don't have a daughter.'

'Yes, apart from that. But your job is everything to you, isn't it?'

Her eyes were warm, her gaze was slow, and whatever was going on inside her rolled across her face in super slow motion, delayed by the idling of intoxication.

'Oh, do shut up and come over here. I'm horny.'

He wanted to. He didn't want to. He got up and went over to her, kissed her greedily and angrily because she had turned up and stirred his desire, messed up his newfound order, and reminded him how fragile it was. He thrust his tongue into her warm mouth, which tasted of rotten cherries, letting her tongue wrap itself around his. He got even angrier. He grabbed her and turned her around so his hands had access to everything, she raised her arms and interlaced her fingers behind his neck, he touched her on the breasts she didn't have, pinched her nipples as she gasped, let his hand wander down, no knickers, to her cunt, across her pubic hair to the wetness between the lips, he slipped a finger inside her, it was too much, he bent her over the table. A red wine glass crashed onto the floor, he pulled up her skirt so it bunched up around her waist, entered her from behind, not gently. He placed his hand at the top of her back, pressing her body against the table and making her arse stand out more.

She moaned, saying 'yes, yes, yes' louder and louder as he thrust into her. He put his hand over her mouth, making her groan even louder.

'Shut up, you'll wake Emma,' he hissed.

He parted her buttocks, entered her as deeply as he could, grabbed her shoulder and yanked her towards him. She put her hand on the small of her back, and he grabbed it like you would hold someone whose arm you're twisting while he fucked her in cold, hard thrusts and stuck a finger up her arse. He came. And hated it.

They stood there, him half-bent over her as if he had stuck to her with his last thrust, and she collapsed over the small café table. He stood up. She pulled her skirt down, drained her wineglass.

'Oh, that was good,' she said. 'That was exactly what I needed.'

He needed her to leave and yet he was surprised when she got dressed. She tucked her blouse into her skirt, continued out into the hallway, put on her stilettos and picked up her jacket. She scratched at some mascara in the corner of her eye with a fingernail and took out a small hand mirror.

'Thanks for that,' she said. 'I'm going home now. So you can work.'

The balance of power had been inverted. He had assumed that he was giving her something, that she needed him, but there was more inside her, a desire separate from his, more willpower than he had expected, something hard – or maybe it wasn't hard, but it triggered his fear of rejection. He smiled ironically.

'OK. Was that the only reason you came here?'

She laughed. She pouted to comfort him.

'Was it that bad for you?'

'No, it was good.'

She walked up to him and kissed him. Placed a hand on his dick and squeezed it.

'Bye for now. See you later.'

He returned to the kitchen. The bottle of red wine was still there. The lump of cannabis resin was left behind on the table.

CHAPTER 24

Sunday, 29 June

When he woke up, his mouth tasted of metal. In an attempt not to smoke cannabis while Emma was with him, he had attacked the red wine instead and emptied the bottle. He wasn't used to drinking, but that hadn't stopped him and now his brain was fizzing with impulses and ideas he couldn't control. The run-in with the men on Islands Brygge, Kaspersen's phone call and Dorte's subsequent visit refused to leave him alone – they filled him with an urgent, restless energy that didn't mix well with lying on the carpet playing shoe shop with seven Barbie dolls. He needed to get high. Or work. Being with a six-year-old girl demanded calm and presence – two things he wasn't capable of right now. And Emma quickly picked up on that. She refused to play anymore. She just wanted to sit on his lap. 'Daddy, my Daddy, my Daddy,' she kept saying. In an attempt to find some relief from her and his colossally guilty conscience, he asked if she wanted to watch television, knowing the answer in advance, and a minute later she was completely absorbed in some foreign cartoon channel.

He had to get back to the nitty-gritty of the cases and ignore the sodding DNA tests and his conversation with Kaspersen. He sat down again with the descriptions of the technical evidence.

He found the pile of shoe prints from the three historical cases. The shoe prints taken in connection with the rapes of Lulu Linette Larsen in the allotment garden in 2003 and Line Jørgensen in Nørrebro Park in 1996 didn't match, but the shoe size was the same. He took out Anne Marie Zeuthen's file and found copies of shoe prints from the windowsill and on the scaffolding. The prints on the scaffolding didn't match the two other cases, but a quarter-shoe print from the windowsill matched one of the most frequently recurring prints from the Line Jørgensen case. A trainer with a long gash across the ball of the sole. He felt a rush of adrenaline. The trainers having the same sole was one thing, but a gash in the exact same place turned the print from circumstantial into direct evidence. Maybe not enough to secure a conviction, but the chances of two different soles having identical rips were practically non-existent. That was good news for him, but shoddy police work. Unsolved serious sexual assaults in the same area should have been cross-referenced down to the smallest detail.

He spread out the finger and palm prints in front of him and went through them one by one. In the Line Jørgensen case, her fingerprints were the only ones at the scene, but in the rape of Anne Marie Zeuthen they had found a partial palm print on a windowsill, which they had been unable to identify. The heel of the right hand where the thumb meets the palm. The hands and fingers of scaffolding workers and everyone who had been to Anne Marie Zeuthen's flat had been printed, without any matches. It could have come from a window cleaner, or from the factory where it was manufactured, or from a resident who had leaned out of the window. But it was also possible that her attacker could have left it, since he could have entered through a window as Jeanette Kvist's rapist had. From the rape of Lulu Linette Larsen they had also found several finger and hand prints from the allotment shed. Axel flicked through page after page of prints, and could see that the vast majority belonged to the owner of the shed and his wife. There was nothing to be had there.

He fetched a strong lamp from the other room and a magnifying glass. Then he placed the palm print from Anne Marie Zeuthen's flat on the table and started comparing it with the other prints in the files. He didn't get a positive result until he reached the very end of the Lulu Linette Larsen file. On a piece of paper showing a print on a door frame were four fingers and the palm of a right hand. The print matched the half-palm print found on Anne Marie Zeuthen's windowsill. It was the same hand. His heart began to pound. 'Yes!' he whispered. 'I've got you, you bastard.'

Except that on the paper it said that the prints belonged to the owner of the allotment shed, a man who would have been 67 years old at the time. Axel called HQ and asked them to run a criminal records check on the man. He gave them the man's civil registration number and waited.

'We haven't got him.'

'What do you mean?'

'He doesn't have a criminal record.'

'Can you look up his civil registration number?'

'Sure, hang on.'

Axel waited. He was shocked that the attacker could have been overlooked, but also baffled because the man would be 72 years old today. It didn't match Jeanette Kvist's description at all.

'He's dead. He died last year. 22 February.'

Axel was thrown. But he returned to the prints taken in connection with the 2003 investigation, and found the sheet with the late allotment shed owner's finger and palm prints. He compared them. The fingers on the door frame were a match, but not the palm print. Yet another mistake. Whoever had examined the prints had assumed that the palm print belonged to the four fingers on the door frame and left it at that. But the palm print on the door frame belonged to the rapist. This was progress. He had connected two of the rapes, those of Anne Marie Zeuthen and Lulu Linette Larsen, with a palm print, and two others, those of Anne Marie Zeuthen and Line Jørgensen, with a shoe print. He had evidence of the same MO. He had a location. A time. A signature. And two pieces of forensic evidence linking the cases. The same cruelty. He had a case to present come Monday morning.

He was finally able to give his full attention to his daughter, who was draped zombie-eyed across the armrest of the sofa watching Scooby Doo and his friends having an adventure on the television. They were together for the rest of the day at the playground, on the floor with her Barbie dolls, at the table with felt tip pens, and finally he found an old sheet, cut holes for her eyes, she drew a mouth that could compete with Munch's *The Scream*, and then she chased him, grinning, round the flat screaming 'boo!' until it was time for bed.

CHAPTER 25

Monday, 30 June

In Nørrebrogade, he held his daughter's hand as buses thundered past them and a stream of scantily clad cyclists whirled over the melting tarmac. She was wearing her summer cap and a pair of pink sunglasses with tinted lenses, she had a lollipop in her mouth and a rucksack that made her back sway and her tummy stick out, bare legs, red sandals, a skirt and a Diddl cartoon T-shirt. A plastic bag in one hand. Ready for her summer holiday with her mother and Jens Jessen. Her hand felt tiny in his and he didn't want to let go of it. A car horn sounded across the street, a big Ford Galaxy. Cecilie got out, pushed her sunglasses up into her hair with one hand and waved with the other as she smiled. She crossed the street while Jens Jessen rolled down the window and waved as well. Axel nodded to him.

'Hi, sweetheart, ready to start your holiday? Hi, Axel, was everything OK?'

She was wearing a loose fitting summer dress, and Axel could see her cleavage when she bent down to give Emma a kiss. Cecilie removed her sunglasses when she straightened up.

'Yes, we've had a great time. We went to the Harbour Bath and played with Barbie dolls, Emma was a ghost.'

'Don't tell them any more about that, Daddy.'

'No, I won't.

'I'm going to scare them, but it's going to be a surprise.'

Cecilie laughed and looked inquisitively at Axel, who had been ordered not to say that the big plastic bag his daughter was holding in her hand contained one of Axel's old sheets with two holes in it, and that her mother and stepfather were in for a treat.

'What's in your bag, sweetheart?'

'Nothing. It's a secret,' Emma said, looking excited and stern at the same time.

Cecilie reached out her hand and squeezed Axel's bicep as if the two of them still had something together.

'So are you are ready, sweetheart? Jens is waiting in the car. We're going to the zoo today, and in a few days we'll go to the summer cottage.'

Axel bent down and picked up his daughter. She was tall. He inhaled her scent for the last time, kissed her cheek, and put her down. Cecilie took her hand. They said goodbye. He waved as they crossed the street. Jens Jessen was still sitting with the window down, looking at him.

'What's this I've been hearing?'

Darling came storming into Axel's office. He had a piece of paper in his hand.

Axel looked up.

'I don't know.'

'You can wipe that smile off your face right now and remember what I said last Friday. You went behind my back with Forensic Services. Three men worked on your old cases for 12 hours, as a result of which the examination of evidence in several others has had to be put on hold. And now you submit a request to BB asking him to examine hundreds of DNA traces from 13 different cases. Two murders, nine rapes and two assaults. I hope you have a really good explanation for this.'

'I do. Have we got the DNA results from the two cases from last Friday?'

'No, they won't be ready until this afternoon.'

Axel briefly outlined what he had discovered, and then showed him the summary he had made of the victims, matching evidence, signature and MO:

Line Jørgensen. Aged 19. Raped. Summer 1996. Nørrebro Park. Nørrebro.

Connecting evidence: Shoe print.

Connecting MO: Mask. Knife. Stranglehold. Forced to reveal her name and civil registration number. Threatened on her life if she doesn't stay silent.

Anne Marie Zeuthen. Age 22. Raped. Summer 1998. Brohusgade. Nørrebro.

Connecting evidence: Hand print. Shoe print.

Connecting MO: Scaffolding. Gloves. Knife. Stocking mask. Forced to reveal her name and civil registration number. Threatened on her life if she doesn't stay silent.

Signature: Forced to choose how she wanted to be raped.

Lulu Linette Larsen. Aged 17. Raped. Summer 2003. Borgervænget. Østerbro.

Connecting evidence: Hand print.

Connecting MO: Knife. Stranglehold. Condom, which he takes with him. Forced to reveal her name and civil registration number. Threatened on her life if she doesn't stay silent.

Marie Schmidt. Aged 18. Murdered. Summer 2004. Ørsted Park. Central Copenhagen.

Connecting evidence: DNA.

Connecting MO: Strangulation.

Jeanette Kvist. Age 23. Raped. Summer 2008. Refsnæsgade. Nørrebro. Connecting evidence: DNA.

Connecting MO: Scaffolding. Stocking mask. Knife. Gloves. Condom, which he takes with him. Forced to reveal her name and civil registration number. Threatened on her life if she doesn't stay silent.

Signature: Forced to choose how she wanted to be raped.

Quick as a flash Darling identified the weaknesses in the cases. First it was the evidence linking the Blackbird investigation to Jeanette Kvist. Then it was the missing link between Blackbird-Jeanette Kvist and the three other rape cases.

'And you think the DNA samples will give us that?' he wanted to know.

'I hope so, but it's not crucial, as far as I'm concerned. It is the same man. There can be no doubt. There are way too many things that match. The time. The place. His MO of gloves, mask, knife, access by scaffolding, his threats to kill them if they don't do as he says. He makes them tell him their name and telephone number, and then there's the condom which he takes with him. And last, but not least, his signature, which makes him unique: he forces them to choose how they want to be raped. There are too many coincidences.'

'And all this has been lying in our archives waiting for a nerd like you to find it?'

Yes, Axel thought, and it doesn't stop there. There was also the DNA evidence in the Lone Lützhøj case, but he decided to keep that to himself for the time being in order to not to muddy the waters.

'Yes. And meanwhile the victims have been living without certainty or closure. It's not something we should be proud of.'

'Nor is it something we want to shout from the rooftops. Though I do see that there's a pattern here.'

Yes, you'd be blind not to, Axel thought, but again he said nothing.

'There's no need to meet with the others to decide whether to allocate resources for this. I'm making that decision now. I'll put together a team for you. Good job. We'll meet at 12 noon.'

Axel thought this was his cue to leave, but he wasn't getting off that easily.

'But none of this changes the fact that I will not have you going behind my back and telling BB the evidence is related to a terror investigation. It's a really stupid thing to lie about, Axel.'

'No one would listen to me. You would never have given me permission.'

'No, but I'm doing so now. Not on the basis of the DNA analysis, though.'

'No.'

This information gave Axel an unexpected opening.

'So can I assume that your decision to allocate staff to these cases doesn't depend on whether or not there's DNA to connect them?'

'Yes, but that's not the point. I don't want you causing any more trouble, do you hear?'

'Yes.'

He turned to leave, but Axel could see that something had made a trip round his brain first. Now it came.

'Incidentally, we had a really nice time on Friday with Jessen and Cecilie.'

'Glad to hear it,' Axel said, trying to sound completely casual.

'Yes, and I sang your praises. Told him about some of our cases. And your dedication. While the women were out.' He looked embarrassed.

'I don't need you to sing my praises.'

'Don't say that.' There was something about Darling's tone that gave Axel an uncomfortable feeling that there was more to it.

'By the way. Jens Jessen is insisting on this idea he had the other day. He wants to shadow a homicide investigation.'

'Great. Then send him along when someone gets a new case.'

'He has asked specifically to shadow you.'

Axel's mobile rang.

'No fucking way, John.' He answered the call.

'It's Kaspersen from the DNA unit. I have good news and bad news. Which would you like first?'

'I've had enough bad news from you this weekend. Just tell me, for God's sake!'

'The good news is that we found DNA from your perpetrator in the rape of Anne Marie Zeuthen. It's the same DNA profile as in the cases of Marie Schmidt and Jeanette Kvist.'

'Bloody hell.'

'The bad news is we got nothing from the tests from Lulu Linette Larsen.'

'Doesn't matter. We've connected it to the others with a palm print. Thank you. You've made my day.'

A crucial link had just been made. Now they could prove that the man had operated for a period of 12 years. It was a major case. A serial offender. A minute ago he had two sets of cases that weren't connected by technical evidence. He had believed all along that they were connected, his instinct told him that, and it also told him that there was more. 12 years of rapes and murder. It could be their biggest case ever. Hunches were enough for him. It was his fuel, but it was hard evidence that would get the cases across the finishing line. And that was still a long way away. They had five cases that were connected in a variety of ways. They had no suspect. But tonight they would try to find one.

CHAPTER 26

They came to his office at 12 noon. Darling congratulated him on the DNA match. Present were Tine Jensen, Axel, Darling and three other investigators. Bjarne Olsen, a motorbike fanatic on the wrong side of fifty with as many prejudices as he had wrinkles. He was one of the country's best interrogators because he spoke the criminals' own language. And Axel appreciated that. Tonny Hansen, an experienced and monosyllabic 60-year-old investigator who always wore wooden clogs and never revealed anything about his life outside HQ. Vicki Thomsen, the youngest member of the group, apple cheeks, close-set brown animal eyes, an analytical woman from Funen in her late twenties who chewed gum constantly.

It wasn't a bad team. Darling introduced Axel as the head of the investigation. Tine Jensen sent him a look that Axel couldn't fathom.

Axel summarised the five cases. Line Jørgensen, Anne Marie Zeuthen, Lulu Linette Larsen, Marie Schmidt and Jeanette Kvist. Then he presented the technical evidence the cases had in common.

'Before I introduce our strategy, Tine will account for the case which is the reason we're here now. She can take the credit for that.'

Tine looked at Axel with surprise, but soon pulled herself together.

'Last Friday we carried out further door-to-door enquiries in the area where Jeanette Kvist lives. We also sent officers out as part of a reconstruction to see if anyone had seen the attacker four weeks ago.

And someone had. A woman returning home from an evening shift had seen a man wearing a hoodie walk down Refsnæsgade. She noticed him because he had pulled up the hood, which seemed odd given how warm it was. It was a light anorak or a sports jacket, she thought. She tried to see his face, but he turned his head away to avoid her. We showed her the picture of the man from Nørreport station, and while she didn't dismiss it outright, she couldn't identify him 100 per cent either. However, she did think that the man she had met had been dressed in a similar fashion to the man on the CCTV footage.'

Axel interrupted her.

'He's at the top of our list now. I'll get back to him. Anything else, Tine?'

'Yes, I've been in touch with our colleagues in Sweden, Norway and Germany last Friday to give them information about our perpetrator's MO, and I have heard back from Sweden. Still waiting to hear from the others. Three cases, one from Malmö, one from Østersund and one from Helsingborg. All within the last five years. And then there's feedback from police districts in the rest of Denmark. Axel has been informed of three homicides, nine rapes and six assaults which might be related to this case. There's no DNA, but potentially other pieces of relevant evidence.'

It was good news, but they had to make the obviously relevant evidence from the Copenhagen cases their priority.

'We need to assign tasks, ongoing ones and individual operations. I suggest that you – Tine – take the lead on case management. There will be more information coming from different police districts. I would like you to organise it and at the same time act as the liaison officer for the whole investigation, OK?'

Ambitious police officers always vied for that area of responsibility. Axel had realised that he needed to set aside his past differences with Tine Jensen and offer her a titbit he knew she would want. But his ulterior motive was to get her away from interviews and fieldwork after her fiasco with Jeanette Kvist. He didn't trust her.

'We have five cases which are connected. That's more than enough. I've no doubt that this piece of shit has more to account for, but we'll have to look into that later. We need to find him now.'

'What about the victims?' Vicki Thomsen asked.

Axel deliberately avoided looking at Tine Jensen.

'We need to inform them that we're reviewing their case. And they must be interviewed in detail again on the strength of what we know now. Would you deal with that?' Axel said, addressing Vicki and Bjarne, who were the most obvious contenders as far as he could see.

They nodded.

'Our perpetrator is always in total control, he takes a dangerously long time and enjoys subjecting his victims to psychological terror. This may be blatantly obvious to those of you who have worked extensively with sexual assaults, but my meetings with Jeanette Kvist, who has stayed seriously strong, have made it clear to me that this bastard is carrying out some of the worst kinds of violence imaginable. He doesn't inflict major physical injuries on his victims, but he terrorises them. She felt that he had got under her skin. And he humiliates them.'

'Is he a sadist?' Darling asked.

'He's definitely a sadist, but not in the sense of wanting to inflict physical pain. The knife is his weapon of choice, of course, because it's the weapon women fear the most, and we must assume that he also used a knife when he raped and murdered Marie Schmidt. Everything seems planned, but he also exhibits a high level of improvisation, such as with Jeanette Kvist, where he toys with the idea of being caught and uses props which he finds in situ. When we catch him, we have to hope that I'm not having one of my bad days because I won't stop at beating the crap out of him.'

There were smiles all around, Darling's was strained.

'I would like to release the picture from Nørreport station now,' Axel continued. 'We're dealing with a serial offender, who has committed at least one homicide and four aggravated sexual assaults. He operates in a limited geographical area in Copenhagen. We have an adequate description of him. He's aged between 30 and 50. I think that's enough to make an announcement. We should brief the media on all five cases, make public aspects of his MO, DNA evidence and issue a description of the man. Cast the net wide. And DNA test everyone brought to our attention. What do you think?'

Darling shook his head. 'I think not. We can't scare the entire population. It's way too risky. Every nutjob will be ringing us round the clock. You have to work this investigation without media support. That's an order.'

Was it the ghost of Holsted haunting them? Every police officer over the age of 45 knew the case. A man who had raped and abused four old women ended up killing his entire family while police were awaiting the results of DNA tests. He was one of several hundred men who were being tested, but the knowledge that he was about to be exposed had made him commit a triple homicide before he committed suicide. This wasn't something that worried Axel. Of course their perpetrator had to be forced out into the open. But what exactly might he do? Throw himself off Rundetårn? Unlikely – guys like him didn't have the guts for that. No, he would start sweating and hope to God that a girlfriend he had tried to strangle one time too many during sex wouldn't shop him.

'I disagree, but let's leave it for now. We have pictures of a man we need to find. We have been able to place him at Nørreport station twice. It supports the theory that the station might be his hunting ground, it's where he spots his victims, follows them home. And we're starting tonight. At Nørreport. We'll look for him. This involves everyone. From 6pm until 2am tonight. We'll meet at 5.30 this afternoon on Israels Plads. Bring service pistols and communication equipment.'

The mood was buoyant when they left the office. Normally Axel would have protested about Darling's fear of the press and the many limitations senior management was imposing on his investigation, but now he had something to do. If they didn't catch him tonight, they would send people there every day. It was a long shot – if he really was their man, the chances he would decide to lie low or change his behaviour following his encounter with Axel were high. Axel looked forward to tonight's assignment, but first there was something he had to get out of the way.

CHAPTER 27

Denmark's most serious offenders serve their time either side of Roskildevej, less than 10 km outside of Copenhagen. If you turn left, you reach Vridsløselille, a star-shaped four-storey brick monster from the mid-19th century, where murderers, kingpins, drug criminals, bikers and gang members serve long sentences in one of the country's toughest prisons. If you turn right, you reach Herstedvester, its low, two-storey 1930s buildings hidden behind a wall. Here 130 inmates serve out their sentences in the 'secure unit'. They are criminals who would struggle to survive in other prisons – sex offenders, child killers, rapists, paedophiles and psychopaths. There is also a small section for women serving long or life sentences. Axel had delivered a handful of offenders to the secure unit during his 12 years as a homicide investigator – lifers and people serving indeterminate sentences – many so dangerous that they would never be let out.

He turned right to Herstedvester and drove up in front of the gate, where he parked. He showed his warrant card and was let in. Handed over his service weapon, jacket, keys and went through two metal security gates.

He waited in a visiting room for 12 minutes before Max Arno Anborg Peters arrived. The man shuffled through the door and sat down on the other side of the laminate wood table into which inmates or visitors had wasted their precious time by scratching names, dates, curses and a variety of terms for the female sex organ. He wore a green tracksuit and moved with the lethargy of a prisoner.

'You're from the police.'

Axel looked at the man who could put the rape of a 10-year-old girl at the top of his CV. He took a deep breath.

'Yes.'

'I haven't done anything.'

If that was true you wouldn't be here, Axel thought to himself.

'I'd like to talk to you about the case for which you were convicted in 2004. An attempted sexual assault to which you confessed.'

'I've already done my time for that.'

'We have found evidence of another man in the same case, and he's wanted for a serious crime.'

'I don't understand. I did it on my own.'

'Have you ever been in contact with other sex offenders?'

He scratched his head as though he had head lice. Thought about it. Axel had a bad feeling about it all.

'Never, well, apart from in here. This place is full of them.'

'In the 24 hours leading up to the rape in 2004, were you in contact with a man about your age, perhaps 1.8 to 1.85 m tall, slim?'

'Not that I know of.'

'Have you ever been friends with or acquainted with a man who was dominating and sadistic towards women?'

'Not apart from my dad.' Rotting teeth behind his grin.

'And if you had, you wouldn't tell me, would you?'

'Anything in it for me?'

Axel struggled to control his revulsion.

'There might be. Good behaviour isn't enough for the parole board given your track record, is it? Me putting in a good word for you will help, but that means you have to give me something.'

He was silent, mulling something over. From time to time he looked up at Axel.

'I didn't do it.'

'Didn't do what?'

'The one in 2004, the one you're asking about. I didn't do it.'

'Give over. Your skin cells were found under her fingernails. Her blood was on your jacket.'

'She attacked me. She had just been assaulted, and she thought I had done it. She lost her mind. Someone else got away with it. The real guy is out there. The same goes for the 10-year-old. I was set up.'

'Of course. You're innocent. Someone's out to get you. It's a conspiracy.'

'That's right, officer. That's exactly what it is.'

Axel got up, smiled and walked over to him.

'I hope someone fucks you up the arse with a carving fork tonight, you loathsome little shit.'

He knocked on the door and looked hard at the man. The temptation to beat him up was strong. Coming here as an outlet for his frustrations hadn't helped. He didn't know whether it was those wretched sexual assault cases with their stellar cast of deranged perpetrators that was getting to him, or whether it was the DNA profile from the Lone Lützhøj case that was threatening to derail his entire investigation. But he would have to address it soon and contact Claus Sigurdsson to get to the bottom of what it could possibly mean.

CHAPTER 28

'Jens Jessen will be joining you tonight. He wants to see how we do it.' Darling had popped his head round Axel's office and was failing to conceal his schadenfreude. 'You'll make a cute couple.'

'You have got to be fucking joking. That moron isn't going anywhere with me.'

'It's not up for discussion.'

They sat in Axel's car. They'd be making their way to the station platform in half an hour. Darling had posted six uniformed officers with pictures of the man at the two Metro exits from two o'clock that afternoon.

Four days ago Axel had sat in Ørsted Park, wallowing in memories of Cecilie. Now he was in a car with the man who slept in the same bed as her. Just thinking about her was practically giving him a hard on, her body which he still knew so well, the look in her eyes when he had proposed to her and she had said yes – nothing he had done had ever made anyone so happy. Except when she had lain in the bed at the maternity ward at the Rigshospitalet with Emma at her breast. And he had known that they belonged together. Then. And for ever. That was what she had said. The lying bitch. That nothing could separate them. But they had separated. And the reason was sitting right next to him, testing his headset with a smug smile, humming to himself. Fuck, he could really do without this. How it had got this far was beyond him. It felt as if Jens Jessen was actively seeking him out. He had asked to shadow Axel and no one else. What the hell was that all about?

Axel stayed silent. He had greeted Jessen when he arrived, introduced him to the others, explained why he was there, and that he was shadowing Axel. Everyone had looked gobsmacked. Axel presumed that the story of his divorce was common knowledge, and how often did you get the chance to witness the lead rivals in action right in front of your eyes?

'We'll get in our cars and test the earphones and mics. Once we're good to go, we'll leave at two minute intervals. Two people at every staircase, two people on the platform focusing on the Metro interchange. Six hours, are you ready?'

Everyone had nodded and gone to their cars.

Jens Jessen had stayed where he was, grinning like an imbecile.

'Fascinating. Military precision. I'm learning all the time,' he had exclaimed.

'Get in the car,' was all Axel had said.

Why was the idiot here? He could be having dinner with Cecilie and Emma right now instead of playing cops and robbers and fucking up Axel's operation.

'Are you sure you want to take part in this?'

'You don't think I can handle him?' Jens Jessen asked him in a frosty voice, and Axel shivered at the thought of the Deputy Commissioner trying to arrest a serial offender at Denmark's busiest traffic hub.

They had tested their headsets. Jens Jessen was wearing a suit that looked a little too big for him.

'That's not what I'm saying, but he's dangerous. And I don't suppose you had many lessons in combat sport when you read law.'

'Oh, if only you knew what I learned when I read law,' he said.

'I'm not interested.'

'What's the problem? Don't you think I can defend myself?'

'It's not about whether you can defend yourself. We might be about to arrest a serial offender, and we have to do it in such a way so that neither we nor anybody else, including him, get hurt.'

'Are you saying no one ever gets hurt when you arrest them? That's not what your HR file says.'

'Why the hell did you read that?'

Jens Jessen flashed him a disarming smile.

'Don't you worry about that now. But let me put it this way, you should thank your lucky stars that I have the job I have.'

Axel wanted to throw him out on his arse on the cobblestones of Linnésgade and then run him over with the car, but he kept his mouth shut.

'How are you going to run after him in those shoes?' He pointed to Jessen's black shoes, polished to within an inch of their lives.

Jessen pulled up one foot and said:

'Crepe rubber soles. I have thought of everything.'

Axel strapped on his service pistol.

'What are you going to do if he runs at you on the station platform?'

Jens Jessen looked at Axel as if he were an idiot.

'Stop him, of course.'

'Sure, but how?'

'There are lots of ways, aren't there?' Grab him, shoulder tackle him, trip him up.'

'He'll be gone before you've made up your mind. This is a bad idea. I suggest you come with me purely as an observer. I don't want you getting involved.'

'Axel, let me tell you how this is going to work. I am in charge. And if I want to be here, then I will be.'

Axel heaved a sigh. Took out his pistol and checked it. Jens Jessen watched him, mesmerised.

'What are you going to do if he's armed?'

'Easy now. Then I'll leave the scene to you. I promise to behave myself.'

But Jens Jessen's eyes were lit up with something Axel didn't trust.

They were in position with two officers at both sets of steps leading down to the platform and two men on the platform itself. It was going to be a long night. During the day the suffocating heat had descended into the underground and mated with diesel fumes, piss, vomit, smoke and oil. Axel wore a pair of grey army shorts and a loose-fitting shirt. The shoulder strap of his pistol stuck to his skin and sweat was pouring from his upper body. The injuries to his face had almost healed and he had been to his local barber in Stefansgade, a former colonel in the Iraqi army. In order to be on the safe side he wore a black baseball cap. He hoped the man wouldn't recognise him.

He took the first shift with Jens Jessen on the platform itself. Every now and then they made eye contact. He had to just cross his fingers that Jens Jessen wouldn't get in his way. Jens looked deep in concentration, a little too concentrated not to draw attention to himself, but he complied with Axel's instructions about where to look. Both of them kept to a section with an unobstructed view of both sides of the platform, where they could see the steps leading down to the Metro interchange.

The time passed unbearably slowly, softened up by brake noises from trains that knocked politely on the rails as they came to a stop and pushed their passengers out onto the platform. Axel lit a cigarette and looked at the faces without seeing them.

They switched positions every half hour. Tine Jensen brought coffee at nine o'clock. Was it all a waste of time? It was a thought that always occurred to him during a surveillance operation when he started to tire. His experience got him back on track, but his colleagues were reaching their limits. The only one not complaining in the headsets was Jens Jessen.

Axel had spent much of his working life standing, waiting, watching and monitoring. He had briefly worked as a personal protection officer, and although he ultimately hadn't had the patience for the deadly dull job of accompanying VIPs in limousines around the city to meetings, hotel rooms, poker bars, conferences, dinners and airports, the many surveillance assignments in public situations had given him invaluable training. He had learned the art of scanning large crowds without losing himself in individual details. Back then it was weapons, irregularities, rage or concentrated expressions that were the target of his attention. This time it was a face.

It showed up at 11.10pm.

CHAPTER 29

Jens Jessen wasn't tired in the slightest. He had been standing on the platform for five hours, studying faces without seeing the man in the pictures Axel Steen had given to him. But he found it interesting to see the city from a whole new perspective. He had never really seen anything the few times he had waited for a train, always lost in a world of his own. He could have been the man over there with the briefcase, black suit and white shirt, blue speckled tie, staring vacantly at the soot-blackened wall. He had met three former colleagues whom he had greeted briefly and then got rid of by saying that he was on assignment with the Homicide Division.

The police officers in the group had looked surprised to see him. They had looked him up and down and concluded he was overdressed. What was he really doing here, their eyes asked. He had smiled amicably and thanked them for allowing him to come along.

His initial plan to experience the reality of every division had completely slipped his mind. He wasn't going anywhere else. He was here on the platform with Axel Steen. It was incredibly exciting. And he had eyed a solution to his problem. He would get close to him. There was something they needed to talk about. He just needed to pick the right moment. He looked at Axel as he stood leaning against the grey ceramic tiled wall 30 to 40 metres away from him. His tall, muscular figure in the oversized shorts and Hawaiian shirt, the cap, his scarred face, the concentrated expression that wandered around and around and around. Then it stopped. He heard his voice in the headset.

'He's here.'

He tried to make eye contact with Axel, who looked utterly indifferent as he spoke.

'Jens, behind you. 50 metres. Turn around and walk past him so he can't get away, then I'll take him.'

Axel Steen started to walk towards him. Jens Jessen turned around as Axel had told him and walked down the platform.

'The rest of you, move down the stairs and block them off.'

The man was 20 metres away from him. He was attractive, well groomed, wearing a tracksuit jacket, tight dark blue running trousers, trainers. Wasn't that the perfect camouflage for a rapist? Short hair, narrow face, his eyes kind and calm. The man tried to catch Jens's eye as he passed him, and smiled. What was going on?

Jens Jessen carried on another 10 metres before he turned around. The man hadn't quite reached Axel when he stopped and took a step back. They made eye contact. Jens Jessen could tell that from Axel Steen's face. Axel Steen held up his warrant card in one hand and smiled. At this point the man turned and started running towards him.

'Police, stop,' Axel Steen called out as the man came towards Jens Jessen as if in slow motion. At this point a gun would have come in handy.

CHAPTER 30

The train on which the man had arrived had nearly emptied of passengers when Axel made eye contact with him. He held up his warrant card. Waved it. You're not going to get away this time. He couldn't help smiling. The moment the man recognised Axel, he stopped. He turned around and started to run, but this time Axel wasn't off his face. He gave chase before the man had even had time to turn around. He saw Jens Jessen standing very still a little further down the platform.

The man pushed aside some young girls in jangling gold and silver necklaces, and a large bottle of Baeardi smashed against the tiles. The train started to pull away. He had almost reached Jens Jessen. Axel was five metres behind him. He would get him.

Ahead of him he saw Jens Jessen suddenly move to the side just as the man tried to pass him. The man crashed into his shoulder and was thrown diagonally across the platform towards the tracks where the train was leaving. Axel could see what was coming next. The man hit the side of the moving train, a window, a door, and then collapsed in a panicky attempt to get hold of something with his arms and legs. He was about to get trapped in the gap between the train and the platform, but Axel threw himself down alongside him and yanked him violently onto the platform.

'What the hell is wrong with you, man?' he roared into the face of the man, who looked to be in shock.

The other officers had reached the platform, where the public was crowding around.

'Is he hurt? Hey, let him get up. What's he done? What are you doing to him?'

Drunk locals about to boil over with sudden altruism, who wanted to be sure the police weren't harassing anyone. Axel hated them.

'Get lost. And you, you're coming with us. We need to talk. Bring him in,' he said, addressing Tine Jensen.

They left with their suspect. Axel turned to Jens Jessen, who smiled and flung out his hands.

'What did I tell you? Shoulder tackle. Works every time.'

'You could have killed him.'

CHAPTER 31

They brought him into Axel's office. Sat him down in a chair with a view of the noticeboard, where Axel had put up pictures of all the rape victims, plus a photo of Marie Schmidt taken right after she had been pulled out of the lake.

He looked at them quickly. Then he averted his eyes. Was he shocked? Axel was fairly sure that the man they were looking for wouldn't be upset by the photos, but he had been wrong about offenders before – intuition was his compass, but it could also be a faithless lover.

'What's this about?' the man had asked as they drove to HQ. 'I demand to know why you've assaulted me. Why are you doing this to me?'

It was the classic reaction of people unused to being in contact with the police. It came in all varieties and was mixed with a healthy portion of indignation and incredulity.

Fortunately he had managed to get rid of Jens Jessen. Now he sat with Tine Jensen facing the man. Axel took his time studying him before he said anything. He was approximately 1.8 m tall with broad cheekbones, a small nose, dark hair with a dash of grey. All of it matched Jeanette Kvist's description.

'We need to get formalities out of the way first.'

'Why am I here?'

'Take it easy. We'll get to that. What's your name?'

'Bo Langberg.'

'Your civil registration number?'

'290164-0113.'

He had already told them this in the car and they had run him through various databases and looked him up online. He had no criminal record. He was an architect, taught part-time at the School of Architecture and owned a graphic design company. He lived in Emdrup, had a wife and three children, two from a previous marriage. His annual income was on the comfortable side of one million kroner. Not exactly the archetypal background of a sadistic rapist and killer, but one detail that made all the difference to Axel. The man's office was in Nansensgade, only six doors down from the home of Marie Schmidt. He must have been checked out in connection with her murder back in 2004. They had spoken to more than 500 residents and business owners in that street alone.

'You don't know why you're here?'

'No, how could I?'

'Sometimes people know exactly why we want to talk to them. You might be one of those people.'

'Am I under arrest?'

'No, you're not. In fact you're free to leave right now if you want to, but I would advise against it. We're investigating a series of aggravated sexual assaults, and in connection with that you have come to our attention. We have quite a few things we need to clear up. We would like to interview you as a witness. If during this interview information comes out which is problematic for you, I will let you know. Then we'll get you a lawyer.'

'I don't want a lawyer. I just want to go home.'

'Do you need to call anyone to tell them you're here?'

'No.'

'Not even your wife?'

'No.'

'Where were you going?'

'Why do you want to know?'

'Please just answer the question.'

'I had been for a run. I was on my way to my office to pick up some things and have a shower.'

He looked up into the air, tensed his body and then relaxed after he spoke. He didn't look like a man trying to remember, but a man trying to come up with an answer.

'Let me make sure I've got this right. You live in Emdrup, you go for a run, then take the train to Nørreport station, still wearing your running clothes, at midnight, to have a shower?'

'I do a lot of running. I like running in the city. Along the Lakes.'

'Where were you the night between Friday and Saturday 31 May?'

'I don't know. At home, would be my guess.'

'Are you able to check that now?'

'I can check my diary.'

He pulled out his mobile.

'I was at the office. We had guests. I caught the train into town. Went for a run. Then I went to my office and worked for a few hours.'

Tine Jensen interjected.

'On a Friday night? Is that normal for you?'

'Yes, like I said, I enjoy running. Afterwards I sometimes go for a walk to relax and enjoy the city.'

'And what does Mrs Langberg say about that?' Tine Jensen wanted to know.

'Nothing.'

'How long have you had an office in Nansensgade?'

'Four years.'

'Do you know who Marie Schmidt is?'

'No.'

'The Blackbird investigation, does that mean anything to you?'

'She was the girl who was killed in Ørsted Park, wasn't she?'

'Yes.'

'A terrible tragedy. I've read about it.'

'OK, you were at your office. When approximately?'

'Which day?'

'Friday, one month ago.'

'I would say that I got there about 11pm. That's the time my wife and children go to bed, and I guess I worked for a couple of hours. I don't remember exactly.'

'So you catch the train to the city centre at 11pm, you go for a run and then you work afterwards?'

'Yes, I went for a run and had a shower.'

'How long have you been married?'

'Eight years.'

'Where did you go for your run?'

'Around the Lakes, I think.'

'And afterwards you went to your office in Nansensgade, took a shower and worked. For how long?'

'A couple of hours. I caught the train home around 2am.'

'You didn't do anything else in between?'

'No.'

'You went for a run around the Lakes, had a shower, worked, went home.'

He wavered.

'I think so. Perhaps I went for a walk.'

'Did you or didn't you?'

'I don't know. I often go to the city centre to run and work. The days merge into one another.'

'Have you ever come into conflict with the law?'

'No, though I was a witness in an assault case once.'

'What happened?'

'A young man was beaten up at Nørreport station.'

'You spend an awful lot of time there, don't you?'

'Every day.'

'Do you take a lot of trains once you're in the city centre?'

'I catch the train there and back. I go running. That's all.'

Axel tossed two surveillance footage stills onto the desk.

'Take a look at these. They're from Friday night at 11pm. You get on the train at Vesterport station and you get off at Nørreport station, two minutes later. How does that fit in with what you've just told us?'

More thinking.

'I had pulled a muscle. So I decided not to run to my office. But take the train.'

'Leave it out. Those two stations are equidistant from your office. I've seen the CCTV footage. You're not limping. You're walking purposefully, at a comfortable speed. The question you need to answer is where were you going?'

'Nowhere.'

'No, so you say. Except I don't believe you. Someone got off at Nørreport station at the same time as you.' Axel noticed that the man now looked frightened. 'And this person was brutally raped only half an hour later.'

'Who was she?'

'A 23-year-old woman was raped by a man who looks like you.'

He looked flustered and his face went red.

'Do you know this woman?' Axel said, showing him a picture of Jeanette Kvist from the surveillance footage.

'No.'

'She's the victim, and right now we're pointing our spotlight on you, so I think you should provide us with an explanation as to what you were doing there.'

'Like I said. I had pulled a muscle and I certainly wasn't following anyone. I got off the train at Nørreport station to go back to my office to bandage it up.'

There was no doubt that he was lying. He had gone from remembering only the outline of a fairly recent event to remembering specific details, except he hadn't done so until he was confronted with facts that forced him to change his explanation.

'Why did you run away from me last Thursday?'

He looked at Axel with a frown.

'I got scared. You looked like you wanted to hurt me.'

'I asked you for a light.'

'Your face was crazed. You said you wanted to talk to me. I didn't want to do that.'

'I called out to you that I was a police officer. Repeatedly. And you still ran.'

'Anyone can say they're a police officer. It was two o'clock in the morning in Ørsted Park and you had blood all over your face. Your eyes looked crazy.'

'Why did you run when you saw me just now at Nørreport station?'

'I didn't know you were a police officer. I got scared. If I'd known, then of course I wouldn't have run.'

'Have you been interviewed by the police before?'

'No.'

'Not even in connection with the murder of Marie Schmidt?'

'No.'

'Is it possible that you're hiding something which has nothing to do with this case at all?'

'What might that be?'

'Well, that's for you to tell me. An affair, infidelity, that's the most common. If that's the case then you need to tell us now.'

'I'm not hiding anything.'

'OK. We don't think your answers are very good.' Axel got up. 'To be blunt, I think you're full of crap. This happens all the time, but I'm telling you now because if I'm right, it will have consequences for you. We're investigating sexual assaults and a murder, and you're in the spotlight, so I think you should put your cards on the table now and tell me what really happened.'

'But I've nothing to do with any of that.'

Axel raised his voice and Tine Jensen turned from Bo Langberg to look at him.

'Jeanette Kvist, a 23-year-old medical student, Refsnæsgade, Nørrebro, you don't know her?'

'No.'

'You didn't follow her to her home, gain entry to her flat and rape her for two hours?'

'No.'

'So what the hell did you do?'

'I—'

'Cut the crap about running and pulling a muscle and tell me why the hell you travelled on exactly the same line as her and followed her once she got off the train?'

'I didn't follow her.'

'How well do you know Nørrebro?'

'I know Nørrebro quite well. I'm an architect. I go there often.'

'Nørrebro Park. Brohusgade. Borgervænget. Are they places you go often or used to go often?'

'What do you mean? Of course I've been to Nørrebro Park. I don't know Brohusgade. Borgervænget, I thought that was in Østerbro?'

'Look up at the noticeboard.'

Bo Langberg looked up at the pictures of the young women, four living, one dead.

He looked frightened.

'I don't know them. It has nothing to do with me. I wouldn't dream of it.'

For the next two hours they scrutinised his movements on the night. Three times. Was there an electronic lock to his office that registered the time people came and went? No. Had he sent emails, been online or done anything else at his place of work at the time of the crime, which could place him there? No. Then they moved on to the other dates. In respect of the oldest ones, he thought that his then wife might be able to provide him with an alibi if they could find the days in question in old diaries. The children had been young, he hadn't had an office in the city centre back then, but spent a lot of time at home. However, they did live in Brønshøj, a 15 to 20-minute cycle ride to both crime scenes. Eventually Axel put extreme pressure on him about the Blackbird case.

'I don't go to Ørsted Park,' he said. Not surprisingly, he couldn't account for his movements at the time of the murder four years ago. They got nothing more out of him. Axel was convinced that he was lying, but he didn't know what about. Either he was lying about the crimes or about something that meant so much to him that he could not be persuaded to tell them – even with a murder charge hanging over his head. That didn't automatically make him a killer. Everybody lied about something or other when they were interviewed in connection with a case. The lie rarely concealed a crime, but the criminal always lied.

Finally they took a DNA swab from his mouth and photographed him full face, profile and full figure. Pictures they would be showing Jeanette Kvist the next day.

They were done with him at 3.23am. He was allowed to leave.

Axel cycled home through a practically deserted Copenhagen. They had made another step forward. Axel had recorded the interview. If Jeanette Kvist could recognise Bo Langberg's voice, he would arrest him. Then they would have to wait for the result of the DNA swab and get a search warrant for his office.

If Jeanette Kvist didn't recognise him, they were back to square one – back with the cases, the five interconnected cases. It would mean that the monster was still somewhere out there.

The light was warm and friendly. The Roskilde festival had drained Nørrebro of young people, leaving behind only the night owls, the confused, the lost and the scruffy, who fell asleep in booths in kebab shops, who sniffed around public bins or carried out drunken conversations with people who weren't there.

CHAPTER 32

Jens Jessen lay wide awake in bed next to Cecilie. The windows were open and the curtains billowed lightly. The heat was unbearable. He looked at the moon.

He hadn't told her anything about his evening excursion with Axel – only that he had had meetings at HQ. He was still on cloud nine from the operation on the station platform. He had caught the man. The fact that the guy had almost ended up on the train tracks was a minor detail, but the feeling in his body, the feeling of brain, body and muscles combining to act on instinct, had been, well, how could he put it – the best trip ever, he guessed you would say if you were a junkie. Cecilie had gone to bed before he came home, after sending him a text message with the three oldest words in the world. That was good. Now he lay here by her side, he could hear Emma snoring in the bedroom next to theirs, everything was as it should be, but still he couldn't get back down to earth. The ecstatic atmosphere he found himself in was hollow. And so his fears returned quietly, one after the other.

Had he made a mistake today? He had requested passenger lists from Copenhagen to The Hague. Three specific dates when Axel Steen had flown down there to pick up his daughter – give or take three days. It was a slippery slope to go down, a rollercoaster, but he had already hopped on and the ride had started.

And then there was seeing Axel Steen this morning when they went to pick up Emma. Cecilie had got out and dashed across the road, she had chatted to Axel for quite some time, she had laughed twice and squeezed her ex-husband's arm. This morning she had suddenly been in a brilliant mood, in contrast with the weekend, where she had flared up over nothing. Was it because she knew she would be seeing Axel? He had asked her what they had talked about when she returned to the car with Emma. 'Oh, nothing. A surprise that Emma has prepared with her daddy, isn't that right, Emma,' she had said and smiled to her daughter in the back. A surprise? Surprises had never been his cup of tea. Especially not one that involved Axel Steen.

They still hadn't made love. Not that it meant anything physically. Sex was, well, what was it for him? Once a week would do him, but still, it was a statement. About love. About fidelity.

In two days she would go to Hornbæk with Emma to start their holiday. He would have to commute there and back – his work demanded it. They would have time together up there in his parents' old holiday cottage by the beach. But they still hadn't made love. 'I guess it's normal that the intensity falls a little after the first few months,' she had said to him when he had asked about it one day. Caressed his cheek gently, smiled the way you smile to a child who has to accept there will be no more sweets, and asked if he couldn't feel how much she loved him.

Checkmate. Yes, it probably was normal after the initial infatuation had died down, but what did you do when it didn't happen? When that infatuation was still as priapic as a lighthouse?

They still hadn't made love.

CHAPTER 33

Tuesday, 1 July

July brought no change in the weather. Summer was still brutal and persistent. Copenhagen was trapped in a bell jar of exhaust fumes and dry heat that didn't suit the city at all. Axel opened a window overlooking the street, showered and drank cold water instead of coffee. Before visiting Jeanette Kvist, he had a phone call to make.

'I enjoyed our lunch,' Ea Holdt said.

'Likewise.'

'I hope I didn't scare you off.'

'Not at all. It was nice to spend time with you.'

'Nice, that good?'

'Yes. I'm calling because we've identified the man we found on the surveillance footage from the train station. I'd like to show your client pictures of him and play her a recording of his voice.'

'That's fine by me. Who is he?'

Axel briefly told her about the man, his name and family situation. Ea Holdt was on her way to court, so she was unable to come with him. Axel felt a dart of disappointment, which passed when she said:

'Was that the only reason you called?'

'No. I still want to discuss that case we talked about earlier, Lulu Linette Larsen. If it fits in with your work, perhaps we could meet later this afternoon for a beer.'

'I would really like that, but I'm taking my sons to football, so perhaps early evening?'

'Yes, that's fine.'

'The café in Kongens Have, how about that?'

'Yes.'

'I'll text you the time. Is that OK?'

It was more than OK.

He met with Vicki Thomsen, who had been tasked with informing the victims in the historical cases. Together they drove to Jeanette Kvist's flat.

'What do you think? Is he our guy?' Vicki asked him in the car.

'I don't really want to say. If he is our guy, then he's a totally new type of serial offender – wife, children, house, job, commitments. They tend to have more disjointed and damaged lives. But his explanation sucks, he has no alibi, no one can vouch for him, so he's a definite possibility.'

'So this is it?'

'If she recognises his voice, we can nail the coffin shut.'

'Then we'll have him remanded in custody?'

'Yes.'

'And the next step would be the result of the DNA test?'

'Yes, if it's positive then he's up to his neck in it.'

When they were sitting opposite Jeanette Kvist, there was no small talk. Axel was sure she could feel how tense both investigators were. She looked at the pictures of the suspect, one after the other.

'I'm sorry. I don't recognise him. Perhaps if he'd been wearing the stocking.'

The same thought had crossed Axel's mind yesterday, but there was no chance her identification would stand up in court if he did that, so he had dropped the idea.

'I didn't dare look at him very much. He ordered me not to.'

'It's OK. I know. I'm going to play you a recording. Let me know if you recognise the voice.'

She closed her eyes and Axel prayed that the next moment she would open them and start to cry, break down on recognising the voice of the man who had turned her life inside out in two hours and transformed it into a living hell.

'I do a lot of running. I like running in the city. Along the Lakes.'

Jeanette Kvist widened her eyes after the last sentence.

'That's him.'

Axel stopped the recording. It was too soon. Too quick. He had recorded many more of Bo Langberg's sentences.

'You're sure? You recognise it?'

'Yes, I think so. Yes.' She wasn't crying.

'I'll play you some more. Try concentrating. I know it's horrible for you to remember, but it's very important. Try to listen for a little longer.'

'I don't know. At home, I would guess. I can check my diary. I was at the office. We had guests. I caught the train into town. Then I went to my office and worked for a few hours.'

He stopped the recording.

'I would like to play you a little more. It's the same man, but he's speaking in a different tone of voice.'

'I demand to know why you've assaulted me. Why are you doing this to me? Why am I here?'

'It's him, I'm sure.'

She broke down.

Vicki winked at him. Axel tried to smile in return, but he was too tired. He felt utterly flat.

'Jeanette, you've been a huge help today. It means a great deal that you were able to do this. It isn't hard evidence, but it's another step along the way. On its own it won't be enough to convict him, but everything points in the same direction. We'll have the results of the DNA test in a few days.'

'And what happens now? Will you lock him up? Will you put him away?' she wanted to know.

'We'll bring him in for another interview. I promise to let you know if there are any developments.'

They said goodbye and left.

'Bloody hell, we have him now, don't we?'

Vicki Thomsen wanted him to high-five her, but Axel ignored her.

'What's wrong?'

'Nothing. It was fine. But we have a long road ahead of us. I won't celebrate until I'm sure.'

'You don't believe her?'

'It doesn't matter whether or not I do. It's a step in the right direction, it's not proof yet. Proof will speak in its own clear voice.'

'Do you always have to be such a killjoy?'

CHAPTER 34

They parked the car on a residential road that led down to Emdrup Lake. Axel had briefly had a dream about an idyllic life in suburbia while he was with Cecilie – or had that been her dream? – but he was quite sure that he would go crazy if he had to live out here in the silence, and that his wife and child would one day come home to find him staggering around the garden brandishing an axe and a bottle of vodka. Anyway, that wasn't something he had to worry about any more. Given how things had worked out.

The house was an elegant 1930s box, simple and functional, the garden immaculate, the lawn as well-kept as a golf green. The area was only a 10-minute drive from Axel's flat, an island of detached houses that lay between the motorway to Helsingør and wealthy Hellerup on one side, and on the other a gloomy neighbourhood with factories, the Bispebjerg Hospital and endless rows of social housing. The elderly, dropouts and junkies had been relocated there from Vesterbro and Nørrebro in the name of inner-city regeneration in the 80s and 90s.

They walked up the garden path and rang the doorbell. The door was opened by a woman in her thirties. She wore make up, she was skinny, her eyes exuded control.

'How can I help you?'

'We're from the police. We would like to talk to Bo Langberg, is he here?'

'No, he's at his office. Has something happened?'

'Please may we come inside? We have some questions we would like to ask you,' Vicki Thomsen said.

'I'm actually on my way to work. Can it wait?'

'No, we would prefer to do it now.'

'Then I need to make a phone call. Will this take long?'

She let them in.

Axel asked if he could use the loo. He was shown to a small lavatory. He had a pee. Called Tine Jensen. He checked the bathroom cabinet while he spoke to her. It contained a toothbrush, toothpaste, deodorant and aftershave.

'He's not here. He's at his office. I want you to pick him up. We'll have a preliminary talk with his wife.'

Meanwhile Bo Langberg's wife was standing in the living room with her arms folded across her chest. Impatient. And confused.

'What do you do? What's the job that you need to call?'

'I'm the managing director of an insurance company. Has something happened? Has something happened to Bo?'

'Nothing has happened to him, we have some routine questions. Bo Langberg has been seen near a crime scene and we would like to ask you some questions regarding his movements. We've already spoken to him and we need to have some of what he said confirmed.'

'You've already spoken to him?' she looked shocked. 'When?'

'Yesterday. Hasn't he told you?'

It stank to high heaven. Why hadn't he told his wife that he had been interviewed?

'No, I haven't seen him since yesterday. He slept at his office. He's very busy with a major project.'

'That's not unusual, I gather. Him being out at night. How many nights a week does he go out to work?'

'Two, three, maybe four times a week. Has he done something wrong?'

'No. What time in the evening?'

'Once the children have gone to bed. Between 10pm and 11pm, I would think.'

'Isn't that quite a lot?'

'Like I said. He's busy.' She wrung her hands.

'Does he then come home or does he spend the night there?'

'He often comes home after midnight. He stays over at the office occasionally.'

'Isn't that strange?'

'Strange how?'

'To go to the centre of Copenhagen late at night, work for a couple of hours and then go home and sleep? Why doesn't he just work from home?'

'His office is there. He's an architect. He needs a lot of space.'

'But you have plenty of space here, as far as I can see.'

'Have you come here to discuss the size of our house?'

'No, have you ever noticed anything peculiar about him when he came home from his nocturnal work?'

'Peculiar, what do you mean?'

'Has he been agitated? Dirty. Injured. Does he change his clothes, does he wash his clothes?'

'What's this about?'

'Please would you answer the question?'

'No, he has not been strange. He's usually relaxed and happy on the few occasions I've been awake. He's a good man.'

She hesitated.

'There was one time when he came home. About a month ago, he had been assaulted. He was very shocked. It was just a scratch, but he said that he had been attacked by some young men, immigrants, at Nørreport station.'

'Why?'

'That was why he was so shocked. There was no reason. They just went for him. It was completely unprovoked.'

'What about the running?'

'He's a keen runner. We both are. We do half marathons.'

'But you don't run together?'

'No, because we have children. We have four from our previous relationships and together we have a daughter of six. We train independently. Bo likes running at night.'

'But why go all the way into Copenhagen to run?'

'Why not? That's what he likes.'

'Why doesn't he run out here?'

'Ask him. Is there a law against that?'

'Does he use his office as often in the summer as during the rest of the year? Does he go for his late night runs all year round?'

'No, he does it mostly when the weather is warm.'

'We're investigating a crime that occurred the night between Friday and Saturday 31 May. Was he here?'

'I don't know. I would have to check my diary.' She fetched her bag and took out an iPhone.

'We were at home. The whole family. My sister was visiting us. She left at 10pm. Our daughter and I went to bed, and Bo went for a run. I don't know when he came back.'

'When did you see him again?'

'The next morning.'

'How was he?'

'He was completely normal. The way he always is. What are you suspecting him of?'

Axel interjected:

'How is your sex life?'

'What do you mean?'

'Didn't you understand my question?'

'Is it routine to ask people that?'

'Yes, and it's important. Just answer the question.'

'I don't think I want to.'

'How is he in bed? Is he violent, sadistic, does he try to strangle you?'

'I don't believe you have the right to come here and ask me such questions.'

'Do we look like we think this is funny? Your husband has been seen in connection with a very serious sexual assault. It's never routine. I'm not asking because I think it's funny, so please just answer the question.'

She gulped.

'I find this all very unpleasant. Bo has never done any of the things you've just mentioned.'

'Do you have sex?'

'Do I really have to answer that?'

'Not if you would like to spend the rest of the day at Police HQ with a lawyer by your side.'

'Yes, we have sex. He has never hurt me.'

'Thank you. That's all from me.'

Axel looked at Vicki, who also stood up.

'I apologise for the inconvenience and the questions. It's part of the job,' Vicki said.

'I have one final question,' Axel interrupted her. He could see that the woman was completely crushed. 'Do you have a key for your husband's office in Nansensgade?'

'No.'

'Do you ever go there?'

'No.'

'Never?'

'Rarely.'

'Why not?'

'It's his space. I have my own job.'

She ushered them out without saying goodbye. She had her mobile in her hand. Axel had no doubts that she would call her husband the moment the door closed behind them. They hadn't learned anything really significant, but they had come away with several small pieces of information that fitted the picture of Bo Langberg as a possible attacker. He primarily went for his evening and night-time runs in the summer – the same period when all five rapes had been committed. He had his office all to himself, and he had a spouse who didn't seem to mind in the least that he was away from their home for four to five hours every other night, which Axel found unusual. He wondered why Bo Langberg hadn't told his wife about being interviewed by the police last night.

CHAPTER 35

Bo Langberg had been picked up at his office and was now waiting to be interviewed for the second time while the investigation team held a quick strategy meeting. He had repeatedly turned down the offer of legal advice.

Everyone was delighted that Jeanette Kvist had positively identified his voice. They had a suspect. Now what they needed was incriminating evidence.

'What's the theme for the interview?' Darling asked.

Axel got up.

'We need to go through everything with him again, but I suggest we focus on the rape of Jeanette Kvist. Yesterday we asked him about the other cases. We need to put pressure on him regarding Jeanette Kvist, because he's lying. We need to make it clear to him that his voice has been recognised and that he's in serious trouble. And the trump card is his wife. She had no idea we brought him in last night. He only sent her a text message saying he would be spending the night at his office. So I'm hoping that might put the cat among the pigeons. She knows he's a suspect in a rape case. He needs to know that she knows. I don't have strong feelings about taking the interview myself. I'm happy to leave that to Bjarne and Vicki, if that's OK with you. The wife didn't give us anything that incriminates him – nothing except his bizarre habit of leaving their home every other night in his running clothes and not returning until after midnight, which in my eyes is enough for us to make him our prime suspect when we throw in the location of his office and his presence at the same train stations as the ones Jeanette Kvist was at on the night she was raped.'

They nodded.

'And then there's his running clothes. It's the perfect excuse for lurking around the city. Copenhagen is full of panting morons in Lycra, so no one would bat an eyelid at a 44-year-old man out and about in that outfit at two o'clock in the morning.'

'When will we get the DNA results?' Darling asked.

'In two days. I've asked them to make it a priority.'

'We'll hold off raiding his office. We don't have enough on him yet. Once we have the DNA result, we can carry out a search,' Darling declared.

DNA was the God of the modern police investigation. And Darling was a serious worshipper. As far as Axel was concerned, DNA supplemented the groundwork: investigation, tracking down witnesses, interviews, technical evidence which formed the basis for rebutting lies, for gathering puzzle pieces which looked chaotic to begin with, but which would in time fit together and form a picture. In the old days they would have got a search warrant based on what they had now, but today you waited for the DNA test – an attitude to police work Axel regarded as soft. But he had accepted he would have to learn to live with it a long time ago. And without it. Because no one could stop him from carrying out any investigation he deemed necessary on his own, while the rest of them sat twiddling their thumbs waiting to hear from Forensic Genetics.

'It means we'll be searching a place he'll already have had plenty of time to clean up,' Axel said.

'I don't recall us ever working a case where the perpetrator didn't forget something or other,' Darling said in defence.

'True, but nor do I remember a case where they didn't remove something given half a chance.'

'What about the victims, Vicki?' Darling said.

'I tried all three yesterday. One of them doesn't even have a current address listed with the National Register of Persons, that's Line Jørgensen. Her most recent address is a hostel in north-west Copenhagen. I couldn't contact Lulu Linette Larsen. She has been hospitalised with depression several times. Three suicide attempts. The only one I managed to contact was Anne Marie Zeuthen. I have emailed everyone a summary of my interview with her.'

'Do they normally fare so badly?' Darling asked, he sounded concerned.

No one said anything. Then Vicki broke the silence:

'Being raped isn't as bad as being killed, but it comes pretty close… Well, not that I would know, but so they say. And it's not unusual for victims to struggle to move on.'

CHAPTER 36

Axel left HQ after the meeting without telling anyone where he was going and rode his bike to Ørsted Park. He sat on the bench on the viewing bridge and smoked a cigarette before continuing towards his real goal: Nansensgade. A village high street in the city with cafés, restaurants, antiquarian bookshops, galleries and a few surviving rough bars and shops from before the arrival of the credit card.

He liked doing things on his own, but the days when that was possible were long gone because of the huge number of different tasks in any investigation, especially those created by modern technology. As team leader he had to delegate some tasks, not just because of the sheer volume of work and the need for specialist knowledge, but also to keep the group happy. The interview of Bo Langberg was currently at the heart of their investigation – it was a job that every ambitious investigator would want. It was one of the reasons he had handed it over to two of his colleagues, but a less noble reason was that after last night's interview he didn't think they would get very much more out of him today. And in contrast to Darling he had no intention of waiting for the result of the DNA test, and so he parked his bike outside number 39 and rang the bell for the fifth-floor flat.

He had deliberately not phoned ahead because he preferred carrying out his interviews without people having had the chance to prepare. The time was 2.30pm and he didn't think that anyone would be in, but there was and he was admitted.

This wasn't going to be easy.

He remembered how he had laid the pressure on Marie Schmidt's father during an interview until he had broken down, sobbing, unable to utter anything other than an agonised: 'I love my daughter, I love my daughter, I love my daughter.'

When Axel reached the top of the stairs, he was surprised to see him standing in the doorway with a friendly smile. But then again, Tine Jensen had been there last week, so he had been informed that they had new evidence in the case.

'Axel Steen, I've never forgotten you.'

'No, it's not the first time someone has said that to me.'

'I guess you were only doing your job.'

'That's a matter of opinion, but I was trying to find your daughter's killer. Please may I come in?'

'Of course. Any news?'

They walked down the hallway through the enormous apartment, which had a roof terrace with a view of most of Copenhagen. The father was a concert pianist, he remembered. And he had inherited money. Occasionally he would see posters of him around town and wonder how he had been able to go on living, recover from the loss of first his wife and then his only daughter, but every time he had told himself it was a sign that people could survive anything.

'Yes and no. We're investigating someone, and I wanted to ask you about them.'

Axel couldn't help looking around the apartment for signs of Marie Schmidt. And as he couldn't see even one picture of her, he grew angry with her father. This profoundly unfair feeling hit him like a bullet, and he realised once again the extent of his obsession with her. Finding her killer had meant everything to him – an 18-year-old girl whose life had been snatched from her just as it was about to begin. It was utterly wrong. There could be no doubt about it. But then so were his feelings about her, especially given that he had very nearly killed his own daughter the same day they had found the body of Marie Schmidt, and that he had subsequently lost his wife and daughter at once.

The thought had barely crossed his mind before he suppressed it. He took three steps down the hallway past the father and opened the door to the room that had been Marie's. It was completely changed.

The father looked at him guiltily.

'I've tried to forget. I couldn't carry on living with her everywhere.'

'It's OK. It's not my business how you handle your grief. I apologise.'

'Let's go up on the terrace, it's a little cooler there,' the man said.

They walked up an internal staircase and emerged onto the roof. Axel had to balance across two planks of wood because the entrance area was in the process of being renovated, and scaffolding had been erected right outside the door. He took a deep breath and turned around. Copenhagen everywhere, Nørrebro right behind him and all the city centre spires, tower blocks and hotels like random fixed points scattered across the otherwise flat horizon. He turned and looked at the father. That was how he thought of him. Not Jacques Schmidt Jensen, which was his name, but the father.

'Have you ever heard of an architect called Bo Langberg?'

Axel studied him. His blond hair was shorter, but it hadn't gone grey, the beard was gone, and he had gained a little weight. His face was red, especially his nose, which made Axel suspect that he was a drinker. The pores stood out like greasy craters. He had to be around 55 years old now.

'Yes, I think so.'

It could be a coincidence. After all, Langberg's office was only six doors away from the apartment where they were now.

'You think so?'

'Yes, it rings a bell.'

'Where have you heard about him?'

'Here in the street perhaps. Who is he?'

'He has an office in this street. And he has become a person of interest to us in connection with another investigation.'

'The rapes?'

Axel didn't know how much Tine had told him. He personally believed that next of kin should be informed quickly, clearly and unequivocally when there were developments in a case, but in order to protect the father, he would have omitted to tell him that they were working on sexual assaults.

'Yes.'

'Was he a suspect back then?'

'No. And he isn't a suspect today, but we're investigating him and mapping his movements.'

'OK.'

'His name is Bo Langberg, and like I said, he has an office in this street. Try to think back: Marie, did she ever mention that name or talk about an architect?'

'It's funny you should mention it. I think it rings a bell. She told me once that she had looked for a job at several of the offices and cafés in our street. That she had gone to the office of an architect and she didn't like him. Could it be him?'

Axel was shocked. He had already checked if Bo Langberg's name had figured in the original investigation. How could they have overlooked it?

'Did you mention this when we investigated the case?'

'I'm sure I did. Maybe not to you, but to your colleagues.'

'What did she say about him?'

'She definitely didn't want to work for him even though he offered her a job, I believe.'

'This is the first I've heard of it. Can you remember precisely what she said?'

'No, but she came home and told me that she had looked for work up and down our street and tried many different places, Bankeråt, Sticks'n'Sushi, Casablanca, a firm of solicitors and an architect. And that he had been irritating. I don't remember.'

Axel's head was spinning.

'I've never heard this before. Can you remember anything else?'

'No. What happens now?'

Axel got ready to leave. He felt uncomfortable, not because he didn't like the father, but because he couldn't tell him anything more.

'How have you been?' he managed to ask at last.

'I've tried to move on, but it's difficult. I visit Marie's grave often, lay flowers, remember her.' He looked mournful.

'Do you live on your own?'

'Yes, but I have a girlfriend now. She stays here sometimes. She's French, a violinist.'

'Congratulations. And listen, I'm sorry I was so hard on you back then.'

'Don't be. I hope I've been able to help. It would be a huge relief if you were able to find my daughter's killer.'

'Yes. It would.'

Axel was confused as he walked downstairs. He decided to call Darling and brief him on the new information.

'Do you remember anything about that from the investigation?'

'No, not off the top of my head. But I'm sure that if he told us, then we investigated it.'

'The case file is in my office. Get someone to start checking it.'

'Will do.'

'You haven't let Bo Langberg go yet, have you?'

'No, they're still busy interviewing him.'

'I'll make my way to the office, then I would like to try this out on him.'

'Of course. I'll let them know.'

Rather than cycle back to HQ Axel walked to number 23 and found Bo Langberg's office. It took him 35 seconds to gain entry using his lock picks. He checked out the office, which consisted of a large room, kitchenette and a bathroom. It was extremely neat and tidy. He turned on the computer, which was password protected. He looked around the bathroom, finding nothing but ordinary toiletries and a variety of over-the-counter and prescription drugs. Then he searched the hallway, the kitchenette and the office again, cupboards, drawers, he searched everywhere in the hope of finding a stocking, a knife, a pair of jeans, shoes, something which could give him a clue. 20 minutes later he was in luck. In a drawer he found a packet of condoms. Thin latex. Three were left. Probably not for wifey back home in Emdrup.

CHAPTER 37

'Let's go over this once more.'

Bo Langberg sat passively opposite Bjarne and Vicki Thomsen on one side of the desk in the latter's office when Axel entered. It was Bjarne, who was speaking in his most laid-back, matter-of-fact voice, which almost made Axel want to sit down and simply enjoy the spectacle unfold.

'First you told us that you went to Copenhagen, ran around the Lakes, went back to your office, had a shower and worked until you went home at 2am. When you were shown surveillance pictures from Nørreport and Vesterport stations, where you walk quite normally, you remembered that you had sprained a muscle and caught the train from Vesterport to Nørreport to protect your leg, although this wouldn't make the walking distance to your office any shorter. How do you yourself think this sounds?'

'As far as I'm concerned, Vesterport is further from my office than Nørreport.'

'May I take over?' Axel said.

Both his colleagues nodded.

'New information has been brought to our attention,' he said, pulling up a chair and sitting down by the desk.

Bo Langberg looked kindly at Axel.

'One month ago you returned home with injuries to your face. What had happened?'

'I was attacked. By some young men. By Nørreport station.'

'Why?'

'I don't know. It just happened. It was entirely unprovoked.'

'Scratches, cuts. The kind of injuries a man sustains when his rape victim fights back.'

'It's like I said it was.'

'Why didn't you report it?'

He rubbed his face.

'It was nothing serious. I wasn't badly hurt.'

'Even though your wife told us you were very upset.'

'I don't know why she would say that.'

Axel was convinced he was lying.

'When we spoke last night, you said that you didn't know Marie Schmidt, but only knew the case from the media. Is that correct?'

'Yes, that's true.'

'You've never met her?'

Axel placed the picture of Marie Schmidt in front of Bo Langberg, who studied it closely. As did Axel, and just seeing her face made him want to punch the idiot sitting opposite him, who was behaving as if none of this was real.

'No, I've never seen her.'

'But she's seen you. She went to your office to look for a job, and you offered her one.'

Bo Langberg smiled, but looked shocked, as if he had just been the victim of an elaborate hoax.

'I've never seen her before. That just isn't true. No one has ever come to my office to look for work. I'm a one-man band. It makes no sense.'

'So you maintain that you've never met her.'

'Yes.'

'We have a witness who disagrees. How is you and your wife's sex life?'

Bo Langberg looked awkwardly from Axel to the two others.

'Why do I have to answer that?'

'If you want to leave here, I think you ought to answer all my questions.'

'I don't want to.'

'Really, your wife was very helpful.'

Bo Langberg looked surprised.

'I don't believe you. She wouldn't want to discuss that.'

'She said that—'

'But why?' Bo Langberg interrupted him.

'It is to some extent relevant to the case. Even more today than it was yesterday.'

'What do you mean?'

Axel could see that he had touched a nerve for the first time, so he slowed down the interview.

'It's odd that you can't explain what you're doing. That weird story about taking the train to Copenhagen, going for a run here rather than at home in your comfortable neighbourhood, and you working here at night. I don't believe it for one second. And I think it's an excuse, a cover story. Your office looks completely untouched. And you keep condoms in your desk drawer. What were you doing the other night when we let you go? Did you go back to tidy everything up? The knife, the clothes, the shoes, the tights? I've got news for you, you forgot about the rubbers!'

Axel tossed the packet in front of him.

'You've used seven.'

'You're not allowed to search my office.'

'Bollocks to that. How would you explain that?'

'I don't have to. I haven't done anything.'

'Who did you use the other seven with?'

'Nobody. I haven't killed that girl or raped anyone. I wouldn't dream of it.'

'Fine, have it your way. You talk a good game, but it explains nothing. And for me it fits perfectly the picture of a calculated, sadistic rapist, well-educated and knowledgeable, who wears a condom in order not to leave DNA on his victims.'

'I use them with my wife. We don't want more children.'

'Are you sure about that?'

He made no reply.

'Because in a moment my colleague will step outside to call your wife and ask her about it.'

'This is a nightmare! Surely having condoms lying about isn't a criminal offence.'

'No, it isn't. Nor is using them. Why can't you get it into your thick skull that we're not here for the hell of it or to bother you, but because we're investigating a number of very serious offences, and you've been seen in connection with several of them, and the more we look at them, the more you crop up. And that's strange, don't you think? It's strange that you can't provide us with an explanation for any of it.'

'I don't know.'

'I'm running out of patience. If you can't come up with a good explanation now, then my next step will be bringing you before a judge to have you remanded in custody charged with four rapes and a homicide.'

'But I've got nothing to do with any of it.'

'Then you have to stop lying and tell me the real reason for your train trips, the running, the rubbers, the work that isn't work, and your meeting with Marie Schmidt four years ago.'

'It's not against the law.'

'Don't you get it? It's not against the law, but it is our duty to investigate and get to the bottom of everything relating to crimes of this nature.'

'What about the DNA test?'

'What about it?'

'That will prove I didn't do it.'

'You all say that. And then when there's a match, you can't explain it. But it won't help you if you can't explain all these things. So what will it be?'

He fell silent.

Axel got up, looked at Bjarne, and Vicki nodded.

'Bo Langberg, in accordance with sections 237 and 216 of the Penal Code I'm charging you with murder and sexual assault. You do not have to say anything. You have the right to legal advice. Would you like a particular lawyer?'

'This is a nightmare.'

'Call a lawyer. Put him in a cell. We'll resume the interview tomorrow. Call his wife and tell her what has happened. And ask her about his so-called work. Ask her where the money comes from. If the money is flooding in from all the work he carries out at night at his office in Nansensgade? And ask her again about their sex life. In detail. This time ask her about the condoms. Ask what he uses them for. If he uses them with her.'

Axel looked at Bo Langberg as he said the last bit. He didn't look comfortable.

'You may well think we're being tough on you now, but that's nothing compared to what's going to happen next. We'll be turning your life upside down, everything will be brought out into the open, phone calls, online activity, secret hiding places, and we will find what we're looking for. And that's a promise.'

He left the office, while Bo Langberg sat with his head in his hands.

CHAPTER 38

Axel let himself be sucked into the cool shade of the lime avenue in Kongens Have; on the lawns around him were tourists and locals who had met up for a beer or a picnic after work.

He walked towards the Hercules Pavilion, which housed a café. From afar he could see Ea Holdt pacing up and down with a cigarette in her hand in front of the Roman god flanked by Orpheus and Eurydice.

His phone rang.

'It's Darling. We have a problem. The prosecutor doesn't think we have enough to charge him. I agree, I think it's borderline.'

'What an idiot. So what do we do?'

'Well, that's the end of that.'

'It's impossible to investigate anything with all the obstacles you put in our way these days.'

'It's called proper legal procedures, Axel.'

'I don't give a toss what you call it. What about the search warrant, can you get that?'

'I can try.'

'I suggest you keep Bo Langberg where he is and get a search warrant for his office. That's the most important thing. If there is anything, then that's where it'll be. We need crime scene technicians out there to go through the place with a fine-tooth comb for biological evidence. Then you can let him go afterwards.'

'I'll try, but I doubt we can pull it off.'

Axel said goodbye and turned off his mobile. It was eight o'clock and he had finished interviewing Bo Langberg two hours ago. He had spent the time reviewing the interviews from the Blackbird case. He concluded that Bo Langberg might well have spoken the truth when he had said that he hadn't been interviewed in connection with that case. There was nothing about him in the file, but that didn't rule out the possibility of Marie Schmidt's father mentioning him and a careless colleague failing to log it in the report. Tine Jensen sprang to mind.

'Hi.'

Jeans, high-heeled light brown leather sandals, blue silk blouse with deep cleavage, canvas bag, a smile, and when the sunglasses were removed, grey-blue eyes and a shy, slightly hesitant gaze.

They ordered beer and sat down in the shade at one of the small café tables.

'How's the case coming along?' she asked.

Axel told her about Bo Langberg.

'Do you think it's him?'

'I don't think anything, but he's our best bet right now. He's certainly lying about his whereabouts.'

'But is he the type? The type to torture their victims, ice cold?'

'Not at first glance. But that doesn't mean anything.'

They spent some time discussing the rape of Lulu Linette Larsen. It didn't get them any further, but confirmed the emerging picture of victim prejudice by police investigators hampering a proper investigation.

'Why do you really do this? Investigate homicide? Wade around misery and unhappiness?'

'Why do you? I imagine you come across worse things than I do.'

'Is it a work-related injury that you answer a question with a question?'

'I could say the same to you.'

'It's very common among psychologists and lawyers. I didn't know it also applied to police officers.'

'I guess it's common among anyone who doesn't want to answer the questions they've been asked.'

Ping-pong – the conversation danced across the table. Small teasing remarks and sparring until she insisted on her original question:

'I'm asking because I'm interested in what drives us beyond the obviously meaningful.'

'What's obvious about it?'

'Helping other people, securing justice for the victims. The sense of justice being done. All that.'

'Isn't that enough?'

'Yes, but there's much more to it.'

'Such as?'

'That's just a rational explanation, a convention. I think we're driven by something else, a deeper and more personal motive.'

'Motive is something I associate with crimes.'

'Yes, and for that reason I imagine you're very good at seeing through it.'

'And what drives you?'

'There it is again. Answering a question with a question.'

'I'm just trying to work out what you mean.'

Axel was attracted to her, but she was also heading somewhere he wasn't sure he wanted to follow.

'Would you like to know?'

'Yes,' he lied.

She drank some beer, lit a cigarette and fell quiet. Did he really want to know? He felt uneasy and even more so as shadows of grief, vulnerability, solemnity and nervous laughter flashed across her face.

'My stepfather raped me from the age of 11 until I was 14. I grew up in Southern Jutland in a family with addiction issues. My four siblings and I were alone. Except for when our stepfather took care of us in his own special way, that is.'

'I didn't mean to—'

She cut him off.

'There. Now you know. Seems only fair, given that I'm sitting here forcing you to bare your soul.' She looked quizzically at him. 'Was that more than you needed to know?'

'Yes. No, I mean… I'm really sorry to hear that. I don't know what to say.'

'I don't know why I told you. It's not something I usually talk about. I'm just interested in hearing what's behind all the scars. And now I've gone and frightened you off with my tragic back story.'

'You haven't frightened me off.' But he was frightened. 'I don't really know what drives me other than the wish to right a wrong.'

'I don't believe that. I think we all know exactly what it is, but it's not something we talk about.'

Axel was still shocked. Her cheerfulness had returned, but it was like a layer of new ice that creaked every time she tried to smile.

I do it because I don't know what else to do, he could say. It was true, given the way his life was now, but it wasn't a proper answer.

'I do it because it makes a difference. I like it. It's not that I like people getting killed, but I like that I'm there, that I can do something about it given that it has happened. I'm good at my job. It means something.'

The slightest hint of a scrubbed-up, fragile smile, but no words for him.

'I don't have a closet full of skeletons driving me. I have an ordinary Danish family background mixed in with a little divorce, alcohol and cold showers. I have made many mistakes in my adult life, but they have nothing to do with my job. What spurs me on is closing cases, finding the guilty party, getting justice for the victim.'

He had exposed more of himself than he had done for a long time. And now he wanted to turn the conversation in a totally different direction before she dug deeper into him. She leaned back in her chair and fixed his gaze.

'That might not stand up in court, but it's good enough for me.'

They sat in silence for a while. Exchanged glances, gazed into each other's eyes for longer and longer, happy and absurd at the same time. Her hand grenade of a family background was an invitation – perhaps the oddest he had had in his life, but also the most honest – and he liked that.

'I'm too curious. And you're Axel Steen. Everybody knows you. And they know you're one of the best. And the most awkward. I've heard – and read – quite a lot about you, so I'm interested in finding out who you really are.'

He didn't want to ask, but he couldn't stop himself:

'What have you heard?'

'Oh, you know, there was a lot of press coverage about you last year after the Youth House case. And I've heard a thing or two at the office when Cecilie worked there.'

'You shouldn't believe everything you hear.'

'I know how to filter. Cecilie and I never got on terribly well.'

Is that my appeal? And if she has said something unpleasant about me, does it only reflect badly on her? Axel enjoyed being with Ea Holdt, but their conversation had a tendency to move in directions that made him feel uncomfortable. On the other hand, he was curious to know how the woman who had dumped him was viewed from another's point of view.

'She's a cold bitch, I think,' she said.

That's my line and not one I want to hear from others, he thought, when he sensed his irritation.

'So what have you learned from our talk?'

'That I very much want to get to know you better.'

'That's mutual,' he said, and felt stilted.

They paid for their beers and walked through the park towards Gothersgade, strolling along as if the things they had discussed were light and easy – or at least that was how she behaved. At one point she slipped her hand under his and her touch made him tingle all over. Her tanned skin, the pale fine hairs, the slender wrists.

She stopped in the middle of the path before they left the garden and looked at him.

'Do I scare you?'

She studied his face closely. It was almost too much.

'Do I scare you?'

'And here we go again, answering a question with a question. We'll have to do something about that. No, I have a good feeling about you, that you mean well, but that you don't want to expose yourself very much. That's OK.'

She fixed his gaze. Flirting and open. His abdomen bubbled and he felt as if his insides were laughing out loud. It was liberating. They gazed into one another's eyes, one minute, two, three, perhaps. There were people around them on the path, and their conversations faded away when they passed them. The yearning was like a howl in his stomach. And the pleasure of standing here prolonging it was almost unbearable. I'm reaching my hands out into the blue, he said to himself without knowing why.

Then he bent down towards her, placed one hand on her shoulder, his fingers felt something under the thin fabric burn them as he opened his mouth slightly and kissed her, not just lips against lips, nor a greedy French kiss either, but something in between. She didn't close her eyes and he could see them, the hazy warmth of their grey darkness so close by, like laughter, a caress. It was a different woman who received his kiss.

'You couldn't wait any longer?' she whispered between his lips.

'No.'

There was live jazz at Jazzcup in Gothersgade. They could hear a trumpet and they drifted towards the sound. It was packed inside, humid and boiling hot. Axel ploughed his way to the bar, bought two draught beers and they stood close to the door to the street, listening to the music without saying anything, looking at one another, at the band, then at one another again, sipping their beers. They took their glasses outside and smoked. The night was generous, they'd lost all sense of time, the words came effortlessly. She told anecdotes about senile judges and jurors who fell asleep during her closing address, he parodied the morons in the management corridor at HQ, including Jens Jessen, and made her cry with laughter.

They lingered for a while in the silence, smoking. The band had finished and Ea fetched another couple of beers. Everything had this carefree and crisp lightness of summer and longing about it, and now one jazz standard after another flowed from the loudspeakers, through the door, out into the street where it floated away on its wing of sweat over the forgotten quarters of Gothersgade. Miles Davis. Art Pepper. Chet Baker's late version of 'Bye Bye Blackbird' from the album *Candy*.

'Why do you look so sad?' she wanted to know.

Axel had let go of Ea Holdt the moment he heard Chet's trumpet.

'It's nothing,' he said, and knew that the memories wouldn't leave him alone until he had closed the case.

She bent across the table and took his hand. Reached out her other hand to caress his face, he thought, but instead she put it on his neck and pulled his face toward hers, closed her eyes, parted her lips. He had to use all his willpower to move from sadness to the kiss.

'Why don't we give ourselves a few hours off from everything, bad memories, revenge, victims. And go back to my place?' she suggested.

CHAPTER 39

Wednesday, 2 July

The mobile. Very close to his ears. An ice pick of sound. He was smeared in juices. The smell of sex was everywhere. Glimpses of last night flashed disturbingly in front of his eyes. Cecilie's voice on his phone.

'Axel, where are you? I'm downstairs, outside your flat. We're on our way to Hornbæk. You have Emma's swimming costume. Please could you bring it down?'

She sounded fraught. Where was Ea? He could see her hair sticking out from under the duvet. He had to get out of here.

'I can't.'

'Have you had a look for it?'

'No, I'm not at home. I don't know if it's there.'

'Where are you then?'

Again he looked at Ea Holdt, who opened her eyes at that very moment.

'I'm at work.'

'The poor child is crying her eyes out because she doesn't have it.'

'There's nothing I can do.'

'I think it's about her missing you. She's been talking about you a lot. Ever since she last visited you.'

Visited you? Was that what Emma was doing when she came to his home? So it would appear in Cecilie's eyes. Axel felt rage rear its black head. Ea Holdt studied him. Then slowly pulled down the duvet so that he could see her body. The smell of sex, a lot of sex.

'And now you expect me to move heaven and earth because of a bikini? Or is this about how you can't cope with the life you've forced on her making her miserable?'

Ea Holdt pulled the duvet back over her head.

'Stop it, you idiot. I'm thinking about our child. Unlike you.'

She rang off. It was 8.30am. He had to get up, out of that bed and away from that night.

'Aren't you going to work?' he asked her, and heard how remote and distracted his voice sounded.

'I'm not due in court until 1pm. Are you OK?'

'Yes. It… yes.'

'Are you sure?'

'Yes.'

'And about last night? You don't think—'

'No.'

She reached out for him. He bent down and kissed her, desperate to get away.

'You're the most gorgeous man in the world, you really are,' she whispered into his ear.

She held onto him and he pulled back. For a second it was a replay of last night.

'How about you get back into bed with me?'

He wiggled out of her embrace and stood up. Picked up his clothes. How could he leave without hurting her? He had to get out. Last night had been far too much. He was saved by his mobile. It was Bjarne calling.

'I have something for you. We couldn't keep him, but we were allowed to search Bo Langberg's office last night.'

'And?'

'There's so much porn and sex chats on his computer that it's practically wetting itself.'

'Anything useful?'

'You want to know if there is anything useful? I think we can safely say that. There's enough to make all of Ørsted Park moan. The creep looks at dicks 24 seven. Big guys in leather chaps with shaved balls fucking each other up the arse. You'd be scared to go to the bog for years after seeing those films. He's a fudge packer. I've been up all night watching this filth in the hope of finding just one tiny little picture of a woman being raped.'

'And?'

'I'm going to have to disappoint you, I'm afraid. No can do. It's pure fudge packing. And bare backing too.'

'Bear packing?'

'No, bare backing. It's English for no glove. In fudge packer lingo it means to bugger someone without a rubber.'

'Does his Internet activity provide him with an alibi?'

'Not immediately, but it might explain why he's lying and what he has been up to. And that's quite a lot. There are loads of chats with men he then arranges to meet in Ørsted Park. There are also more than a handful of films of him sticking various objects up his arse. You wouldn't believe what he can find room for. He even manages to get—'

'Thank you, Bjarne. Spare me the details. I'll be there shortly. And we need him brought in. When will we get the result of his DNA test?'

'This afternoon.'

'Will you bring him in?'

'I really don't feel like it, but I could always put on my crime scene gloves so I won't have to—'

'Oh, give it a rest, will you, just bring him in. I'll be there in 30 minutes.'

CHAPTER 40

He was greasy and sweaty when he stepped into Tine Jensen's office 20 minutes later. Saying goodbye to Ea Holdt had proved easy, because he hadn't contributed anything other than a mixture of panic and distracted distance, which she would most likely interpret as him fleeing last night's intimacy and tenderness. Sex and words, loving words. Far too many.

'Have you just been to the gym?' Tine Jensen asked him. And before he had time to answer, she continued:

'I've found another two cases that are similar. I've informed Darling of my discovery.'

She looked up at him meaningfully. *My* discovery? Oh, you'll make something of yourself. You'll probably make yourself a laughing stock in the canteen, would be my bet.

'They're from '07 and '06. One in the spring, the other in October, but the weather was warm on both occasions. One in the open air, one where the perpetrator entered a basement flat through an open window. One in north-west Copenhagen, the other in Utterslev Mose.'

They were both a perfect geographical match for the home of Bo Langberg, but Axel had already eliminated him. If he was right, Bo Langberg wasn't a serial offender – the only serial about his life was his sexual encounters with men in Ørsted Park, and God knows where else. He had been screwing around. Big time. The fact that his partners were men made no difference to Axel. And he presumed that Bo Langberg had kept his infidelities a secret from his wife and family. Again, that didn't matter to Axel. What did matter was that he had wasted their time with his lies. The police can keep secrets, but if people's shame or guilty conscience makes them lie, then everything will be brought out into the open. Axel was pissed off with Bo Langberg, and he intended to tell him so.

They were back to square one. A complex caseload of multiple investigations that had to be reviewed carefully and then compared. To what extent could they hone in on the attacker by cross-referencing locations, times, accessibility, MO and signature? That was their task now. And so he had come to Tine Jensen's office to get her to organise every detail from the individual cases so they could meet up this afternoon and brainstorm once they were done with Bo Langberg.

His mobile vibrated in his pocket.

'It's Bjarne. You need to come down here now.' His voice sounded very odd.

'Yes?'

'I'm at Bo Langberg's office. He's hanged himself.'

'Shit.'

'No goodbye letter, no nothing. Though he might have sent one to his wife. I've called for crime scene technicians and Jönsson and the whole caboodle.'

'Are you sure it's a suicide?'

'Well, it certainly looks like it. Nothing suspicious about this death.'

'Fuck.'

'Fuck indeed. Darling and the others are going to blow their tops. He's an architect, remember! And his wife is a managing director.'

'What the hell was he playing at?'

'I don't know. But at least we can cross him off our list. And I'm pretty sure his wife won't make a fuss. I can't imagine she'll want it known that her husband has been buggered by half of Copenhagen—'

'Stop it.'

'She should have known he wasn't training for a marathon, is all I'm saying—'

'Will you shut up, Bjarne. Her husband is dead, they have a child who has lost her father, and he has two other children. I don't want to listen to any more of your crap. Get the scene processed. I'm coming down to have a look, and then we need to tell his wife. And you're coming with me!'

Axel walked down to his bike with a tight feeling in his chest, the heat was suffocating and he was thinking about yesterday afternoon when he had reviewed the Blackbird file in order to link Bo Langberg to it. A complete dead-end. Was he losing his instinct? His grip? Had his intuition dried up?

CHAPTER 41

The Swede was taking down the body just as Axel entered Bo Langberg's office. The only sound was the clicking of the police photographer's camera. A crime scene technician helped place the body on a tarpaulin sheet. Everyone had donned white coveralls, face masks and gloves.

The body was wearing the familiar running clothes that Axel had seen him in earlier. His face was pale and the tip of his tongue stuck out, dry, between his lips.

The Swede nodded to Axel, then bent over the dead man. He opened the eyelids and the mouth, examining the body from head to foot. He untied the rope around Bo Langberg's neck, and Axel could see ligature marks in the skin, high up on the neck.

'There's very little doubt, gentlemen, and I don't believe I need to tell you that. He died from what we call a complete hanging. It means that he hung freely without touching the ground.'

He turned and pointed to an upended chair.

'My guess is that he climbed up on that. The rope was suspended from a pipe right above it. It was tied tightly around his neck.'

Axel slipped on a pair of gloves and did a round of the office and the kitchenette, where he found two wine glasses with red wine crystals in the bottom and a glass of water with traces of white powder. He picked it up and sniffed it. Medicinal. Then he examined the cupboards without finding anything of interest. In the bathroom he found what he was looking for in a cabinet. A whole shelf of various pills: sleeping pills, happy pills, benzodiazepines, a small freezer bag with coloured ampoules, which he took to be poppers.

He went back to the office and grabbed the crime scene technician.

'There are some glasses in the kitchen, which I want checked for medication, and pills in the cabinet bathroom.'

He turned to the Swede.

'Are you sure he killed himself?'

'Hanging is very rarely murder, Axel.' He picked up the body's hands and studied them. 'And there are no defensive injuries to his hands or bruises from blows or injuries to his face. It's very difficult to get someone's head into a noose and hang them unless they're willing to cooperate. It requires a defenceless victim. Either a child, which he wasn't, or you restrain your victim somehow – again, that's not the case here. The third option, which I'm guessing is what you're hinting at, is medication. And sedation. We'll have to wait for toxicology to tell us that.'

He pulled up Bo Langberg's training top. Took out a small camera.

'Bruises,' he said as he started taking pictures.

'I can't exclude that we're dealing with murder disguised as suicide, but it's very rare, and this looks tidy. Genuine. It doesn't feel staged.'

'OK.' Axel turned to Bjarne. 'How did you get in?'

'The door was open. I could see him dangling through the window.'

'All these questions,' the Swede said. 'Why do you think he might have been killed?'

'I don't think anything. I just saw a glass in the kitchen, which was used to wash down medication. And I don't suppose that you sedate yourself before you hang yourself. If that's your intention you want to be fairly clear-headed, don't you? After all, it requires a certain level of determination to stick your head in a noose and kill yourself. And then there are two red wine glasses, which had both been used. If he's so tidy, why are they still there?'

'I never speculate. Do you have a suspect?'

'No,' Axel lied. But from the moment he entered the room, he regretted telling Marie Schmidt's father about Bo Langberg.

CHAPTER 42

'What do you think? Is it worse for a woman if her husband is unfaithful with another man?'

They were on their way to Emdrup. Axel was driving Bjarne's car because Bjarne was eating a hot dog. Axel wasn't in the mood for small talk, Bo Langberg's death had rattled him, and he couldn't let go of his suspicion that it might be murder.

'I don't know,' he replied absentmindedly while trying to organise his train of thought.

'It reminds me of a woman I fucked once. She was shit-scared that I might be queer, can you believe it? Are you gay, she asked me the first time she came over to my place. Just because I had lit a couple of candles and tidied up.'

'She thought you were gay?'

'I know! She had been buggered about by a guy who was. If you get my drift.'

'Yes, thank you, I get it.'

'And she thought he had been doubly unfaithful to her because it was with a poof.'

They drove across Dronning Louises Bridge, the bridge that connected Nørrebro to the inner city, and down Nørrebrogade.

'I can see why.'

'What?'

'Why she thought you might be gay.'

Bjarne's mouth froze, framed by a moustache of neon yellow mustard and a piece of bread roll.

'What the fuck—'

'I mean, you're obsessed with them, aren't you? You go on and on about poofs and fudge packers so much that I can't help wondering whether this is really about you needing to get fucked up the arse so hard it shuts you up.'

Bjarne dropped the rest of his hot dog onto his brown gabardine trousers.

'Fuck.'

His voice was incredulous and pleading.

'What the hell are you talking about? You're taking the piss, aren't you? You're having a laugh, Axel, you can't be serious.'

'Well, you know the old saying about how if you can spot it, you've got it.'

'I don't mind poofs. Or dykes. Or Pakis. Or Social Democrats. Or do-gooding liberals. Or that gay mayor. Or squatters. And—'

'Thank you. Put another record on, will you? I'm fed up with your prejudices. And we have a serious job to do.'

Bjarne folded his hands and offered him his obsequious undertaker smile.

'What do you think about Bo Langberg's suicide, is it all good?' Axel then said.

'You mean, did someone kill him?'

'Yes.'

'I couldn't see anything suspicious. And you heard what the Swede said. It looked like suicide.'

'I also heard him express reservation.'

'What the hell do I know? It certainly looked like a suicide,' Bjarne slurped.

221

Axel wasn't convinced. Giving the name of their suspect to Marie Schmidt's father was a rookie error – what the hell had he been thinking? He was really losing it, he had become careless, he would never have done anything like this in the past.

He had to call the Swede and find out when the post-mortem would be taking place. But before that he needed to speak to Marie Schmidt's father again.

'Once we get there, you shut your mouth and let me do the talking. Nothing about how it never rains but it pours or how everything has a silver lining.'

'Got it, boss, though it might be true in her case. Now she can start over. It can't be much fun living with a guy who fucks—'

'Just shut your trap once we get there, Bjarne.'

Axel thought about it. Relationships and secrets. Two words married to one another, and in contrast to all the others, they couldn't be separated. And they both had a lifelong mistress called the lie. It made him sick to his stomach. But it had to be done. They had called ahead. She was at home and was expecting them. But she wasn't expecting their message.

Axel once had a colleague who used the indirect method to inform the next of kin that their loved ones had died. You asked to come in, you said you had something serious to tell them, but you didn't mention what it was. Instead you insisted that the next of kin sat down and so they already knew what was coming before you spoke the words. It wasn't something he had ever wanted to emulate. For him there was only one way. Tell it to them straight. Immediately. Look the person in the eye and be ready to hold him or her, if they needed it.

He rang the doorbell and she opened the door. The skin on her face was hidden behind a thick layer of foundation, discreet eyeshadow and mascara, but he could see that she was on the verge of falling apart.

'I'm sorry to have to tell you this, but your husband is dead.'

'What are you saying?'

Her left hand closed around her chin and mouth.

'Please may we come in?'

She touched her throat, her cheeks, she looked as if she hadn't taken in what they had said. She sat down on the sofa, invited them to sit down as well.

'Would you like some cof... No, what are you saying? What has happened?'

'We found him an hour ago. In his office. It looks like he killed himself.'

'But why?'

Bjarne looked beseechingly at Axel as if he wanted to tell her, but Axel signalled with a gesture for him to stay in his basket.

'He didn't leave a letter so I can't answer that question. Was he prone to depression?'

'No... yes, he was on happy pills.'

She thought about it.

'But up until two days ago everything was normal. Ever since then he has been very introverted. Since you got hold of him and accused him of being a rapist? Is... was that what he was?'

'No, there's nothing to suggest that.'

'So what did you do to him?'

'We didn't do anything to him. We interviewed him and we asked him to account for some irregularities in his movements that were important to us. He refused. So we got a search warrant for his office, we picked up his computer yesterday and examined it. And after that he committed suicide. That's the short version. I'm very sorry to have to give you news like this.'

'But that's not an explanation. Why did he kill himself? He might have been depressed, but Bo wasn't suicidal. Is it because you started prying into his life?'

'I can't know that. I didn't know your husband, and he lied extensively to us because he wanted to hide something which turned out not to be relevant for our investigation.'

'What?'

Axel took a deep breath. There was no escape.

'He lived a double life. He had a large number of sexual encounters in Ørsted Park. Were you aware of it?'

'Bo? In Ørsted Park? You're telling me my husband was gay? Oh, come on—'

'There's substantial evidence on his computer. I'm very sorry to have to tell you, but he has been having sex with many different men. For a long period of time.'

It was as if her lower jaw had no contact with the rest of her face, her eyes widened. She looked at him with a crazed expression.

'Why are you sorry to tell me that?' she retorted aggressively. 'Isn't that exactly the kind of thing you love telling people, like when you were here last and questioned me about our sex life? So now you know. We didn't have one. And now this. Bo is dead. And he's gay, you say. And he was unfaithful. What kind of person are you? Why didn't you just stay away? Then he would have been alive today.'

There were hundreds of things he could say in his defence, but there was no need for any of that now.

Axel fixed her gaze.

'I don't know why he took his own life, but I presume it was because he couldn't handle the fact that his double life had been revealed. To my mind that's the only explanation for your husband's suicide. If you can provide me with another one, I would like to hear it.'

'You bastard. What you've come here and flung in my face is disgusting. You killed him. I'll make sure you're punished for it.'

Her grief took over. She bent forwards and croaked:

'I want you out of my home. Now.'

'We'll leave. Do you have anyone who can be with you?'

'Like you would care,' she screamed. 'Get out.'

CHAPTER 43

This was awkward. Jens Jessen had been summoned by the Police Commissioner for a carpeting – police speak for a bollocking. It would be done on the quiet. 'Lie down and take it,' she had said. He had briefly wondered where in her brain she found her metaphors. It wasn't a pleasant image, but it was probably him and his pent-up, overheated libido and yearning for Cecilie that prompted him to hear it the way he did. He had that confirmed when she carried on: 'In a situation like this, all you can do is roll over and apologise.'

Afterwards he had called Darling. Was it Axel Steen again? Yes, it was, to some extent. He was now banned from further contact with the widow, and they would just have to engage in some damage limitation. Jens was going to visit her tonight and Darling would be coming with him.

It was far from being a perfect day. On top of that there was Cecilie's call to him this morning about Axel. Something about a swimming costume. She had been livid. She had gone to Axel's flat to pick it up. But why? What was she doing there? Without calling ahead to find out if he was at home. What was that all about? She was furious with Axel. Jens didn't understand her rage. If she was really over her ex, why did she get so wound up over a pair of forgotten swimming trunks? It made no sense at all. And Scarface hadn't been in, of course. Was he out on a job, Cecilie had practically screamed at Jens down the phone.

He hadn't had the energy for it. It was the final straw and he had lost his temper, something that rarely happened. Had he actually sneered at her? 'I'm not his line manager, Cecilie. The ways of your ex-husband are inscrutable. My guess is he's out on another conquest,' he had said. She had slammed down the phone, or at least it had felt that way. Like a big, black five-kilo Bakelite handset from the golden age of the landline. Slam.

He had called her back and she had apologised, but he could feel that she was still completely beside herself.

What on earth was going on?

CHAPTER 44

The mood in Darling's office had hit rock bottom. He had summoned everyone to talk about the death of Bo Langberg and the investigation. Axel had seen Jens Jessen leave Darling's office just before the meeting. His guess was that the two of them had come up with a strategy to prevent the death of Bo Langberg blowing up in their face in the press. And he was right.

'I never thought it was Bo Langberg,' Darling opened the meeting. 'I refused to release the picture of him, and I wanted to wait for the DNA result before we put further pressure on him. The DNA result has arrived. And it exonerates him 100 per cent. Not that it's any use to him now. He's dead. Not in our custody, but you couldn't blame his widow and the media – God forbid that they find out about it – for reaching the conclusion that we contributed to his death.'

'But we didn't,' Bjarne interjected.

'No, but we could have acted differently.'

Axel loathed this use of the benefit of hindsight.

'How?' he demanded to know.

'That's what I want to ask you. Did you press him too hard? Could you have seen it coming?'

'I can't know what people might decide to do. I've never known. I couldn't have handled it any differently.'

He had led the first interview with Tine Jensen, while Bjarne and Vicki Thomsen had conducted the second one until he got involved. The blame couldn't be apportioned to him alone, but he had an inkling it was heading that way. It had Jens Jessen's name written all over it.

'No, but you're the one who pushed hard from the start. You saw a link to the Blackbird investigation, and you pressed him hard about it.'

Press my arse, Axel thought. It's what we do. If a nice little chat would do the trick, we wouldn't need warrants, interviews under caution, preliminary examinations. Either Darling had read the print-outs or Tine Jensen had told him about the interviews. Axel didn't feel that he had done anything wrong.

'Before we all dress ourselves in sackcloth and ashes in response to our failure, take a moment to remember where the investigation was at. We had a man who was lying big time about his movements on the night Jeanette Kvist was raped. He couldn't come up with a convincing explanation. We offered him several ways out. We said that if he was hiding something else, say an affair, then he could tell us about it. He couldn't provide an alibi and he refused to say why. Besides, he had an office in Nansensgade close to where Marie Schmidt was murdered, and his home in Emdrup is a 10-minute drive away from all the other crime scenes. Of course we put pressure on him. Of course I went for him. It was the right thing to do.'

'But why the rush? Why not just wait for the DNA result?'

'Because I'm a police officer, for fuck's sake. I'm not a bloody pen pusher. Have you forgotten what it means to investigate a crime? DNA on its own is never enough to convict. Police work is more than just crossing your fingers and hoping for the best. What if the DNA sample had been a match? Then we wouldn't be having this conversation, then we would have been accused of gross negligence if we hadn't already done all the things we just have.'

The mood had been level with the linoleum floor when the meeting opened, and his criticism of Darling hadn't lifted it. Darling got up and took such a deep breath that his shirt strained across his chest and his skin-tight trousers threatened to split.

'Besides, we can't be sure that Bo Langberg killed himself,' Axel said to distract everyone's attention from his outburst.

Jaws dropped collectively as they stared at him.

'Why would you say that? I've seen the preliminary post-mortem report. It says nothing about the death being suspicious,' Darling said.

'No, it doesn't, but Bo Langberg had bruises to his body and there was evidence of medication being consumed at the office, so the Swede couldn't rule out that something suspicious had been going on.'

'That's not the impression I got,' Bjarne said.

'Maybe not, but we have to wait for the result of toxicology tests before we can say for sure that he took his own life,' Axel said.

They looked at him as if he were a giant pain in everybody's arse.

'You and I need to have a talk about this later,' Darling said.

Vicki spoke up.

'I agree with Axel. We did our job. Bo Langberg made a choice. It wasn't about us, but about his life. We didn't harass him. We tried to get him to tell us the truth, and he refused.'

Bjarne added:

'Besides, I doubt we're in trouble because of this. When the wife discovers what happened, she won't want it splashed all over the tabloids that her husband waved his bare arse around Ørsted Park every night. After all, that was why he killed himself. Because he didn't want people to know.'

'That's not for us to speculate about. I'll be meeting with his wife later today, so I'll deal with that. She has complained about you, Axel,' Darling said.

'Posh cow,' Bjarne muttered, earning himself a harsh look from Darling, who continued:

'We have many other priorities. Gang attacks are escalating. I can't allow your time to be taken up with this case any longer. That goes for you too, Axel.'

'That's outrageous. I'm just as upset as the rest of you that Bo Langberg is dead, but we are still conducting a multiple case review, which indicates that a serial rapist and killer has terrorised Nørrebro for the past 12 years without being caught. We're the Copenhagen police force, for Christ's sake. We can't just shelve it. Especially not if it gives us a chance to catch a killer.'

'We'll talk about that in private. You'll all keep a low profile from now on. And not another word about Bo Langberg. Meeting over. Axel, you stay here,' Darling said.

When the others had left, he walked over to the window. Axel looked at the door to the small room. On the back of it was a tabloid newspaper cutting about unsolved murders of women in Copenhagen in the last 15 years. The room itself contained the Division's Holy Grail: the archive of all unsolved homicides in the capital from the last 20 years. Eight, the last time he had checked. While Darling prepared to read him the riot act, he looked at the pictures accompanying the article: Mirlinda, Stina and Rajan. And Marie Schmidt. She gazed at him with hopeful green eyes from under her leaver's cap. There was no bloody way he was dropping this case. He got up, crossed the room and flung open the door.

'Take a look at this, John, look at these faces. You have children of your own, teenage girls. Is there anything more important than this? How can you seriously tell us to downgrade work that might lead us to catch Marie Schmidt's killer? Have you forgotten what the two of us have worked on for all those years? Have you forgotten why we're here?'

Darling spun around furiously.

'Sit down!' he thundered.

Axel sat down in the chair in front of the desk. Darling studied him closely.

'What's wrong with you, Axel? You seem completely unhinged.'

Am I? Axel wondered. He was breathing through his nose and could smell his own acrid sweat and Ea Holdt. Am I fucked up? Or am I just trying to solve my case? He needed to get out of these rooms, into the sunshine, sit on the quay by the harbour entrance and light a joint. But he didn't have any. Perhaps he could get one from the Drug Squad. Christ, I really am on a slippery slope when I start to think like this, he thought to himself.

'What do you mean?'

'Take a look at yourself. You look like a madman. And you mouthing off to me in front of my staff. I've warned you about it. But you just plough on. As if you have no shame or humility towards our profession. A man has just killed himself and you act as if you don't care, as if all you want to do is carry on working the case.'

'I do care, but it's not our responsibility what people get up to in their own time. That includes killing themselves because we – not unreasonably – asked them a number of questions in connection with a homicide.'

'You can't see it at all, can you? You've lost your sense of proportion, of what's reasonable, and when it's wise to keep your head down, Axel. Not that it ever was your forte. You need to take a long hard look at yourself. You're wearing yesterday's clothes, you look like death. What's really going on?'

'What do you mean?'

'I'm your boss. I can help you if something is wrong. We have resources to support staff with problems.'

'What the hell are you talking about?'

'I'm talking about you. Your career. Your life. We're old colleagues. I would like to help you if I can.'

'You can help me with one thing.'

'Yes?'

'Let me carry on working my investigation.'

'There it is again. Your investigation. As if it's personal. It's not on, Axel. And I'm ending this now. As of today, we'll change the reporting structure of the team. Tine Jensen will head the investigation and she'll report directly to me. She investigated the first rape, which is the reason we're now re-examining several old cases. I know you outrank her, but that's how it's going to be. If you don't want to work for her, I have plenty of other things you could be doing.'

Normally Axel would have protested, but he kept his mouth shut. His heart was in his throat. He glared icily at Darling.

'Anything else?'

'No.'

'You're a fucking moron.'

CHAPTER 45

He picked up his jacket from his office and left, tumbled down the cylinders of the rotunda, into the colonnade, out through the main entrance, crossed Polititorvet and walked down behind the Falck building until he reached the harbour. His chest felt tight, as if his heart was being gripped by an iron glove. The heat was horrendous.

He sat down on a black mooring bollard from a time when there were still ships in the harbour, felt the metal burn underneath him, and lit a cigarette. This case. He had to focus on it, he tried to convince himself, in an attempt to ignore his body's distress signals. His heart was pounding alarmingly.

Today was a 24-carat shit show. Bo Langberg's wasted life. All because of lies and desires. Wouldn't we all be so much happier if everything was out in the open? If everybody knew who they were, so no one had to go around thinking that everyone else was perfect, so that no one had to hide their secret life? But the thought of having to show himself as he truly was made him hyperventilate. He could never do that. All that crap about letting it all out was bullshit – every experience in his career as a police officer told him so. He and his colleagues would be rushed off their feet if people gave in to their true feelings. It would cause a pandemonium of violence and rage. The truth always came at a price. Or there would be no need to lie.

His pulse terrorised him so he could feel nothing else. He hated his body, its life, its pain and weakness. He tried to breathe calmly, but only became more aware of the pounding heartbeat beyond his control. He pressed a finger against his neck and felt its hectic rhythm, counted the strokes – it was fast, much faster than normal. This was bad. He threw his cigarette into the water, looked across to the Harbour Bath where he had spent Saturday afternoon with Emma. What was happening to him? He rubbed his face. The smell of Ea Holdt's cunt on his hand. She had straddled his face, touching herself while he had licked her, he had looked up at her body, her moving fingers, her pubic hair, her stomach, breasts heaving and sinking in tune with her breathing. Her face had studied his with undiluted pleasure and desire. And later. When he took her while she lay on her back, her arms reached over her head. She took the initiative in order to be taken, she was active in order to become passive. How did that add up? It didn't add up at all, if you thought about it. Nothing did. She was loving and tender, showing him devotion and eventually surrendering to her own lust, in a way that excluded him because it was so pure. He was there. And at the same time, he wasn't. Last night had ambushed him this morning like a naked movie with him in the leading role. He felt exposed and vulnerable in a way he couldn't handle. He couldn't have this. He had shown himself to her. Surrendered. He wasn't ready. Would he ever be ready again? Would he ever manage it before his heart put a stop to it all?

And then there was this sodding DNA profile from their killer, which had ended up on a 17-year-old girl from Ballerup, Lone Lützhøj, who was almost raped by that piece of shit Axel had visited at the secure unit two days ago. He tried to visualise it, but saw only chaos and disorder as the case slipped through his fingers. A few days ago he had been given a second chance to find Marie Schmidt's killer. Now he was back to square one, fumbling in the dark, nightmares, failure.

His left arm hurt and he thought he felt the pain spreading to his neck and back. He knew all the symptoms of a heart attack. He tried to make it go away, but his heartbeat pursued him. When had he last had an ECG? Was it four months ago? Did he really have to go there again? Was he dying?

He walked up to the Fisketorvet shopping centre, stepped out onto the road without warning, raised both hands and stopped a taxi, which screeched to a halt in order to avoid hitting him. There was a passenger in the back seat.

Axel tore open the door to the front passenger seat.

'I need this car. Your passenger needs to get out. Call him another taxi. Take me to the Rigshospitalet. Fucking do it. NOW!'

He pulled out his warrant card and showed it to the taxi driver.

The passenger looked at him nervously.

'What's the problem?' he asked in a feeble voice.

'Get out. This is an emergency. The driver will call you another taxi.'

Axel got into the back.

'Trauma centre. Go!'

He tried to take deep breaths, but couldn't get any air into his lungs. It was another symptom. Things were very wrong indeed.

He saw Copenhagen glide past outside the window in summer yellow, super slow motion yet fleeting. Was this the last time he would see his city? Past the central railway station, which even in the sunshine looked like something from an old black-and-white movie and made his heart ache with its drunks, taxi drivers and backpackers, prams, families going to and from places in their lives. But he was heading to intensive care with his heart galloping out of his throat, he couldn't breathe, past Tivoli's parade of sunglass-wearing tourists, people sitting outside in the sunshine enjoying cold beers and nothing else.

'It's like I'm disappearing,' he whispered, his soul piss yellow from fear.

'Don't you need an ambulance, mate?' the taxi driver called out to him in broken Danish. 'You don't look too good. You're not going to throw up, are you?'

'Just fucking drive and shut the fuck up!'

He closed his eyes and tried to get air into his lungs, opened them again in Nørrebro, his city – everyone he had loved was there, Cecilie, Laila, Emma and Ea, what about her, no goodbye, would he just be a ghost in her life? He looked at the street life on Nørrebrogade, up along Fælledvej. Shit, this wasn't what he wanted. He touched his neck again. His pulse was very fast. If he survived this, he vowed he would change his life.

At the basement level where the trauma centre was he jumped out of the taxi, throwing 200 kroner at the driver, and half ran to reception.

A nurse looked up at him.

'Yes?'

'I'm having a heart attack… I think.' Even he could hear how crazy it sounded.

She got up and came over to him. Very calm. Called out a name over her shoulder.

'Sit down. Relax. Are you able to breathe? Where's the pain?'

Another nurse arrived.

'What's your civil registration number?'

Axel pulled his health insurance card out of his wallet and gave it to her.

She checked his pulse.

'Yes, it's quite high. Can we put him in bed two, Susanne?'

'Yes, that's free.'

'Have you been here before?'

'Yes, way too many times,' Axel panted.

CHAPTER 46

He lay in bed, his upper body raised. There were electrodes on his body, a pulse oximeter on his finger and an oxygen mask over his mouth and nose. A doctor had questioned and examined him. Blood tests had been taken. On the table by his side was a piece of paper with his civil registration number. 'Sinus rhythm leftward axis, otherwise normal ECG', over a horizon of sharp regular peaks, each indicating a heartbeat.

He was alone. Very calm. He was alive. And he needed a cigarette. He had thought he was dying. And now he lay here, surrounded by electronic sounds and the sterile smell of medication, disinfectant and artificial life. He listened to the sounds from the trauma centre. A man groaning, a gunshot victim being carried in. A hostel for Copenhagen's dying and suffering. He was healthy. And yet he was sick. In his head and everywhere else. Except in his heart. He heard the sound of clogs approaching. A Buddha gaze from the same doctor who had examined him earlier. He had Axel's medical records tucked under his arm. He picked up the ECG printout on the table and sat down with reassuringly rosy cheeks arranged either side of a superior smile.

'Axel, how are you?'

He hated strangers using his name, and it was worse in a situation like this where he subconsciously felt that the doctor had held his life in his hands, and now sat here juggling with his fear of dying in a condescending manner.

'Good, I'm good.'

'Your pulse is slightly elevated. But that could be down to a number of factors. Do you have any questions?'

'Am I OK?'

'There's nothing obviously wrong with you, Axel, but then again this isn't your first visit here.'

'No.'

'It's the fifth time in three years, once with the burns to your face, do they bother you, by the way? No? And four times about the heart. And during that same period you've had nine ECGs. Without us finding any kind of heart arrhythmia or anything else wrong with you. And we have scanned you. You have been examined for pleurisy and reflux. Nothing there either. And I don't think there's anything wrong now. And that's why I want to talk to you about—'

Axel's mobile rang.

'Hang on.'

It was the duty officer from HQ. He put it on silent.

'Are you stressed?'

'No.'

'Do you have addiction issues?'

'Addiction issues? Are you joking?' he let out a hollow laugh.

'Because your pulse is slightly elevated, and it could be what's causing it.'

His mobile lit up once again. This time it was Darling calling. Had they been informed that he was here? How could they know?

'You're a police officer, aren't you?'

'Yes.'

'Then you also know that you—'

His mobile rang again. Axel turned his attention from the doctor to the display. The duty officer. It meant they didn't know he was in hospital. It had to be about something else.

239

The doctor looked disapprovingly at the mobile as Axel placed it on the duvet in front of him.

'The reason I'm asking about addiction issues is that we found traces of cannabis in your blood.'

His mobile rang again. Axel looked at the doctor as if he were from outer space.

'I'm sorry, I really do have to take this call,' he said, and picked up the mobile again. The doctor's self-assured smile of compassion was replaced by a frown of irritation.

It was Darling.

'Yes? What is it?'

'There has been another rape. It looks like he's struck again.'

'This is an emergency admission ward, you don't just interrupt the doctor's round,' the doctor interjected.

'Just be quiet, will you,' Axel said and sat up in bed.

'Who's that?' Darling said.

'No one. Where is it?'

'Where are you?'

'That's not important right now. Where did the rape happen?'

The doctor looked angry. He threw down Axel's medical records on the bed. If I haven't had a heart attack before, these two morons will certainly give me one, Axel thought.

'Nørrebro. By the Lakes. Læssøesgade. A 19-year-old girl. Last night. She's at HQ now.'

Axel started removing the electrodes from his chest.

The doctor walked up to him and placed a hand on his arm.

'What on earth are you doing?'

Axel threw him a fierce look and he quickly snatched back his hand.

'I'm going. We have an emergency.'

'But you've been admitted for observation for a heart attack. You can't leave now.'

Axel got out of bed.

'What's happening? Axel? Axel?' Darling's voice sounded like a feeble cry from the bottom of a well as Axel removed the mobile from his ear and turned to the doctor.

'I thought you just said there's nothing wrong with me?'

'Yes, but we need to keep you in overnight so we can see the result of the tests. You can't just leave.'

Axel stuck out the arm with the cannula towards him. He hated needles.

'Just take this out of me,' he said. 'Now.' The doctor stared at him incredulously, then did as he was told.

'This is unbelievable. You can't leave.'

'I'm sorry, but I have to.' He put on his shirt. 'I appreciate everything you've done for me. I really do. And if those tests show anything, then I would very much like to be told, but I'm afraid I've got to run now. I have a case.'

'But you can't.'

'Watch me,' Axel said and half ran out of the ward. He carried on up the street. Took out his mobile. He was about to make a call, but discovered that he hadn't ended his conversation with John Darling.

'Are you still there, you fool?' he whispered tentatively into the handset.

'Axel, are you talking to me?'

'No, no.' He had overheard his conversation with the doctor.

'I'm at the Rigshospitalet. I'll explain later. Have the crime scene technicians got to Læssøesgade yet?'

'Yes.'

'I'm going there now. Email me her statement. I'll come to HQ afterwards.'

'Tine is interviewing her, Axel. We have talked about that.'

'I don't give a toss. There's only one thing I want to know. Is there scaffolding?'

'Yes.'

CHAPTER 47

Axel walked the 500 metres to Læssøesgade and read the preliminary summary of the interview with the victim as he walked. Ida Højgaard was surprised in her bed by a man at 1.30am. She had come home from a night out one hour earlier. Didn't think that anyone had followed her. She had been raped for one and a half hours by the attacker, who had threatened her with a knife he had brought with him. The attack was just as violent as the one Jeanette Kvist had been subjected to, and similar to hers on several crucial points. She had also been forced to choose how she wanted to be raped. The word 'choose' was absurd because there was no opt-out – it was merely a question of the order of violations. Her attacker got off on the humiliation. Axel could feel himself shaking with anger. The rapist had worn a condom, which she hadn't seen as she had had a pillowcase over her head, but she had heard it, and he had worn gloves, which she had noticed because they were so unusual in the heat. No stocking over his head, but a hoodie and a scarf tied around the lower part of his face. And a revolting and chilling sadism that had scared the living daylights out of Ida Højgaard. It all matched. Axel thought about Marie Schmidt. Had she been subjected to the same treatment in the bushes of Ørsted Park four years ago?

The attractive Læssøesgade stretched from Blegdamsvej down to Lake Sortedam. The nearer the lake, the more expensive the flats. Ida

Højgaard was a student and lived in a small flat at the cheap end – or less expensive given the part of Nørrebro it was in.

The scaffolding was enclosed at street level by thin Masonite boards, and a stairwell had been constructed on the outside of it. The door to the stairwell tower was padlocked, but the deck of the first-floor scaffolding was so low that a man who wanted to could climb up there. There were no crime scene technicians on the scaffolding, but he could hear builders higher up on the roof. He examined the lock. It didn't look as if it had been tampered with. The rapist could be on the roof right now. He recognised a familiar feeling in his stomach, the excitement, the chase, like a predator scenting its prey, it was as if all his nerves were electrified. He felt energised, as if he had been given a body other than the one he had hysterically handed in to the Rigshospitalet only a few hours ago. He followed the scaffolding all the way round and explored ways of scaling it. It was possible but difficult, and there was a risk that you might be seen or make a noise.

He rang the bell and was let in. It was a first-floor flat. BB was busy with the windowsill and three of his colleagues dressed in white coveralls, disposable gloves, shoe covers, face masks and hairnets were silently processing the flat.

'So, Axel, you managed to get us moved to one of your rapes after all.'

'I haven't moved you anywhere, but I would like to move you out onto the scaffolding.'

'We haven't been told to sweep that.'

'No, but that was how he got in. And I want all of it checked. Hair, particles. Shoe prints. It's important. I don't want you to just examine the way he most probably arrived, but all of the two lower decks. He could have climbed up onto it in many places. You have to get prints from everyone who has been on the scaffolding since this morning. I can hear that builders are working higher up. I'll go talk to them now. Do you have a spare pair of gloves and shoe covers?'

One of the technicians opened a bag in the hallway and handed Axel a set, including a hairnet and a face-mask, which he donned.

Axel went down to the street to a spot where the scaffolding was covered with canvas to reduce dust. He assumed that the attacker would have chosen a spot with easier access, and so Axel wouldn't be disturbing any evidence. He had to pull himself up with his arms and then swing one leg up onto the scaffolding. Then he climbed up on the outside so as not to leave prints on the deck of the scaffolding itself until he reached the second floor. He continued up the ladders and by the time he reached the uncovered roof, he was soaked in sweat. Four builders wearing protective face-masks were laying down Rockwool insulation. They wore cut-off work shorts, two of them were bare-chested, the other two in T-shirts. Axel saw them before they noticed him, and one by one they stopped what they were doing and came up to him.

'Axel Steen, Copenhagen Police. You may have heard that a woman was raped in this building last night. I would like to talk to you one at a time about what you've seen, if you've noticed anything, and what time you arrived here.'

Everyone was helpful. They had turned up for work at 7am when police were already here, but no one had prevented them from starting their work, so any evidence on the scaffolding had probably been destroyed – Tine Jensen, was Axel's immediate thought. Careless and ambitious. Two qualities which when put together made him feel sick.

The scaffolding was locked, but it was possible to scale it, as he himself had just proved, and in the three weeks it had been up, the builders had twice seen the ladder pulled down, and the site had had visitors outside working hours. Axel got the dates. Three people had a key to the scaffolding, one of them was present, and Axel got the names of the two others and of the man from the firm that had erected the scaffolding.

Then he hailed a cab and went home, showered and changed his clothes. He called Vicki Thomsen.

'Hi, Axel.'

'Hi, who is doing the interview?'

'Bjarne and Tine.'

'What are you doing?'

'I'm reading up on the cases. Later I'm going to Nørrebro to do door-to-door enquiries. We're hoping someone saw him climb the scaffolding.'

'Do you have time to look at something else?'

'Ye-es, although I guess it's Tine who decides what we do now.'

Axel ignored her objection.

'The two cases where the perpetrator entered via scaffolding. Anne Marie Zeuthen and Jeanette Kvist. We need to establish his access routes. Could he have come in using a key or was it easy to climb the scaffolding from the street?'

'Sure. I'll check it out.'

'And we need to find out who had access to the scaffolding, caretakers, security firms, scaffolding workers, builders, housing association representatives. And check up on any cases of burglary via scaffolding on Nørrebro in the last 15 years.'

'Why?'

'He could have been on many scaffolding sites throughout the years, perhaps he was tempted. Perhaps he started off being a burglar and then came across a sleeping woman and seized his chance. It's certainly one possibility.'

'I won't have time to do all of that before going to Nørrebro with Tonny.'

'No, but if the two of you could get started, then I'll be there in an hour and take over.'

'We're on it.'

'I'll inform Darling so you don't get into any trouble.'

He called his boss. Darling had no objections, but he had questions.

'Is something wrong, Axel? Why were you at the Rigshospitalet?'

'Everything is fine. Just a regular cardio check-up.'

'It didn't sound like it.'

'I'm OK.'

For the first time in a long time, what he felt and what he said married up.

CHAPTER 48

He went to the kitchen, found the hash that Dorte Neergaard had brought with her when she stopped by Saturday evening, and flushed it down the toilet.

He shaved. Studied his face in the mirror. The swelling and the bruises after the fight in Ørsted Park were completely gone. The scar tissue on the other side still glowed white. He went down to the courtyard to get his bike. Checked the time on his mobile and thought about Emma. It was almost 4pm. Where was she now? On the north coast with her mother and friends and Jens Jessen in his smart holiday home? He could imagine Cecilie on a leisurely shopping trip in Hornbæk, wearing expensive sunglasses in her hair, a summer dress and flip-flops, holding Emma's hand. For once, he wasn't thinking about his ex-wife's face or body, but his daughter's smile and eyes, her voice, which he knew better than his own.

He rang Cecilie.

'Hi. Please can I talk to Emma?'

'She's in the garden.'

'How is she?'

'She's fine.'

'Is she missing me?'

'She probably is. She doesn't say so. Or talk about you.'

'I'd like to see her.'

'You'll have a week's holiday with her in 10 days.'

'I know that, but before that.'

'I'm not driving down to Copenhagen with her.'

'No, but perhaps I could visit, go for a walk with her, go to the beach, buy her an ice cream.'

It was all wrong. What was this? She was his kid. What kind of messed-up, sick society was he living in where a father couldn't see his kid?

'It's not convenient. I think it'll only make her more confused. But if she starts talking about you, I'll suggest it to her. I think it needs to come from her.'

Convenient? I'm not convenient.

'Please may I speak to her?'

'She's busy with something. I don't want to interrupt her play. I can get her to call you later.'

Axel said goodbye. Took a deep breath. Got on his bike and rode his longing away at a furious pace down Nørrebrogade. It didn't help.

His phone rang on Dronning Louises Bridge and he stopped and held onto one of the old lampposts while answering the call with his other hand.

'Axel, you came to visit but didn't drop in on your old friend?'

'I didn't think you wanted to see me again.'

'No, but I worry about you when I don't hear from you.'

'I thought I'd get clean first.'

'You haven't lost your sarcasm, I can hear, but you sound better.'

'I'm fine.'

'Yes, perhaps you are. Though the story I heard from my colleague makes me think otherwise. Cannabis-affected police officer rips off ECG electrodes, cannula and pulse oximeter and runs half-naked from the trauma centre in the middle of the doctor's round to solve his case.'

'Half-naked? I was fully clothed.'

'Even so.'

'Hang on, Lennart, are you telling me that you swap confidential information about your patients over coffee and sandwiches, or have you looked up my medical records?'

'I didn't even have to ask him the patient's name when I heard that story. I knew it was you. And then there are the burns.'

'Well, then your worst fears have just been confirmed.'

His mobile beeped to indicate that he had received a text message. He moved the phone from his ear, Ea Holdt. He had time to read the first three words, 'lovely sexy man', before he quickly pressed the mobile back against his ear. He preferred the Swede.

'Or have they? After all, cannabis stays in your blood for quite a long time.'

'Yes, and it's several days since I last took drugs. Why are you really calling me?'

'Don't be so gruff. I'm not calling to check up on you, but to offer a suggestion. I'm sure you'll be pissed off with me, but all this stuff that's dogging you, cannabis, imaginary blood clots in your heart, perhaps it'd be an idea to get some help?'

'What do you mean?'

'There are some excellent therapists who specialise in panic attacks or addiction issues or a combination of them, which isn't unusual either, as it happens. It might do you some good. You might even start to feel better.'

'You must have swallowed a box of scalpels. I'm not seeing a bloody shrink. I'll handle this on my own. I'm fine. I haven't smoked for five days. And now, if you don't mind, I have crimes to solve.'

He ended the call and got off the bike, pushed it over to the granite parapet that led down to the lake, parked it, sat down on the wall and read Ea Holdt's text message.

'Lovely sexy man. You disappeared far too quickly this morning. Fancy meeting for a quick coffee? There's something I would like to talk to you about. Ea x.'

More than anything he wanted to forget, and he had no wish to find out why she wanted to talk to him, but he felt obliged to reply. The only problem was he had no idea what to say. He looked across the lake shimmering in the afternoon sunshine, the small ripples on the surface, the muted sound of cars from Vester Søgade, the smell of exhaust fumes, bicycle tyres against the tarmac and summer. It could be different, couldn't it? He could be with her. Enjoy life. Surrender. If he were a different man.

'Thanks for last night. I'm busy today. No time. Will get back to you. All the best, Axel', he wrote.

CHAPTER 49

Jens Jessen was in his car. The swimming costume had turned up. Cecilie's mother had found it in their flat. And then Cecilie had called him again. And cried. She had been inconsolable. He didn't understand a word of what was going on, but he had driven to Hornbæk with the swimming costume. To find out what was wrong or comfort her. And he had done that. But she had barely dried her eyes before Axel Steen rang. After which she didn't give him a second glance, but stepped outside on the terrace to continue the conversation.

He didn't understand their relationship, her mood swings, her rage, he was sure it was a cover for something. She said that she didn't care about Axel, but you didn't get that mad at someone you didn't care about. And why wasn't he allowed to hear what they were talking about? She looked quiet and deep in thought out on the terrace. Why did she always conduct phone conversations with Axel in another room? If all she was really doing was putting him in his place? No, it didn't make sense.

He floored the accelerator down the Hillerød motorway while he tried to review the development of their relationship from passionate infatuation spiced up with problematic divorce to everyday life, them talking about having a child together – OK, so that hadn't happened, yet their life was good in many ways, Cecilie's new job, his time with Emma, everything was fine. And yet something grated. It had started a year ago. Their relationship seemed to have stalled. And for the first time he had started to doubt. He had been away with work for a couple of days. Cecilie had been to see Axel, who had Emma – what had it been about on that occasion? A pair of Wellington boots? But was that the only thing she had given him? He refused to believe it, but the suspicion had started to grow, and it was corrosive like acid because he had phoned home. Several times. Without her picking up. Afterwards she had been furious with Axel. She had told Jens that he was irresponsible, an addict, that she suspected he smoked cannabis. How could she have known any of that, if all she had done was drop off a pair of Wellington boots? He hadn't questioned her any further, of course he hadn't, because she had also been turned on, given him attention, kissed him and held him for longer than usual.

Maybe he was making a mountain out of a molehill. And yet. He had just received the airline printouts. Axel Steen had flown to The Hague three times. To pick up his daughter, of course, but what kind of grown man does that? It was totally over the top. But that wasn't the real problem. The real problem was that every time he went there with plenty of time to spare. The first time the day before, the next time seven hours before, and the third time two days before. Was he with Cecilie when he went to The Hague? On one of the occasions Cecilie had hired a babysitter the same evening her ex-husband had been in town. It wasn't proof, but it was circumstantial, as they said in the English justice system. And it was all beginning to mount up, wasn't it?

CHAPTER 50

When Axel reached HQ, he turned left on impulse and went up to the management corridor. He knocked on the door with the sign saying Deputy Commissioner and opened it when a voice from the inside called out 'enter'.

Jens Jessen looked up, surprised.

'Axel Steen... right, do come in.'

'Thank you.'

'What can I do for you?'

'There's been another rape.'

'Yes, so I hear.'

'So now we have six cases which are connected. All committed within a radius of a few kilometres. Focusing on Nørrebro. Two within the last five weeks. In three of them he used scaffolding to gain access to the flats where the women were raped.'

'You want to issue a press release?'

'No. And yes. It's about protecting the public. And the media as a means of informing them. When I leave your office, I'll go and see Darling to talk media strategy with him. He's very defensive. And I just don't think that we can afford to be. We have to take action now. And we need to warn women not to leave any windows open when they go to bed – especially if they live in a building that's undergoing renovation. If we don't, the media will find out anyway, and you'll get precisely the kind of flak you're desperate to avoid. And once they decide to do a hatchet job on us, I'm sure they'll spot countless errors of judgment in the cases.'

'What do you mean?'

'Careless handling of evidence, superficial interviews of victims, our failure to compare cases that obviously have much in common. These cases aren't new, they've been lying around for years waiting for someone to notice them. And you don't need to be a journalist to find that remarkable.'

'I haven't heard anything to that effect yet.'

'No, and I'm guessing you wouldn't like to.'

'So you think we should take the initiative and announce that we're hunting a serial rapist?'

'Yes. On my desk are stacks of other cases, more than 10 rapes and three homicides, which this man could also have committed. It could be our biggest investigation in recent years, and it'll keep growing.'

Jens Jessen stretched out while he considered it.

'After Bo Langberg, we're very careful about drawing attention to ourselves.'

'Yes, but this is the right kind of attention. The media will bend over backwards for us as long as we're in control.'

'Hmm. You have some experience of sharing information with the media, I seem to recall. So are you asking me for my support?'

'No, I just want to make sure that you're open to the idea and have heard my reasons before I take it up with Darling.'

'What's that supposed to mean?'

'When I last suggested something along those lines, you and Darling stomped all over my idea like a couple of power-hungry elephants trying to outdo one another in a pissing contest.'

Jessen smiled, but there was something more behind his smile.

'I don't recognise that description of our meeting. I'm not biased. I'll listen to your request and consider it. Anything else?'

Had he offended him?

'No.'

'Good. Nice to see you… Oh, by the way, I would like to come with you a few more times. Last time things went a bit crazy, but I would like to join you on some more routine assignments.'

If that was the price he had to pay, then Axel was close to changing his mind.

'There's nothing routine about what I do.'

'No, of course not. But say we were to go public with this, won't we be inundated with calls?'

'Probably, and we'll just have to trawl through them. We have a good description. We have his height and approximate age. There will be many, but we can narrow them down.'

'And what do you do then?'

'We collect mouth swabs from anyone of interest for DNA testing. See if that gives us something. It'll require quite a lot of officers.'

'Will you be doing it yourself?'

Hell no.

'Yes, some of them. I'll visit anyone of special interest to us and we might bring some of the men in here to interview them.'

'Good. Really interesting. If John agrees with your suggestion, then I'm ready to go with you. You just let me know when and where. It'll be interesting.'

'Tell me, what's this really about? Are you bored?'

Jens Jessen laughed out loud.

'Not often, but occasionally, yes. Aren't you?'

'No.'

'Who would pass up the chance to accompany the legendary Axel Steen?'

Axel couldn't decide if Jens Jessen was making fun of him.

'No, I'm serious. It's quite simply essential for me to know more about how you work, and you're one of our experienced officers whose knowledge I hope to draw on. At the same time you can give me some inside information about the relationships between the divisions, conflicts, alliances.'

So you can cut staff numbers. I don't think so, Axel thought to himself.

He heaved a loud sigh. Said goodbye, went down to his office and turned on his laptop. He read the interview with Ida Højgaard. There was a chance of DNA, but they wouldn't know for several days. Axel didn't care. As in the attacks on Jeanette Kvist and Anne Marie Zeuthen, the rapist had asked her where she 'wanted it'. Gloves, dark running jacket or anorak, a scarf in front of his face, jeans, trainers, height and use of language – it all matched. Axel thought about his timetable:

1996. 1998. 2003. Homicide in 2004. Two rapes, one month apart, 2008. What did that tell him? That the man had been active for at least 12 years. The biggest gaps between the reported dates were five and four years. The four years after 2004 could be because the murder of Marie Schmidt had shaken him. But that wasn't Axel's impression of this man. It was more likely there were cases they had missed. Or his personal circumstances had reduced his urge, a girlfriend, children, a posting abroad, a move. But what alarmed him the most were the two most recent rapes five weeks apart. American studies of serial offenders had shown that they often increased their frequency the further into their offending they were and the more demanding and insistent their obsessions or voices became. Now that could be the case here, but Axel didn't think of this perpetrator as disturbed. He thought of him as a sadist who enjoyed cruelty and psychological terror and was perfectly aware of what he was doing. And so he could provide no other explanation for the random jumps in time: the man had committed many more offences. That right now in Copenhagen, there were several more women who had been raped by this man. Unsolved rapes or unreported. Every police officer knew there were many of the latter. Criminology surveys indicated that for every reported rape at least one went unreported. Axel consoled himself by thinking that these figures didn't cover this type of aggravated stranger rape, but rapes where the victim was a spouse, boyfriend, friend or family member. He looked at the dates and returned again and again to the two most recent rapes, five weeks apart. It was worrying. It suggested that the killer would soon strike again because if the treatment he had subjected Jeanette Kvist to didn't dampen his urge, it was because it was peaking. He hadn't mentioned it to Jens Jessen, but he would use it to argue his case with Darling.

It proved unnecessary. Jens Jessen had already set things in motion. Darling had been a good colleague of Axel's for years and saved his arse many times, but he was also so ambitious that you could hear his heels click loudly the moment a senior manager came to his office.

Now he wanted to talk strategy. And he was usually good at that – press handling had always been one of his strong sides. He was dignified. He invoked trust. He was serious. He was the right person to stand in the colonnade, face the assembled Copenhagen media and tell them about the perpetrator of five rapes. Darling summoned the team to his office.

'We need the DNA test from the new investigation, and then we go public.'

'You have got to be joking!'

'No, I don't want to say anything until we're sure. Surely you can understand that after Bo Langberg. If there's no connection between the two cases, then we can't say that there is.'

'But there's a clear match in his MO. It has to be the same man.'

'That's what you said about Bo Langberg.'

'I don't want to hear another word about Bo Langberg. What about people who live in Nørrebro, don't they have a right to know, to be warned?'

'And they will be. Once we're sure. This isn't up for discussion. It's not as if the media isn't writing about the rape already. And I'll be happy to say that people ought to close their windows if there's scaffolding around their building, but I'm not saying anything about us looking for a serial offender until we have the DNA test result. We'll have that in two days, and then I'll be more than willing to go out and say that we're hunting a man with five rapes to date and possibly even more.'

'And a murder,' Axel interjected.

'We'll keep that back for now. We can use it against him if we get him. Or we can go public with it if the calls taper off. It's one of the most-high profile killings in Denmark and it'll get huge coverage. But it's not our strongest card, because we have no evidence. And we tried asking the public for help several times back in 2004. It's the rapes that'll give us something. We can always play our trump card of Marie Schmidt later.'

Darling was right, although everything in Axel wanted to link Marie Schmidt to the other cases.

The others had arrived. Darling shared his thoughts with them.

'My question is: what we do until we get the result of the DNA test? Tine, what's your view?'

'We're investigating the scaffolding companies from the three cases involving Anne Marie Zeuthen, Jeanette Kvist and Ida Højgaard. Who had access? Who works there? We will re-interview the victims to strengthen the description. And we're still waiting for quite a lot of forensic results from the new crime scene. So that'll keep us busy. What about you, Axel? What are you doing?'

'Why are there no attempted rapes?' he wondered out loud.

'Are you saying we're missing something?' Tine Jensen said.

'Isn't it common with rapists who commit multiple rapes, that they fail sometimes – that they actually fail quite often?'

'Yes, that's quite common,' Vicki Thomsen said, as Tine Jensen seemed to be pondering whether what Axel was saying now implied a criticism of her.

'So what does it mean that we're not considering any attempted rapes?'

'That he's prepared,' Bjarne said.

'He has local knowledge. He's very well prepared,' Vicki added.

'Operates at specific times. Doesn't take any risks,' Tonny Hansen interjected.

'Yes, or we've overlooked some. Attempted rapes, I mean. Has he ever had to give up? We should be able to find that out quickly if we limit our search to Copenhagen. Perhaps Vicki could help me. If you don't mind, Tine, then I would like to check it out.'

'No, of course not. The rest of us will follow up the scaffolding line of enquiry. I'm fairly sure we'll find him in Kansas work wear with tattoos all over his body. It sounds just like him.'

'I'm afraid you're completely wrong about that,' Axel said. 'He's not some oik who drives an old moped with a milk crate at the back, who strikes whenever he gets the chance. And I don't think he's a working-class guy with a deep hatred of women because his mother made his life hell. He's organised, articulate and willing to take risks, intelligent. He might prove to be well educated, he might even have a wife and children. He could be one of us.'

Tine Jensen fell silent.

'So your guess is, Axel?' Darling asked.

'I'm not guessing. All I'm saying is we mustn't allow ourselves to be blinded by one theory yet. He doesn't seem like a man who is tormented by voices or some type of borderline schizophrenic but an intelligent, calculating sadist, who enjoys what he's doing, he might enjoy it more than the sex itself. And he could turn out to be anyone. He may be single, perhaps with a very active sex life, which also shows traces of his proclivities. The moment we point the spotlight on him and dig through the layers of his life, we won't be in doubt.'

Darling closed the meeting.

'I agree with Axel. We mustn't fixate on anything yet. That's enough for today. We have an early start tomorrow morning.'

Axel was tired, but he had one more thing to do before he could go home. He had called ahead, and Marie Schmidt's father was once again waiting for him on the landing outside the top-floor apartment.

'Any new developments?'

'Yes, but nothing I can tell you about yet.'

They went into the big living room. The father remained upright.

'So what do you want?'

'Bo Langberg, the architect, remember we talked about him?'

Axel deliberately didn't say why he was there, because he wanted to see the father's reaction when he heard the name. If he had had anything to do with the death of Bo Langberg, then he would be expecting this visit. And he would have prepared his poker face – yet it was often in a conversation's best prepared lies that the cracks would show.

'Yes, the architect. Of course I remember him. I even remember her pointing him out to me in the street one day.'

The father was calm. If he had killed Bo Langberg, his performance was worthy of an Oscar – and that wasn't quite how Axel remembered him from four years ago when he had bared his broken heart to them several times.

'How did he look?'

'Very ordinary, dark hair.'

'Do you remember when it was?'

'No, not precisely, maybe six months before Marie died. Or three months.'

'What was the weather like when she pointed him out?'

The father looked confused.

'Why do you want to know that?'

'Because you told me that she pointed him out to you in the street, and if you can recall the situation and the season, it can sometimes help you to remember when it was.'

The father looked up into the air. Thought about it.

'It was spring. Probably April.'

'OK. I need to ask where you were between 10pm last night and 8am this morning.'

'Why?'

'I'll get to that in a moment. Please would you tell me?'

'I'm getting the feeling I had when you interviewed me four years ago, that I'm the suspect.'

'Much of my work is about eliminating people. As I told you back then. Please would you tell me where you were?'

'Yes, I went to a concert in the DR concert hall. It finished around 11pm. Afterwards I went to 90'eren for a drink with two friends and stayed until 2am.'

'And then?'

'I went home on my own.'

'Did anyone see you come home?'

'What's this about? I deserve to know, don't you think, why are you asking me all these questions? I went out. I haven't killed anyone.'

Axel looked into his eyes, which didn't look away, but still had something questioning in them.

'Why would you say that?'

'Say what?'

'That you haven't killed anyone?'

'I don't know. It's just a figure of speech, I guess. And that is your line of work, isn't it?'

'Have you ever been to Bo Langberg's office?'

'No, I've no idea where it is. You said that it was in this street, and Marie told me the same back then.'

'You're quite sure about that?'

'Yes. What's happened?'

'We have your DNA profile from 2004, and if you have been to his office in the last 24 hours, our technicians will find traces of you. I'm telling you this because the next thing I'm going to tell you is that he was found dead this morning.'

'And you think that I—'

'We don't think anything, but we have to investigate everything. That's what I'm doing now. I'm sorry that it's done like this, but there's no other way to get to the bottom of the case. It looks like he committed suicide, but we can't rule out that he was killed.'

'But why? Why would he commit suicide? Was it because he knew he was about to be exposed?'

'No, far from it. DNA evidence has eliminated him. He had nothing to do with the death of your daughter.'

The father looked visibly disappointed. Axel couldn't blame him. Not only was he suspected of killing a man believed to be the killer of his daughter, now it turned out that the man had nothing to do with the murder, and the chance of getting closure after four years of hell had slipped away once again. Axel knew that next of kin never gave up hope, but it was a fact that many police visits ended in yet another disappointment, and that disappointment propelled them back into grieving.

'I'll return as soon as I know more. I know this is stressful, but I'm sure you can understand why I need to ask you these questions when a man who was suspected of involvement in Marie's death is dead himself, and you're one of the few people, apart from us, who knew that he was of interest to us.'

He got the name of the two friends the father had been out with. There was still a window of four to six hours where he had no alibi. Axel had no clear reading of the father's reactions, some of which had the smooth veneer of a lie, but he couldn't put his finger on what was wrong. He wasn't ready to rule him out just yet.

He hadn't eaten since last night. He took a box and filled it with files from the Blackbird investigation, went down to his bike, attached it to the back and rode home. On his way he stopped off at the Indian in Nørrebrogade, the only place in town you could get a classic vindaloo with vinegar and plenty of green chilli. Raita, poppadum and naan bread. He would be doing nothing but lying on the sofa and reading through the interview files from the Blackbird case.

No hash, no sex, just rest.

He ate with open windows as the darkness crept in. And with it followed cool gusts from the street, half an hour of a gentle breeze that felt like a blessed relief. He lay down with the Blackbird case and started reading, but soon surrendered to sleep.

CHAPTER 51

Thursday, 3 July

He woke up at 3am, tangled up in a blanket he had battled for a couple of hours. It was too short to be a duvet and he had had a constant urge to cover himself up, but it was also too hot to be underneath it. The part of him that had craved safety under the blanket had won last night's struggle because it was wrapped around him, clammy with sweat, as were his T-shirt and underpants. The temperature in the room was closer to 25°C than 20. He got up and went to the bathroom. Peeled off his clothes and took a long, icy shower. Naked, he walked back to the living room. He lit a cigarette and opened the Blackbird file again. He was going to HQ in four hours. They would have a brief morning meeting before they headed out to talk to the scaffolding workers, builders and caretakers, whose names Tine and the others had compiled yesterday. They wanted to see if they matched the description and get a DNA test if they did.

Axel wanted to review the entire Blackbird case before they caught the perpetrator so that he would be fully prepared when he came to interview him.

The moment he delved into the files, he was four years back in time. And it wasn't a good place to be. He flicked through the interviews with Marie's next of kin almost on autopilot. Her father, who had lost the last person he had, but today looked as if he had come through it. Her paternal grandmother, whom he had interviewed several times, and whom he was sure was holding something back despite him having pressed her very hard. Marie had trusted her and there was something she hadn't wanted to tell them, something about Marie's relationship with a boyfriend, and no matter how much Axel had impressed on her that her granddaughter was dead and that it wouldn't help anyone to protect her secrets now, he hadn't been able to make the grieving old woman open up. He skimmed her classmates. Boyfriends. Niels Bak, the guy she had arranged to meet that night. Her other sexual relationships.

There was one person in particular who had been on his list of suspects for a long time. Rasmus Berndt, aged 18, who was in the same class as Marie. His parents were divorced but rich, he was an arrogant son of a bitch, lots of loud, overexcited teenage partying, buying spirits by the bottle in smart bars in central Copenhagen and a coke habit that placed him in the weekend addict league. He had wanted to pick a fight with Niels Bak because he thought Marie was his. Those were his very words during the interview. Axel took it out.

'Were you in a relationship?'

'No, but she was mine. She liked it when I ordered her about.'

Even at this point Darling, who had two teenage daughters of his own, had started to shift restlessly in his chair.

'How?'

'She was a bad girl. Up for anything.'

'And what's that?'

'Oh, I don't know. Different things. I had sex with her in a classroom during a party once.'

'Yes, so we gather. We also know that you bragged about it. Let me read this to you: "I fucked her on the teacher's desk, I slapped her and then I came in her mouth, what a hoe".' Are those your words?'

'Whatever, I told you she was a bad girl, didn't I?'

'Is it true that you hit her?'

'I just slapped her arse during sex. She liked it.'

'We've been told that you slapped her across the face several times one night when you also had sex. Where you allegedly had anal sex with her.'

'I did have anal sex with her, that's true, she liked it. The other bit is not true.'

Darling had got up and was leaning his entire body over him.

'Listen, you little turd, your DNA is on her clothing and that's enough for us to lock you up and throw away the key, so stop showing off and tell us the truth.'

They had all loathed him. Homicide investigators used to interviewing the most depraved psychos without letting it get to them, they had all wanted to wipe Rasmus Berndt's smug, privileged smile off his face with their fists. Axel told Darling to leave the room.

'I agree with my colleague. Why did you hit her?'

'She stepped out of line, didn't she? So I had to teach her a lesson.'

'She stepped out of line. How?'

'I had fucked her up the arse, hadn't I, not many girls will let you do that, but then she said she already tried it before, that she had had other men, older men, and then she asked me if I thought that was stupid.'

'And then?'

The fat outer layer of self-assurance began to melt.

'Well, that's when I hit her,' he raised his voice, 'and I told her to shut the fuck up. I didn't want to hear about that.'

And so it went on. Meaningless porn sex between two teenagers. Everyone was sickened by it. They had spent weeks trying to identify these older men, but to no avail. One of her male teachers had been interviewed for 36 hours because a girl had said that he had fancied Marie, but it turned out to be a lie. The girl had only made the allegation because the teacher had turned her down.

Axel read on. Rasmus Berndt had left Bellevue beach in his convertible half an hour after Marie Schmidt, and driven to Østerbro, where he lived in a big house with his father. Mobile phone information from transmitter masts confirmed this. Then he had driven to a party on Amager, where he had been seen by several people at 1.30am. There was a time window where he could have murdered her, but it was tiny. They had nothing on him. Nothing except him being a loathsome little shit, as Darling had called him in a rare moment when he lost control of his feelings.

Axel had reached the list of tip-offs. 663 in total. Calls about absolutely everything between heaven and earth which had been logged. He started going through them. Could their killer be hiding behind one of those? Could a witness have seen him around Ørsted Park, or might he even have been one of the people who was interviewed but not DNA tested?

He remembered coming home to the flat one evening and how Cecilie had paced restlessly around him. It was unusual because she was normally ice cold. He had given it no further thought, exhausted as he was after working 16 hours straight on the Blackbird investigation. The next morning he had noticed that their landline had been unplugged. He had plugged it back in, thinking no more about it. In the next few weeks there were little clues which he also hadn't picked up on until later. On one of the rare evenings he had been at home with Emma, Cecilie had gone out for dinner with some girlfriends. The next day in the laundry basket he had spotted underwear he hadn't seen for a long time, a G-string, a corset and stockings from Aubade, which she had worn several times when it was in the air that they would be having sex. He had thought that she intended to wash it because she wanted to make love with him. But no. She worked longer and longer hours, her mother looked after Emma increasingly often. Her smile on the sofa one evening when she read a text message and afterwards looked up at him as if she didn't know who he was.

Then she had called him one day and said that she had left work early, Emma was with her parents. Would he be able to get home soon? He had thought they would be having sex. He was wrong. She was moving out. She had met someone. It was a done deal. She had gathered up all the trash from their relationship into one big pile and reviewed it mercilessly. His absence, his workaholism, the Blackbird investigation, and the final straw, his carelessness and irresponsibility towards Emma. Their daughter's hospital admission, which was his fault. She couldn't live with him any longer.

'When I was at the hospital, at the ICU and I couldn't contact you, I knew I had nothing more to give you. I've tried to find my way back, but I can't, Axel. I'm sorry, but it's over.'

He couldn't think about it any longer, the pain was too great. He cursed himself for having got rid of the hash.

Cecilie had moved out with Emma one week after what in Axel's life was now known only as 'the conversation'. They had met up once more to talk, but it had been a disaster. Everything was done and dusted and she moved into a four-bedroom apartment in Holbergsgade which Jens Jessen had found for her. Axel couldn't let go of the feeling that he had been tricked, that everything had been arranged behind his back. And for a long time that was all he could see. He stayed in their flat, with Emma there for four days every other week. The Blackbird investigation, which for a long time he had been the only one working on, sucked him in and he lived for nothing else. Day and night. He stayed at work long after the others had left, slept across his desk, he took the files home with him at the weekend, wandered around Nørreport, Ørsted Park, made the trip from Bellevue beach to Copenhagen. Night after night. Until his boss forced him to shelve the case. And the Swede told him he had to find meaning in something other than a dead girl, whose killer he would probably never catch. He had humoured them, but he had promised himself that he would find him. One day.

He went to the bedroom and got dressed. Now he was going out to get the bastard who had killed her. He might have lost everything back then, but at least he could fix this one thing. Give her peace, put things right.

He didn't know whether it was Cecilie or Marie Schmidt he had in mind.

CHAPTER 52

The list contained the names of 47 men, all current or former employees of construction companies that could be linked to the three rapes where the attacker had gained entry to the victim's home via scaffolding. Everyone under the age of 30 had been eliminated because the first of the five rapes was 12 years ago, and every victim was of the opinion that their attacker was an adult male.

Jeanette Kvist's description of her attacker narrowed it down even further. They were looking for a man who was 1.82 to 1.83 m tall. Slim. Possibly muscular. Strong. The stocking made her facial identification dubious, but Jeanette Kvist had said that he had hair on his head, that the shape of his head was ordinary, not pointed or narrow, but with rather broad cheekbones. Small nose.

Axel reckoned that at least two thirds of the 47 men could be ruled out based on the height and build criteria, although they had decided to test everyone who was between 1.75 and 1.85m tall.

Five teams had been dispatched. Axel had made sure to get the list of men who lived in Nørrebro or north-west Copenhagen. There were eight of those. He was going with Bjarne, who was still giving him the silent treatment after the gay quip.

His phone rang as they walked down to Bjarne's car. It was Ea Holdt, and Axel asked him to hang on for five minutes.

'Hello.'

'Hello, it's Thursday and I'm childfree.'

'Me too.'

'Perhaps we could do something together. Go for a meal. A movie. Or you could show me your lair.'

'Yes.'

'How about we meet at 7pm? By the Lakes?'

'Yes. Or how does Blågårdsgade sound to you? Kate's Joint, if you like foreign food.'

'Good. Right in the middle of the Nørrebro jungle. I like it. Are you busy?'

'Yes. New developments all the time.'

'I'm aware of it. I have a new client. Your latest victim. I think it's about time you caught him.'

'So do I.'

'7pm. See you later.'

Bjarne had been eavesdropping.

'Someone's getting their leg over?'

'Oh, fuck off!'

'It's nothing to be ashamed of.'

'Just shut up and let's get going.'

'I'm not the one holding us up. You miserable old… fucking burns face, you know how to suck the joy out of a room. I've had it up to here with you! You think you can get away with anything, don't you? You're happy to call people gay, but if anybody ever says anything to you, you bite their heads off.'

'Don't be so sensitive, Bjarne, you sound like a little bitch.'

Lundtoftegade. 1970s concrete tower blocks so hideous that the architect who designed them ought to be in jail. 70 flats overlooking Copenhagen's busiest stretch of motorway. Not even the supermarket, the nursery schools, the green open spaces and the playgrounds could hide that Lunden, as it was commonly known, had ended up blighting the cityscape. As far as Axel and his colleagues were concerned, it was eight storeys of ghetto crime, hash, hard drugs, violence, theft, robberies and the odd homicide. Every officer knew Lunden. And they all hated it.

Even in the car park they were tailed by the local youths, pale, light and dark-skinned young men with too much time and energy on their hands and nothing to do with it. When they followed them inside the stairwell, Axel turned around and held up his warrant card.

'Get lost!'

'We live here, man, what are you doing?'

'We're here to talk to someone and you'll stay out of it.'

'Who are you looking for, pig?'

It was a delicate balance between a show of strength and talking the situation down, but at this point they had few options other than to show some muscle, which luckily came easily to them both.

'It's none of your business. And the next one to mouth off is nicked. Now piss off.'

Axel and Bjarne had the lift to themselves, but when they reached the gallery, there they were again, five or six young men with their hands stuffed in the pockets of their cut-off jeans, basketball vests, baggy trousers, caps, gold chains and mobile phones. They were nudging one another as they watched Axel and Bjarne.

'Ignore them,' Axel said to Bjarne.

They found the door they were looking for. The young men followed them.

'Get lost,' Bjarne shouted.

Axel placed his hand on Bjarne's arm, then pulled out his mobile and pretended to make a call while he walked towards the young men, looking hard at them.

'I need three vans, one patrol car and a paddy wagon for five or six young men in Lundtoftegade who are preventing us from doing our job. Yes, Block D facing Lundtoftegade, we're on the third floor. No, no, just get here. I think they really want to see the inside of a prison. Great. Thanks.'

'You got your wish, boys. Our lads are looking forward to meeting you.'

The young men started to retreat. Before they reached the lift they had invited Axel to screw his mother, his grandmother, his daughter and Bjarne, but they left.

Axel and Bjarne knocked on the door to Flat 31e. The occupier had been employed by the scaffolding company that had renovated the property where Anne Marie Zeuthen was raped ten years ago. The door was opened a crack. Axel thrust his warrant card into the gap.

'Open up. We just want to talk.'

Bald. Bare-chested. Covered in tattoos. Sleepy eyes with tiny, piggy pupils. The murky flat behind him reeked of skunk and rubbish. The man was unwashed and revolting to look at, but probably a little too fat to do what their attacker had done. Still, he was the right height, and Axel exchanged glances with Bjarne, who nodded.

'What if I refuse?' said the guy in the doorway when they asked him for a mouth swab.

'Then I handcuff you, charge you with murder, raid your drug den, drive you to Vestskoven and beat the crap out of you,' Bjarne said while calmly slipping on his disposable gloves.

He had previously written the man's name, civil registration number, date and location on the FTA card that came with the DNA swab.

The man gaped at him as if he couldn't take any of it in. His gaze moved to Axel as if he was looking for confirmation that this was really happening.

'He means it,' Axel said.

'Open your mouth, you tosspot!' Bjarne said, taking the mouth swab with the foam head out of the wrapping and holding it up in front of the gobsmacked man.

'We haven't got all day.'

The man opened his mouth. Each cheek must be swabbed for 20 seconds, and whether it was the time, Bjarne's grip on his jaw or the situation in general that got too much for him was impossible to say, but after a short time he started to groan and squirm. Axel looked over his shoulder and saw that three of the young men were back at the lift.

'Oi, pig, what the hell are you doing?' they called out.

'Argggg-gy-gy-gy,' the man gurgled.

The young men threw something along the gallery, and a firecracker exploded a short distance away from them.

'I'll deal with them,' Axel said, and ran towards them. They instantly scarpered down the stairs. He walked back to Bjarne, who had finished, and was now asking the man to sign the FTA card. Then he turned it over, tore off the protective flap, placed the foam head of the mouth swab on the absorbent paper and pressed down as he wiped the head from side to side.

'Hold this,' he said to the man, thrusting the mouth swab at him. He looked as if he still didn't understand what was going on.

Bjarne pulled a small envelope out of his jacket pocket, placed the FTA card in it, and sealed it.

'Nice doing business with you,' he said to the man's gawping mouth.

'What about this?' the man said, waving the mouth swab.

'It's a present for you,' Bjarne called out as they started walking along the gallery.

Axel glanced over his shoulder and saw the man hurl the mouth swab onto the ground and stamp on it angrily.

'It's not him, but I'm guessing he was nervous because he knows he'll come up in the DNA register as being wanted for something else, a burglary or car theft. I love buy one get one free,' Bjarne said contentedly.

'Let's get out of here before the young thugs feel the need to express their disappointment that the forces of law and order didn't rock up after all.'

They were hassled all the way back to the car, which hadn't been scratched or had its tyres let down. All in all, a successful visit.

The next stop was Hejrevej in north-west Copenhagen. A yellow housing block from the 1940s. The linoleum on the stairs was brown and cracked. The walls painted an ugly curry yellow. The occupant had worked as a builder on the property where Jeanette Kvist was raped, and he wasn't at home. They tried a neighbour, who told them that she had seen him the night before and thought he was probably at work. They called his boss and were told that he was fitting windows in Valby. They drove there. His height and build matched. He willingly provided them with a DNA sample and expressed the hope that they would 'soon catch the bastard'.

A site manager who lived in a flat in Rantzausgade had to have the seriousness of the situation bent in neon tubes before he agreed to the mouth swab. He had the right height, he was slim and bald with a sticky pinprick gaze in his dark blue eyes. He was defensive and suspicious.

'What happens if I refuse to give you a sample?'

'Then we charge you with murder and then we have the legal right to take a mouth swab from you on the spot. If you refuse, we'll take you to HQ, get you a lawyer, whom you will end up paying for, and then take the mouth swab with or without your consent.'

'Are you serious?'

'Yes. So wouldn't you rather we came inside and dealt with it now?'

'I see no reason for that. I have nothing to do with this.'

'I also have a few questions,' Axel said.

'Yes?'

'And I'm not planning on asking them out here on the landing. Either you let us in or we take you to HQ immediately.'

He finally admitted them. He showed them to the kitchen, but when Bjarne made to wander around the flat while Axel asked the questions, the man interrupted him and blocked Bjarne's path to the living room.

'I won't allow it. You've no right to snoop around my home without a search warrant. You can ask any questions you want to out here, or I will call the—'

'Police?' Bjarne smiled.

'No, my lawyer.'

'You really have one?' Axel said.

'Yes.'

'Why?'

'I just do.'

'Where were you the night leading up to Wednesday?'

'I was with my girlfriend and some friends at Amager Strandpark.'

'How long?'

'We were there until 2am. Then we went back to her place.'

'Have you got her number?'

'Why?'

'So I can check the information you've just given me. This is a regular police investigation into several serious criminal offences. Please give us her number so we can verify your information.'

He did. Bjarne made the call.

'This is insane,' the man said.

'Just do as I say and answer the questions, and we'll be out of here in no time and you'll probably never see us again. If you haven't done anything illegal, that is. Where were you the night between Friday and Saturday 31 May?'

On that occasion he had also been with his girlfriend, who confirmed his alibi. Bjarne carried out the mouth swab and they left.

CHAPTER 53

After six hours, seven DNA tests and one man they couldn't find, they returned to HQ. The other teams were also back. Two of them had brought people in and interviewed them. Axel skimmed the summaries.

Darling entered.

'I've managed to accelerate the testing of the DNA sample from the rape. We'll have the result tomorrow morning. If it's positive, I'll go public with it right away. We'll have 10 people manning the phones. So you'll be busy. I hope you're right that this is how we catch him, Axel, because we'll be inundated with calls.'

'What are you going to say?'

'I've prepared a press release. I'll tell them what we know about the perpetrator, the area where he operates, how many cases we're dealing with. How he operates. I'll encourage women in Copenhagen to be careful, keep their windows closed, not walk alone in parks or along deserted paths, be extra careful in Nørrebro, and then I'll ask anyone who has even the slightest idea of who the attacker might be to contact us. I'm going to say that he is wanted in connection with five sexual assaults, but that we believe he has more to answer for, and that we're reviewing homicides and sexual assault cases from the past two decades.'

No one said anything. Everybody knew that the scaffolding workers, builders, caretakers and security guards they had spent today tracking down were only the first stage in their search. It would have been too good to be true if the attacker was to be found among them – his callousness didn't indicate that. Now they were spreading the net much more widely, and the chance of catching him would increase significantly.

'Please would you call Lennart Jönsson, Axel, and ask him to keep an eye on suicides once we get started? So that our man doesn't commit suicide once the net tightens and we don't hear of it until we get his DNA result?'

The Swede was his responsibility, everybody knew that. What they didn't know was that the two of them currently weren't speaking, but Axel would have to find a way around that. He considered not informing the Swede, because he was certain that the rapist would never consider killing himself. He was far too arrogant for that.

He returned to his office and sat down with the list of unsolved attempted rapes in Nørrebro in the past 10 years, which he had got his colleagues at Bellahøj police station, under which this area of Copenhagen fell, to draw up. He was meeting Ea Holdt in four hours and he was looking forward to it.

But he wasn't looking forward to the meeting he had to set up now. He called the head of Forensic Genetics, Claus Sigurdsson.

'Axel Steen, more whisky?'

'No, I'm afraid not. When are you leaving work today?'

'In just under an hour. And I'm not working late because of you. What's this about?'

'I'll tell you when I get there. I have some questions.'

Claus Sigurdsson listened to him with his elbows resting on the desk and his hands folded under his chin. His sad eyes didn't move at all; they stuck to Axel as he accounted for the attempted rape of 17-year-old Lone Lützhøj in Ballerup in 2004 and the DNA sample from that investigation that matched the DNA of the man who had killed Marie Schmidt and raped Jeanette Kvist and Anne Marie Zeuthen. DNA which for reasons unknown had ended up on Lone Lützhøj, even though they could prove that another man was guilty of the attack on her.

He sat still for a long time before he answered.

'I can't explain it. Either your rapist and killer accidentally bumped into Lone Lützhøj and left his DNA on her—'

'And what are the chances of that?'

'It's possible, of course, but nothing I'll swear to in court.'

'Or?'

'Or the samples were contaminated.'

'What do you mean?'

'I mean that your perpetrator left his DNA on the sample taken from Lone Lützhøj's blouse when he was handling it. Or later.'

'Where?'

'It can happen in many places. At the police station, at the hospital if the girl was examined there, it can happen here and at Forensic Services. It happens a lot. It's impossible to avoid. That's why we keep a record of our own staff members' DNA samples as well as samples from every technician and police officer who attend crime scenes.'

'And?'

'And there was no match at all. We have a staff DNA register. I'm sorry, but I would have known.'

'Does that mean this man's DNA accidentally ended up in a rape case he had nothing to do with?'

'Yes, I can't think of any other explanation.'

'It can't be one of your staff?'

'Good heavens, no. No one gets to work here without giving a DNA sample first. We're very thorough.'

'Any other explanations?'

'I can't see any, but you look as if you can. What are you saying?'

'Is it possible that one of your staff who worked the Marie Schmidt or the Jeanette Kvist case was sloppy and transferred our perpetrator's DNA from those cases to the Lone Lützhøj case by accident?'

'I'm sorry, but you're really clutching at straws here. That's not how it's done. It's impossible. Case samples don't just lie around the lab. They're handled in accordance with extensive safety procedures, precisely so that something like that can never happen.'

'And you're sure of that?'

'Beyond reasonable doubt.'

'Then how do you explain this?'

'I always say that we're the witnesses of a DNA profile – not how it ended up where it did. That's your job. I'm sorry.'

Rather than go straight to his car, Axel took the lift down to the basement to the Swede's office. The big man was wearing a headset and swaying in his chair.

Axel knocked on the door.

Lennart Jönsson looked up, held up a hand and said 'hang on!' His hands danced gently in the air for a little longer. The he took off the headset and said:

'Fredrik Åkare, what can I do for you?'

'Fredrik who?'

'Doesn't matter. It's just a ballad I was listening to. Cornelis.'

'Have you performed Bo Langberg's post-mortem?'

'Yes, I have.'

'And?'

'I haven't received the toxicology report yet, but if it's murder camouflaged as suicide, then it's very well done. There's no evidence of force or violence. The bruises to the side of his torso were several days old.'

'So there's no doubt it was a suicide?'

'No, I don't think so, but let's wait for the toxicology results. He could have been sedated, though I very much doubt it. And even if he had been, there would still have been marks on his body. It's not easy to haul around a man who weighs 80kg and hang him in a noose one metre above the floor without leaving any signs of it, especially to his neck, where the ligature marks were completely clean.'

'OK.'

'You look a little tired. How are things?'

'All right. The case is becoming more complex.'

'I wasn't referring to the case. But to you. How are you? Do you still get high or are you starting to get a grip on yourself?'

'I'm not high or on anything.'

'Have you thought about what I said yesterday when you hung up on me?'

Axel was in need of advice, not a psychologist, but he was unlikely to get the former if he said that out loud.

'Yes, and I'm still thinking.'

'Well, that's a start. So tell me about your case?'

Axel told him the reason for his meeting with Claus Sigurdsson.

'That's bad. Either it's a coincidence, a very, very unlikely coincidence, so unlikely that we don't even operate with it in science, though I've no doubt that a defending lawyer could make something out of it.'

He fell silent. Scratched his chin, fiddled with his tin of chewing tobacco.

'Or your rapist is someone in the system. And that has to be the explanation.'

'But everyone has been tested, according to Claus Sigurdsson.'

'Claus is a big girl's blouse. He would say that, wouldn't he? You have to go to management with this. You need to have it investigated fully. All samples must be re-examined. All staff members must be retested. It would ruin everything if someone on the inside is mixing up DNA profiles while running around the streets raping women. God Almighty, Axel. You've opened Pandora's box here.'

The Swede shook his head.

'Why can't you just occasionally find yourself a nice little case and solve it without upsetting the apple cart? You have to take this to Jens Jessen. It has to be investigated without anyone knowing about it.'

CHAPTER 54

He went home and showered, changed his clothes, shaved. He had tidied up the flat when Emma came last weekend, and it was still clean enough that all he had to do was change the bed linen.

Nørrebrogade was deserted because of the Roskilde Festival. A languid evening mood had descended on Blågårdsgade, the café tables on the pavement were sparsely occupied, greengrocers and butchers still generated a little life in the street, but the sense of an abandoned neighbourhood was everywhere. At Kate's Joint he got a table outside and sat down to wait. Ea Holdt texted him to say that she was running 15 minutes late. He spent the time scrolling through old text messages. Looked about him. Two young immigrants were standing across the street by a café, looking at him, talking on their mobiles. Suddenly they were five, then six, eight of them. And they were all watching him. Too late he recognised one of them as the pipsqueak who had pissed on him in Ørsted Park, now with his arm in plaster.

Axel assessed the situation. Just how outnumbered was he? He could see two really tough guys and then five or six younger ones. They had divided into two groups. He was unarmed. He didn't stand a chance. He opened Ea's text message and quickly wrote 'Stay away. Trouble.' Had time to send it before they went for him. Four guys from two angles, while the rest of them kept a lookout or got ready to join in. He saw the knives. They approached him from the side and front and covered his obvious escape route out of the neighbourhood towards Nørrebrogade. He had to find another way. He bent down as if reaching for a gun concealed on his ankle, which caused them to hesitate for the fraction of a second he needed to hurl the table at the two men closest to him, grab the chair behind him and attack the two others. They had started moving towards him again, but they stopped when he came at them with the chair. He knew that they could tell from the look in his eyes that he intended to hurt them. He threw the chair at them. And ran. Down towards Pladsen. Their home turf. He ran. Turned the corner, up across Pladsen, through the gap into Blågården, out onto Stengade. He ran. And while he ran, he could hear footsteps slamming down on the tarmac behind him. When the hell were they going to give up? They weren't gaining on him. Folkets Park. He saw a cluster of drug dealers with mobiles 100 metres away. When they noticed him, they started running. Cut off his access to Assistens Cemetery. Just when he thought he had lost some of them, another group appeared. Along Stengade towards Nørrebrogade. He ran.

There was shouting. It sounded like there were just two of them now. Should he take them on? He abandoned the idea and ran and ran and ran out of his own city. He hated it, but he ran. Nørrebrogade. The footsteps behind him had ceased. He looked back and saw the reason: a police car had turned up at the other end of Stengade. It would soon be alongside him, but he acted as if everything was fine. He had things to do. And they didn't include reporting threats and an attack. He would deal with that personally. Later. He walked up towards Dronning Louises Bridge. Gasping for air. Glancing over his shoulder. He took out his mobile. Called Ea. No reply.

He stayed on the corner of Fælledvej. Sent her a text message. 'I'm ready now, but we need to find a new place.'

Then he spotted her. She came walking towards him from the Lakes with a cigarette in her hand. Sunglasses, light-coloured chinos, high-heeled sandals and a dark blue shirt with two buttons open. Her bob fitted her head like a brown helmet. He made eye contact with her.

'What's wrong?'

'Oh, nothing.' He grinned and looked over his shoulder. 'Just a little exercise.'

'No really, what's wrong with you? You're acting strange and you're sweating.'

He looked around.

'Strange how?'

'Who are you looking for? What's going on?'

She started looking around too.

'Oh, nothing, I just bumped into some old friends. And then—'

'And then what? What was that text message about?'

'And then we decided to go for a run. Race one another. It doesn't matter.'

'What about our dinner at Kate's?'

'Change of plan. The atmosphere sucked. And they didn't have a table.'

'I haven't got time for this, Axel.'

'Me neither. I promise. I ran into some morons who threatened me. A lot of them. I had to run. I've been looking forward to seeing you. Let's find somewhere else. It's not important.'

He put his arm around her and walked her down the street towards the Lakes. She checked him out.

'You look good. White shirt. It suits you.'

'Yes, it does, doesn't it? Come on, let's go.'

They crossed the bridge. The sky was yellow and orange and red, and the colours reflected in the windows of the mansions buildings on Søtorvet that rose imperiously towards the city with their spires, towers and mansard roofs.

'How is the hunt coming along?'

'Slow and steady, but not quite as I had expected.'

He couldn't tell her about the contaminated DNA. And he needed to forget about the case, the rapist who was out there somewhere. And the Blackbird investigation.

There was a light and bright scent about Ea Holdt. Her hair had a faint reddish tint, it was silky and kept slipping in front of her cheek and eyes. At regular intervals she would raise a hand and tuck it behind her ear. Only for it to slip forwards again. She smiled when she saw him notice it.

'So where are we going to eat? We could try something new Nordic? Fancy that?'

'I'm not a huge fan of bladder wrack and wild garlic. I know a super place in Nansensgade where they do great couscous, how about that?'

'Hmm, that sounds a little heavy, can we meet halfway. Sticks'n'sushi. Do you like sushi?'

Axel hated raw fish, but he felt he had used up his quota of alternatives, and so he smiled. It was fine.

They walked down three steps and got a table at the back.

She ordered sushi, he ordered a platter labelled 'Food for men' consisting of different types of meat on small skewers. Beer.

They talked about the Roskilde Festival. To Axel's enormous surprise, she was going there tomorrow.

'I'm there every year. I volunteer as a stage guard.'

'Are you having me on?'

'No, I've been doing it for 15 years. It was how I met Jakob, the children's father. We're a group of old friends who go there every year for the weekend where we work and party.'

Axel thought about old friends. Did he have any apart from a surly old Swede? Yes, but he had to go back a long way to find them. He felt envious, or was he jealous of her ex-husband? Could he be more primitive?

'It sounds interesting. I've only been there once when I was 20.'

'Yes, you're more the melancholic jazz type,' she laughed.

He laughed as well. No one had ever called him that before. He looked about him.

'So what did you want to talk to me about?'

She fiddled around with something that looked like green pea pods and removed the green beans one by one while she mulled it over.

'The other day. When you left. It was as if you had turned into someone else. As if you had closed the door to something.'

'I was a bit stressed, distracted by my investigation.'

'Yes, and your ex-wife's phone call. But there was more. I might be wrong, but I've thought about you, and I see you—'

'As what?'

'As someone who never emerges fully. Or someone who disappears. Our night. You were so close to me. That morning too. And now. You're closed up. Won't you come out? From in there. I don't bite. I really like being with you. I really like you. It's as if I can feel you, and then I can't feel you, as if you become visible, and then there's just a shadow.'

He was saved by the waiter bringing two rectangular plates of food. Everything was so attractive and stylish. He felt out of place and under pressure.

'I do want to,' he heard himself say. He didn't know where that had come from or where he would go from here.

She placed her hand on his and looked at him.

'But you are here. I can feel you through your job, your calling, all the feelings you invest in it. I like that it gets under your skin, but I imagine it must be tough.'

'What do you do?'

'I detach myself. You have to when you deal with violence. I don't think about what they were subjected to, I think about them as people.

I can't allow myself to be ruled by my emotions. It's OK if it fuels you, but I guess it can also be dangerous.'

They ate. He talked about the case, about how they would be announcing a major manhunt tomorrow morning, and that he thought they were close to catching him. But he could feel that her interest was waning, and eventually she interrupted him and said:

'How do you feel about a perpetrator like him?'

'I don't feel anything about him.'

'But doesn't it affect you when you know what they have done?'

Axel didn't want to carry on in the direction she was steering their conversation.

'I don't think of them like that.'

'How very professional,' she said ironically.

'OK. I regard them as weeds that must be pulled up. And when I look at what happened to Jeanette Kvist, I don't think any punishment is too harsh. On the contrary. Far too many punishments aren't harsh enough.'

'How about the old police motto: You hunt an animal, but catch a human being. Do you believe in that?'

'Humanity in this guy? He's not a human being I have any kind of understanding of or feel any compassion towards. What's your point? Your job is to take care of the victims, and now you sit here playing the bleeding-heart liberal.'

She snorted with her mouth full of sushi, spraying grains of rice onto Axel's shirt, and that made her laugh even more. She tried to apologise at the same time, shielding her mouth with the back of her hand and nodding repeatedly while she finished chewing.

'No, I'm not, but my job also gives me an insight into the mind of the perpetrator. And this has taught me that there are no evil people. There are, however, all too many losers. Children who drew the short straw from the second they were born. It doesn't have to be beatings with a leather strap and rapes. Human coldness and neglect are enough. And you always find that in the perpetrators' backgrounds.'

'Says who?'

'Says I. Says the cases.'

'Says the perpetrator himself. To the police. And to the court-appointed psychiatrists. And when he's in court. Because he thinks it'll reduce his sentence. And because your colleagues tell him so. If we told people their sentence would be reduced if they joined the Jehovah's Witnesses, they would do it.'

She laughed out loud.

'Your cynicism is alive and kicking.'

'I've seen it too many times. The criminal's actions speak for themselves, they speak louder than any words he can say. It's as with everything else in life. Their words are just… words. And their actions demand a response that is effective and understood. And they don't get that from us feeling sorry for them because they had an unhappy childhood.'

'What does that mean?'

'It means making them see that their actions have consequences. For people other than themselves. And they have to pay for that.'

'What with? Their life?'

He was unsure. Most killers were just wretches caught in the high beams of the car crash that was their life. At one moment in time they would do something seemingly logical that turned out to be fatal – but there was also another type, the planner, the sexual predator. And there were grey zones and exceptions. And he was fed up with the conversation.

'Child killers, offenders who enjoy and are turned on by their victims' terror and helplessness. They have to be removed. First we need to get them off the streets. But ultimately I feel that they deserve to burn in hell for what they've done. All that bullshit about rehabilitation and starting over, you can stick that up your arse as long as it's their victims who are paying the price. You know the cases. When it comes to the worst of them. I feel that—'

'…that they should die, be exterminated?'

He had no answer. She shook her head faintly. He could see that he had said too much, been too brutal. And he did have doubts, but he wasn't going to dissimulate in front of her.

'I don't know.'

Was she shaken? She stared into the air for some time, then said:

'I have a younger brother.'

'Yes. I have a few of those too.' He smiled. She didn't.

'Mine is in jail.'

'What for?'

'Possession of child pornography.'

Axel fell silent. Was that what all this was really about?

'He's not evil. He gets turned on by looking at pictures of young children being abused by adults.'

'Has he himself…?'

'Fiddled with anyone? No, not that I know of. He has described it as a kind of obsession. Once he started downloading the images, it just carried on and on and on. He couldn't stop. He sat in front of his computer collecting and swapping images for two months until the police came knocking on his door. He was sentenced to one year in jail.'

'How do you feel about it?'

'Terrible.'

'Are you in contact with him?'

'Yes, I am. I know him, I remember him, I know what he was subjected to as a child. And I know who he is essentially. He's not evil. Of course he has to be punished, but it doesn't do him any good. Now he's in Herstedvester with all the other sex offenders, and I'm sure he gets plenty of good ideas in there. The alternative is a different prison where the other inmates would beat him up. Is that the kind of justice you're looking for?'

Axel looked at her. He had no answer. The truth was he was measured and rational towards most criminals, but the sexual murders of children and women or aggravated stranger rapes ate him up from the inside.

'If we merely punish and torture those who commit the assaults, it'll never end. It's the only thing they know, and it doesn't cure them,' she said.

'Do you think they can be cured?'

'My younger brother, yes, I think he could. And most of the others, yes.'

'And if they can't be, if they get out and commit fresh assaults, do we just start all over again?'

'Yes.'

'I thought you were on the side of the victims.'

'I am. All victims.'

She pushed a lock of hair away from her forehead, but her finger carried on repeating the movement without any hair to move. She continued:

'Sometimes I feel like you do. In my gut. I haven't forgiven my stepfather for what he did to us, or my mother for letting it happen.' She fell silent and slipped away, then she came back, and Axel knew exactly how it looked, the place where she had been. 'Why don't we go outside for a cigarette?' she said.

They went out into the street. People sitting outside looked at her. He could see why. She lit a cigarette. She looked at him in a way that ached all the way down to his stomach.

'It's possible that my choice of career, my view of offenders and victims, is my way of containing my own experiences.'

The light summer mood was gone and Axel felt queasy. He wasn't a cold-hearted avenger, but he had feelings that came to the surface when he was confronted with the most evil criminals. He felt pressured by her openness, it was almost too much. A joint would calm him now. Ea Holdt drained her beer glass and smoked while she glanced around. Then she looked straight at him again with a clear, slightly challenging expression.

'When you say that the worst of them don't deserve to live or should be exterminated—'

'That's not what I said—'

'No, but that was what you meant, wasn't it? I can follow you emotionally. I think the worst are parents who abuse and rape their own children. In a way that's worse than everything else, it's crossing the final line, it's the ultimate betrayal of someone who trusts you unconditionally. Sadly, it's all too common.'

Axel pondered what she had told him about her childhood the last time they were together. It made sense in the middle of this pointless discussion that he normally never entered into. He was all about the chase. If he focused on the perpetrator's wickedness, he couldn't devote all his energy to capturing him. And that was ultimately his goal and his fuel, but could he really swear that he didn't feel like taking the life of the sickest bastards?

They went back inside. Axel wanted to pay, but she insisted that it was her turn. They took a taxi back to his place.

She left her jacket in the hall, and he followed her as she strolled into the bedroom, where she unbuttoned her shirt slowly, looking up at him.

'Will you give me a guided tour afterwards?' she grinned.

Kisses. Skin against skin against lips against lips. Eyes very close. Without seeing. He lay on top of her. Slipped inside her. Squelching juices. Movements like waves. Quietly and gently. She pulled up her legs and locked them around his back, and she held him, held his shoulders and turned her face towards him, and he felt her open lips on his cheek, wandering across it, teeth and tongue, and she kissed him, her body underneath him, her thighs, shins, heels, her skin, her hips, her breasts, all of her, while her cunt tightened around him until he couldn't hold back any longer, and it crawled up inside him from every place, a huge, grotesque sense of relief, growing, spilling over. He screamed. He came.

Her hand in his hair. His head on her shoulder. The last thing he was aware of was that he was drooling.

CHAPTER 55

Jens Jessen was standing on Hornbæk beach, watching the sun go down over the fiery Kattegat. He had received Cecilie's mobile phone records. Calls and text messages to Axel Steen's mobile in the last six months. Was it many or few for a divorced couple with a six-year-old daughter? They spoke every other day! That was too much, considering how frosty Cecilie claimed their relationship was. But what should he do with the information? And what did it all mean?

Was he losing her? He found it harder than usual to read her signals. He didn't want it to be true, but something was definitely wrong.

Axel Steen had flown to The Hague three times to pick up his daughter. Every time he had spent an unnecessary amount of time between his arrival and departure. Jens had asked Cecilie if she had met with him.

'No, are you mad? Why would I waste time on that idiot?'

But was she telling the truth? Could he trust a woman who had been unfaithful to her husband for five months before she confessed and demanded a divorce? And what was the real reason for the five months? Was she road-testing me? Had it been ice-cold calculation? Did she want to see if I would make the grade as a stepfather and future husband? If I was interested in reproduction and had fatherhood potential? What about love?

Stop it now. He hated himself. Cecilie had never given him cause for anything other than trust. And here he was drowning in acid-green jealousy. Paranoid because of that bloody Axel Steen, whom he had even promised her to shield for Emma's sake. Christ Almighty, what was going on?

Axel had called him earlier that evening. As if things weren't bad enough already. Jealousy, hash and now suspects who hanged themselves? Trust Axel Steen to create a shitstorm. He had called about one of those things Jens hated most of all. Evidence in a rape case that pointed internally. Ultimately the attacker might not prove to be one of their own, but mistakes had been made somewhere. And they were dangerous mistakes. He had quickly analysed the possibilities. And they were as follows: either it was a grotesque, almost impossible coincidence that a man responsible for five rapes and the murder of Marie Schmidt had accidentally transferred his DNA to another victim, one he hadn't raped. It was bordering on the unthinkable, but he already considered this scenario as a possible explanation, if they couldn't keep the matter in-house. The other possibility was that staff handling the DNA had been sloppy with the samples and cross-contaminated them. The thought made him shiver with cold in the heat. It would undermine confidence in the entire system. Defence lawyers would milk it for years to come. The thought was unbearable. The third possibility was that the perpetrator was one of their own – someone who had come into contact with the DNA samples as part of his job and left his DNA on it by chance. This was just as bad. In fact, it was catastrophic. And so he had had to draw his sword and face the knight of justice, the truth-hungry Axel fucking Steen.

'We need to keep this secret from everyone. If it's one of our own, it could undermine the whole system,' he had said to him.

'Is that all you care about?' Axel had responded.

'And is all you care about wreaking havoc? What will you do if the public stops trusting the uniform? Or our procedures? If every rapist and killer you catch is set free by the courts because we've been compromised? Don't you believe in the value of your own work? Don't you believe that we're doing a good job?'

'Yes, but I don't believe we should cover up our mistakes.'

'How can you say that? You of all people? You bet we should. I'm thoroughly fed up with your chronic opposition to everything. Don't you understand? This is about more than you and me, and what we're working on right now. This is about trust. If we lose trust in the system, it's the end of everything.'

'Boo-hoo.'

'So you'll investigate this with the utmost discretion, do you hear me? Or there will be consequences.' He paused, but Axel said nothing. Jens could sense his contempt right into his ear. 'You're a brilliant police officer, but surely even you can see that this is something we need to keep very quiet about. If you refuse, I'll have you suspended right now.'

There had been silence on the other end of the handset. Then the reply had come completely deadpan:

'I'll find him – no matter where he is. The rest is your problem.'

'You find him. And I'll handle everything relating to the DNA samples, are we clear?'

It had been liberating to shout at someone, especially at Axel Steen, who was doing precisely what? Was he busy stealing his girlfriend? But there was nothing liberating about the reason for his call. It was a curse.

CHAPTER 56

Axel woke up in the dark with a jolt. The nightmare. The hunter and the hunted. Every time he reached his prey, the dogs caught up with him. He had screamed. He sat up. He was scared. Wet and cold. A hand on his arm. He snatched back his arm. And stared at her.

'What is it?'

He knew things were bad. He was going to pieces, it was as if there was only a thin membrane between him and some unknown and inexplicable insanity where everything would dissolve. He needed that joint now. Why the hell had he thrown it out?

'What's wrong, Axel?'

He swung his legs out of bed. The heat was unbearable. What had they talked about last night after making love? They had shared a bottle of wine, got a little tipsy, she had told him about her childhood, she had called him an Old Testament eye-for-an-eye, tooth-for-a-tooth avenger. But with a smile. Was that a problem, he wanted to know.

'No. I have a good feeling about you, of something good, that you want to do good. But I can't accept revenge. I understand the feeling, but I think it's wrong. And I would never be able to live with someone who crossed that line.'

He had tried to screw and then sleep the feeling away, but she had got to him. So much purity, so much decency. He couldn't cope.

She sat up in bed, put her arm around him.

'What is it?'

'The cases, the details, they live inside me. All the time. When you say that you don't think about all the things your clients were subjected to… I can't imagine that.'

He shifted away from her.

'I do think about it. But the details, they don't interest me. I keep away from them.'

'They interest me. I can't afford to ignore them. I can't allow myself that luxury.'

'No, but—'

And then it came. It was one of those conversations that just spiralled into the darkness as if he was programmed with a script from hell – the victims, the abuse and the bodies came tumbling out from the darkest recesses of his mind.

'Let's start with the man I visited on Monday in Herstedvester. He raped a 10-year-old girl last year. After two previous convictions. I want to smash him. She was only 10, Ea. She was tied to a bed and raped by a 29-year-old man, who bit into the breasts she didn't have, who shoved a toothbrush and a bottle up inside her, pissed on her, licked her and called her 'my little sweetheart' while he abused her. Afterwards he left her there. Tied up. Unconscious. If someone hadn't found her by accident, she would have died. And you're telling me that they're all human beings.'

She wanted to say something, but he didn't let her speak. He reeled them off. Details from 10 years of working with homicide. Precise and visceral details, which for him was wickedness written in flesh and blood. A jet of tar he vomited all over her. He didn't know for how long he had been speaking, shouting, ranting. But when he stopped, she was crying.

He lit a cigarette. Daylight had started creeping in between the blinds.

'You're so raw. It's as if you're enjoying telling me this. The details you pick out.' She shook her head. 'It's as if you don't care at all.'

'You said you wanted to feel me.'

'I don't believe that's the real you, Axel. I think I got too close to you. That's OK. But you have to look after yourself. So it doesn't eat you up, so it doesn't end up infecting you. Because if it does, if we become victims of our emotions when we deal with those people – and they are people – then we become like them. And I can't and won't accept that.'

'But we are like them, you say. They are people. So what's the problem?'

'Fuck you, you idiot. I've experienced what the victims were subjected to on my own body. I don't need your pain. It's OK that I got too close, but it's not all right for you to hurt me, to mock me like that.'

She got up and started picking up her clothes. He couldn't do anything other than sit there staring into space. Avoid her eyes. Wait until she was gone.

CHAPTER 57

Friday, 4 July

He was in his office at 6am, reviewing first the Blackbird case and then the attempted rape of the 17-year-old girl in 2004, for which Max Arno Anborg Peters had gone to prison. He wanted to make a list of every police officer who had been present during the investigation of both cases, and anyone who could theoretically have left DNA traces in connection with the investigation. Afterwards he wanted to find out which staff members at the Juliane Marie Rape Crisis Centre had been working on the day the girl had been examined. Jens Jessen had contacted Claus Sigurdsson and the head of Forensic Services and asked them for lists of every employee since 2004 – every staff member, and not just those who had worked directly on investigations – so they could check if any staff could have come into contact with the evidence. Once they had the finished lists, Jens Jessen would draft a letter ostensibly from Forensic Genetics, explaining there was a problem with the register and that they had to ask a number of employees to make themselves available for a new DNA test. Then they would run them manually through the system to see if any of them matched the perpetrator's profile. It could take weeks.

Claus Sigurdsson and the head of Forensic Services had been told the true reason and had accepted it. Jens Jessen had stressed yet again that it was crucial to keep this investigation under wraps.

Axel's list comprised 89 named colleagues. In the attempted rape of 17-year-old Lone Lützhøj, that number was 11, but in the Blackbird case they had cast the net wide and numerous police officers had worked the case in the early days. It was unlikely that many of them had been in contact with Marie Schmidt's clothing, but Axel was taking no chances. In order to find the names he had gone through the crime scene log with a fine-tooth comb. And one name kept recurring. His own. Yet again he was reminded of the worst day of his life. He would have to relive it soon. Maybe try to talk to Cecilie about it. About his... betrayal. But it also reminded him that he might now be further away from solving the murder of Marie Schmidt than he had ever been. Because seeing as DNA from the perpetrator of the five rapes had also been found in the case of attempted rape of a 17-year-old, whether by accident or due to an error, it might also be an accident or an error that had cause it to end up on Marie Schmidt's leaver's cap. The thought made him feel sick. He promised himself that no matter what happened, he wouldn't shelve the case this time. As he did the last time. From one day to the next. He owed it. If to no one else, then he owed it to himself. And Marie Schmidt.

As expected, the DNA sample tested positive. The man who had raped Ida Højgaard had also raped Jeanette Kvist and Anne Marie Zeuthen. And the technical evidence linked him to the rapes of Line Jørgensen and Lulu Linette Larsen. The same man had smashed up the lives of five women and possibly killed Marie Schmidt.

Darling had called a 10am press briefing in the colonnade facing Polititorvet. The media had been issued with an embargoed press release, so they knew what was coming. The place was packed. There were TV, radio, every newspaper, several reporters from every outlet. The silly season was well and truly over. It was breaking news. A serial rapist was at large in the capital, they had DNA evidence of at least five aggravated rapes, and there was more than that, Darling said, but refused to specify what that was, 'until we have finished all the technical examinations,' as he put it.

Darling spent the entire day in front of rolling cameras and reporters making notes. Calls started pouring in at HQ. As early as noon more than 100 people had called with tip-offs and information. It was pandemonium. Some people had seen something, others suspected an unknown person, some gave names, quite a few ex-girlfriends called to say that it was the sort of thing 'he' might well get up to.

Police officers had forms with five questions about the attacker. Name? Age? Address? Height? Why do you think it's him? The plan was to visit every man whose name matched the age criteria. If a man was under 1.5 m or over 2 m tall, there was no need to test him. But this wasn't all the hotline had to deal with. Some called about rapes or attempted rapes they had never reported, and they were noted down and a team of investigators began to look into them.

The hunt had begun and it made Axel forget last night, his thoughts, his fears, everything that was caving in on him and screaming at him that he had to do something about his life, all of that was set aside. He launched himself into doing what he did best.

The forms with details of potential suspects were passed on to Axel, Bjarne Olsen, Tine Jensen, Tonny Hansen and Vicki Thomsen as they arrived. They were prioritised, several could be eliminated quickly, quite a few were dubious but couldn't be written off altogether, and eventually they had a pile of 35 out of the first 100 calls. At 2pm they set off in separate teams.

Axel drove with Vicki Thomsen. 12 names. Two of the men didn't meet the height requirement and one weighed 150kg, which he was unlikely to have gained in the few days that had passed since the rape of Ida Højgaard. Many of them had heard about the case and were deeply offended that someone had pointed the finger at them, but nobody refused to give a DNA sample. And if they even so much as hinted at that, then Vicki Thomsen would make it clear to them that the alternative was being charged with rape and a visit to HQ. No one was interested in that option.

At 5pm they pulled up in front of a house in Brønshøj. It was rented by a man called Mark Lira Poulsen. They had got his name from a woman who had called in to say it could be him. An ex-girlfriend. He was into rough sex, she had said, and he had acted out a rape fantasy with her several times; it had frightened her because he seemed as if he had tried it before. According to the Office for Civil Registration Numbers, he was 41 years old. He had been convicted of three counts of vehicle theft in the early 1990s and charged with assault in 1993, but the case had been dropped.

They knocked on the door, which was opened immediately by a man slightly shorter than Axel. He had strawberry blond, very short hair, pale blue eyes, very blond eyebrows and eyelashes that made his face look bland and colourless. He studied them closely, first Axel, then Vicki, then he smiled – it wasn't a hostile smile, but neither was it warm.

'Let me guess. Jehovah's Witnesses or the police?'

Nor was his voice hoarse. His chest was pushed out as if he was holding his breath, he wore a thin gold chain around his neck, his body language was guarded.

'Copenhagen Police,' Vicki said. 'As you may have heard in the media—'

'I haven't heard anything.'

'…we're requesting DNA samples in our hunt for a serial rapist who has been active in Nørrebro for the last 12 years.'

There was no reaction to be detected in his face.

'Well, that sounds like a very worthwhile thing to do, but what do you want from me?'

'We have had hundreds of tip-offs and one of them was about you. We would like your permission to take a DNA sample so you can be eliminated from our enquiries.'

'Who reported me?'

'No one has reported you, but your name was mentioned in connection with a tip-off. We're looking into everything.'

'What did they say about me?'

'I can't tell you that because I don't know. We're just here to ask for the DNA sample. And even if I did know, I wouldn't be allowed to tell you.'

He didn't say anything.

'So please can we have the sample?'

'I don't see any reason for that.'

'If you don't cooperate, we'll have to charge you with rape and force you to give us the sample.'

'I don't intend to obstruct you, of course, but I'm concerned about civil liberties, and I regard this as an intrusion into my personal freedom.'

Axel got involved:

'I know five girls who can tell you all about intrusion into their personal freedom. They were tied up and raped by a psycho. He didn't ask them for permission. So do we get going or would you like a trip to HQ?'

The man looked him as if he were the dirt under his shoe.

'Yes. All right. Come in.'

They entered a house practically stripped of furniture.

Vicki Thomsen looked about her.

'Have you just moved in?'

'No, I've lived here for a while.'

Mark Lira Poulsen let Vicki Thomsen take the mouth swab. His eyes followed Axel the whole time. In the centre of the living room was a steel desk with a tower computer, printer and other hardware – Axel thought it was a hard disk, a scanner and photo equipment. Blinds

305

covered the windows. A 24-inch flat screen which was on, showing TV2News, dumbbells, a hammock, a football poster with FCK's 2007 Premier League team and an old leather sofa.

'Was that it?' Mark Lira Poulsen wanted to know, and Axel tried to put himself in his shoes. If he was the killer, he would be on red alert right now, shocked that his life of crime now had an expiry date. He would want to get rid of the police as quickly as he could, so that he could assess his situation and explore the chances of getting off the hook. There were no options. Mark Lira Poulsen, however, didn't appear to be thinking along those lines. He seemed completely calm.

He signed the FTA card.

'Anything else?'

Vicki thanked him and Mark Lira Poulsen walked them to the hall. Just as they were leaving, Axel turned around.

'Just a moment. We haven't finished. I want to ask you about some dates.'

And that was when he saw it. Something furious and cold that slipped past the man's gaze before he managed to control it.

'Is this a formal interview?' Mark Lira Poulsen said, his voice slightly raised.

'You can call it what you will. And you can drop the offended act. We're not doing this to harass you, but to solve a crime, and it could help eliminate you.'

He bowed his head and showed them back inside.

'So what do you want to know?'

'Have you always lived in Copenhagen?'

'No, I've also lived in Helsingør.'

'Where did you live from the age of 18?'

'Different places in Copenhagen, Amager and Nørrebro.'

'How long did you live in Nørrebro?'

'Until six months ago. For 15 years.'

'Where were you in the summer of 2003?'

'I don't know. In Copenhagen, I think. I like the Danish summer.'

Just then the TV2 news anchor said: 'Copenhagen Police are asking the public for help with their investigation into five rapes so far. Our reporter, Dorte Neergaard, is at Police HQ, but first here's a summary of this very unusual and distressing case...'

Mark Lira Poulsen glanced at the screen and then looked back at them. His face was completely devoid of expression. The story had been on the news all day and he must have heard of it.

'What about the summer of 2004. Were you in Copenhagen then?'

'Yes, I was.'

'Late June 2004. Where were you then?'

An illustration came up on the screen listing the five rapes. Years and dates. Nobody in the living room said anything. Mark Lira Poulsen looked at Axel, who stayed silent while the news anchor reviewed the cases. Mark Lira Poulsen's face was completely unreadable, but he had picked up that the year 2004 hadn't figured in the review on the news.

'Why do you want to know about 2004?'

Axel didn't take his eyes off him for one second.

'Because a woman was murdered in Ørsted Park by the same man who committed the five rapes. Marie Schmidt. Aged 18. Raped and strangled.'

'I don't know anything about that,' he said, but Axel detected something in his eyes. It looked like fear – for the first time, he showed something almost resembling emotion when confronted with the murder. The ultimate crime.

They went over the two most recent dates and his alibi. He accounted for his whereabouts. He worked from home providing support for an IT firm, and had no alibi for the two nights this year when the women had been raped, but he believed that the log on his computer could document that he had been at home at the times in question.

Vicki Thomsen seized her moment when Axel fell silent.

'What about your criminal past? Have you put it behind you?'

'I was just a kid back then. I fell in with bad company. I stole a couple of cars. I haven't done anything since.'

'There was the assault,' Axel said.

'I was charged, but the charges were dropped. Does that still make it a case of assault?'

'It does to me. Do you find it hard to control your temper?'

'No, does it seem like it?'

No, it doesn't, Axel thought, and for an innocent man you're very difficult to provoke and so you fit our profile to a T.

'I wouldn't want to comment on that after only knowing you for 20 minutes.'

'I haven't been in conflict with the law since.'

He escorted them out. In the hallway Axel turned around again. Looked him right in the eye with the coldest stare he could muster.

'Have you ever raped a woman?'

The man was completely unruffled when he said:

'No, I wouldn't dream of it.'

'That's not what I hear,' Axel then said.

'We'll be in touch,' Vicki said.

'How soon?'

'In just under a week.'

'Goodbye.'

'Bye for now.'

'Yuck, he was creepy,' Vicki said as they got back in the car.

'Yes, he was. And he lied about not knowing about the case. And he fits the description. Do you think he reacted when I mentioned Marie Schmidt?'

'Yes, he reacted, I just don't quite know how. Because otherwise he didn't react at all. He was completely cold. Seriously creepy.'

But so are many people. Axel's gut feeling told him that Mark Lira Poulsen could easily be their man. But then again, he might just be a callous, unpleasant individual. He decided to investigate him further.

They returned to HQ. Mark Lira Poulsen wasn't the only man who had attracted their attention, but they agreed that they had to collate all the names, submit the DNA samples and then wait. When Axel entered his office there was post. He had asked the National Police for the files of the three unsolved homicides that investigators from other police forces had mentioned when he sent them his MO email last week. Now the case summaries had arrived in three removal crates on the floor.

Vicki Thomsen entered.

'I thought that went well. What do you think? Is that how we're going to catch him?'

'I don't know. I never bet on things like that, but he's our best offer. For now.'

'What does that mean? Will we get a better one?'

Axel was sure there would be another chance once the staff DNA tests had been carried out, but he couldn't say anything about that to her. It was like sitting on a ticking time bomb. If the man they had now asked the public for help in finding turned out to be working for the police here or for Forensic Services, there would be a huge outcry. He could imagine the headlines. But it wasn't his responsibility – it was for Jens Jessen to clear up.

'No, but if we don't get him this way, we soldier on. Then we have to find him some other way.'

Vicki Thomsen looked at the summaries.

'Old homicides?'

'Yes.'

'Unsolved?'

'Yes.'

'You're still looking for him?'

'Yes.'

'Why?'

'Because I think he's there somewhere.'

'But aren't five aggravated sexual assaults enough?'

'Not if he's a killer.'

'And that's what you're hoping?'

'Yes.'

'Why do you say if? Do you have doubts?'

'No.'

'But there's nothing in the rape cases to suggest it, is there?'

'No.'

'So those cases, they're your link to Marie Schmidt?'

'Yes.'

'Is that what you really care about? You're not going after the rapes. You want Marie Schmidt's killer.'

'Yes.'

'What is it about you and that case?'

'I couldn't solve it.'

'But there has to be more to it. Tine clams up whenever I ask her about it.'

He looked up at her.

'That case blew up in my face. Everything blew up. And that's your therapy session done for the day. Anything else you and I need to talk about?'

She held up her hands.

'No, that's it for today. Will I see you tomorrow?'

'Yes, early tomorrow morning.'

Axel looked down at the three crates. It would take him the whole weekend to work through them. But he had other plans.

CHAPTER 58

Axel drove home and changed his clothes. Hoodie. Sunglasses. Jeans. Trainers. He had received an email from Forensic Services about the two red wine glasses found in Bo Langberg's kitchenette. The deceased man's finger and lip prints were on both. That didn't surprise Axel. If it wasn't a suicide but a camouflaged murder, it would have been incredibly carefully executed, and the killer wouldn't have been so careless as to leave potential DNA evidence on a red wine glass. This line of enquiry would now stand or fall with the toxicology tests.

He walked down the street and sat on the kerb, waiting for it to get dark. He smoked two cigarettes. As the swallows dive-bombed around the church spire and night began to colour the light blue sky, he went to his car and drove to Brønshøjvej. He parked 50 metres from Mark Lira Poulsen's house and waited. It was 10.30pm, there was no moon, and the darkness was dense enough for him to sit in his car without anyone noticing him.

A text message. It was Jens Jessen: 'Call me.'

He looked towards the house. He could see the blue glow of a TV, but no movement. He made the call. In the background he could hear someone laugh. Was it Cecilie?

'Yes, hello. Axel. Hang on a minute… I'll have the staff lists from Forensic Genetics and Pathology tomorrow. I've already had them from Forensic Services. I just wanted to ask you who should carry out the tests. I've an old PET colleague, Henriette Nielsen, remember her?'

'Yes, and that's a bad idea. You have to get someone in-house to do it so no one gets suspicious. It should be someone who started working for us after 2004, and therefore couldn't have caused the contamination. And someone you trust completely.'

'I don't know anyone I trust completely.'

'It must look as if it's pure routine, and it has to be someone who won't talk. Ask BB, he must know a colleague who can do it. Also, it seems less conspicuous if it's someone from Forensic Services who collects the samples.'

'I get you. I'll do it Monday morning.'

'It needs to happen quickly. You must get Claus Sigurdsson to speed things up. If the perpetrator is one of our own, then he'll have been alarmed by the press coverage, and anything could happen.'

More laughter in the background. Cecilie's voice: 'Jens, are you coming, Jens?' It sounded as if he removed the telephone from his mouth and said something which included Axel's name.

'Yes, Axel?'

'Anything else?' Axel wanted to know.

'Yes, there is, as it happens.' The background noise was gone – Jens Jessen must have stepped into another room. 'We have unfinished business. When can I come with you again?'

'I'm going out collecting DNA samples tomorrow.'

'Great. I'll come with you.'

'It's going to be dull.'

The light went out in Mark Lira Poulsen's house.

'I have to go now.'

'What's happening? Are you out on a recce?'

Recce, God help us. Did he still think he was with PET?

'I'm out on a job. We'll have to organise this later.'

'What job?' he heard Jens Jessen say before he ended the call.

Mark Lira Poulsen appeared, pushing his bike. He was wearing running clothes, a bum bag around his waist. He got up and rode his bike towards Axel without even looking at him. In his rear-view mirror Axel saw him continue down towards Brønshøj Torv. Axel started the car and turned it around. Followed him calmly. Mark Lira Poulsen riding his bike presented a problem. There were many places where Axel couldn't follow him in a car without drawing attention to himself, especially if he cycled to Nørrebro, where much of the neighbourhood had been turned into a nightmare of one-way streets.

Lira, as Axel had already nicknamed him, turned right at Brønshøj Torv and headed into Copenhagen. Axel watched him while he waited for the lights to change to green. Then he drove around the corner and down Frederikssundvej, a depressing straight stretch of road with a car breaker's yard, a Turkish pizzeria, boarded-up shops, a second-hand bookshop whose display hadn't changed for years, then on to Bellahøj. He saw the city in front of him, a sea of flickering light and life. Lira stopped before the Bellahøj junction, drove up onto the pavement and got off his bike. Axel had to abandon his car immediately. Lira was in no hurry, but calmly crossed the cobblestone and walked down a path between the tower blocks. Axel locked his car and half ran after him. The area between the blocks was open, so he could follow him at a distance of 100 metres. Lira got back on his bike and rode slowly through the Bellahøj estate, then disappeared behind a house where the path curved. Axel caught up and saw Lira disappear behind the estate into the green open space and marsh area behind it.

He spotted him 100 metres further down the path. Axel walked calmly. If Lira was out hunting lone women, he would be checking for other people in the area, so Axel couldn't get too close to him, but neither could he be too far away should he suddenly change direction. He saw him get off the bike and lean it up against a bench. Axel retreated behind a tree. Lira began his stretching exercises. An old man came walking with his dog behind Axel's back. He looked at Axel with an angry face as if he were the new media bogeyman, 'the scaffolding man' as their perpetrator had been nicknamed by the online press. Oh, if only you knew, grandad.

Lira continued his stretching on the bench. Then he sat down and lit a cigarette. Axel felt tense all over.

Five minutes later, Lira locked his bike and started walking further along the path and in between the trees. Axel followed him. He lost sight of him, then he reappeared. He tried to follow Lira, but then he disappeared in between the trees once more. Axel jogged towards the spot he had last seen him, but he was gone. He waited for a while. He couldn't risk bumping into him. Lira would recognise him immediately. Then he would know they were on to him. All he could do was wait and listen. Lira could be hiding behind any of the trees in the thicket in front of him. Axel looked at the branches, touched some birch leaves, which were crisp and dry. He couldn't bear staying where he was, so he withdrew behind some trees, into the darkness in order for his eyes to get used to it. Then he moved through the bushes as softly as he could. He listened out. What was that noise? Moaning, whimpering? He stood very still. It sounded like a woman whimpering. He ran towards the sound. He stopped. He listened out again. It was coming from the thicket 20 metres away from him. He stormed towards it.

The back of a man in the process of taking a woman from behind. She was naked from the waist down and panting. Axel pulled the man away, but saw instantly that it wasn't Lira.

'What the fuck are you doing?' the man exclaimed. He was young. The woman barely 20.

'What's going on, Niels?' she said.

Axel grunted an apology.

'I'm a police officer. I thought you were being raped.'

The woman tried to cover herself up.

'She's my girlfriend, you idiot,' the man said. He sounded shocked.

Axel ran from the thicket. Then he started to walk. He pulled up his hood. He was tense. He had to relax or he would end up making a mess of this. He reached the clearing and continued until he reached the open-air theatre. He looked around the amphitheatre's semicircle of rows of grass seats. Lira sat smoking in the last row furthest away from him.

Axel asked himself if the rape victims had smelled smoke on their attacker. No one had mentioned it. He turned around and walked back, then zigzagged behind the trees until he found a spot from where he could watch Lira, who was sitting very still. Had he noticed him?

20 minutes passed. Lira smoked another cigarette. Then he got up and walked in between the trees. And was gone. Axel stepped out close to the open-air stage, and ran along the trees. He walked in between them in the same place as Lira, but the man was nowhere to be seen. Axel stopped. Was he here? Right next to him? Or was he stalking the area, hoping to bump into a lone woman? He heard a car pass by on Bellahøjvej. But there was no sign of Lira. He searched the bushes in between the trees several times before giving up and conceding that he had lost him. He wandered around for half an hour. He met a young woman hurrying through the green area. He decided to follow her at a distance. She was Lira's target group. Prey that could attract the predator. She glanced over her shoulder and Axel wondered what it must be like to be a woman alone in a dark place, feeling scared. Surely it must be even worse to be home alone in your flat, safe and relaxed, and suddenly be confronted with a man in your living room? He knew that most rape victims soon moved away from the place they were raped, and that none of them ever felt safe in their home again.

The young woman disappeared out into the road by Degnemose Allé.

He walked back to the place where Lira had left his bike. It was still there.

315

15 minutes later Lira reappeared. Running. Maybe he really was just a runner.

Axel hurried back to his car. He drove down to the junction by Bellahøj Lido. Saw Lira emerge between the tower blocks, drove down towards him and turned right into town. The time was 45 minutes past midnight. He had been out for a long time. Axel followed him down Frederikssundvej, north-west Copenhagen turned into Nørrebro under the overground train line, Lira rode on, the streets were filled with young immigrants, they hung around on street corners, by their cars, swinging key chains in their hands, joking, smoking and chatting, but apart from that Copenhagen was still empty of young people.

Axel stayed 50 metres behind him. It bothered several other drivers that he drove so slowly. Two gave him the finger and a car with four young immigrants drove up alongside him and lowered their windows. The man in the passenger seat called out to him.

'What's wrong, old man? Having a nap? People like you shouldn't be allowed on the roads.'

Axel looked at him. He could almost reach out and touch him.

He pulled to the side to let them pass. At that moment he saw Lira turn onto the cycle path down towards Nørrebro Park via the old railway yard. He couldn't follow him. He accelerated down Hillerødgade to wait for him there. Lira appeared on his bike, but continued onto the cycle path by Nørrebro Park, so that Axel was forced to drive to Stefansgade via various side streets.

He parked 100 metres from the dealers where he usually bought hash. He watched them. He waited.

But Lira didn't come. He waited for 20 minutes. He had lost him. He got out of the car and walked up to the dealers. Bought two joints, got back in his car and waited another 15 minutes before he drove past Lira's house, which was dark. There was no sign of the bike.

He drove home.

His flat was like a sauna, he opened the windows and sat in the bay window. Smoked a cigarette. Took out the joint. It would help him sleep. Perhaps that was what he was missing. He tried to count back to last week. Three to four hours every night. Plus a few nights with Ea Holdt when he had hardly slept. The days merged into one.

Just as he was about to light a joint, he remembered something. He called radio control at HQ.

'It's Axel Steen. Has anyone reported an assault or anything like that in the area around the Bellahøj estate last night and tonight?'

'Let me have a look. There was something. Here it is: a couple was approached by a man who claimed to be a police officer hunting a rapist. He attacked the man when the couple was embracing.'

Axel laughed.

'That was me. They were fucking. I did apologise, several times. Pass it on to me if it needs further attention.'

'Right you are. And then someone out walking their dog phoned to say that he had seen the scaffolding man in the bushes, scouting for girls.'

'The public really are keeping their eyes peeled. That was me as well.'

'I did dispatch a patrol car, but they didn't see anything.'

'Anything happening in Nørrebro?'

'No, it's a quiet night because of the Roskilde Festival.'

He thanked him and ended the call.

Axel lit the joint. Axel inhaled. Axel smiled. Axel into the landscape and out again. Axel disappeared.

CHAPTER 59

Saturday, 5 July

He overslept. It was 10am when he woke up. He was well rested and he showered in an attempt to wash away the hash. Then he knocked back a mouthful of cold coffee and went down to the courtyard to get his bike, took it to his car and attached it to the rack at the back. He picked up a croissant from the bakery, then drove to HQ.

The meeting was over and everyone had gone out to collect more DNA samples. Vicki Thomsen had left a message saying that she had gone in the car with Tonny Hansen. Axel's mobile rang. It was Jens Jessen.

'I'm coming in this afternoon. Then the two of us can go out together,' he began optimistically.

'I'll be done with today's assignments by then.'

'You'll be done by four o'clock?'

'I do have a life outside this job.'

'Right, let me see what it says here: Axel Steen contacts radio control at 1.30am asking for information on rape in Bellahøj. He approached a couple who felt harassed by him. And he was spotted by dog walker. That has recce written all over it in my book.'

'I wasn't recceing anyone. I was following a man who had given a DNA sample.'

'Precisely. That's what I call a recce. Have you given up on him? Or do you have your eye on someone else?'

'I haven't given up on him, but I prefer to work alone.'

'Nonsense. I'm coming with you. What time do I need to be there?'

'On one condition: I make the rules. You do as you're told. None of that I'm-management-bullshit. We meet at 10pm tonight. Outside HQ.'

Axel ended the call.

He went to the front office and picked up a pile of today's papers. The media had jumped at the story and it was on every front page. As usual, reporters had been out interviewing terrified women. Ekstra Bladet featured a map of Nørrebro where the crime scenes had been circled under the headline 'sex sadist will be found here'. BT had printed almost the same map with the variation 'rape monster's hunting ground'. The media coverage had increased the pressure on the police not only to solve the case, but also to answer, deal with and sift through the many calls, and investigate any that were relevant. The calls went straight to a call centre that Darling had set up on the fourth floor next to radio control.

Axel thought about Mark Lira Poulsen and his movements and decided to investigate him more closely. He looked up various registers and pulled out information on him. He had worked many different jobs, he gone to medical school and studied at Denmark's IT University. He had changed his address many times, but it pretty much matched what he had already told them: Nørrebro with a few detours. He was unmarried, but had an 18-year-old son. Axel looked up the boy in the criminal records register. Nothing. He lived with his mother on Amager.

Then he sat down and started reading through the three historical homicides in the hope of finding similarities between them and the murder of Marie Schmidt or the rape investigations. But it was slim pickings, because the victim in a homicide for very obvious reasons can't give any information about their killer's MO, language or appearance, so everything is based on technical evidence and the analysis of it.

His mobile rang. It was Cecilie. He answered the call.

'Hi, Daddy.'

'Hi, sweetheart.'

'I can swim now.'

'That's great. Have you been swimming in the sea?'

'Yes. And in a swimming pool. I can swim in the sea a bit, but Jens taught me to swim in a pool. I can swim with my head under the water. And I can dive. Without holding my nose. I'm a diver.'

'That's great. I miss you.'

'I miss you too. I'll be seeing you soon, won't I?'

'Yes, next week. Then we're going on holiday.'

'Oh, Daddy. What will we be doing on our holiday?'

He had promised himself to organise something, but it had totally slipped his mind.

'I'd like to go somewhere with a swimming pool. Where it's warm. And where there's a disco. Just like when I went to Spain with Mummy and Jens.'

He visualised himself at a poolside with Emma in the water in full diving kit. He couldn't afford to take her to the Mediterranean.

'Perhaps we can find a camping site in Denmark with a pool.'

'Will we be sleeping in a tent?'

'Yes, we will. Would you like that?'

'Yes I would, Daddy. I'm going swimming now. Bye bye.'

His longing for her nearly tore him apart. He could feel Emma right into his marrow, his eyes welled up and he felt guilty that he hadn't organised anything and allowed his entire life to drift, in the hope that somebody or something would pick it up along the way.

He spent the next hour searching the Internet for camping sites. He found one with a swimming pool in Gudhjem on the island of Bornholm. They could also ride their bikes there. Not bad at all.

At 6pm he wandered over to the central railway station and ate two hot dogs. Then he returned to his office and carried on reading up on the homicides. He had received a text message from Ea Holdt. 'Please call? Hugs Ea'. The joy went straight to his stomach. Maybe he could make up for his death trip the other day. He called her immediately.

'Hi. It's Axel.'

Music in the background.

'Hi.'

'How is Roskilde?'

'It's great. And it's nice to have something else to think about. But I'm sorry. Sorry about how our last date ended.'

'So am I. It was my fault.'

'Mine too. I go at it too hard. Can we fix it or are you done?'

'I'd like to try.'

'I'm really glad to hear you say that. So would I. Why don't we meet up? Give us a chance?'

'Yes.'

'I'll call you when I know when I'm free. I'll probably also have the boys for a few days when I'm back, but next week is good. Perhaps you could pick me up from work one day. If the weather is nice, why don't we go for a drive out of town? To a beach or a forest. Try to talk about it all.'

'Just give me a call.'

At 9.45pm he went down to his car. He smoked a cigarette and waited.

The Deputy Commissioner appeared on the stroke of 10 in his family car. He was tanned, wearing jeans and an expensive shirt, tennis shoes. He walked up to Axel and shook his hand.

'Are we ready?'

'I am.'

'OK, let's go.'

'We'll take your car. No one would ever suspect a police officer of driving a Galaxy. Let alone a Deputy Commissioner.'

Jens Jessen clapped his hands together.

'Fine by me.'

'I'll drive.'

Axel attached his bike to the rack on the back of Jens Jessen's car.

The temperature had dropped a few degrees and the air was clean and crisp. They drove out of Nørrebrogade, heading for the orange red glow over Brønshøj, the most beautiful sight he knew in Nørrebro. Just before the night descended upon the city, the setting sun dyed the western sky, and you could feel the embers of the day burning out, still hot, but fading, it was like a coming down from a high.

They parked in the same location as where Axel had sat yesterday. The summer holidays had begun and there were few cars around.

'What are we waiting for?' Jens Jessen wanted to know.

'We're waiting for him to come outside.'

'And then what?'

'And then we follow him.' If you say recce one more time I'll knock your block off, Axel thought. 'We'll follow him from a distance. Do you know anything about that?'

'It *is* a recce. We follow him, but he mustn't see us. I didn't work in intelligence for nothing.'

'This is about moving naturally, never stopping to watch, making it plausible that you're heading somewhere. Then he won't notice you, unless he has training.'

'Does he?'

'No, he trained in only one thing.'

'Which is?'

'Raping young women. He'll probably take his bike. That's what he did yesterday. I'll follow him on my bike and you drive after us in the car. We'll keep in contact via our mobiles. We can't wear radio equipment. You mustn't get too close to him.'

'What are we doing?'

'We just want to make sure that he doesn't do any more damage than he already has.'

'What do we have on him?'

'Nothing.'

'So the fact that we're sitting here is down to Axel Steen's famous intuition.'

'You can call it that. It's him. I'm sure.'

'Just as sure as you were about Bo Langberg?'

'Quite honestly, what the hell are you doing here? You wanted to come with me. I said yes as long as I don't have to listen to your crap. You're my boss, but on this assignment, I'm in charge. And if you can't handle that, then I'm out of here.'

Jens Jessen fell silent. Stared out of the window. The mood was tense. Axel was hoping that Mark Lira Poulsen was now so stressed by having provided a DNA sample that he would go out on a few last desperate rape raids and that he could catch him in the act. He was prepared for the task ahead, but he hadn't factored in the deluge of questions from Jens Jessen, and he had a vague feeling that learning the ropes wasn't the real reason Jens Jessen had wanted to come along, that there was more to it. He was loath to admit it, but he was warming to the man. He wasn't the stupid bastard that Axel in his jealousy had tried to turn him into.

'I don't mind your language, it's your style. And I wasn't being critical. I'm genuinely interested. What separates him from Bo Langberg and the other men who've been DNA tested?'

'I didn't think anything about Bo Langberg. I wanted him to explain himself after I saw him on the CCTV footage. And when we caught him, he told us one lie after another. Now this one: a young woman made an anonymous tip-off because he was a creep to her in bed. Rape sex. A game or for real? We don't know. So we've sampled his DNA. He matches our rapist in terms of height, build and age, he has lived in Nørrebro all his life. He fits some of the typical characteristics you would expect of a man like that. He's single. He has worked several different jobs. He doesn't settle down. But that's not the real reason we're here.'

'Then what is it?'

'I've met him. He's as cold as ice, and he lied about not knowing about the case from the television.'

'But can't the same be said for many of the other men people have been calling us about?'

'Probably, but there's another tiny detail that makes me sure.'

'What is it?'

'When I followed him yesterday, he left his home precisely at the time our perpetrator starts hunting. Wearing running clothes. On his bike. With a bum bag around his waist. I'm guessing tights, gloves and a knife—'

'…but you're just guessing.'

'Yes, but hear me out. I followed him. He rode his bike into a park in Bellahøj, parked his bike there and did some serious stretching while he kept looking about him. 10 minutes' stretching of his legs, a little bit of arms. When he was done, you would expect him to start running. Instead he smoked two cigarettes. I don't know about you and your friends, but it's the first time in my life I've seen a runner stretch out before smoking a cigarette and then wandering around some trees.'

'OK. I agree that is strange, but is it enough?'

'It's enough for me.'

'So what happens if you're right? If it is him? If he goes out looking for another victim tonight? If he actually finds another victim?'

'Then you'll have an experience you'll never forget. And I will catch him. And I've been looking forward to that for four years.'

Jens Jessen fell silent again.

'Four years. Is it the Marie Schmidt case that's still haunting you? Cecilie has told me you went completely—'

'I don't want to know what Cecilie has said about anything, is that clear?'

'Suit yourself. I just thought we were starting to get to know one another.'

Axel opened a window and lit a cigarette.

'I would prefer you not to smoke in my car.'

'I've opened a window. Just leave me alone for five minutes, would you.'

He sat in silence in the car next to the man who had replaced him, thinking about what Jens Jessen had just said about Cecilie, whom he had loved more than anyone else. The woman he couldn't get over because she had left him. Because he had dared to love her. That was how he felt. But was it true?

He remembered the calamitous night. The night he had done everything to forget, which he had hidden somewhere inaccessible deep inside himself.

'I don't want to hear another word about that sodding Blackbird. You spend more time with her than with us. Your daughter and your wife. You're running around every night hunting... hunting what? A dead girl. What's going on with you, Axel? You nearly killed your own daughter, for fuck's sake!'

'I didn't. Don't say that.'

'Why not, what are you going to do? Hit me?'

'Don't say that again. I've never hurt Emma. Don't say that ever again.'

He had wanted to hit her. Make her shut up. But he wasn't like that, was he? No. He didn't hit women. He took a deep breath, knowing it was a lie, dropped his voice two octaves.

'It was an accident. I just forgot.'

He closed his eyes. He couldn't bear to think of that night. His daughter, his own daughter.

'You're very far away,' Jens Jessen said. 'Does it distract you that I'm here?'

Axel looked at him.

'No, it doesn't.'

He fell silent and heard Cecilie's voice once more.

'An accident? There's no room for accidents in my life. A grown man, a responsible father doesn't leave a whole jar of codeine tablets on a table where a two-year-old can reach it. And when she complains that her tummy hurts, he doesn't bloody drop her off at nursery and say she has a stomach ache and go to work. A father doesn't do that, Axel, don't you get it?'

'But nothing happened. She got over it. She's all right now.'

'But it happened, Axel. She could have died. Because of you. She's only two years old, for Christ's sake. She could have died.'

She had pushed him away in sadness, anger or rage, he didn't know which. He had tried to hold her, but she had just pushed him away and carried on shouting. And then his hand swooped in as if it were the hand of someone else. He slapped her across the face, sending her flying across the floor. He walked up to her, raised his hand again and didn't stop until he caught her eye.

'There's something I want to talk to you about,' Jens Jessen said.

'Do we have to talk all the time?'

'No, but perhaps I had hoped for a little more conversation, if I may put it like that, I mean not small talk, don't get me wrong. I do know that you... well, that you think of me as a somewhat—'

'I don't think about you at all. You're here. That's your choice. I'm at work.'

'But we're colleagues now and we also share other things. I spend a lot of time with Emma. And I really like her.'

'I hope for your sake that you do.'

'Yes, indeed I do, and so perhaps we could chat in a more relaxed way.'

'About what? What would you like to talk about?'

Jens Jessen gave him a look Axel had never seen before.

'Have you come here to talk about Emma? Cecilie? Our marriage? Forget it. I'm not interfering in your private life.'

'Aren't you?' he said. The suspicion in his voice made Axel throw the cigarette out of the window and look at him.

'Aren't you, Axel Steen? That was exactly what I wanted to talk to you about,' he said in a firm and completely different voice, looking into Axel's eyes with a gaze that was just as dark as the night sky above them.

CHAPTER 60

'You think I'm a prat, don't you?'

Axel had thought so many times. For years. But he didn't think so now.

'Perhaps. Why do you ask?'

'Because. I'm not. I take good care of your child. In fact, I treat her well.'

'You don't *treat* my child. You're with her.'

'I'm no fool.'

'You're the one using that word. I never called you that. So why are we talking about it?'

'Because you and I need to have a conversation. And it'll be on my terms.'

'What the hell are you on about?'

'I want you to stay away from her, do you understand? For ever. I don't want you wrecking my relationship.'

'No, really, what the hell are you talking about?'

'I'm talking about the calls. You make her sad. You need to stay away. I know you haven't given up hope of getting her back. After all, didn't you fly to The Hague to pick Emma up? Wasn't that one way of getting closer to her?'

'No, it bloody wasn't.'

'Don't lie to me. I'm not an idiot. I know that you've never been able to let her go. But you have to, do you understand? Or I will destroy you.'

'What are you talking about?'

'You may think that the ice will always be strong enough to take your weight, but not for very much longer. I hold your entire career in the palm of my hand. All the complaints made against you. You're addicted to hash, and no, I haven't said anything to her, but I will if you don't leave her alone.'

'What do you think you're doing?'

'I'm talking about Cecilie. You're done with her, do you understand?'

He looked at Axel, his gaze burning and intense, his body very calm. Axel thought this man would make a brilliant interrogator or police officer, given his ability to control himself. The contrast between his words and his body language made him feel sorry for him.

'I'm done with Cecilie. And she's done with me, and you know it.'

'I know that you've been with her when I have been away.'

That one time, had she really told him?

'I don't know what you're talking about.'

'Why the hesitation?'

'What do you mean?'

'That's what you do, isn't it? You say something you know isn't true. You bluff. I didn't actually know, but I do now. I can tell from the look on your face. Now answer me!'

Jens Jessen grabbed his collar and pushed him up against the window.

This can't be happening, Axel thought, while he felt Jens Jessen's hands move up to his throat. He didn't think about it consciously for a second, but swung his elbow up against Jens Jessen's left arm. And punched him hard and quickly on the jaw with his left fist, sending him into the side window. But Jens Jessen was strong. He slammed his right fist into Axel's face. This can't be happening. Axel elbowed him in the ribs, and Jens Jessen lashed out at him again, hitting his temple. Axel pinned him up against the side window with his forearm and prepared to smash his left fist into his face as many times as it took to make the man calm down.

'Relax, for fuck's sake. You crazy bas—'

The light went off in Mark Lira Poulsen's house.

'Stop, stop it. He's coming out.'

Jens Jessen froze, stared at Axel and then followed his gaze towards the house where a man was now letting himself out and locking the door.

'You… you… complete bellend, what the hell do you think you're doing? It was me who ruined it. I… I hit her. Do you get it now?'

'But—'

'There's no but! Sit still, for fuck's sake! He's passing us now.'

They were still holding on to one another, but they didn't move. Mark Lira Poulsen cycled past them, wearing exactly the same outfit as last night.

'I'll get on my bike. You'll follow him in the car. OK? Like I told you to do!'

Axel jumped out of the car, ran to the back and removed his bike. He jumped onto it and cycled after Mark Lira Poulsen. The night was beautiful and pure, starlight and moonshine.

Mark Lira Poulsen went the same way as last night, and tonight Axel felt completely clear – and rid of the handicap of the car. He took out his mobile and called Jens Jessen.

'Stay on the line at all times. I'll do the same. All you have to do is watch me. And follow my instructions.'

It turned into a round trip of Nørrebro that lasted an hour. Mark Lira Poulsen cycled round and round. With no apparent aim. Jens Jessen asked twice what he was doing, but apart from that the Deputy Commissioner was uncharacteristically silent. Axel knew there was nothing aimless about Mark Lira Poulsen's movements. He was a hunter circling and searching his territory. Axel saw him scout, his gaze scanning like radar around Nørrebro Park, the deserted streets in the Hans Tavsen quarter, Fælled Park, the Panum Institute car park, Nørre Allé and De Gamles By. He cycled close to Ida Højgaard's address.

Looked up at specific flats, stopped up on the cycle lane, pretending to check his mobile, but Axel could see that he was watching any windows where the light was on. He guessed that Mark Lira Poulsen might have spent a long time searching the area. He had done a recce, as Jens Jessen would have put it, and perhaps he had several potential victims to choose between. Axel presumed that it was his MO, which explained how he had got away with it for so long, that he carefully examined the locations until he found the right one. He reckoned it was too early for him, it was only 11pm, and he had never struck before midnight.

At 11.55pm he parked his bike and entered a passage by Nørre Allé, which would take him to the vast residential complex of corridor flats built by Håndværkerforeningen. Axel knew that Alderstrøst, the name of this complex, had recently been renovated, but he thought that work was finished. The moment he rounded the corner, he realised that he was wrong. Skips loomed up to two storeys high, and the first of the two five-storey blocks, which had consisted of 250 small flats before the renovation, was wrapped in scaffolding and tarpaulin.

Mark Lira Poulsen was nowhere to be seen. Axel ran into the first courtyard, where there was a small landscaped area with trees to his left. He looked up at the scaffolding, took his mobile out of his pocket and said to Jens Jessen:

'You'll have to drive around to the Møllegade exit and try to enter that way on foot. You can take a look around. He doesn't know you.'

'Right you are,' Jens Jessen replied.

Axel had rounded the corner of one building when he finished the conversation and was now looking down the elongated courtyard flanked by the two old buildings clad in steel pipes and tarpaulin. He looked towards the exit to Møllegade that went through two archways. Jens Jessen had yet to arrive, and there was not a soul to be seen in the courtyard. Were there other exits? He didn't think so. He stood still and listened out. Voices were coming from open windows somewhere.

There was music, shouting and partying. He was at a loss. Should he climb the scaffolding and give himself away? Then again, if he discovered Mark Lira Poulsen wandering around the scaffolding, he could definitely arrest him on the grounds of reasonable suspicion. But what if he was here for entirely legal purposes?

His telephone buzzed. It was Claus Sigurdsson from Forensic Genetics. Axel paused the open conversation with Jens Jessen and took the call.

'Hello, I'm sorry for ringing you so late, but it's important.'

'This had better be good.'

'I've found him.'

'Who?'

'I've worked out what happened. I reviewed the DNA profiles of everyone who has worked here since 2004. Unfortunately it turns out that quite a few members of staff took their own DNA sample. We never thought of it as a potential criminal issue but as a way to eliminate contaminated profiles.'

'Just get on with it.'

'I checked the staff samples. Everyone had given a mouth swab, I looked up the profiles and one stood out. This man's genetic profile matched that of an Asian woman, but no Asian women have ever worked here.'

'What the man's name?'

'Bo Poulsen.'

'You're sure it wasn't Mark Lira Poulsen?'

'No, his first name was Bo.'

'Do you have his civil registration number?'

'Yes.'

'Call this number and ask them to look him up.' Axel gave him the number of radio control. 'If this is what I think it is, then his first name is Mark. Text me if I'm right. When did he work for you?'

'January 2004 to September 2004. He joined us on a research programme that never really took off, and did some shifts as a temp. Then he left.'

'I bet he did. He must have realised that he risked being exposed if he littered his DNA profile all over different cases. Or he took the job with you purely to tamper with the samples. Is that possible?'

'No, but of course we have to try to map what he has done. It's the guy who made a packet from selling his flat in Nørrebro, he was on that picture in my office, I pointed him out to you.'

Axel tried to recall the photo of the winter bathers from Helgoland Lido in Claus Sigurdsson's office, and was convinced that it had to be the same man who was now somewhere up on the scaffolding.

'Fuck.'

'I'm sorry. This is a disaster.'

'We're tailing him right now. We'll have to clear this up later. Got to run.'

Axel ended the call.

He saw Jens Jessen enter through the archway from Møllegade. He ran towards him. It didn't matter if he saw them now, Mark or Bo Lira Poulsen, it didn't fucking matter. They just had to get him.

'It's him,' he said to Jens Jessen. 'It's his DNA profile, I've just heard from Forensic Genetics. He used to work for them. Call radio control and get them to dispatch every patrol car in the area to this address. We have to catch him now.'

Axel stepped out into the courtyard, put his hands together to form a cone around his mouth and was about to call out when he heard a scream. Where was it coming from? He looked about him, then up at the scaffolding, as if he could locate the sound by sight. He thought it came from the block that overlooked Møllegade.

He called out:

'Mark Lira Poulsen. This is the police. Step forward and surrender and nobody gets hurt. I know you're up there somewhere.'

Jens Jessen was turning around, checking out the two buildings. He had a cut to his cheek.

'You take the scaffolding over there,' Axel said, pointing to the other block. He started climbing the scaffolding covering the entire side of the block that faced Møllegade. He looked along the bottom deck of the scaffolding. Why the hell hadn't he brought his torch? He started to jog across the metal sheets, which reverberated underneath him as he peered into each flat. He continued upwards to the next deck via a slim metal ladder. Ran along the next level. There were people in the flats, but no sign of Mark Lira Poulsen. He focused on any windows which were open or not on the hasp. On the third floor he spotted a window to a dark flat. It was ajar. There was a fine white layer of renovation dust everywhere, and on the windowsill he saw a shoe print. He opened the window fully. Then he called out:

'Mark Lira Poulsen, are you there?'

He listened. Then he looked inside. He tried to adjust his eyes to the darkness. He listened out for breathing. He had no doubt that someone was in there. Not in the first room, which was a living room, but further inside the flat. Before the renovation the flats had been one or two bedrooms, but now it was impossible to say how many more rooms were hidden deeper into the darkness.

Axel climbed up onto the windowsill, checked out what was in front of him, pushed a pile of books to one side with his shoe, pulled up his other foot, then stepped down from the windowsill. Now he was in the room, but he was distracted by outside noises, a man shouting, it was Jens Jessen's voice. Axel concentrated on listening towards the rooms. The sound was clearer now. It was like a strained hissing. He guessed it was Mark Lira Poulsen's terrified victim, whose mouth was covered. He felt an overwhelming sense of calm. His body relaxed for a second. Then he entered the flat. And walked towards the sound.

Jens Jessen climbed up onto the first scaffolding deck and started walking along it, looking into the flats. It was a crazy night, and he was out of his depth, but this was definitely more fun than anything he had ever done. There were people behind the windows. Some of them spotted him and looked confused. One man opened the window when he walked past, calling after him: 'What the hell are you doing here?'

'Police,' he called back and carried on. He had no idea whether he should knock on the windows that were dark or where he couldn't see people – in fact, he had no idea what he was looking for. How could Axel Steen know? He seemed to act on instinct all the time. As if he knew what to do at any given point. What should he do now that they had heard the woman scream?

Jens Jessen ran. He remembered that he had forgotten to call for backup. He would do that in a moment. A woman, who had just stepped out of the shower and was wrapped in a towel, dropped it from the shock of seeing a strange man look into her flat. Then she screamed. He opened the window fully and called out that he was from the police and that she should stay calm. What had he got himself mixed up in?

Their fight in the car. Why had he shown Axel all his cards? He had planned to put pressure on him as regarded Cecilie, but not show him his hand. What was he going to do with the information? Would he use it against him? Go to Cecilie with it? No, it was unthinkable. He had to process it later, analyse the risks. He ran.

When he had checked every deck, he started walking back down. He listened and greeted the odd resident, who had stuck their heads out of the window, and advised them to keep their doors and windows closed. They were hunting a rapist. There would soon be more police officers turning up.

When he had reached the ground, he walked across to the scaffolding covering the other block. He could hear legs coming down through the darkness towards him.

'He wasn't there, Axel, is that you?'

Axel inhaled before he stepped into the room with his pistol drawn. It was dark in there, he had been able to see that much from the hallway. Many police officers would have hesitated, considered calling for backup, but more would have followed their instinct, although it was rule number one at the police academy that you did not go into a room without backup, if you didn't know where the threat was or the nature of it.

He found him standing up against the window of a bedroom with the woman in front of him as a human shield. The stocking over his head, a gloved hand holding her hair so that he could pull her head backwards and expose her throat. He was holding a knife across it. A flick knife. He stood completely still, only the woman's body was alive, trembling, frantically breathing. His face was hidden behind the woman's head, which told Axel that he must be aware of the pistol.

Axel had been wrong on one point. Mark Lira Poulsen hadn't covered her mouth with his hand. He had been fast and got quite far in his preparations. She was gagged with several scarves around her mouth and a T-shirt had been tied around her head, covering her eyes. He thought about how terrible it must be behind the fabric, and wanted to kill him.

'Easy now. I'm a police officer. I'm here to rescue you.'

He didn't move, he looked at Mark Lira Poulsen.

'Let her go. It's over. You're finished.'

'Stay where you are. Or I'll cut her throat,' Mark Lira Poulsen said, showing no signs of emotion. 'Put down your pistol. Or she dies now.'

Axel lowered his pistol.

'Put it on the floor.'

Axel did as he was told. Then they both waited. He estimated the distance. He couldn't reach the man without jeopardising the woman's life. Mark Lira Poulsen straightened up. He let go of the woman's hair and slowly pulled the stocking from his head. His gaze rested on Axel.

His eyes were utterly dead. The woman's head slumped a little, but she quickly straightened it up when she felt the knife press more firmly against her throat, and she gasped. Axel could feel who he was dealing with right in his gut. Mark Lira Poulsen wouldn't be surrendering. Right now it was about pacifying him, making sure the woman was safe, then he would deal with Lira.

'Stay where you are,' Lira said. 'And kick your gun over to me with your foot, but stay where you are.'

Lira leaned back, then pushed open the window behind him.

Axel wanted to get closer to him. He took a step forwards while he tried to work out what Lira was going to do now.

'Stay where you are,' Lira said again. 'And kick the gun over to me. Now.'

He was aware of Lira's body tensing. It was a matter of seconds. Axel looked down at the pistol and got ready to pounce the moment he had kicked it. Something in Lira's eyes changed.

Then the woman was shoved towards Axel, and Lira squeezed himself out of the window. Axel had to choose between picking up the pistol or trying to catch Lira. Shooting into the courtyard, in Lira's direction, was too risky. He swept the woman out of the way, threw himself at the window and grabbed Lira's leg, which kicked out at him, connecting with his shoulder and jaw, but he didn't let go. Then Lira stopped kicking, and Axel saw the knife come plunging towards him. He jerked his head to one side. He felt a warm wetness on his cheek and shoulder and knew that it was his blood. He let go of Lira's leg, the warm wetness running into his eye, and fumbled for his service pistol on the floor, but when he had found it, Lira was gone.

'Police officers will be here shortly to take care of you, you're safe now,' he called out to the woman, and tumbled out of the window without looking. Lira had escaped. He looked both ways, then ran along the deck. There were two ways down, and he chose the closer one, stopped and listened when he got there, looked out over the railings. Nothing below him. But at the other end, 100 metres away, Jens Jessen was looking up into the darkness. Then there was a crash and Jens Jessen was knocked over. Axel threw himself headlong down the ladders.

CHAPTER 61

The figure in the darkness climbing down the ladders was in a hurry, and Jens Jessen realised it couldn't be Axel. But it was too late for him to react. His assailant had a knife in one hand, and Jens was so focused on the weapon that he misread the attack and prepared himself for a stabbing as the man turned sideways and swung his leg round, kicking him in the chest. He fell backwards onto the flagstones and before he could get back up, the man kicked him in the head and ran.

Jens Jessen was one big adrenaline rush. His face hurt, but everything inside him powered up at the same time. He chased after the man, who had disappeared out of the archway to Møllegade. When he emerged into the street, he saw him round a corner into De Gamles By, an estate of sheltered housing for the elderly and nursery schools for the young. He might be a runner, but I have the advantage, I'm in better shape than him, Jens Jessen thought. He ran as fast as he could, and spotted him some distance ahead. Mark Lira Poulsen ran under the streetlights on the pavement, but Jens Jessen ran in the middle of the road on a high. The old buildings disappeared behind him. He felt the strength of his body. He was gaining on him, he reached a church, but then lost sight of him. He ran around it and stopped for a brief moment. He had come to a lawn. He ran across it. Sensed something living in front of him. What was it he could hear? Animals? The first 'baaah' nearly gave him a heart attack, and he couldn't help giggling. Sheep? In the middle of the city, in the middle of Nørrebro? He walked across the grass.

It was a large, open, green space with trees and benches. An enclosure with sheep. He looked in all directions, moving forwards as he had been taught in the army, calmly scouting from left to right. Then he heard a grating noise. He couldn't see anyone, but he ran towards the sound. Metal hitting metal. Mark Lira Poulsen was trying to scale a tall, barred gate leading out of De Gamles By. He was 10 metres away. He would catch him. He reached the man's legs. You're going nowhere, my friend, he thought, and pulled hard.

CHAPTER 62

Axel reached the courtyard between the blocks and ran towards the place where Jens Jessen had been standing. Called out his name, but got no reply. His mobile was lying on the ground. He picked it up and checked the last call. It was to him. Why the hell hadn't Jens Jessen called radio control for back up? Axel started running as he made the call. He shouted into his mobile:

'This is Axel Steen. Officer requesting assistance at Møllegade/De Gamles By. In pursuit of rapist. Dispatch all units. Now!'

That would get them to pull their finger out. He stopped and listened out again, and thought he could hear running inside De Gamles By. He continued towards the sound. He entered through a goods entrance and ran towards the middle of the large estate. He stopped and caught his breath. He could hear the sound of metal against metal over by the enclosure where sheep were grazing next to a nursery school. He ran on, vowing to himself that he would definitely start to exercise again, something he had stopped for fear of his heart. It was the third time in a week that he could taste blood in his mouth because of his pathetic fitness level. He reached a grassy area and stopped.

Then he saw them.

CHAPTER 63

Jens Jessen pulled down Mark Lira Poulsen, who landed on top of him.

'Stop, you're under arrest,' he panted, aware that he didn't have the right verbal skills for a situation like this. He pushed the man away, kicked out at him without connecting, got halfway up to standing, then he rose in full and lashed out at Mark Lira Poulsen, who floored him in that instant with a punch to the face. Mark Lira Poulsen climbed back up onto the barred gate, but Jens Jessen staggered to his feet and grabbed his legs again.

'You're going to jail,' he said. But he got no further with his thoughts before Mark Lira Poulsen came crashing down on him again, knocking the air out of him. Then the man was astride him, he kicked him in the head, stamped on him, grinding down with his foot with the knife in one hand, one, twice, three times, something cracked, Jens could taste blood in his mouth, there were black explosions in front of his eyes, he felt dizzy and the pain was severe. He tried to defend himself with his hands. Nausea surged in his throat, choking him. The man transferred the knife into his right hand and took a step towards him. Mark Lira Poulsen raised the hand holding the knife. Jens watched the movement in dull slow motion, the moon behind his attacker in the sky, the stars twinkling brightly in the night, the stars that he would never see again. What did he think he was doing coming out here?

The knife plunged towards him.

CHAPTER 64

'Drop the knife or I shoot. Now,' Axel shouted.

Mark Lira Poulsen turned to face him. He was seven or eight metres away. Axel had a clean shot.

'Drop it, for fuck's sake!' Axel screamed.

He heard the sirens behind him. There was no time for a warning shot. Mark Lira Poulsen looked at Axel. He smiled. Then he plunged the knife towards Jens Jessen's body.

Axel fired. He knew at that second that Mark Lira Poulsen was expecting, and hoping, that he would kill him, but it was easy for him to shoot him in the shoulder of the arm holding the knife. Lira collapsed with blood pouring from his splintered shoulder.

Axel quickly walked up to him. Kicked away the knife. Stood astride the whimpering man.

'You don't get off that easily. There are a lot of sick bastards in prison who can't wait to meet you,' Axel said.

Then he turned away from the hyperventilating, groaning body. There were blue flashing lights everywhere in De Gamles By. No one had spotted them yet, so he called out:

'Officers, over here. One officer wounded. One perpetrator badly wounded. We need two ambulances. Now!'

He walked over to Jens Jessen and pulled him to his feet.

'Right, Deputy Commissioner, that's the end of you playing Rambo.'

'What happened, Axel?' He sounded dazed.

'You caught him, Jens. You did it. I had to shoot to incapacitate him.'

Jens Jessen looked at him in wonder, then he nodded.

'I thought I heard a gunshot.'

Axel helped him towards an ambulance.

'You're bleeding quite heavily from your face,' one of the paramedics said to Axel.

'That'll have to wait.'

'It'll need stitches.'

Axel walked over to the other ambulance, where Mark Lira Poulsen was lying on a stretcher wearing an oxygen mask. Axel looked him in the eye and felt at peace. He turned to a fellow officer.

'He'll need an armed police officer in the ambulance and a police car following them. He's capable of anything.'

CHAPTER 65

Sunday, 6 July

Axel Steen was standing in the bay window with a cup of coffee, looking down at the Sunday summer lethargy in Nørrebrogade. His overactive brain had woken him up, trains of thought he was trying to organise, uncertainties that had turned into questions that needed answering.

It was 10am. He expected to be interviewed by the DPP later today, which was standard when a police officer had discharged his weapon. He had had to give a preliminary statement to an investigator from Bellahøj police station at 2am. He had had time to say that he had fired his gun in an attempt to incapacitate Mark Lira Poulsen, but Darling had come in and interrupted the interview. 'Axel Steen has saved a young woman and a colleague's life and he's bleeding all over his face. Leave him alone, he needs taking to the hospital now. You'll have to do all this tomorrow.' Axel had heard heels clicking as he spoke and knew something had happened that was above his paygrade.

But he didn't care what they concluded and whether it would result in an inquiry.

He had done what needed to be done.

He had been to the Rigshospitalet and left with eight stitches to his face, a final greeting from Mark Lira Poulsen, a cut from his hairline on one side of his forehead and down the middle of his cheek, and six stitches to the skin above his collarbone where the cut ended. It would leave a scar, the doctor had told him.

Jens Jessen had called an hour before and told Axel he backed his version 100 per cent.

'I don't have a version,' Axel had said.

'Yes, you do. I've read your preliminary statement. You shot him. You warned him, and then you shot him when he didn't react. That's what happened.'

Axel hadn't had anything to say to that.

'One last thing: Thank you!'

Axel had ended the call without saying goodbye. He couldn't stand the man, but he had saved his life and his experience had taught him it could make people do the strangest things. Or was this about something else? What would happen if there was an inquiry? Then it would come out that Copenhagen Police's second most senior legal professional had insisted on tagging along on a dangerous assignment where he had risked his life, and that a police officer had had to save him. And that was unlikely to reflect well on Jens Jessen.

Axel turned on the television, found TV2News and followed the story, which was being broadcast constantly. Dorte Neergaard was in her element. She had been to De Gamles By last night, and was now standing with a serious and concentrated face and a big microphone outside HQ, where Darling was giving a press briefing.

'Following an operation last night, we have arrested a man who we believe has committed at least five sexual assaults in Nørrebro over the last 12 years. He was apprehended by two police officers when he was in the process of committing yet another sexual assault, and a struggle ensued during which he almost killed a police officer with a knife, but was fortunately incapacitated by another officer. The suspect sustained a gunshot injury to his shoulder when he refused to surrender. He's expected to survive. He has been remanded in custody for four weeks in absentia, as he is currently in hospital being treated for his gunshot injury.'

'Is he suspected of other offences?' Dorte Neergaard asked.

'Yes. We're investigating him. And we'll review a long list of other cases which have yet to be solved.'

'Does that include murder?'

Darling hesitated.

'Yes, it does.'

Axel heaved a sigh. His mobile rang.

'Axel Steen.'

'It's Ea. Was that you?'

'Yes.'

'I saw it on TV. Are you hurt?'

'No.'

'You got him?'

'Yes, we got him. He won't be sending any more clients your way.'

'That's wonderful. I'm really pleased to hear that. And you didn't even kill him. Perhaps there's hope for you after all.'

Axel didn't know how to respond to that.

'I was only joking. But perhaps there's hope for us, what do you think?'

'That's right, we were going to meet up. When?'

'Wednesday, I think, I'm childfree then and hopefully I'll have recovered from the Festival.'

'Works for me, text me when and where and I'll be there.'

'I want you to know that it truly means a great deal to me, what you've done.'

He couldn't thank her. He had done what he was supposed to do. He was used to people valuing some of his actions and hating him for others. Their approval or lack of it could never be what drove him.

They said goodbye. Axel went to the bakery, bought a buttered roll, and ate it as he walked down Nørrebrogade. In front of Netto he saw a young woman he had twice called an ambulance for. The supermarket was closed, but she was half standing, half sitting on an electricity meter box next to the sliding doors with a paper cup for change in her hand. He stopped. The roots of her hair were very dark, the rest of it was golden. Her white scalp, visible through the centre parting, was covered in dandruff. She had a newspaper tucked under her right arm, her hand picked at her chin mechanically, her eyes were semi closed, a side effect of drug abuse and liver failure. Every time she surfaced enough to sense her surroundings, she would reel off the sentence 'support-the-homeless-buy-the-big-issue-support-the-homeless-buy-the-big-issue'. She wasn't far enough gone for an ambulance to be willing to take her to a hospital. He put 50 kroner in her cup and walked on.

A little further down the street outside the kiosk, the owner's son, a young Pakistani, was wearily watching a scarecrow of a man with long shiny black hair and a leather jacket who was sitting on a milk crate outside the kiosk with a strong lager in one hand and a cigarette in the other while he spoke into a mobile, his voice slurred from drugs.

'…for fuck's sake, Mum, I told you to pay the money into my account…'

It was Sunday morning in Nørrebro, junkies, the homeless, the mentally ill and the lost drifting aimlessly round the streets. This afternoon and evening when the neighbourhood's young people returned from a week of partying at the Roskilde Festival, the streets would assume their normal face once more.

Axel crossed the Runddelen junction and headed for the Guldberg quarter. Five minutes later he rang the entry phone to Jeanette Kvist's flat.

'Who is it?'

'It's Axel Steen from Copenhagen Police.'

He was buzzed in immediately.

She was in the doorway when he reached the flat. Her blue eyes looked expectantly at him.

'Is it him?'

'Yes, we've got him.'

'Come in.'

There were removal crates all over the flat.

'Please excuse the mess. I'm just here to pack.'

'It's fine. I won't stay long. I just wanted to tell you in person. He won't hurt anyone again.'

'Are you sure it's him?'

'We'll have the result of his DNA sample in two days, but I'm sure. Absolutely sure.'

'What will he get?'

'A long sentence. Not just for the rapes, but also for the attempted murder. I can't tell you how long, but he'll pay.'

She smiled nervously.

'There was something else I wanted to say. I know how powerless you felt, but you did many things that helped us catch him. If you hadn't noticed so many details, the saliva, the condom he put on, we never would have connected your case with the others. It was crucial.'

She was silent.

'I know it can't give you back what you've lost, but it will stop him from hurting anyone else. And one more thing. You read him correctly and realised that resisting could cost you your life. You did the only right thing you could in a totally wrong situation. You were able to save your own life. Don't ever forget that.'

Jeanette Kvist's eyes were not as dead when he left, but her face was still drawn and Axel knew that it would be a long time before that fear was healed.

When he emerged onto the street and checked his mobile, he saw that he had missed calls from Cecilie, Dorte Neergaard, the Swede, Jens

Jessen, John Darling and Vicki. Text messages and voicemails. They all wanted him to call. Cecilie was coming to Copenhagen tomorrow and would like to meet him for a chat.

Jens Jessen said that he had given a statement concerning the shooting incident to John Darling, and that Darling would be contacting Axel. The Swede wanted to hear if he was all right. He had got the result of Bo Langberg's toxicology tests and could inform him that Bo Langberg had had nothing but happy pills and a glass of red wine in his blood. The cause of death was suicide. Dorte Neergaard wanted to meet up and get all the details. She had learned that it was Axel who had stopped Mark Lira Poulsen.

He called Vicki.

'Hi, Axel. How are you?'

'I'm OK.'

'We'll be interviewing Mark Lira Poulsen tomorrow. Are you coming?'

'We?'

'Darling has let Bjarne loose on him. He has gone one round with him already. He denies everything. I'll be sitting in from tomorrow, but I thought it might be an idea for you to take part as well as you're the only one who knows what happened last night.'

'When is it?'

'Tomorrow morning. I can pick you up at 10am. I'm guessing you're not coming into HQ. You'll be taking a few days off, won't you?'

'I won't be taking any time off. But please come pick me up. I'd like to be there.'

Then he called Darling, who immediately became very circumspect, something Axel wasn't used to.

'I know I wasn't there, but Jens Jessen has given his statement to me as his presence last night makes things a bit awkward. And I just wanted to go it through with you because there might be details you remember differently.'

Go through it? It was quite normal for police officers to discuss their statements, but it was unheard of for Mr Clean, and it confirmed Axel's suspicion that this would prove to be the least problematic shooting incident of his career.

'What do you want me to say?'

'Let me read it to you.'

Darling proceeded to read aloud Jens Jessen's account of the incident. Axel had no objections. Including when it came to the conclusion.

'…the perpetrator was standing over me and was holding a knife. He was warned twice by Axel Steen, who made it clear that he would discharge his weapon unless the man dropped the knife. When he attempted to stab me, he was shot. I didn't see where he was hit as I was dazed. He fell. Without Axel Steen's intervention, I would have been killed.'

'Now, now, how about we dial down the melodrama a little?'

'Yes, of course, but you did save the man's life. So do we agree that this is how it happened?'

'If you say so, John.'

'Great. You'll be hearing from the DPP sometime today and they'll ask you for a statement. This is a completely straightforward case. I can't imagine that there will be any problems.'

Axel had nothing to add to that part of the investigation, but there was one other matter he wanted to raise.

'I can't have any more wannabes coming with me on assignments in future, Darling, no more have-a-go lawyers, all right?'

'Yes, of course. I think everyone would agree after this. By the way: we'll have the result of Mark Lira Poulsen's DNA test tomorrow night or Tuesday morning. Then we'll have another press briefing. The press are asking to speak to you about what happened, is that something you're willing to do?'

'No.'

'I thought as much. It's probably not a very good idea either, but we could consider a television interview about what happened.'

'I'm not interested.'

'No, all right. Well, I just wanted to say thank you. And congratulations. You got him. Again.'

'No, *we* got him. If Jens Jessen hadn't chased after him, he would have got away. Besides, there's also the murder of Marie Schmidt.'

'Yes?'

'I'm not sure he did it.'

'Axel, please don't start that again. We don't know that yet. Let's deal with one thing at a time. We have his DNA on that case.'

'He didn't do it, Darling. I know he didn't.'

They ended their call. Axel was sure that the answer would become clear once they had reviewed the DNA evidence and discovered how the contamination had occurred, but he had no intention of waiting for that.

He had known as early as last night that he wouldn't be allowed to interview Mark Lira Poulsen on his own because he had chased after him, caught him and shot him. But the fact that he had been given the chance to take part in tomorrow's interview might just provide him with an opportunity to speak to him alone.

In front of them lay months of work and regular confrontations with Mark Lira Poulsen whenever they made a fresh discovery, and Axel had no doubt that many more things would come out, more victims, damaging witness statements, women he had been with, new technical and DNA evidence. It would be a long haul. He would take an interest, he would follow up the DNA side of the investigation, but he was ultimately not a part of it anymore, and he was all right with that. He was done with the case. And the less he had to look at Mark Lira Poulsen's icy, deadpan mug, the better.

He was back home. He walked up to his flat, opened the windows and lit a cigarette. He smoked it by the window, wondering why he had told Darling that Mark Lira Poulsen hadn't killed Marie Schmidt. It had been eating him up all night.

When he had finished his cigarette, he went to the dining table where the case file lay. Just as unsolved now as it had been a fortnight ago, sadly, but he was going to have one last try.

He had three reasons for thinking Mark Lira Poulsen didn't kill Marie Schmidt. Firstly, he suspected that Mark Lira Poulsen had left his own DNA on her leaver's cap when he worked for Forensic Genetics – so the transfer was purely due to contamination. As Claus Sigurdsson had explained, contamination by staff was common.

Secondly, there was the murder itself. No matter how hard he looked, there was nothing to indicate that Mark Lira Poulsen was a killer. He was a lot of other things, but Axel had been unable to find another killing to support his theory. The third reason weighed most heavily with him: Mark Lira Poulsen's expression, his surprise when Axel had spat Marie Schmidt's name into his face when they first met him in his home. Mark Lira Poulsen had been on the verge of protesting, but then he had stopped himself. It was the only crime he had acknowledged and denied. The five rapes, which Axel was sure he had committed and with which he had also been confronted, he hadn't reacted to at all. Axel had mentioned Marie Schmidt and said that she had been raped and strangled. 'I don't know anything about that,' Mark Lira Poulsen had replied.

He was meeting Ea Holdt in three days. He looked at the case file with Marie Schmidt's name on it. He hoped to solve the case before seeing Ea.

He knew who to go for. Where there were weaknesses. Rasmus Berndt. The time window between Berndt leaving Bellevue beach, going to Østerbro with his father and continuing onwards to a party on Amager meant it would have been difficult but not impossible for him to go to Ørsted Park and kill Marie. He would try some of her classmates to hear if anything had come out since then. It was a long shot, but it happened that people got careless, that something emerged after a long time.

And then there was the grandmother. He remembered interviewing her very clearly. How he had sensed that there was something she was hiding, something she wouldn't say. About a lover or a boyfriend, perhaps.

And then there was the father. He had to try to interview him about Rasmus Berndt. He had to tread carefully because he had crossed the line once already, but their recent meeting made him hopeful that they would be able to talk again.

He started rereading the interviews. It took him all day. He picked up a doner kebab from the place round the corner before making a list of the people he wanted to talk to and looking up the addresses of Marie Schmidt's girlfriends on the Internet. Half an hour later he had found the three who had been closest to Marie, and had it confirmed that her grandmother lived at the same address as in 2004. He continued reading up on the case. It was midnight and he went to bed. With a goal. Cecilie was coming tomorrow. He was excited. And not just about the case.

CHAPTER 66

Monday, 7 July

The thirteenth floor of the Rigshospitalet has a secure ward where people under guard are admitted. When Axel and Vicki arrived, Bjarne Olsen had been at it for an hour. Vicki knocked on the door and he came out to join them in the corridor. A police officer was sitting on a chair next to them.

'We're having a very nice chat, but the idiot is denying everything. He says he got scared when you started chasing him around the scaffolding and did a runner. He knows nothing about any rapes, and he won't hear talk of the murder. He's a cold son of a bitch.'

'And what's your impression? Can you make him talk?'

'No, we'll get sod all out of him. He doesn't give a toss. Even now when all the evidence points to him, he's denying everything I ask him about. I doubt I'll be able to break him.'

'How is he physically?' Axel said.

'He's OK.' Bjarne laughed. 'His shoulder has been patched up. Good shot. Nicely placed. You could have taken the bastard out and no one would ever have batted an eyelid.'

Yes, I could have, he thought. And not for the first time. The possibility had flashed through his mind in the crucial seconds before he pulled the trigger.

'Do you want to go a round with him about what he was doing in the flat with that girl in Møllegade?' Bjarne wanted to know.

'Yes.'

They entered the side ward.

Mark Lira Poulsen was lying in bed with a view of the lower of the hospital's two main buildings. He looked up at them when they came in, his eyes wandered from face to face, but he didn't react to Axel.

'Where is his lawyer?' Axel asked Bjarne.

'He doesn't want one. He says he's innocent.' Bjarne shook his head. 'I've told him he can have one, but he says no.'

'I would like to interview you about what you were doing Saturday evening and night. Is that OK?' Axel said.

Mark Lira Poulsen merely looked vacantly at him with his pale eyes, which had lost some of the life Axel had seen in them the first time he met him. He straightened up slightly in bed.

They reviewed the whole chain of events. The denials queued up, mixed with a series of sick explanations about how he had taken fright when Axel had shouted out to him in the courtyard between the apartment blocks, and how he had fled into a flat, where the girl had become hysterical and he had had to put his hand over her mouth. He hadn't had a knife. He hadn't threatened her, but Axel had threatened him. Then he had done a runner because he feared that Axel was a biker gang member intent on beating him up. He had previously had problems with Hells Angels. Axel soon tired. He didn't have the energy to listen to Lira's pathetic explanations, which were so overwhelmingly contradicted by the facts and witness statements – his own, Jens Jessen's and, not least, the woman in the flat, whom Mark Lira Poulsen had been in the process of raping.

'Why didn't you drop the knife when I warned you that I would shoot?'

'I did drop it. But you shot me anyway.'

Axel smiled indulgently.

'I'm done here. I'm not wasting any more of my time on him,' he said to Bjarne, then aimed his gaze at Mark Lira Poulsen. He remembered Ea Holdt's words about everyone being human. He wasn't sure that she was right.

'In the next 24 hours we'll get the result of your DNA test. And then you're finished. It doesn't matter what kind of stories you come up with, it's over for you.'

He put his mobile on the chair, then turned to his colleagues.

'Is that it?'

'Yes,' Bjarne said, and they left.

'I need a cigarette. Are you coming?' Bjarne said.

They started walking down the corridor.

When they reached the lifts, Axel said:

'Shit, I forgot my mobile. I'll just go get it.'

He walked back down the corridor. Nodded to the police officer sitting outside the side ward, opened the door and locked it behind him.

Mark Lira Poulsen looked up at him. His eyes glowed with hatred.

'You! What are you doing here?'

'We need to talk.'

'I'm not talking to you. But when I get out, I'll come for you. If it's the last thing I do.'

Axel drew his pistol and walked up to him.

'You want to die, don't you? It was what you wanted last night when you tried to kill my colleague. This is your chance. All you have to do is answer my questions incorrectly. And lie still, you piece of shit!'

Axel placed his hand on Mark Lira Poulsen's injured shoulder and gave it a light squeeze. It worked. He pressed the pistol hard against his chin.

'Marie Schmidt. What did you do to her?'

He was frightened now, pure fear cascaded out of the pale blue eyes. It delighted Axel and he let Lira see it.

'I don't know who she is. I haven't done anything.'

Axel flicked aside the safety catch.

'Oops, wrong answer, but you got lucky. The safety catch was still on. It's off now. And if you get it wrong again, I'll decorate the ceiling with your sick brain. Why did you kill her when you only raped the others?'

'I haven't killed anyone. I didn't do anything… to her.'

Axel pressed his pistol deeper into his jawbone. Looked into his eyes. His gaze was enough for Axel to know he was telling the truth. Then he let him go.

'You're lucky. And you come find me when you get out. I'll be waiting for you. Come get me with your Zimmer frame. Because if it works out as I expect it will, you'll be given life. Until then I hope you rot.'

He walked over to the door, locked himself out, nodded to the police officer and headed down the corridor.

'What took you so long?' Vicki wanted to know.

'Was I a long time? Oh, the suspect had a question relating to the sentencing guidelines for the crimes he's accused of. And I explained it to him in a very professional manner.'

CHAPTER 67

He had two and half hours before Cecilie arrived. Enough time to visit one of Marie Schmidt's friends. She lived at Bispebjerg Kollegiet, two U-shaped blocks next to the train station with a view of the railway yard for the Nørrebro line. Agnete had known Marie Schmidt ever since they started school together, years before her mother died. She lived at the top, on the eighth floor, and Axel stood overlooking the area where the previous year he had stumbled out of a blazing container and had his face burned while fighting a killer. He touched the stitches on the other side of his face. Yet another scar.

'Any news?' Agnete wanted to know.

'Not really, but there's one thing I would like you to tell me again. About Marie, how she was before she was killed?'

'Not a day goes by without me thinking about her. She was such a good and sweet person, and then she changed, but all the time I could still see the old Marie inside her. And then she was killed. It just doesn't make sense, does it? What happened to Marie, I mean.'

She wiped away the tears.

'How did she change?'

'She became miserable. I mean really miserable. She would binge eat and then make herself sick. She was bulimic. I knew her all her life. She was a happy girl until her mother died, and then it was as if everything fell apart for her. And her father. The atmosphere in their home was like… dead. It was completely dead. She was utterly destroyed.'

'But she was also very extroverted, wasn't she?'

'Yes. Once we started sixth form, she went off the rails, she would drink herself senseless and have sex with anyone, she did coke, she changed, she became desperate for validation, I could barely recognise her.'

'Tell me about her relationship with Rasmus.'

'Rasmus, he was a dick. I told her that he was just using her, but she wouldn't listen to me. All the boys were crazy about her. In that porn star way, not for the right reasons, but because she was up for anything. It was scary to watch her stagger around in a stupor with those glassy Bambi eyes and everyone groping her. It wasn't her style at all. She was never like that.'

'Do you remember anything about Rasmus or have you heard anything since?'

'No, I haven't seen him since school. What a loser. He couldn't care less when she died. All I've heard is that he was thrown out of Copenhagen Business School for dealing. He was a tosser, but I never thought he did it.'

'Why not?'

'I think it must have been some random guy. Or that man. At one point she told me that she was seeing a man who did things to her that hurt. But she also felt sorry for him so she didn't want to say who he was. If she went to the police about him and told them everything she knew, then he would go to jail.'

Axel clearly remembered the mystery man, the adult lover they had tried to find, but had finally had to dismiss as the fantasy of an unstable girl who had wanted to come across as interesting to her peers. But now he was no longer sure he didn't exist. But where? Who was he?

'And you never had any idea of who he was?'

'No, it was something she told me once at a party when she had been sick in the garden and I was holding her afterwards and she was off her face. I tried to talk to her about it later, but then she just dismissed it as the alcohol talking.'

Axel tried several approaches, but there was nothing more. He could feel the case like a lump in his stomach.

'It's a real shame. I mean it would be for anyone, of course. But Marie was so close to her mum, she was the one who called her Blackbird, and when she died, it was as if her whole life was pulled away from underneath her. The light went out. And her father could never give it back to her. Although he tried. She really deserved another life than the one she got.'

Back in the flat, he tidied up. He had a call from BB from Forensic Services telling him that they needed Axel's service weapon for examination. He promised to stop by later today. Cecilie called and told him she would be there in half an hour. Her voice sounded soft. When she rang the doorbell, he was sweaty and nervous. She walked up the stairs and appeared in front of him.

'You look a sight.' She raised her hand to his face. Smiled.

She looked at him like you look at someone you once owned. Just one look from her and he was ricocheted back to their past life together. 'Axel!' She shook her head. 'What have you talked my boyfriend into doing?' It was said in a way he was neither used to nor had expected. With a smile.

'Goodness. Jens says you saved his life,' Cecilie said when she had made herself comfortable on the sofa. He remembered the last time she had visited him in the flat. Just over a year ago. It was during the Youth House riots, and the charged silence of the street had spread to the flat. It was one of the most beautiful nights of his life. And the worst morning. They had made love and argued. Since then they had barely been on speaking terms. She looked like her old self as she sat there watching him. A loose summer dress in some kind of black fabric, buttoned at the front, her hair piled up with cheap grips, her skin tanned. The yellow flecks in her brown eyes, which were warm and alive. And filled with joy. He loved her.

'I would like to talk to you about the future. I've been wanting to do that for a while, but I decided to wait for…' she trailed off.

For what? Are you leaving him? Axel thought about the other day. About Jens Jessen, who had feared that Cecilie still had feelings, love even, for Axel, which she couldn't get over. He had believed that Axel was a threat to their relationship. And now what? Was it possible that he really was a threat, he just didn't know it yet?

'…well, for a few things. To fall into place. And now I've made up my mind that we'll be moving back to Denmark six months sooner than planned. We'll be moving home in August, which essentially means that we're back for good now.'

He felt joy deep in his stomach. She was coming home. And his daughter was too.

'I'm glad we're talking,' he began. Say something, anything. 'I think Emma has been suffering. The Hague, our disagreements. I want to work on making things better. And if you and Jens are now…'

He didn't know how to continue. Should he say: Are now splitting up? No, she would have to be the one to tell him.

'I'm so pleased to hear that. That you feel that way. I hope we'll get on better from now on. You can see Emma a lot more if you promise we can agree a proper schedule. I'll need help, and she will need somewhere to let off steam.'

Axel's heart was beating faster and faster. Could they possibly rekindle their relationship? And where did that leave Ea? Had Cecilie just come here to sweep all the pieces off the board? Was Jens Jessen merely some rebound affair she had embarked on purely because he was everything that Axel wasn't? Yes, it was. Of course she wanted him back. In spite of everything. Despite the accident with the codeine tablets. Despite him leaving Emma in the mortuary. Despite the hash. Despite him hitting her. Despite, despite, despite…

'Emma might find it tough when the baby comes.'

'What baby?'

'I'm pregnant, Axel, Jens and I are having a baby. In December.'

She looked at him. In wonder.

'Oh, I thought you had guessed it after what I've just said, I mean… Axel. No.'

Now he could see his own expression reflected in her concerned, slightly pitying gaze. He felt dizzy.

'I've just had it confirmed this morning. I've had a scan and everything is fine. Nobody knows yet. I've only just told Jens.'

He congratulated her, congratulated them both, then went to get himself a glass of water.

He steeled himself at the sink. You idiot! What were you thinking? He started to laugh. At the absurdity of it all.

Then he re-joined her.

'Jens has said so many nice things about you,' she said.

'And it… it's been eventful to get to know him.'

'As it happens, he and Emma are picking me up. Perhaps you would like to come downstairs and say hi. I know you'll be seeing her on Friday, but she misses you.'

Together they walked downstairs.

'Does she know yet? That you're pregnant?'

'No, not yet. We'll tell her later.'

Jens Jessen's Ford Galaxy was parked in Gormsgade. Axel walked there with Cecilie, the car door opened and Emma jumped out and ran towards him with her arms outstretched.

'Daddy!'

That was exactly what he was.

Jens Jessen got out of the car as well. He had blue bruises around his eyes, cuts to his cheeks and black lines under his eyes caused by having his nose broken when he fought Mark Lira Poulsen.

'Honestly, the pair of you,' Cecilie said, looking from one to the other, and at this point Axel decided he had had enough. He had the most important person in his arms, but this bromance was starting to make him sick. Jens Jessen stood there looking like what he did best, a slightly manic boy scout with blinking eyes and an embarrassed smile that spread across his blissfully happy, beaming face. He kept trying to make eye contact with Axel. Axel remembered Jens Jessen's jealous outburst in the car the other night. Just enjoy it, you fool, he wanted to say to him, but he stayed silent.

When they had said their goodbyes and were about to drive off, Jens Jessen got out of the car again and walked over to him.

'Have you spoken to Darling?'

'Yes.'

'I want you to know that I'm 100 per cent behind you.'

'Yes, you said so.'

'There's another thing.'

He squirmed in his expensive clothes. Out with it, for Christ's sake.

'Yes?'

'I very much regret losing my temper with you. I mean, I didn't know… Please forget it, forget everything I said.'

'I already have,' he lied. He was about to leave, then stopped himself and looked at Jens Jessen. He wanted to say 'take care of them!' but the sentence stuck in his throat. Take care of my wife and my child – it sounded nauseating, but that was how he felt. For the first time in three years.

Then he left. He waved as they drove past him. Everything fell into place after talking to Cecilie. He had made some progress recently, shifted away from the constant longing, something he had experienced before, but this time it felt true. But the wound was barely healed and could soon start to bleed again. And after Jens Jessen's outburst in the car, Axel had opened up yet again and let hope in – a ridiculous, totally unrealistic and vain hope that had made him believe that a woman whose husband had nearly killed their child, whose husband had hit her, who was now living with another man who provided her with all the stability and security she had craved all her life, that a woman like that would simply do a U-turn, even though every signal, every word, every action told him the opposite, that she would fall in his arms, the arms of Axel Steen, the junkie, the violent psycho, the workaholic who was terrified of death.

He looked down Nørrebrogade. Something was different. The heat was gone and the leaves on the trees were suddenly busy fluttering in all directions. Then the rain hit the tarmac like hammer blows. Sharp and violent. He stayed where he was as it soaked him, turning his face towards it. It stopped as suddenly as it had started. Axel took a deep breath right down into his stomach. The air was pure like alcohol and tasted the same. In grief, there was relief.

Instead of walking back to his flat, he headed down towards Runddelen, past the shaded side streets and open archways into courtyards where children played hopscotch on wet flagstones in the yellow light, down to Assistens. The cemetery was filled with young people, parents with children who had dragged picnic rugs under the trees to shelter from the rain, but were now heading back out onto the grass to enjoy the sun in between the overturned gravestones. He went over to the urn section and found the stone. It lay untouched in the sun. No flowers, nothing, just the words: Marie Schmidt 1986-2004. A bronze blackbird sat on the rough granite stone as it always had. Axel had watched it change colour during the last four years from dark golden to dusty grey, black and finally verdigris as it was now. A thought relating to the case crossed his mind briefly, something he had overlooked, something the grave reminded him of. He couldn't hold onto it, no matter how hard he searched for that tiny little detail that had prompted it.

He remembered that Marie had performed her favourite song 'Bye Bye Blackbird' at the end of the sixth form leavers' ceremony, silencing the audience with the sense of longing and loss she induced in them, that her singing teacher had called her extraordinarily talented, and said that she had dreamt of singing jazz.

She never would. He heard the melody in his head, its melancholic notes of farewell, and knew that he, too, would soon have to say goodbye. But it wasn't time to say goodbye to Marie Schmidt just yet. There was something he needed to do before he could move on.

CHAPTER 68

Jens Jessen was sitting behind his desk at HQ. Cecilie and Emma had returned to Hornbæk. He had a few outstanding matters to deal with before he could join them and enjoy the last three days they had with Emma before she went on holiday with Axel. The DNA result was back, and it was a complete match for Mark Lira Poulsen. The case would be investigated in depth and more offences were likely to emerge, as Darling had predicted, but that didn't worry him. He needed to clear up the mess with the contaminated DNA samples and Mark Lira Poulsen's employment with Forensic Genetics without leaving any damaging traces.

He had met with Claus Sigurdsson, who informed him that they had discovered that Mark Lira Poulsen had avoided detection by submitted a false DNA sample. When he was hired and was asked to submit a mouth swab, he had gone to the loo and got a cleaner from Thailand to open her mouth and had taken the scraping from her. This explained why they had never found him in the register. He had worked for them for nine months in 2004, and they were busy reviewing every case he had had access to, but as he hadn't been a full-time employee, the number was limited. He had called himself Bo and been employed under that name – something which in itself suggested that he always intended to disguise his identity. A fellow employee recalled him being very interested in the safety procedures surrounding the storage of DNA tests and how he had expressed strong disappointment when he realised that Forensic Genetics was never told the names of victims or perpetrators, and that any connection between the tests and actual individuals was made only by the police. It was therefore reasonable to presume that his intention had been to see if he could find his own samples and tamper with them, but that he had had no choice but to abandon his plan when it proved impossible to identify them. Shortly afterwards he had quit his job with them and dropped out of studying medicine.

They had agreed that the two DNA samples that matched his profile and which had been collected from the Marie Schmidt case and the Lone Lützhøj case, for which someone had already been convicted, had to be there due to contamination. They couldn't say for certain, but the most likely explanation was that Mark Lira Poulsen had accidentally left saliva or cells on objects from the two cases while he worked for Forensic Genetics: Marie Schmidt's leaver's cap and Lone Lützhøj's blouse. It meant that they had to be removed from the final charges against Mark Lira Poulsen, but it wasn't a major problem from a trial point of view. They already had him for five aggravated sexual assaults and the attempted murder of Jens Jessen, plus possibly also the attempted rape of the woman in Alderstrøst, but that was for the DPP to decide. The attempted murder alone would mean a long sentence. He could think of only one person who would protest, who would in fact blow his top if they removed the two cases: Axel Steen and his accursed Blackbird obsession. He would deal with that later.

He had agreed with Claus Sigurdsson and BB that they would remove all evidence of Mark Lira Poulsen from those two cases and forget all about it. True, this wasn't entirely by the book, but they couldn't risk a pedantic defence lawyer using it in court one day in order to get a guilty person off by casting aspersions about the DNA register. A mistake had been made, but they had identified and fixed it. And apart from the three of them, it was only Mark Lira Poulsen and Axel Steen who knew anything about it. Time to move on. They had already introduced new procedures for collecting mouth swabs from staff. In future these would always be taken by independent staff, that is to say, people not working for the same organisation as the person being tested, and control samples would be taken. All staff had to have their existing samples redone. It would cost millions, but he would just have to find the money somewhere.

He was satisfied with that conclusion to the case. He thought back on that morning. Cecilie had gone to Copenhagen early. She had a doctor's appointment, she had said. An annual check-up. He hadn't been aware of anything amiss other than her being a little more distant than normal, but things hadn't been normal for a long time and so he hadn't read anything into it.

He had gone into the living room when she had returned from Copenhagen. Emma was playing in the garden and Cecilie was sitting with her back to him as he came in. Her shoulders were trembling and he could see that she was crying. Was she about to break up with him, he had thought for one terrifying moment.

He had sat down next to her and touched her shoulder; he had hardly dared ask, but neither could he wait any longer.

'What's wrong, Cecilie?'

She looked at him with a grimy face, and smiled through her tears.

'I'm pregnant, Jens.'

'But—'

'I didn't want to tell you until I was sure.'

'But why?'

'Why am I pregnant?' she laughed. 'Because you got me pregnant, we're having a baby.'

'But that's wonderful, why haven't you said anything until now?'

'Because I thought I was pregnant once with Axel. Only I wasn't. And he didn't want another baby. And I was so afraid, well, I don't know, are you truly happy? You've been acting so strangely.'

'But it's good news. I don't know what to say.'

'I did a test at home on Monday morning. I was so happy, and then I started to have doubts. What if you didn't want it?'

He remembered that Monday morning when she had been in a completely different mood, when they had picked Emma up from Axel's and he had sat in the car, looking at Cecilie and Axel, and had been jealous and thought she was happy because she was seeing Axel. How blind he had been.

Her hysterics over Emma's swimming costume. Her mood swings. The red wine she had refused to touch. Their non-existent love life. Why hadn't he worked it out? 'Do you think I've gained weight?' she had asked one morning and let her hand glide over her belly. She had flashed him such an odd smile.

Jens you big idiot Jessen. Hormones. And fear. It had made him think that she was leaving him for Axel Steen, who had looked gobsmacked when he had accused him of wanting Cecilie back the other night, accused him of having been with her while she was his. He wanted the ground to swallow him up, he was so ashamed of his behaviour.

He packed his bag. Then he remembered something. He opened the drawer and took out the envelope with the six pictures. He hadn't managed to find out where they had come from. Nor did he think that he would now. But something would happen eventually. Someone somewhere was sending pictures of that nature to him. He wondered what lay behind it. Was it to nudge him into action? Probably. And if he didn't take action, would someone then accuse him of protecting Axel Steen? Yes, probably. But he had a solution. He had already called Axel and discussed it with him today. He reached for a memo he had composed after their conversation and backdated to March 2007. Back when he first made Axel's acquaintance in connection with a PET operation where Jens and his people were monitoring gangs in Nørrebro and were trying to catch the strongest gang in Blågårds Plads and their leader Moussa – without much success. Axel had had some contact with Moussa then, and now Jens Jessen had written this memo referring to an agreement he had had with Axel saying that Axel Steen's job was to make contact with the gang and infiltrate it if possible. In order for his cover to hold up, he had to act like a bent police officer who might be for sale. And now these pictures had appeared. What Axel was doing was therefore entirely in accordance with his cover. He took the memo and placed it with the photographs, which he had copied and locked in his safe, in an internal envelope and wrote 'Police Commissioner. Confidential' on the outside. Then he tossed it into the internal post tray and left HQ.

CHAPTER 69

Tuesday, 8 July

He had dreamt about Marie Schmidt. She had been wearing her leaver's dress. At the cemetery between the trees in the summer sunshine. She had waved to him. Just waved. Then she had turned into Emma. And he had run towards her. Because she mustn't die. He had woken up bathed in sweat. Panicky and fearful until he realised who he was, where he was.

He got up and checked his mobile. There was a message from Darling saying they had had received more calls about Mark Lira Poulsen and were looking into another three cases of sexual assault.

Axel got dressed and went into town, to Løngangsstræde, to visit yet another of Marie Schmidt's friends. She had bumped into Rasmus Berndt several times on nights out, but he had never bragged about killing Marie Schmidt, as Axel had hoped. On the contrary, he had whined and complained about her death because he had really liked 'her potential', and it was outrageous that the pigs had suspected him. Axel got nothing more out of her.

The next friend lived in a two-bedroom flat in Istedgade with her boyfriend. She had known Marie in sixth form, and they had also boarded together at a continuation school when they were 15. That was two years after the death of Marie's mother. The continuation school had been strongly recommended by a psychologist who thought it would be good for Marie to get away from home, Axel remembered.

'She cheered up a bit, but at the same time, she didn't. While she was there she had sex with a guy for the first time. And then more guys. She went home every weekend.'

'Why?'

'Her dad insisted on it. I thought he was really strict with her. Sometimes he would pick her up from the school. It was like he was jealous, I would say, one of those fathers who can't bear that his little girl is growing up. Believe me, I know what I'm talking about, my dad totally lost the plot when I started dating boys. She finally dropped out of that school. She got ill, I don't really know why, but because her mum had died, it didn't seem that surprising. I visited her. She just stayed at home. Eating happy pills. Her dad looked after her. I liked him. And he was nice to her. And he had been through such a lot. And he missed his wife. But there was also something weird going on between them.'

Axel's heart began to pound. Suddenly he remembered that there had been no flowers on Marie's grave, not yesterday, nor on any of the many other occasions he had stopped by her grave in the last four years, although when they met a week ago, her father had told him that he would often visit her grave to remember Marie and leave flowers.

'Weird how?'

'I saw her comfort him once, it was very intimate. He didn't like her dating boys, and that's when she started to change. It was like she had two personalities. One when she was with her dad and another one when she was going out, where she just partied, drank herself senseless and slept around. He wasn't keen on her staying over at other people's places, but he would let her sometimes. Once we had all had a sleepover at a friend's house. Or so we said. We're staying over at Emilie's. What it really meant was that her parents were away so we had a party and crashed at her house. So I walked Marie home and her father watched her like a hawk when he could tell from her eyes that she was drunk and high. She had screwed some boy, she didn't even know his name.

"What have you been doing, Marie? Have you done something silly again?" She just seemed to get more and more sad, as if she wanted to wreck her life, as if she was in a trance, daddy's good little girl, yes, daddy, no, daddy. It was actually a bit scary.'

'What do you think about the relationship between her and her father?'

'That it wasn't completely normal, a bit unhealthy, but then again, her mum had died, hadn't she?'

'Are you saying their relationship was more than father and daughter?'

'That's not what I'm saying, but I have been thinking that it was odd, unnaturally intimate and also a little bit menacing. And then Marie seemed to hit a good patch despite all her self-sabotaging. She talked about moving out and starting to sing. It was her dream, but her dad was against it, I remember. He didn't want her to move out.'

Axel felt his stomach flood with acid, raging at having overlooked it, furious that he had been taken off this line of enquiry. He said goodbye. He knew where he was going. He remembered Marie Schmidt's diary. One of the last entries was: "Now I've told her. Asked her to help me so it will stop." They had never been able to discover who she had told, but he knew now. He had asked her paternal grandmother, but she hadn't known what it was about, and he began to think that there was something she didn't want to tell him. He had pressed her hard – so hard that she had complained and he had been ordered not to visit her on his own for the rest of the investigation.

He drove to visit the grandmother who lived in an old, overfilled flat in Oslogade in Østerbro. He had phoned ahead. She was nicely dressed when he arrived, a brooch with a green gemstone, a pleated, wine-coloured dress with a collar – he remembered that she was the daughter of a factory owner, there was money in the family, she was a woman in her seventies for whom appearances mattered.

They sat in the dining room at a round mahogany table where tea was ready, a pot, two Royal Copenhagen china cups and a bowl of After Eight mints.

He cut straight to the chase.

'What was going on between your son and Marie?'

'My son was a good father. He always took good care of Marie.'

'How good?'

'What do you mean?'

'When I came here four years ago, we talked about Marie seeing a man and I got the distinct impression that there was something you weren't telling me. What was it?'

'I don't understand.'

'Marie would visit you from time to time, wouldn't she?'

'Not often. She was quite a distant girl.'

'But she visited you a fortnight before her death.'

'It's such a long time ago. I don't remember.'

'She visited you, and then she went home and wrote in her diary that she had told you about it and asked for your help so that it would stop. What did she tell you?'

'I have no recollection of that.'

'But you remember her telling you something?'

'I… I don't know anything about that,' she said, putting the stress on that. As if to emphasise it.

'Did your son have sex with his daughter?'

The woman picked nervously at her collar. She looked unwell, pale eyes swimming around too much water in the sockets as if she couldn't focus.

'I see. So that's why you've come.'

'That's what I want to know. Did your son sexually abuse his daughter? Did she come here asking for your help to make him stop?'

'I don't remember that.'

'And did you do nothing?'

'I certainly would have done something if Marie had come here and told me something like that.'

'Did you?'

'It… yes… it… no, but there was nothing. It didn't happen.'

She began to weep.

'She came here and she told you that your own son was abusing her, and you did nothing. And two weeks later she was dead.'

She fell silent. Axel waited. Then she said ever so quietly:

'It wouldn't bring her back to us.'

'And you didn't think it was important to tell us that?'

'I didn't say that. I didn't.'

'No, but you've said enough. Your own son,' he said, and got up. 'Look at me! Your own son, for fuck's sake!'

Then he left.

He drove down to Lake Sortedam and sat on the bench to get a grip on his thoughts. He looked across the lake to Nørrebro. The neon advertising reflected in the dark surface of the water in green, red, yellow and blue and when the colours changed, it looked as if neon lines were being drawn across the surface.

The mystery man. He didn't have a trace of evidence, but he had no doubts. Nor did he have any doubts about what to do next. Try the carrot, then the stick, should it prove necessary. He would bluff, threaten, lie, it all depended on the father's reaction. He remembered what had happened when he was removed from this particular line of enquiry. Tine Jensen had gone to the then head of Homicide and to Rosenquist to complain about him. They had threatened to take him off the case completely. He had obeyed them, but not before losing his temper with Tine Jensen, throwing her against a filing cabinet and calling her 'the most interfering little snitch I've ever met'. No wonder she wasn't an honorary member of the Axel Steen fan club. But he had had a hunch about the father, and behind the pain and the self-pity that had flooded his life at the time, he knew it was wrong that he allowed himself to be taken off this part of the investigation. His hunches were usually right. They were all he had. When he felt something, it was because something was wrong. He cursed himself. He had let it all slip through his fingers because of his despair and rage at a time when he should have kept a cool head and insisted on following up his hunch. His colleagues had let him down, but he had also let himself down. And Marie Schmidt.

Before he was banned from investigating the father, he had visited him at home on several occasions. He had walked from Nørreport station to the flat in Nansensgade. He had rung the doorbell and walked upstairs. Could she have made it home, he had asked. Could she have come home and then gone out again? Without you hearing her? No, that's insane, the father had replied and Axel had believed him, but the father had looked scared.

Perhaps it wasn't insane after all. Perhaps that was what had happened. Perhaps Marie Schmidt had come home. And then what? Had he murdered her in the flat and carried her down to the lake? No, that didn't make sense. Could she have left again? And might her father have followed her?

He didn't know if he would be visiting a killer. But there was something that was just as bad. A father who abuses his child. It was the darkest offence of all. A child is at the mercy of its parents, and Marie was alone with her father, who had used her to satisfy his own lust. Then she had nothing. No safety, no trust. Nothing but the darkness, which ate her up and spat her bones out afterwards.

The questions queued up. Had he always abused her or had he started after her mother's death? Marie's behaviour, which had been attributed to grief at the loss of her mother, he now viewed in a different light. She had lost the most important person in her life, and the one she was left with had destroyed her. She had been alone. No one had been there for her. He felt grief right to his bones for the teenage life she had lived, he could feel it deep in his heart, her sense of abandonment, her sexual escapades, her need to be seen, her relationship with her father. 'I love my daughter,' he had groaned. He probably believed it, they always did, but it was the reverse of love he had shown Marie, the darkness he had allowed to enclose her.

It couldn't be true. But Axel could feel that it was, and his heart was pounding in his chest, he wanted to scream, but he knew that there was no way around this for him. Marie Schmidt was dead – nothing could change that fact, but the man who had ruined her life must pay. Or nothing would make any sense anymore. None of his other feelings in connection with the case meant anything now, the loss of Cecilie or of Emma, his obsession with Marie Schmidt, and his inability to solve her murder. It was possible that he still couldn't, but he could give Marie Schmidt a scrap of that justice she had been denied her entire life.

It was late evening when he reached Nansensgade. He looked up at the flat. The light was on. His pistol was still being examined by Forensic Services, but it didn't matter. Axel took a deep breath and pressed the entry phone labelled 'Jacques Schmidt Jensen'.

'What a surprise, Axel Steen, do come up,' Jacques said in the entry phone. Axel couldn't call him the father anymore.

As he walked up the stairs, Axel wondered whether the grandmother had phoned her son and warned him what was coming. He didn't think so.

Jacques Schmidt Jensen appeared in the doorway with a smile smeared across his whole face. His blond hair was messy, stubble, he hadn't shaved, his face was flushed and his grey eyes red, his gaze glassy. He was drunk.

'Axel Steen. Come in.'

Axel looked at him, thanked him and entered.

'I'm on the roof terrace enjoying a glass of wine, care to join me?'

'Yes, please.'

He followed Jacques Schmidt Jensen up the steps and emerged under the Copenhagen sky; he felt the heat and heard the sounds of the city below him.

'Any news?' Jacques Schmidt Jensen asked him as they sat down on the wicker chairs.

'Yes, I have news. As you've probably read, we arrested a man for the rapes three days ago.'

'But that's brilliant. So you got him. My daughter's killer.'

Brilliant wasn't an appropriate word from a father who had just been told that his daughter's killer had been arrested, but then again, that wasn't what had happened.

'Yes, we can finally close the case. I'm sorry that it took us so many years.'

'Don't worry about that. It has been stressful, of course it has, and yes, there were times when I felt I was being treated as the suspect.'

'I did suspect you. It's part of the job.'

'Why did you?'

'You would be surprised how often the killer is found among the victim's next of kin. The most dangerous place to be isn't a dark alley or a park at night. It's in the bosom of your family. Nine times out of 10 a child is killed by their father. So we have to investigate close family members.'

Jacques Schmidt Jensen looked as if he would prefer to change the subject.

'How long do you usually get for something like that?'

'For what?'

'For killing your child. Does it count as mitigating circumstances that you're related?'

'No, there are no mitigating circumstances when killing your child.'

Axel had been here before. Killers who wanted to discuss their guilt, hypothetically. Usually it was the first step towards a confession, but in this instance he attributed it to Jacques Schmidt Jensen's intoxication. No innocent man would start to fantasise about what would happen if he had killed someone. And certainly not when talking to a police officer, but Axel assumed that the relief that another man would now be held responsible for Marie's murder had made him drop his guard. And it had. After a short pause he said:

'You always thought I did it, didn't you?' He looked at him with swimming eyes.

'Yes, I did.'

'You always had me in your spotlight, Axel Steen, I sensed that from the beginning.'

Yes, and I should never have left the investigation of you to other people, Axel thought.

'But now you have found Marie's killer.'

'Yes.'

Axel looked up at the blue-black infinity of the sky. He considered his options.

He had spent the last hour on the bench by the Lakes checking out some of the things Jacques Schmidt Jensen had told him during previous interviews. Via a contact in the National Register of Persons, he had found out exactly when Bo Langberg opened his office in Nansensgade. It was in June 2004. He remembered Jacques Schmidt Jensen saying that Marie had pointed out Bo Langberg to him in the spring of 2004. Then he had Googled pictures of Bo Langberg. He was, as the father had said, dark-haired when he died, but Axel had found several pictures from architect conferences from April, May and August 2004 where Bo Langberg had shaved his head, which had only strengthened his suspicion that Jacques Schmidt Jensen had never seen him, although he claimed the opposite. That, together with the fact that he could find no trace of Bo Langberg in the Marie Schmidt file, even though everyone who lived in or had an office in Nansensgade had been interviewed, and that the architect himself had denied knowing anything about Marie, convinced him that Jacques Schmidt Jensen had lied about Bo Langberg right from the start. Axel knew only one way forward now. It was all in.

'The only problem is that next week we'll discover that the man we've arrested has nothing to do with your daughter's murder. And then we'll reopen the case.'

'Reopen the case? What are you saying!' he exclaimed and hiccupped. 'But what about the guy you've caught?'

'We haven't caught your daughter's killer. Yet.'

Axel went over to the door through which they had come, took the key from the inside, closed the door and locked it.

'Of all the next of kin I've ever met, no one has ever been more obsessed than you with finding him, but not to ease the pain and get closure, am I right?'

'Eh?' Saliva and contempt were spat out of his mouth, but Axel could see that he had now got to him.

'But in order to frame someone else for the murder.'

'Eh?' he echoed mechanically.

'Why did you tell me that Bo Langberg had met her? Three months before she was killed, isn't that what you said? He didn't even have an office in Nansensgade at that point.'

Jacques Schmidt Jensen looked confused.

'Maybe I was wrong. It's not—'

'You weren't wrong. You were hoping to close the book on your daughter's murder by having another man convicted of it. Just now, when I told you that we had arrested the rapist, you were happy and relieved that another man would take the rap for it.'

'Nonsense.'

'No it isn't. The day we found her, when you came down to the park, I remember you calling out: "It's my daughter down there." How could you know that? We hadn't brought her out of the lake yet. No one knew she was down there. No one but you.'

Jacques Schmidt Jensen drank his wine, then shook his head. Axel continued.

'Where is Marie? Why isn't she on your walls? Is it because you can't live with what you've done? You can't bear to be reminded that you killed her. That's why she's gone. That's why you lied when you claimed you visit her grave.'

'I didn't lie.'

'Yes, you did. Because I visit her grave. And no one has put flowers on it for three years. You haven't been there since the funeral.'

He sat still and stared, paralysed, across the city.

'We have a witness who saw her walk the other way through the park. Did she come home first? Did she come home after the beach party? And did she want to go out again? My guess is you didn't want her to, that you followed her. And then what?'

The father had slumped in the chair.

'I've gathered enough evidence to have you convicted of something which is at least as bad as murder. Once you're locked up, it certainly will be. You'll wish you were dead. So I think I have a strong hand. And I'm not leaving until I've got what I came for.'

'What are you talking about?' He looked genuinely shocked. And sober.

Axel sat down in the chair opposite him.

'I'm talking about you sexually abusing your daughter.'

'But—'

'I've just visited your mother, who has admitted that Marie confided in her that you abused her, and that Marie hoped she would put a stop to it, but she did nothing.'

He sat very still, staring past Axel, who sensed what was coming. Then Jacques Schmidt Jensen jumped up and ran to the door, tearing at it. He screamed: 'Unlock it, let me back in!'

Axel was on him, pulling him away, and when the man kept shouting, he slapped him across the face, sending him careering across the terrace floor. It felt good. He went over, picked him up and threw him into the wicker chair.

'You're not going anywhere until you tell me what happened, do you understand?'

It came, piece by piece, over the next hour. With no sense of remorse. An alcoholic's pathetic confessions from the bottom of the family swamp.

The first time he raped her was three months after the death of her mother. 'She was comforting me,' he said. She was 13 years old.

'She reminded me of Eliza. She was developed, fully developed. I was crushed by grief.'

One night when he had been drinking heavily, he had complained about his loneliness, he had wept and told her how much he missed her mother, physically, how much he needed to hold her in his arms, cuddle her, comfort her. And Marie had cuddled him. Please will you comfort me, he had asked her. And she had. They had cried afterwards and he had apologised.

'And that's what it was. She comforted me. I had nothing more to live for. She helped me through it. She loved me. We loved one another.'

As she got older, she started to object. 'I'm your daughter,' she would say.

'I made her drink. We drank wine together. It made it easier. But she thought it was wrong and yet she comforted me. She was ashamed of me and felt disgusted. But all we had was one another. I did think that it should stop, but I needed her.'

Axel threw up as the father spoke. He vomited all over the terrace until there was nothing left inside him. It was clearly a relief for the father to talk, though his story was told through snot, whimpering and tears.

The summer Marie Schmidt left sixth form she had said stop. Enough. She was moving out. Wanted to live her own life. She rebelled, stayed out late, drank heavily. On the night of her murder, she came home, remarkably sober, and said she was heading out again. They had a row. 'I won't comfort you again, Dad. It's sick,' she had said.

'I knew what it meant, I knew that she was seeing others. So I forbade her to leave.'

Marie Schmidt had gone to bed in her own room, locking the door. One hour later her father heard her sneak out. He followed her into the park.

'I knew she was off to see some boy. I approached her. We argued. 'No, Dad,' she said, 'It's over. If you don't let me leave, I'll tell people what you have done.' That's when I knew she was going to do it whatever happened. It would destroy me. I held her tight. We fought. I dragged her into the bushes. And I clutched her neck. I didn't want to let her go. Suddenly she went completely limp. I tried to wake her. I tried to revive her. Then I panicked. I wanted to leave the park, but I thought there would be traces of me all over her. So I threw her into the lake.'

'Did you rape her before or after you killed her?'

'I didn't.'

Axel thought about Marie Schmidt's final minutes. He could barely breathe.

'She wasn't dead when you threw her into the lake. She drowned.'

'She was dead. She wasn't breathing.'

'She wasn't dead. The post-mortem revealed that she drowned.'

He wept. Tears that Axel had seen hundreds of times before. The pathetic sobs of a criminal who hadn't wasted a single tear on his victim, but felt sorry only for himself.

'I want you to repeat all of this to a judge. I want you to acknowledge your actions, your guilt, confess to it.'

'I can't. I won't,' he bawled, and Axel hated him with his whole heart. He knew it was only one man's word against another, there was no hard evidence in the information he had gathered. It was circumstantial at best; even if he could get the grandmother to testify, it wouldn't be enough to bring a case of incest to court, four years later and with the victim deceased. There wasn't a snowball's chance in hell of a conviction.

He stood up and went over to Jacques Schmidt Jensen.

'But that's how it will be. I've recorded our conversation on my phone, so you're finished. I'm going to go now, but I'll be back tomorrow. And I'll be bringing you in to the station. And you'll tell them what you've just told me.'

He made to leave. He heard Jacques Schmidt Jensen get up. He looked at the refurbishment work on the terrace in front of him, heard the father come running and stepped to the side the moment the man was about to pounce on him. The father continued over the interim railing and crashed through it onto the scaffolding. He landed heavily on the deck and rolled over the edge, scrabbling to get a hold of it, clasping onto a metal pole running along the deck at foot height. Jacques Schmidt Jensen dangled over the courtyard. Axel stepped across the upended wooden barrier. Walked up to him. The father stared at him.

'Help me,' he pleaded.

Axel just looked at him.

There was only fear left in the eyes of the man who had killed his daughter. Not once. But hundreds of times.

Axel saw his fingers whiten around the steel pole, saw them slide, tighten, grip. Then the father let go with one hand, trying desperately to cling to something that could keep him connected to life. But it was too late. Axel saw him slip away and disappear completely. There was a protracted scream, followed by the thud of a body hitting the ground, then silence. He looked down. Then he turned around and gazed into the night over Nørrebro, mobile masts, church spires and the sky behind it all, faintly coloured by the city lights, growing darker and darker the further up he looked.

He unlocked the door, walked down the stairs, out to the courtyard, glanced at the body of Jacques Schmidt Jensen, returned to his car and took out his mobile, which was in his bag. Then he rang 112.

EPILOGUE

Wednesday, 9 July

At 5.50pm he parked his car on Kongens Nytorv outside the editorial offices of the newspaper Jyllands-Posten. He stayed in the car. Looked across the square, where pigeons were flapping around the benches or snatching crumbs from the ground around the sausage stall. Tourists and people who had left work were sitting around the café tables by the old kiosk where they had arranged to meet. He stayed in the car.

At 6.02pm she came strolling across the square from the pedestrian crossing by Strøget where her firm of solicitors was located. She looked happy. She was wearing a light-coloured trouser suit, a white shirt, the same sandals she had worn when they met in Kongens Have. She was tanned. He remembered her skin. Her chestnut hair was silky, it swung back and forth around her face and shone whenever the sun landed on it. He thought that he could feel her gaze, her grey-blue eyes in which he had lost himself.

He stayed in the car as she went to order a beer. He stayed in the car as she sat down and lit a cigarette, and he saw her inhale the smoke, then exhale it with delayed gratification, he saw her sip her beer, then take a big gulp. He stayed in the car and watched her smoke all of her cigarette, watched her check her mobile three times. He saw her make the call and felt his mobile vibrate in his inside pocket. He stayed in the car until she got up and left. He followed her gait with his eyes all the way to the taxi rank by Hviids Vinstue and saw her chuck her cigarette into the gutter before she disappeared in a dark blue Ford.

He opened the glove compartment and took out the CD, Chet Baker's late version of 'Bye Bye Blackbird', and let the sound of the trumpet fill the car. He put the car in gear and drove down the blue corridor of Gothersgade, past the open area by Kongens Have towards Nørrebro where the sun was setting over the rooftops, and the neon Irma hen was busy laying tonight's endless supply of neon eggs. People cycled across Dronning Louises Bridge as if nothing had happened, swallows darted through the air, and the Lakes lay like tinfoil either side of the bridge. He drove down Nørrebrogade, into his city, and let himself be swallowed up by the traffic.

ACKNOWLEDGEMENTS

Claus Buhr and Vicki Therkildsen for their sober and insightful book *Sagen om Amagermanden*, which was the inspiration for a female character in this book.

Det Danske Forfatter og Oversættercenter at Hald for several fruitful stays.

Morgenavisen Jylland-Posten for giving me time off.

Retired police officer Tom Christensen; State Pathologist and Professor of Medicine Hans Petter Hougen at the Institute of Forensic Pathology at the University of Copenhagen; Bo Thisted Simonsen, Head of the Department of Forensic Pathology at the Institute of Forensic Pathology at the University of Copenhagen; city historian Bjørn Westerbeek Dahl. All contributed invaluable specialist knowledge. Anders Bach for his knowledge about cars; Niels Lillelund for his knowledge about wine.

Lene Juul, Charlotte Weiss, Rudi Rasmussen, Nya Guldberg, Camilla Wahlgreen and everyone else at Politikens Forlag, who has helped my book and Axel Steen on their way. A special thank you to my editor Anne Christine Andersen.

Helle Vincentz, Torben Benner, Peter Stein Larsen, Lotte Thorsen and Jakob Levinsen for reading, critiquing and giving insightful advice.

Anja Kublitz and my daughters for all their support.

Also by Mirror Books

UNREST
Jesper Stein

An unidentified man is found murdered in a Copenhagen cemetery, his hooded corpse propped up against a gravestone.

Rogue camera footage suggests police involvement, and Detective Axel Steen links the murder to the demolition of a nearby youth house teeming with militant left-wing radicals. But Axel soon discovers that many people, both inside and out of the force, have an unusual interest in the case – and in preventing its resolution.

With a rapidly worsening heart condition, an estranged ex-wife and beloved five-year-old daughter to grapple with, Axel will not stop until the killer is caught, whatever the consequences. But the consequences turn out to be greater than expected – especially for Axel himself.

MIRROR BOOKS